PARTED BY DEATH

CAROLINE FARDIG

SEVERN RIVER PUBLISHING

Severn River Publishing
www.SevernRiverBooks.com

This is a work of fiction. Names, characters, businesses, places, events and incidents are either the products of the author's imagination or used in a fictitious manner. Any resemblance to actual persons, living or dead, or actual events is purely coincidental.

ISBN: 978-1-64875-473-9 (Paperback)

ALSO BY CAROLINE FARDIG

Ellie Matthews Novels

Bitter Past

An Eye for an Eye

Dead Sprint

Parted by Death

Relative Harm

To find out more about Caroline Fardig and her books, visit

severnriverbooks.com/authors/caroline-fardig

To my son, William

PROLOGUE

Victory. He celebrated by scarfing two handfuls of Cheetos and pounding a Red Bull. Using his favorite shirt to wipe the orange dust from his fingers, he saved his findings on two flash drives—one for his client and one for himself. Nothing wrong with a little insurance.

He'd had a bad feeling about this mission for days, especially once his client had to get a new email account after the old one had been compromised. His work had gone off without a hitch, like any other cyberattack he'd ever orchestrated: infiltrate the target, find all the skeletons in the proverbial closet, and get out without being noticed. But having to sift through this particular information sickened even him, and he'd seen some messed-up shit.

He fired off an email signaling he was finished with his latest hack job, being purposely vague about the specifics, as always. Email servers were notoriously easy to hack into, especially when dealing with amateurs on the other end, so the less said, the better. He did, however, make it clear that he'd gone the extra mile and had a treasure trove of dark secrets to share.

He put on his headset and dived into his preferred world. In *Xanthe's Quest*, he was Rex, general of one of the largest guilds in the game. His character was his complete opposite. Rex was a mountain of a man nearly impossible to beat in hand-to-hand combat, not some scrawny introvert largely ignored by the world. Rex was the ultimate badass sculpted meticulously by his unbeatable gaming skills and countless hours of time.

Once he'd greeted his fellow online players, he'd only had time to walk Rex to the closest pub to meet his hunting party for a tankard of mead before his real-world phone interrupted him. It was a reply to his email. He briefly considered waiting until tomorrow to open it, but then he remembered how much he wanted that sweet new gaming chair he'd seen online, which this job would more than pay for. The sooner he turned over his findings, the sooner he could come back, splurge to overnight himself an ergonomic throne fit for a king and get lost in his preferred world.

The email read, *Sounds like you hit the motherlode. I need the info tonight. Bring it now.*

Groaning aloud, he issued a quick apology to his fellow online players for having to step away so soon, ripped the headphones off, grabbed one of the flash drives, and stowed the other away for safekeeping. He hated being summoned and ordered to run across town at a moment's notice, but that's how the agreement worked, and he was well compensated for it. Maybe this late-night delivery and the extra time he'd invested to wade through all the information would earn him a hefty bonus.

He arrived at the darkened building in record time and parked in the small rear parking lot. He began knocking on the back door as he usually did, but it swung open as his knuckles made contact. That was odd. Usually a pretty lady met him at the door and wordlessly exchanged an envelope full of cash for his flash drive. Sometimes this cloak-and-dagger stuff seemed a bit ridiculous to him. But considering the secrets he'd unearthed, especially this time, maybe it was necessary for the safety of everyone.

He entered the building, calling a "Hello!" down the dark hall. No response. "Anyone here?"

Still hearing no response, he blew out a disgusted breath. "Hey, I brought the flash drive with the info you said you needed tonight." Again, nothing. Angered, he stomped on down the hallway, griping to himself, "If I wasted time and gas driving over here for nothing..."

As he passed an open doorway, grumbling as he went, he slowed and glanced in but saw nothing. Suddenly, a hard shove from behind had him sprawled out on the floor.

"What the hell?" he croaked, tears springing to his eyes as his knees and right wrist exploded in searing pain from his fall. A wrist injury was the last thing he needed. If he couldn't type, he couldn't work.

Before he could get his bearings and raise his head to figure out what was going on, whoever had knocked him down gave him a swift kick in the ribs, shooting a racking pain through his torso. Moaning in agony, he curled into a fetal position, his only defense to stave off any further attack.

A low voice growled next to his ear, "Hand over the information."

He shoved a shaking hand in his pocket and retrieved the flash drive, only to have it ripped from his fingers with unnecessary force.

His attacker slammed his face against the floor, keeping up a blinding pressure that seemed like enough to be able to pop his head like a grape. "Did you tell anyone about this?"

"N-n-n-no," he wheezed.

The pressure suddenly subsided, leaving his head pounding and his ears ringing. Before he could get his bearings and try to crawl away, a thick plastic bag engulfed his head, stretching tight over his face. He clawed at the bag to get free, but with each hitching breath, it sucked closer over his mouth and nose. Each frantic gulp for air burned his lungs more and more, but relief wouldn't come. He got light-headed and everything went dark. He awakened in Rex's body with an odd feeling of weightlessness about him despite Rex's larger frame. He felt as if he were flying, gazing down over the moors of his kingdom at sunset. He could see the spoils of his victories and the throngs of his loyal minions across the darkening landscape. Smiling, he closed his eyes. He was home.

1

My phone buzzed. I checked the screen and shoved the phone back into my pocket without answering or breaking my stride as I jogged with Vic Manetti on the Nickel Plate Trail toward downtown Fishers. For early April, the weather in central Indiana wasn't half bad. It was the first time I hadn't had to layer up for the first mile only to have to shed half my clothing once I got warmed up. The trees along the trail were starting to leaf out again. I was not at all sorry to see this brutal winter come to an end.

Vic asked, "Who was that?"

"Jayne."

"You let the sheriff go to voicemail? I don't know of anyone else in this county who could get away with that."

For the past two months, I'd let all of my calls from the sheriff go to voicemail. Jayne Walsh was my mentor and friend, but at times she was also my boss. I welcomed her personal calls to chat or check up on me. For the professional calls, I needed the extra time a voicemail afforded to come up with good excuses to repeatedly turn down the consulting jobs she offered me.

"I'm kind of busy at the moment," I huffed, our pace a little quick for me to carry on a full conversation.

"Ellie, come on. You're not that busy. What if she has a case for you?"

I shook my head. "Probably a social call."

After a few minutes, catching my breath became easier and I noticed I kept having to slow my speed to stay next to Vic. "You okay?" I asked.

"I'm starting to run out of steam," he replied, his handsome face stuck in a frown. He wasn't sweating or flushed, which were his normal indicators that it was time for me to remind him to take a break. Glancing down at me, he said, "You're getting pretty good at reading me."

I smiled. "Well, when our pace slows to the point where I'm not overexerting myself, I know something's up with you."

Vic was a big-time fitness buff, but after being nearly killed during the last case we'd worked together, he'd had some major recovery to do. He had a long road ahead of him to get his full stamina and speed back, and I'd appointed myself the person to make sure he didn't try to overdo it and he-man his way back into shape while he was on medical leave from the FBI. To my surprise, he'd been positive and, for lack of a better word, obedient. He could've even been described as downright sweet and easygoing. I feared I'd have the fight of the century on my hands to get him to cut himself some slack, but he'd been impressively laid-back.

Slowing to a fast walk, he said, "I think you're selling yourself short. I feel like you could definitely kick my ass in a race."

Even in his weakened condition, I doubted that. "A lesser person would accept that challenge, but I won't."

He laughed and steered me away from the ramp leading to the tunnel under 116th Street, which was always our normal route, turning and taking 116th east instead. "Very noble of you. How about we stop for coffee?"

I eyed him. "Coffee during exercise time? Now I know something's up. Is there something you're not telling me? Is one of your wounds infected again?"

"Relax, mom. My wounds are perfectly fine."

"Then why the stop? We've only gone a mile, and you said you wanted to try stretching it to two today without a break."

"Can't I simply offer to take you to your favorite place for coffee, considering how much of a burden I've been—"

I stopped in the middle of the sidewalk. "You think you're a burden to me? That couldn't be further from the truth."

He wheeled around to face me. "Oh, sure. So it was no big deal when I called you in the middle of the night to drive me to the hospital, only to find out I'd managed to develop a staph infection, which then you had to deal with for weeks?"

"I told you I didn't mind. It was only a bump in your road to recovery, and it was silly to have your sister come back for something I could easily help you take care of. Besides, that was a month ago. I thought we hashed this out already. Where's this coming from?"

Vic's sister had flown in to help him recover when he came home from the hospital. I'd offered to help in any way he needed once he was well enough that she could go home. It was simply bad luck that the stab wound in his gut had gotten infected, and no reason for his sister to leave her family again to run back out here. I'd helped him change his bandage and got food and medicine for him so he didn't have to drive. It was the least I could do, considering I'd caused his excessive blood loss.

"Look, I'm trying to do something nice for you to thank you for everything you've done for me."

And there came today's fresh wave of guilt. I continually blamed myself for having assumed he was dead at the hands of the sadistic killer we'd been chasing and not at least attempting to give him first aid. Helping him recover could never make up for me standing there like an idiot while he bled out, making no move to help because I couldn't get my act together enough to think straight.

I opened my mouth to speak, but he put a hand up. "And don't even think about subjecting me to another monologue detailing what you could or should have done differently at the scene. Either forgive yourself for being human and snap out of your self-inflicted guilt trip, or I'll trump up some kind of bogus charges and arrest you."

I managed a rueful smile. "Okay, fine. No more monologues. But you couldn't arrest me if you wanted to. You're on leave, pal. And, as you said, you probably couldn't catch me." As his eyebrows shot up, I added, "That was not a challenge. We are not racing the rest of the way."

"Party pooper."

As Vic and I settled into a table at The Well with our coffees, he asked, "Are you going to call the sheriff back?"

"Later," I replied. "How's your coffee?"

He ignored my lame attempt at a subject change and suddenly slipped into his no-nonsense FBI agent persona. "How many more cases are you going to avoid?"

Training my gaze on the intricate swan latte art on my drink, I said, "I haven't been avoiding cases, Manetti."

"Bullshit. You passed on a robbery last week and the guy with the buckshot in his ass the week before that."

I took a deep sip of my latte. "I was busy helping you and doing my real job."

He kept his expression neutral, but his eyes held some pain. "I don't want to be the reason you give anything up."

I wished I hadn't said that the moment it was out of my mouth. "Seriously, they didn't need me on a measly robbery and a drunken, out of season hunting accident. Wasn't worth my time."

A smirk pulled at the corner of his mouth. "Oh, because celebrity criminalist Ellie Matthews is too big-time for that?"

I frowned at him, having forgotten over the past couple of months what it was like to go toe-to-toe with the old Vic. "Well, this conversation has certainly taken a turn."

The tough FBI agent schtick falling away, he put his hand over mine and said gently, "Ellie...are you happy?"

Wishing he'd go back to bad copping me instead of whatever this was, I jerked my hand away. "Wait, this isn't coffee. This is some kind of weird intervention. What the hell kind of a question is that?"

"The kind that needs to be asked once in a while, especially when someone is in a caregiver role."

I waved a hand. "I haven't been hardcore caregiver-ing in a couple of weeks. All I've had to do for you lately is make sure you don't keel over while you're jogging. Back when I had to clean out your nasty wound a couple of times a day, maybe I wasn't at my happiest."

"I think you need to go back to work."

"I do go to work. I taught three classes and a lab today."

"I mean to the job you love."

I feigned a little more offense than I actually felt from his remark. "I love teaching at Ashmore College. And now that I'm 'celebrity criminalist Ellie Matthews,' my students actually listen to me. My job is going better than it ever has."

He shook his head. "Maybe it's easier, but it's not fulfilling you. You need to get back out on scene, doing what you do best. I've been watching as you turn down case after case, and I think you don't realize how much you're missing field investigating."

It wasn't exactly the field investigating I was missing...or avoiding. It was Detective Nick Baxter. Because of the circumstances of our last case—he was on the "lead detective who broke the case" side and I ended up not only being dismissed from the case but also landing on the "victim/witness" side—we couldn't begin the relationship we'd both so desperately wanted for months for fear of the defense using it against us and the case suffering. To make sure we stayed above reproach, he and I couldn't have any contact outside of work until the trial was over and done. We hadn't spoken in two months. It had been excruciating to cut him out of my life only hours after I'd told him my true feelings for him. It would stand to reason that I should take any approved opportunity to see him, but I didn't know how I could manage working side-by-side with him, pretending we were merely colleagues and nothing more.

My phone buzzed again. I checked it—Jayne again. I put it back in my pocket unanswered, again.

Vic said quietly, "I think you need to get that."

"It would be rude since we're in the middle of a conversation."

He sat back in his chair and crossed his arms. "No, we're not. I'm not saying another word until you answer that phone."

Growling under my breath, I took out my phone and answered before it had time to go to voicemail. "Hi, Jayne."

She didn't even bother saying hello back. "I need you for a case, and I'm afraid I can't take no for an answer this time."

I glared across the table at Vic, who held up his hands in a defensive gesture and chuckled to himself.

To Jayne, I said, "You're sure Beck and Amanda can't handle this one?"

"It's a homicide."

That word conjured up a flurry of thoughts in my head, most of them centered around Baxter and the endless hours together a homicide case would entail. I was both excited and terrified.

I mouthed at Vic, "Homicide."

He smiled and gave me a thumbs-up. I nearly snickered at his odd response to the word, but I knew he meant it as an encouragement for me to take the job rather than, "Yay, a homicide!"

Vic was right. I did love the adrenaline and challenge that came with field investigation. I needed to get back out there. More than that, I needed to come to terms with my permanently-on-hold relationship with Baxter and find a way to get on with my life. This limbo was killing me, even if it was my own fault for prolonging it.

"Ellie?" Jayne prompted.

"Uh…" I still wasn't convinced this was such a good idea.

Vic nodded at me encouragingly.

I sighed. I had to get back out there at some point. "Okay. I'll do it. Where am I going?"

Now it was Jayne doing the hesitating. "Um…the body was found at… Carnival Cove."

My jaw dropped. "Wait, the scene's at Carnival Cove? Oh, *hell* no."

Vic reached over and grabbed my free hand. He knew going to that venue would open a Pandora's box of emotion for me. It was where I'd found a dead student. It was where my reinstatement into the Hamilton County crime scene unit had ultimately begun. Last but not least, it was where I'd first met Nick Baxter. Plus the clown-themed, long-abandoned water park was creepy as hell on a good day.

Jayne's voice took on an apologetic tone. "I wouldn't have called if I didn't need you."

I could barely process even the idea of setting foot out there again, so I stalled for time. "If this is a joke, it isn't funny."

Her tone turned reproachful. "How many times have I joked about a murder case?"

The sheriff, never. The rest of the department, always. It was how we got through murder cases with our sanity. I got a pang in my heart when I thought about how much less joking around there'd be this time with Baxter and me having to pretend we barely knew each other.

She continued, "Look, I know it's not going to be the easiest place for you to work, but I feel like this one's going to need someone with your experience...and your strong stomach."

I made a face and mouthed to Vic, "Decomp."

He smiled and released my hand to grab both of our coffee cups to take to the dish return, then he came back to usher me out of my seat and toward the door. I guessed he figured I was going to eventually come around and agree to take the case. Or maybe he was going to drag me there kicking and screaming, if need be.

I said to Jayne as Vic and I speed-walked down the street, "The more you say, the less I want to do this."

Ignoring me, she went on, "Oh, and can you have your entomology professor friend come out as well? Dr. Berg could use his help."

"There are bugs, too?" I whined, shuddering.

"I'm afraid so."

I sighed. If I could make it through this case, I'd be fully over any anxiety I had about coming back. Plus, if I said yes, then maybe Jayne would leave me alone again for a while. "Fine. I'll call Dr. Seong, and...I'll come out, but it will take me a good thirty minutes to get there."

She sounded relieved. "Thank you. Bring along a waterproof jacket. It's supposed to rain this evening."

I groaned. This was going to be the crime scene from hell.

2

Vic insisted we run at nearly full speed back to his house, which cemented my theory that our coffee break was a total bullshit move. I hopped in my car and headed toward Carnival Cove, cursing pretty much the whole way. When I got to the parking lot's entrance, I slowed to wave at a deputy sitting in his cruiser, guarding the scene from any unwanted visitors. He waved me through, and I entered the lot and took the parking spot next to the crime scene unit van. I'd arrived later to the party than usual. The coroner's van, another sheriff's department cruiser, Jayne's sedan, and a civilian vehicle were all already there. And, of course, there was Baxter's SUV.

Wrapping the waterproof jacket Vic lent me around myself to stave off the sudden chill I felt, I trudged through the entrance to the park. A tingle of apprehension and unease ripped up my spine as I walked through the gate and past a sign with a laughing, dead-eyed clown. "Welcome to Carnival Cove," my ass. I shivered as I wondered if the owner of this place, my former friend and colleague, Dr. Dudley Cooper, had ever bothered to remove the rest of the clown signage and statuary. I doubted it, given the fact that he'd moved away shortly after I'd found the dead body here, his hopes dashed of turning this place into an outdoor forensic anthropology research facility. Honestly, I was happy his "body farm" idea never came to be. I'd agreed to help him run the place, mostly because he couldn't get anyone else on board. And while the idea of studying the cadavers he intended to let decompose out here in the elements didn't bother me, the fact that he and I had nearly tripped over someone who'd been murdered here did. Every time I came to this hellscape, I would have been thinking about the girl we'd found, as I was doing now.

Trying to shake that off and get my head straight, I continued into the park, which was in the exact state of disarray as the last time I was here. I passed the same sad, rusty picnic tables, the same broken and scattered beach chairs, and the same crumbling and weed-infested retaining walls. It seemed that the only thing that had been done to the place was the removal of the pig's blood the student protesters had used to write "Death to the Body Farm" across the welcome sign at the entrance. Going farther into the park, I gave a wide berth to a peeling statue of a fat clown with a missing nose, picking my way around piles of leaves and garbage. I slowed my pace as the snack bar came into view. Now brown and faded, the message written in pig's blood on the wooden siding of the snack bar was still visible: "Dr. Death Sucks." I remembered every detail of the look on Dr. Cooper's face when he saw the vandalism. Seeing the hurt in his eyes as he realized how much the Ashmore students were against him going ahead with his research facility had been tough to stomach. And only moments later, we were calling in a homicide on a student we both knew quite well.

I willed myself to breeze past Kiddie Land without so much as a glance. If I caught a glimpse of the stained concrete where I'd found that poor girl, I didn't know if I could lock it down to do this job. Pressing on, I walked toward the tall, imposing water slides, now covered in vines and graffiti. I could see and hear people milling around just past them. And then of course there was the smell I kept catching a whiff of as I forged ahead. I was definitely going the right direction.

Gathering my courage, I headed through the "Wild Slide" section of the park, past the pool in the center where all four slides deposited their riders. The pool, if you could still call it that, was a big concrete bowl, its deep end holding a couple of feet of murky water and leaves and its shallow end dusty and cracked from years of baking empty in the hot sun. The bitter aroma of stagnant water and algae was soon blotted out by the unmistakable sweet-rotten stench of decomposing flesh, no doubt coming from the human-sized lump lying in the far shallow end of the pool, near the edge. My colleagues were gathered at a safe distance, watching from above as the coroner and his assistant performed their field examination of the victim. Both men were covered head-to-toe to protect themselves not only from the decaying body but also from the thick cloud of flies swarming it.

I stopped to greet a deputy holding a clipboard and signed the scene entry log. There was none of the usual crime scene tape denoting an inner or outer perimeter here. It would have been a waste of tape since we were way too far into the park to worry about keeping the looky-loos at bay. As I scanned the area, I noted nothing unusual, except of course for the dead body. There were no bloody footprints or discarded weapons. The only items strewn about were tables and chairs and trash cans that had been here already. Trying to fingerprint anything out here would be an exercise in futility. Not a whole lot of work for me to do, as far as I could tell. The less evidence to gather, the less time I'd have to spend here, and that was fine by me.

Jayne broke away from the group and came toward me. "Thank you for agreeing to take the case, Ellie. I know it's a big deal for you."

"Yeah, yeah," I replied, shaking my head. "This place is every bit as creepy as I thought it would be."

"I don't disagree."

An image flashed in my brain of all the clown faces that had leered at me on my way in. On top of everything I'd had to endure here, I had a mild phobia about clowns. I knew the images of them in this park weren't going to magically come to life and attack me, but I still didn't want to come nose-to-nose with one in the shadows.

"You think we'll get out of here before dark?"

She smiled. "Considering there's not a lot of visible evidence and nothing looks terribly suspicious, I'd say you have a decent chance."

Called that one. "Any signs of struggle near the body?"

She shook her head. "Not that we've been able to find yet. But I'll wait for you and Ms. Carmack to work your magic. Oh, and there's also no ID in the victim's pockets, so it should be extra fun for everyone."

"Good times."

Jayne and I walked over to join the group, which consisted of Baxter, criminalist Amanda Carmack, Detective Jason Sterling, entomologist Dr. Ben Seong, Coroner Dr. Everett Berg, Assistant Coroner Kenny Strange, and a couple of deputies who were likely the first responders.

A jolt of electricity went through me. This was it. Not only did I have to do my job, which was going to be smelly at best and frustrating at worst, I had to do it without openly staring at Nick Baxter's handsome face, which was all I wanted to do since I hadn't laid eyes on him in two months. He didn't glance in my direction as I approached; he seemed deep in concentration on what Dr. Berg and Kenny were doing.

They finished their examination and climbed the steps to exit the pool. Dr. Berg approached us, his expression solemn as he removed his respirator mask to address us. A consummate professional, he paid the utmost respect to the dead and demanded nothing less from the rest of us while he studied, handled, and moved bodies at crime scenes.

"Good afternoon, all. I'm afraid that due to the length of time since death and the decomposed state of the deceased's body, it will be impossible for me to determine the time of death." He nodded toward my fellow Ashmore professor, Ben, who I'd called at Jayne's request as Vic and I were jogging back to his house. "But with the help of Dr. Seong, we should be able to provide the date of death at least."

Frustration was already forming in Sterling's eyes. He saw in black and white, never letting feelings cloud his judgment. He wanted clear-cut, hard evidence and only accepted the most airtight of alibis. Having to work a case with a twenty-four-hour window for the time of death was going to drive him nuts. That was where Baxter would come in. He was good at all the gray areas. A big TOD window wouldn't throw him off his game—he'd simply come at it from a different angle. And I'd be right there beside him... maybe. I wasn't sure how things would work in our "new normal," for lack of a better term.

Dr. Berg went on, "As I'm sure you've noticed, the deceased's body is fully in the autolysis stage of the decomposition process, which can begin at any time after seventy-two hours postmortem and last up until day ten. I believe we're somewhere between days four and six."

I finally took a good look at the victim. When I came onto a scene, I tried not to focus on the corpse right out of the gate. It was too easy to get distracted by the gore or saddened by the circumstances. This was one of the "distracted by the gore" situations. The poor man was blown up like a balloon. In life, he probably would have been a fairly small man, short and with a thin frame. But at this stage of decomposition, aptly named the "bloat" stage, he looked as if he'd swallowed a whole other person. His too-tight skin was a sickly greenish color, peeling off in sheets from the pressure of the bloating and lack of moisture and natural oils. And then there were the flies. Lots of flies. I was thankful Ben had trucked over here as fast as he had. Now he would have to weather the swarm to collect bug and larva samples instead of me.

I glanced at Ben, who was doing a terrible job of hiding his glee. I understood his excitement over gaining the privilege of consulting for the county, plus the real-life experience in his field. The lab experiments he and I manufactured so our students could do hands-on study of insects and forensics didn't hold a candle to the real thing. And the rush of collaborating on an actual homicide investigation was impossible to recreate.

Dr. Berg said, "I noted some petechial hemorrhaging in the eyes, which suggests asphyxia. However, between the overall distension and the presence of a fair amount of postmortem animal attack, it's pointless to even speculate about the cause of death until I perform the autopsy. I've collected the deceased's fingerprints and will forward them to the lab in hopes of verifying his identity. We've found nothing in the clothing pockets, no jewelry of any kind, and no visible tattoos or birthmarks on the exposed skin. Again, I'll do a more thorough examination during the autopsy."

Now that I looked even more closely, I noticed scratch and bite marks on the victim's arms, neck, and head. At least the poor man was already dead while his body was being mauled by small animals. Chunks of flesh were missing, the gooey holes left behind fast filling with maggots. Most disconcerting was a jagged hole in one of his arms, and I would go so far as to describe that arm as deflated. I'd read about raccoons scavenging for muscle tissue, leaving limbs like empty tubes, but had yet to see it in person. Another perk of field work versus lab work: you never knew what you were going to see, and subsequently be unable to unsee. I had a strong stomach and could look at most anything without feeling ill, but I would on occasion become uncomfortable if I let my mind think too much about the mechanics of how certain atrocities occurred. This was not one of those situations. I was fascinated by the deflated arm and couldn't rip my eyes away.

Dr. Berg concluded, "We'll vacate the scene for a bit while we gather our equipment, if you all would like to take photos and study the area."

Baxter immediately pulled Sterling aside and began speaking to him, his back to the rest of us. I guessed our hello would have to wait.

My fellow criminalist, Amanda Carmack, gave me a warm welcome. "Hey, Ellie!" she said, giving me a one-armed hug and steering me toward a tarp on the ground laden with two field kits and a big duffel bag. "I can't tell you how happy I am that you're back."

Amanda and I had become friends during our time working together and had stayed in touch while I took my two-month break. I'd told her all about my ordeal from our last case—well, almost all of it. I left out everything about Baxter and me.

As I retrieved a jumpsuit from the bag and began stepping into it, I smiled at her. "Is Beck working your last nerve?"

She grimaced. "Honestly, I don't know how much longer I can deal with him."

The county's head criminalist, Beck Durant, was a total fool, and even though he outranked Amanda in title only, he took every opportunity to be the big man and boss her around. When I worked as head criminalist for the county, he had Amanda's position, and most days I essentially did both of our jobs. Things hadn't changed—Amanda complained of having to do his job as well. He was famous for taking hourly smoke breaks where he pretended to vape in order to get out of working. Complaining about him would get her nowhere—his mommy was a county court judge with enough connections to keep her baby boy in a job no matter how much he sucked at it. Although the department was shackled with him, Jayne had found a way to keep him out of the way when it mattered by bringing me in as a consultant on all homicide and high-profile cases.

As Amanda put on a respirator mask and gloves, I asked, "Getting worse by the day?"

She nodded. "I swear, if you hadn't taken this case with me, I would have come and got you and dragged you here by your hair."

I laughed as I put on my own mask and gloves. "It's nice to be missed, I guess." Pawing through the bag once more, I asked her, "Did you happen to pack a hat for me?"

Groaning, she replied, "Sorry, I forgot. Beck was berating me as I was packing, and I was in a rush to get away from him."

I took off my mask and called to the group, "Anyone have a hat I can borrow?"

Baxter flicked his eyes in my direction for a moment but made no offer. Odd, because he had an endless supply of baseball caps in his vehicle and was always happy to share. I knew we needed to play it cool, but surely lending me a hat wouldn't be tantamount to publicly professing his love for me.

Maybe he was being overly cautious. I didn't see how Baxter and I could work together as closely as we always did and keep the appearance of being only coworkers. I wasn't that good an actress. Worse, what if working together kindled that spark (as it always did) and we succumbed to our feelings and got caught together? It would be a disaster, not only for the two of us professionally, but for the department, the case we'd worked on, and the victims, including Vic. I couldn't imagine being able to look him in the eye ever again if I were the one to cause the case to implode.

Ben jogged over, a smile still plastered on his face. "Hey, Ellie. I have an extra." He opened his backpack and handed me an Ashmore baseball cap. "Thanks again for the opportunity to work with you guys. Is it okay to take my own photos to use in class? Do you ever do that?"

I gathered my long hair into a low ponytail and put on the borrowed hat. "Sure, take as many photos as you want. You just have to wait until the case is closed to show them to anyone."

"No problem."

"And by the way, it was the sheriff who asked for you. You must have made a good impression on her with the last case you consulted on."

His grin widened. "That's good to hear. The last one was a challenge, since the corpse was a month old and I had several types of insects to study. This fresh one should be cake, at least for me."

Amanda laughed. "Fresh and cake are not terms I'd use in regard to our victim."

I said to her, "I guess this is probably the least fresh corpse you've encountered, right?"

Since this was only her second job as a criminalist, her initial position having been in a county known for its low crime rate, Amanda hadn't seen much in the way of carnage. But you'd never know it from the professional way she handled herself.

She nodded. "Yes, this is officially the grossest thing I've ever seen."

Sterling strutted up behind us. "You ladies gonna stand around talking all afternoon or do your jobs?"

I turned to him, lowering my mask so I could frown at him. "You, I didn't miss."

"Back at ya, Matthews."

Amanda grabbed the camera and brushed past him without a word. She and Sterling had been dating for months, but things had started to unravel between them a few weeks ago. I couldn't imagine what she saw in him and hadn't expected their relationship to last as long as it had. Now it seemed she was merely another notch in his bedpost (not unlike myself after one particularly drunken night) and would be relegated to his shit list —again, not unlike myself. More polite than I could ever hope to be, she took the high road and didn't engage him.

Sterling must not have gotten the rise he wanted from us, so he followed us and decided to pick at me. "You working for the Feds now, Matthews? Is that why you've been ghosting us the last couple of months?"

"Huh?" I asked, taking out my sketch pad to begin making a preliminary rough sketch of the scene while Amanda took the photos.

"Your jacket."

When I'd borrowed the jacket from Vic, I was way more concerned about protecting myself from getting soaked to the bone than about how wearing an FBI jacket to a county crime scene might be perceived. It wasn't like he'd lent me his official windbreaker with "FBI" in giant letters emblazoned across the back. This was a nicer one Vic had purchased to wear running when there was the threat of rain. The FBI insignia on the left front shoulder was small and unobtrusive, but not enough to escape the eagle eyes of a detective.

"The jacket's borrowed. And as for my absence, I'm sure even you can understand that I needed a break after the last case I worked," I murmured curtly, hoping to end this conversation. Baxter was only a few feet away from us, surveying the scene by himself. He wasn't exactly a fan of Vic's, so I'd always tried not to bring up Vic around him.

Sterling wouldn't let the jacket thing go. "Yeah, borrowed from Manetti. Does that mean you guys are still banging?"

I winced. That was the last thing I wanted to have said within Baxter's earshot. But Baxter seemed to have been either suddenly stricken deaf or in the middle of an Oscar-worthy performance, because he didn't so much as bat an eye at Sterling's comment. Any other time, he would have told Sterling to shut up or at least let a flash of annoyance cross his face.

I quickly replied, "No, we're just friends."

"Like you can be friends with a guy without banging him."

I could have sworn I saw Baxter flinch, just barely.

I snapped at Sterling, "Now who's standing around talking all afternoon and not doing their job?"

"Touché," he replied, smirking at me.

Sterling finally left Amanda and me alone and headed over to confer with one of the deputies. As I worked on my rough sketch, my eyes wandered in Baxter's direction. He still hadn't made any indication that he knew I was here. Not that I had a whole lot of room to talk—I hadn't approached him, either.

I inhaled a deep breath and exhaled slowly to settle my nerves. I took two steps toward Baxter and cleared my throat.

3

"Hey, Nick." The words came out breathless and throaty, my nervousness as plain as day.

Baxter looked my way and nodded. His expression was blank; even his eyes were devoid of any emotion. His tone was flat. "Nice to have you back." Effectively cutting off any further conversation, he turned and walked over to join Sterling in speaking to the deputy.

Okay, so he was playing it cool. Or maybe he was concentrating on the investigation. After all, that was why we were here.

I returned to stand near Amanda, who was almost finished taking photos of the victim. "See anything interesting in the close-ups?"

She shuddered. "Lots of bugs. Your professor buddy is going to have no shortage of samples to collect."

"Better him than us."

"Exactly what I was thinking."

We both startled when Sterling's voice boomed right behind us. "Maybe he's homeless. His clothes are old and filthy. He's got no shoes, no phone, no wallet. We need to search this whole place. If we can find his crash pad, we might figure out his identity."

Amanda and I turned to find Sterling and Baxter now standing not three feet from us.

Baxter replied, "You think he could have been living here?"

Sterling glanced around and shrugged. "Sure. There's plenty of shelter, and the place is always deserted. It's a vagrant's paradise. I'm surprised there aren't more of them squatting in all the empty buildings out here. This could be as simple as a bum fight that got out of hand."

"No signs of a struggle, though," Baxter said.

"So they got into it somewhere else on the property, then he ran away like a little bitch and collapsed here. Or fell in like an idiot."

Baxter studied the body. "His hair is fairly short, and he's got no facial hair. He's not living on the streets if he's shaving daily and getting haircuts."

I nodded. "I thought the same thing, only about his nails. He's groomed enough to definitely not be homeless."

Baxter flicked his eyes at me, but other than that pretty much ignored my comment. He wasn't even being polite, which baffled me.

Sterling completely ignored me, which was par for the course. "If he's not living here, then what the hell's he doing here?" He stalked off toward the deputies, and Baxter followed him.

My heart sank. I'd imagined my reunion with Baxter in my head a thousand times during the past two months, but I'd never dreamed it would play out this way. I assumed he'd be outwardly polite and friendly but have that little sparkle in his eyes reserved only for me. Nothing about him indicated he was happy (or even upset) to see me. He was indifferent, and he was never indifferent. He hadn't even used my name in the few words he'd spoken to me. It made me feel like I was barely an acquaintance, some stranger whose name he hadn't bothered to remember.

I shook my head, reminding myself I was here to do a job. There was no room for relationship drama in the middle of a crime scene. I'd been called to work this particular case because of my ability to lock it down and focus on the smallest of details, and that's what I was going to do. On the surface, my exchange with Baxter had looked nothing short of professional. No one would have suspected there was anything going on underneath. At least now the hard part was out of the way, and I didn't have to wonder anymore about how it would go. It wasn't like it was the first time we'd had an awkward reunion after not speaking for a couple of months. But it was the first time I'd felt like something had shifted in a very bad way.

"Ellie...*Ellie*."

I snapped my head in Amanda's direction. "Sorry, what?"

She pulled her mask down to give me a strange look and make a show of overenunciating, "I *said*, do you mind grabbing a stack of evidence markers? I left them in the bag."

"Oh, sure." I hurried back to the duffel bag, studiously avoiding Baxter.

I really needed to get my act together. Amanda was every bit as detail oriented as I was, and with her being my friend as well as my colleague, it was only a matter of time before she'd figure out something was up with me. I retrieved the evidence markers from the bag and took the surveyor's wheel so I could add measurements to my sketch. I also took out a voice recorder and turned it on, slipping it into the front pocket of my coveralls.

I returned to Amanda and handed her the markers. She was deep in thought, her back to the body and instead focusing her attention on a stretch of concrete that was scattered with dried leaves, pine needles, and gritty dirt. She snapped a couple of photos and then studied them on the camera's screen.

"See that?" She held out the camera for me to look at the screen. I shielded the mild glare that wouldn't last long with the fast-darkening sky. She had taken some mid-range and close-up shots of a few intertwining ruts each about an inch wide that had been carved into the dirt. "Some kind of wheel marks or drag marks, maybe?" she asked.

"Good eye. That wasn't easy to notice until you zoomed in on it."

Amanda's eyes became bright and laser-focused, as they always did when she discovered something at a scene. "Let's follow the tracks."

I stuffed the surveyor's wheel under my armpit to keep my hands free, notating the location of the tracks on my drawing as I followed Amanda across the expanse of concrete. We stayed several feet away from the tracks in order to disturb as little of the scene as possible. The marks were erratic —sometimes intertwining, sometimes straight.

She took a couple more photos and pointed to a place where leaves had gathered, blanketing the concrete. "I lose the trail there." She made a wide circle around the leaves, studying the ground around the area. I followed.

As I stepped off the concrete pad and gazed out across the expanse of weedy grass stretching toward the back perimeter of the park, memories came flooding back to me again—this time, good ones I'd all but forgotten after my last experience here. This part of the park was thankfully devoid of any clown-related nonsense, which was why I'd always liked it best. In my youth, I'd spent countless summer afternoons here stretched out on a towel in the sun with my friends. Back then, the grounds had been well maintained, the grass thick and soft, the perfect place to lie for hours and forget about my shitty home life. A smile tugged at my lips as my eyes landed on a small outbuilding near the edge of the property, its only window now busted and the rusty door hanging at a crazy angle, secured only by its bottom hinge. A seen-better-days chain link fence marked the property line, which backed up against a wooded area.

I pointed in the direction I was looking. "There's a dirt access road that runs along the property line, with a gate just to the left of that outbuilding. You thinking what I'm thinking?"

She cast me a sidelong glance. "I am, and I'm also thinking you must know your way around here better than most people."

I shrugged. "Dudley and I studied the plot plan for the property to decide how we were going to secure the facility, but I didn't learn anything I didn't already know about weak points of entry into the park. Back in my wild child days, I got pretty good at climbing that fence to sneak in because I didn't have the money to pay for admission like everyone else."

"I did my fair share of sneaking into places as a kid, too. I don't miss being poor."

"Same. Another fun fact about me: I lost my virginity in that outbuilding."

Amanda let out a peal of laughter. "You can't just put that out there and not tell the whole sordid story."

I regaled her with the not-all-that-sordid story—it was the first time for both of us, there was a lot of fumbling, and it was practically over before it started—as we trekked toward the back of the property. Last year's brown, dormant vegetation, anywhere from ankle to knee high, crunched under our feet as we picked our way across it, hoping to find more of our trail at some point. While the disrepair and damage to the rest of the park had made it even creepier to me, the neglect of this section only made me sad.

Over a decade later, my sunny oasis was nothing more than a desolate field overtaken by weeds, my first love nest ravaged by time and abuse.

We saw nothing of note until we came up to the parking area, such as it was, a square of dirt with ground-in rocks and, of course, more weeds.

Amanda pointed to the ground and cried, "Aha! More of our tracks. I'm forming a theory here. How about you?"

I nodded. "Especially since there's an excellent set of vehicle tire marks right next to your chair tracks. It must have rained not long before these were made, which is good for us. The tread marks are the perfect depth and will be easy to cast."

Amanda began taking photos, and I started a new sketch of this area, including the gravel/dirt access road and tiny parking area, fence, outbuilding, and tire marks.

Studying the gate, she said, "The lock on this gate is broken, but there's rust around it, so if someone came out here to dump our victim, they didn't even have to break in."

Sterling called to us from fifty yards away, "The hell are you two doing all the way over there?"

"Following the evidence," Amanda yelled back.

"Evidence of what?" he griped, although he started jogging our way.

When he got within non-yelling territory, I said, "We have the makings for proving a body dump."

He shot us an unconvinced glare. "Nobody drove that guy out here to BFE and *then* dragged him all the way into the park. That's overkill."

I replied, "Maybe our killer is an overachiever."

Amanda pointed to the nearby gate. "Actually, there's very easy access back here. The lock on the gate is busted, although it—"

He interrupted. "Could've happened anytime."

She grimaced, her frustration with him apparent. "As I was about to say, *although it looks like it's been broken for a while.* Anyway, a vehicle entered through there and made these trac—"

He interrupted again. "Those tracks could also have been made anytime."

She didn't back down, pointing to our chair tracks. "True, but considering we found this other pattern of tracks both here *and* near the body, we think there's a good chance they're from the same incident."

Sterling bent down and shined his phone's flashlight where she was pointing. "What the hell are these tracks supposed to be?"

"We think they could be from a desk chair with wheels."

His tone dripped with sarcasm. "You think someone rolled our dead guy around out here in an office chair?"

I said, "It would have been a hell of a lot easier than dragging him. For example, if I actually went through with killing you like I do in my daydreams and needed to hide your body, I'd be hard-pressed to drag you even a few inches. But I could totally bungee strap your lifeless corpse to a chair and roll you damn near anywhere."

He sneered. "Like you could get the drop on me, Matthews."

"Oh, I know I couldn't. I'm practical, even in my fantasies. I kill you by poisoning your coffee when you're not looking."

His sneer fell away. Was he actually worried about that? Recovering quickly and putting his normal smirk back into place, he said, "Again, I'm going to ask: why cart a body all the way to the pool? Why not just dump it here? No one could see it."

I gestured to the woods, the brush and trees just leafed out enough to hide anything twenty yards in. "There's a house next door, through those trees. A body dumped here could be smelled from there and would be in full view from the access road. However, cart it a little farther and hide it down in the pool, and, yes, you could probably catch a whiff of it when the wind blows, but you'd never see it unless you were literally on top of it. The perfect location for a body dump." I thought for a moment and ripped off my mask, taking in a deep breath through my nose. "Wait. Like, *really* perfect. I can't smell it from here. Can either of you?"

Amanda took her mask off and took a breath, shaking her head. Sterling also shook his head.

I asked, "How did anyone even know there was a body out here? Who called it in?"

"Some neighbor kid was flying a drone over the park and noticed it."

I shivered. Without that random act, this poor man might not have been found for months or even years. The circumstances of this case were begin-

ning to feel decidedly less simple. I didn't like the increasingly premeditated feeling of the body dump. Sterling was clearly not in a mood to listen
to alternate theories. I needed to speak to Baxter.

Amanda got out her notepad and jotted a quick note. Then she said to
me, "I'm going back to get some casting materials and the fingerprint kit."

Sterling said, "We're going to fan out and search for the guy's crash pad.
We'll let you know if we need you to process another area. In the meantime, don't waste what little daylight we have left on a couple of random
tracks we can't prove are related to the case."

Already walking purposely away from him, she called over her shoulder, "You're not our boss, Jason."

His nostrils flared, but he couldn't seem to quit watching her walk away,
and with a heavy dose of regret in his eyes, if I'd read him right.

I smirked at him. "You let a good one get away, dumbass."

"Shut up, Matthews."

4

While Amanda was gone, I quickly measured the parking lot and all the distances to its perimeter from our two sets of tire marks. From that, I was able to properly show the position of the marks in my sketch. Sterling had taken a quick look inside the outbuilding before stalking off in a huff after Amanda, but I thought I would be remiss if I didn't have a look for myself. I changed my gloves, took out my phone, and turned on the flashlight, illuminating the inside of the place, which looked every bit as sad as the outside. Old tools were strewn about, discarded and broken. Several old tubes from the water slides were stacked in a haphazard pile, all of them at a different stage of deflation. Shards of glass from the broken window littered the floor, along with leaves that had blown in. There was a long-dead raccoon carcass in one corner. I saw no signs that anyone had ever tried to live there—no blankets, clothing, cardboard, or food wrappers. Everything was covered in a layer of dirt. It wasn't like it had been the Taj Mahal the last time I'd been in there, but at least it hadn't looked like a set from a horror movie.

When I exited the building, Amanda was returning with a bag of casting mix, two casting frames, and the fingerprint kit. She snickered. "Reliving your glory days?"

"Hardly. The place is a mess, but I don't think there's anything relevant to our case in there."

She looked up at the gloomy, threatening sky. It was only mid-afternoon, but the cloud cover had become so thick it wouldn't be long before we'd have to break out the spotlights. "You think there's time for our cast to cure before it starts pouring rain?"

I frowned. "Debatable. Once we're done, I'll grab a tarp."

She mixed the dental stone from the all-in-one kit as I removed twigs and leaves from the tire impression. She then pressed the metal frame down into the soil around the stretch of tread mark with the clearest pattern and sprayed it with aerosol hair spray to set the soil. While waiting for the spray to dry, I placed a scale next to the tread mark and took several photos. She poured the dental stone mixture into the frame and smoothed off the top.

Moving on to the chair marks, we both stood over them for a moment debating whether or not it was even worth it to make a cast. Although we had enough dental stone left, which couldn't be reused, a photo would more than suffice. Chair casters were pretty much a standard size and weren't necessarily specific to a brand of chair, and knowing what brand of chair was used wouldn't help, considering how many office chairs there were out in the world. We finally decided on a simple photo with the scale showing the wheels were one-and-a-half inches wide.

Amanda took final photos of the area, and I cleaned up our casting materials. She began studying the gate for fingerprints while I hustled back across the field to our kits to find a tarp. I came upon Baxter, who had his back to me and his phone to his ear. I didn't intend to eavesdrop, but it was fairly quiet out there. And he was speaking at regular volume...probably assuming no one would be eavesdropping.

He sounded apologetic as he said, "I'd planned to head your way this afternoon, but I caught a case." After a pause, he said in a sweeter tone, "I know, but I really wanted to see her today..."

My whole body tensed at one word—her. I forced myself to keep walking. Who was the "her" he wanted to see? Before my unfortunate jealous streak had a chance to rear its ugly head, I reasoned that Baxter probably had plenty of female family members and friends he wanted to see. "Her" didn't have to be a new girlfriend. It could have been an animal or even a boat. And though it pained me to even think it, if he had found a new girlfriend, I pretty much had to grin and bear it. While we hadn't made any promises about putting all romance on hold until we were allowed to date each other again, that was my tentative plan. I didn't want to be with anyone else. I'd assumed he felt the same way, but if he didn't, I didn't have much of a say in the matter.

Concentrating on tamping down the lump in my throat, I grabbed the tarp out of Amanda's duffel bag. On the way back, I passed Baxter again. He was putting his phone back into his pocket, his expression neutral and oddly blank, like it had been before. If I had to give this expression a name, it would be "cop face." Baxter normally didn't do the cop face thing. Vic was a master at it, as was Jayne. Sterling was a loose cannon and didn't care how his disdain, laughter, and sneers affected others. Baxter wore his heart on his sleeve and made no apologies for it.

But not today. And his cop face told me that any personal comments I might make wouldn't be welcome. That didn't mean I should hold back on speaking with him professionally. I needed to bring him up to speed on what Amanda and I had been working on.

"Hey, um...Baxter." Better to be a little less personal than before. "Amanda and I are thinking pretty strongly that this could be a body dump. We found some marks we think came from the casters of an office chair near the body and also near the back gate, like maybe this death was a little more premeditated and planned than—"

He pointed to the sky. "We're kind of on a timetable, here." He started walking away from me and threw over his shoulder, "We can wait on the spitballing until the meeting this evening. I gotta go."

I'd been dismissed, now both personally and professionally. Stunned and finding it a little difficult to breathe, I tore my mask off and trudged back across the field. After unfolding the tarp, I laid it over the cast of the tire impression and staked down the corners.

Amanda was busy packing up the fingerprinting kit. "I dusted several areas of that gate but came up empty-handed on prints." She closed the case and stood, finally looking at me. Her face fell. "You okay? You look like someone kicked your dog."

It certainly felt like it. I shook my head. "My ulcer flares up when I get too hungry. I need to find something to eat." I really did have a self-inflicted ulcer, but it hadn't been an issue since I'd quit drinking and started eating better.

"Now that you mention it, I could eat. I threw in a box of granola bars and some Diet Cokes, figuring we'd miss dinner."

"You're the best."

* * *

Granola bars were a no-go on the Keto diet Vic and I had agreed to do together, which was why I discreetly exchanged a low-carb protein bar from my purse for Amanda's proffered snack, but I gladly guzzled the Diet Coke. While we were out by the edge of the property, Dr. Berg and Kenny had carted the victim away, so we now had our chance to go over the epicenter of the scene for evidence.

Amanda and I put our masks back on, donned new gloves, and got out flashlights. We made a visual sweep from above, but there was nothing on the pool's cracked floor besides a few sheets of the victim's dry skin and a little dark goo—likely blood from the animal attacks or bowel secretions or some other kind of human ooze. There were still a few flies buzzing about, but the bulk of the swarm had moved on. Ben Seong was gone as well, probably speeding toward Ashmore so he could get cracking on his examination of his beloved bugs.

Amanda said, "I don't know what we can do here. There's literally nothing to collect."

I nodded. "I know. Let's take a closer look, but I'm not holding my breath."

"Well, the stinky body's gone, so no need anymore."

We both laughed at her bad joke as we descended the steps into the pool. Even close up, we could find no discernable evidence. I hated scenes like this; it always felt like I was missing something. I would honestly rather have a room full of prints, secretions, objects, and even trash to sift through and collect. At least then I felt like I'd contributed something to the investigation. Juries these days expected hard forensic evidence. Having little to none made it all that much harder on the DA, who never passed up the chance to berate the department for handing him a case that he didn't view as a slam dunk.

After officially deeming this area a bust, Amanda and I headed back to our secondary scene and checked the tire impression cast. It was cured and ready. She took out a marker and labeled the back with the date, her initials, and the case number. I rattled off the photo numbers that corresponded to this impression, which she also jotted down on the back of the cast. She then removed the metal frame, dug her fingers under the edge of the cast, and picked it up, transferring it to a cardboard pizza box for transport with the impression side up.

"Great impression," she said.

Drops of rain started falling. "Ugh," I groaned. "As if this day could get any worse."

As she wrote out an evidence tag for the box, she said, "It hasn't been that bad, has it? I mean, I've been having fun."

Aside from the whole Baxter thing, it really hadn't been that bad out here. We'd spent most of our time in a section of the park that had always brought me joy, well away from the horrors of the rest of the place.

I let out a rueful laugh. "I guess I've been a bit of a Debbie Downer today. Sorry. I came in expecting the worst."

"Considering your history with this place, you get a pass. And while the guys are stuck out here in the rain on a wild goose chase for the victim's alleged crash pad, we get to go get our nerd on in our warm, dry lab."

"Sounds like a lovely end to this not-so-horrific afternoon."

I sealed the box with red evidence tape and scrawled my initials across it in several places. The rain started falling harder, so we wrapped the cardboard box with the tarp to prevent any damage and hightailed it back to collect the rest of our belongings so we could head back to the station.

* * *

We stopped to grab some fast food on the way back, and by the time we arrived at the station, my previous apprehension had faded away. We checked in our one piece of evidence with the evidence clerk, and then we took it to the lab. Having already ditched our jackets and coveralls, we donned clean lab coats and new masks and gloves, ready to dive into examining our meager evidence.

Amanda frowned at the tire impression cast. "I've only examined a tire mark once, and we had a suspect vehicle for comparison. This is a shot in the dark."

"It is," I agreed. "Basically, all we can do is measure the tread width and come up with a possible class of vehicle. Determining a make and model from the tread pattern is way above my pay grade, and I don't think the department bothers paying for access to a database for comparison, anyway."

We'd have to pack up the cast and send it to the Indiana state lab for examination. Before we could do that, though, it would have to be set aside to dry for at least twenty-four hours. And then it would take a good thirty days for them to get us the result, thanks to a constant backlog that had been going on since long before I got into criminalistics.

Amanda grumbled something unintelligible and got out a ruler.

I said, "How about the vic's fingerprints? Any word from Beck?"

"Oh, yeah. I forgot to tell you. He sent me an email earlier. The fingerprints are a no-go. Nothing in AFIS. Our victim is still a John Doe."

I frowned. "Says Beck. I'm doing the second pass before having to deliver that news to the team."

Every piece of evidence we collected had to be examined twice, independently, by two criminalists. When only Amanda and I handled a case's evidence, I viewed the second exam as simply a failsafe. With Beck helping out, it was a necessity. He missed things that were right in front of his face, and that made him even worse at field investigating than lab processing.

I headed for the lab office where we kept the AFIS computer, which was equipped with a huge monitor to blow up fingerprint images as well as our access to the Automated Fingerprint Identification System database. Fingerprinting was my favorite part of the job; I enjoyed both the collection and plotting of prints. To me, it held no frustration factor. Prints were either viable or they weren't, and you had little control over that.

Now that I was in a room with a window, I could see and hear the rain and wind gusting outside. I felt bad for Baxter and the deputies, being stuck at Carnival Cove with Sterling until they either found evidence of our victim squatting in one of the empty buildings or exhausted every possibility. It wasn't like this was the storm of the century, but it would still drench their clothes and chill them to the bone.

Nothing I could do about it, though. I opened a file on the computer, and John Doe's right thumbprint took over the large screen. Great. He was a loop guy. What a surprise that this vic had the most common print type—it went along perfectly with the maddening lack of other evidence we had. Regardless, his fingerprints could still be matched with accuracy to his identity (if they were in AFIS), but it would have been nice to narrow him down to the five percent of humans with arch patterns.

Amanda breezed into the office. "Two hundred thirty-five millimeters. That's the measurement of the tire." She sat down at the computer next to me and started a Google search.

I nodded and went back to work, pulling up the right index print and letting out a happy yelp when I noticed something that stood out.

Not taking her eyes from her screen, she asked, "Getting all hot and bothered over those fingerprints?"

I fanned myself, grinning. "You know it. He's got radials on his index fingers."

"Ooh," she said appreciatively, as only a fellow criminalist would.

There were two kinds of fingerprint loop patterns—ulnar loops (loops opening toward the little finger) and radial loops (loops opening toward the thumb). Most people had all ulnar loops. A small segment of loopers had radial loops, which normally only occurred on the index finger. Finally something to set this guy apart. But again, if Beck had indeed done the first pass correctly and there were no matches in AFIS, our vic was still nothing but a ghost.

Pointing at her screen, Amanda said, "Here we go. Our treads could be from a mid-size SUV or a minivan, which would kind of make sense since we think the killer threw a chair in his or her vehicle along with the body. A compact car or even a sedan probably wouldn't have had that kind of room."

I looked over at her. "So...we're looking for a killer soccer mom, then?"

She laughed. "Yes. This is most definitely the work of a soccer mom."

Pushing back from the computer, she said, "And with that, I'm taking a break. Later."

I bid her goodbye and went back to plotting the fingerprints. When I was almost finished, I got a call from Vic.

"Hey," I said, putting my phone on speaker so I could keep working on my last print and enter the information into AFIS.

He asked, "You still out at the park? This storm's getting nasty."

Thunder rumbled in the distance, making me thankful I could reply, "Nope. A tragic lack of evidence cut my field work short and forced me into the safety and comfort of the lab. I'm running prints and generally wasting time until the pre-autopsy meeting."

"Nice. Does this mean your afternoon wasn't as terrible as you'd imagined?"

I wrinkled my nose. "I suppose not."

Hesitating, he said, "So then...you're not mad at me for nudging you to take the case?"

"No, but I'm not going to lie—your nudging felt more like a sucker punch."

"Sorry. I've wanted to say something for a while." His voice growing warm, he added, "I'm proud of you for getting back out there."

"Thanks. You feeling okay after the run?"

"Yeah, I'm fine."

"Uh-huh. I bet you were fine the whole time."

He cleared his throat. "Okay, good talk."

"Manetti..."

"See you tomorrow."

I chuckled to myself as he ended the call.

The AFIS computer came back with a couple of very low probability matches, which I quickly compared against my John Doe's prints. No luck. On the bright side, Beck had actually done his job well for once.

My text tone chimed with a message from Sterling: *Time for the pre-autopsy meeting. Head over now.*

I had to break the news to him eventually, and it would be way easier over text than telling him in person. *Will do. BTW, our John Doe isn't in AFIS.*

His reply: *Or maybe you just suck at your job. Get your ass over here.*

5

I drove myself to the pre-autopsy meeting, wondering if the detectives had gone straight there from the scene or had come back to the station first. Normally, Baxter would give me a ride to this meeting. In fact, he and I pretty much went everywhere together during the course of a case, but I had a sinking feeling that was not going to happen this time.

When I got to the morgue, Baxter and Sterling were finishing up putting on their protective gear—gowns, masks, and gloves.

The only greeting I received was from Sterling, and it wasn't a nice one. "You struck out hard on the fingerprints. What have you actually got for evidence?"

I stuffed my arms into a gown and tied it around my waist. "The tire impressions and chair tracks we showed you."

"Ooh. So you've got jack and shit. Great job today."

He wasn't wrong. As excited as Amanda had been about finding those chair and tire tracks, there was really no definitive way to tie them to this particular case. It was likely they were linked, but no test could prove it. At best, the track marks were a non-essential piece of circumstantial evidence, a tidbit of information to help flesh out a timeline of events for the detectives to use against their suspect during interrogation, if this case ever got that far.

I fired back, "So I take it *your* search was super fruitful and now you not only know the victim's identity but have also amassed a list of viable suspects?"

"Shut up, Matthews."

I grinned evilly at him as Baxter rolled his eyes and pushed past us. Sterling bailed as well, leaving me to finish suiting up alone.

I entered the morgue's inner sanctum and joined Baxter, Sterling, and Dr. Berg, who were standing silently next to the slab where our still stinky but slightly less bloated victim lay. A crisp white sheet covered the body from the neck down. I wished the head was covered as well. Maggots had done a number on every available orifice. Even though Dr. Berg had removed the victim's clothing and washed the body, there were still a few of them hanging around, most likely having wriggled to the surface after a deep dive in the victim's soft tissue. Sterling's jaw was clenched tight. Baxter looked kind of green, but he was hanging in there.

Dr. Berg said quietly, "We'll go ahead and get started."

"Without the DA?" I blurted out, too mesmerized by the gore to remember Dr. Berg's reverent morgue protocol.

Luckily, Dr. Berg didn't shoot me a frown over my lack of volume control. "Since the victim is at this point a true John Doe, DA McAlister has opted out of this meeting."

Without knowing the victim's identity, there was no one to blame and therefore no charges for DA McAlister to pursue, giving him the luxury of "opting out." Lucky bastard.

Dr. Berg continued, "The autopsy for John Doe will begin at nine o'clock tomorrow morning. Who will be attending?"

Sterling raised a finger in the air.

Dr. Berg nodded. "As I mentioned at the scene, my preliminary determination of the cause of death is asphyxiation. With the body in this unfortunate state, I'm afraid my findings may not be as cut and dried as you might like. Lividity suggests the victim had been in the position where he was found for days. Dr. Seong should be able to narrow down a window for you." He pulled down the sheet to reveal the victim's torso, but all I could focus on was that freaky, deflated arm. "Perimortem wounds include blunt force trauma to the victim's ribcage and what I believe could be scratch marks at his neck from his own fingernails, which would further suggest asphyxia. I will verify the presence of skin cells and blood under the fingernails during autopsy." He went to pull the sheet back up, but it had slid a bit askew. In his attempt to straighten the sheet and recover the body, we got a glimpse of more of our victim than we'd bargained for. Not that we hadn't seen naked victims before, but I had yet to lay eyes on the business end of a corpse in full bloat stage who'd been fully victimized by maggots.

It was more than my strong stomach could stand. Eyes tightly shut, I bent over and clamped both hands over my mask, sealing it tightly over my face, worried what might happen if I got one more whiff of decomp.

Evidently it was more than Sterling could stand, too. "Dick maggots," he choked out on a barely contained retch.

His turn of phrase made me laugh, jarring my stomach and worsening my nausea.

Baxter, who was a million times more likely than either of us to be the first to vomit, was evidently okay, and he sounded pissed. "Get it together, you two," he griped, his voice a terse whisper. In a normal tone to Dr. Berg, he said, "I assume his face is too distended to do any kind of facial recognition or sketch, right?"

Dr. Berg sounded a little tight as he replied, "I'm afraid so, Detective. And even once the distention abates, the face won't return accurately enough to its former shape to be of much help." By now Sterling and I had righted ourselves. Dr. Berg gave us both a reproachful glance as he asked, "Does anyone have questions for me at this time?"

Sterling and I shook our heads.

Baxter replied, "No more right now, Dr. Berg. Thank you."

Dr. Berg nodded. "I'll see you tomorrow, Detective Sterling. Goodbye, all."

We left Dr. Berg and filed out to the changing area. Sterling and I both ripped our masks off and inhaled deep gulps of clean air marred only by the squeaky-clean sharpness of bleach.

Sterling shook his head, his eyes kind of glazed over. "I'll never unsee that. Never."

"Same," I breathed.

Baxter snapped, "That was unprofessional, especially in the morgue. You should both know better."

Sterling scoffed. "You puke at the drop of a hat, dude. I don't wanna hear it from you."

I said, "Pretty sure he's referring to the 'dick maggots' comment." Turning to Baxter, I added, "Come on. You, with the terrible gallows humor, didn't think that was even a little funny?"

"There's a time and place for everything. And this wasn't it." With that, he slammed his used gear into the bin and stalked out of the room.

I turned to Sterling as I removed my gown and gloves. "Pardon the pun, but what crawled up his ass?"

Sterling laughed. "Hell if I know. He hasn't been himself lately. Edgy and pissed off. Kind of an asshole."

"He took over your role, then."

"Hardy-har-har, Matthews. You're funnier than I remember."

A serious compliment, coming from Sterling. But my mind could think of nothing but Baxter and what was making him so upset.

* * *

Back at the station, I headed straight to the breakroom for coffee before our first team meeting.

Jayne was passing by in the hall. Upon seeing me sitting alone sipping my coffee, she stopped and leaned against the doorframe. "How was your first day back? Must have been okay if you're not raiding the vending machine for chocolate bars."

I smiled. "It's been...just okay. A candy bar would definitely soothe my soul, but ultimately I feel better when I don't eat them."

"That's very adult of you."

"I think hanging out with Manetti is rubbing off on me in a good way this time. You can thank him for me agreeing to show up today."

She tried not to smile but failed. "I'll have to do that."

I'd felt like something was up with him earlier, and now I knew. Life is easier when your friends don't all know each other.

She continued down the hall, and I downed the rest of my coffee and followed her to the conference room. I somehow managed never to be first to these meetings, often coming in last, like today, and having to take the only seat left—next to Baxter. I was going to at least smile and nod, but he studiously avoided looking at me, or at anyone for that matter. His head was buried in his phone, and he seemed to be carrying on an active text conversation.

Chief Deputy Sheriff Rick Esparza, who I hadn't run into out at the scene, said to me, "Good to have you back, Ms. Matthews."

"Thanks, Chief."

"How's Agent Manetti's recovery going?"

Sterling chimed in, "Yeah, how's your *buddy* doing?"

He was clearly trying to bait me, but I didn't bite. "He's better. Still on leave from the bureau. It'll be a while before he's back out in the field."

While the chief merely nodded, Sterling jeered, "Too bad for him, but good for us. No chance we'll have to deal with him on this case, even if it turns into a real shitshow."

Baxter hadn't moved a muscle all during this conversation; he merely kept his head down, still glued to his phone.

"Um...yeah," I replied.

Jayne said, "Let's get started. As you all well know, we have very little to go on. No identity on the victim. No TOD or DOD yet. Dr. Seong is working on it and should have something for us soon. Detectives, your report?"

Sterling looked down at the file in front of him, a very short, bulleted list on top of a meager stack of case information. "The scene is secured as best we can, given the sheer area of it. It's ready for your approval for release, Sheriff. We found no signs of struggle and no primary crime scene that we can discern. We found no evidence of the victim's identity on the property. We checked every locker room, snack bar, pump building, outbuilding, and outhouse out there and got nothing. Worse, there have been no missing persons reports filed in the past week in Hamilton, Marion, or Boone Counties for males matching his general description."

This guy really was a ghost. A ghost with no one to realize he was gone. I shivered at the thought.

I added, "I ran his prints, but he's not in AFIS."

Frown stuck on his face, Sterling continued, "We questioned the fifteen-year-old kid with the drone who discovered the body, and we questioned his parents. None of them have any priors, and the kid's an honor student. They all told the same story—the kid plays around with the drone a couple of times a week and often flies over the park. We're getting a warrant to collect all the video footage he took from the past week." He tossed his pen down onto the file. "That's all I got."

Jayne asked, "Speaking of cameras, I'm sure there aren't any traffic cams all the way out there, but are there any private security cameras in use in the area?"

Chief Esparza looked up from the notes he'd been taking. "Not according to any of the neighbors the deputies spoke to. And further, none of the neighbors recalled seeing anyone lurking around the park or any vehicles coming or going from the front or back entrance lately."

Amanda and I shared a glance. That news was no boost for our theory, but just because no neighbors had seen a vehicle at the back gate didn't mean one hadn't been there.

Jayne nodded, making some notes as well. "Did Dr. Berg have any more information to impart at the pre-autopsy meeting?"

Baxter said, "He said he noticed some blunt force trauma on the victim's ribcage and scratch marks on his neck possibly from his own fingernails, which supports his asphyxia theory."

Jayne frowned. "That would seem to point to murder, or at the very least, assault, rather than simply an accident or death by illness. Ms. Matthews, Ms. Carmack, did you find any evidence to support any of that?"

With each investigation we did together, I'd been trying to hang back and give Amanda more responsibility and experience. I knew it wouldn't be long before she'd tire of being Beck's second and go find a job worthy of her expertise. I knew she liked working for the department, but I also knew she craved more. I sat quietly while she gave our report.

"There were no fingerprints to be found at the scene. We did, however, find some interesting tracks near the body and also near the back gate." She slid a large photo of the chair tracks toward the center of the large table. "These look like they were made by an office chair, which could have been used to transport the body from the back gate to the pool." She slid another photo toward the middle of the table, this one of the tire tracks.

"These tire tracks seem to be fairly new and were found near the chair tracks. Based on the size, they came from a mid-size SUV or a minivan. We're sending the tire impressions to the state lab for further identification."

Sterling had been fidgeting while she was speaking, and evidently couldn't keep quiet any longer. "Like I said at the scene, those tracks could have been made at any time."

Amanda glared at him. "Thank you for mansplaining that to me yet again, Detective. But no matter how insignificant, I don't ignore evidence at a scene."

I resisted the urge to reach out a hand to high-five her. When I first met her, she never would have said something like that in a meeting. I noticed Jayne covering a smile. Sterling looked sufficiently put in his place.

Amanda continued, "The victim's clothes just got sent over from the morgue, so that's all we have left to process."

Jayne gave me a pointed look. "Sounds like you two can close the book on today pretty quickly, then." Snapping her fingers as if she just remembered something, she said, "Who spoke to Dudley Cooper, the owner of the property?"

Chief Esparza gave a little wave. "I drew the short straw. At least over the phone, he seemed sufficiently surprised and upset to hear what had happened. He agreed, a little grudgingly, to do whatever we needed to fully cooperate with our investigation. He sent out someone from his maintenance company immediately to unlock all the buildings for our search."

I hadn't considered how the detectives and deputies were going to get into all of the buildings. Not all of them were in the same dilapidated state as the back outbuilding I entered. It was pretty nice of Dudley to be so cooperative, considering the department had falsely arrested him for murder several months ago. For a fleeting moment, I wondered how he was doing these days, but then Jayne's voice broke me out of my thoughts.

"Let's all try to make some headway tonight, if we can, at least on identifying our victim. I need to make some kind of statement soon to the press. Good luck."

Noticing Baxter was back to being engrossed in his phone, I dawdled as everyone else packed up to leave. Soon, it was just the two of us.

I said, "Hey, if you want, I can stay a while and help out. I'll even take the tip line, if it'll help." We all notoriously hated tip line duty, so I was hoping my offer would prove to Baxter that I was more than happy to help.

Looking up with a start, he noticed for the first time that we were alone in the room together. He jumped out of his chair and snatched the haphazard stack of papers in front of him, rumpling them in the process. "No, that won't be necessary." He hurried out of the room without a backward glance, missing the disappointment I was sure was written all over my face.

I gathered my things and went back to the lab, where Amanda was removing the victim's clothes from their paper evidence bag. I put on a lab coat and new gloves and mask and went over to stand beside her to survey our next task.

Her eyes said it all, but she croaked out, "Clothes are never my favorite, but these are soooo nasty...even the shirt."

She wasn't wrong. While we expected there to be some amount of bodily waste on pretty much all of the clothing we processed, this batch was above and beyond. We'd be lucky if we didn't find a few maggots and other assorted bugs that had tagged along for the ride.

I blew out a breath. "Okay, let's get this over with. I'll even offer to let you start with the shirt."

"I'm going to need to go worst to best. Get it over with before it gets in my head."

"Fair enough."

I took the tattered T-shirt over to a workspace and positioned it under a bench magnifier. The material had once been gray, with a mapped area I didn't recognize and the word "Westerley" silk-screened on the front. It reminded me of the type of shirts the college gamer kids at Ashmore often wore. I got the camera and took a few photos, first of the front of the shirt and then of the back. I then began the in-depth examination, section by section. The collar and surrounding area looked like a pinkish/clear substance had run down them, I assumed from runoff from the victim's mouth and nose. Blood dotted the shirt near all the tear marks, presumably from animals picking at the body.

The interesting part was the orange dust and dark-ish smudges I found all over the part of the shirt that would have covered the victim's stomach. The coroner had said the body had been in the same position for a while, on his side/front, which would have at least partially protected the front of the shirt from the elements. I circled the area with a Sharpie and then took out a swab to collect a sample. The bright orange dust looked familiar to me. I took a step back and studied the shirt. The swipes of orange dust and the corresponding dark smudges were kind of uniform...as if made by fingers. In fact, it reminded me a lot of every shirt my three-year-old nephew Nate owned, all of them shamelessly used as napkins when his little fingers got dirty. This shirt looked like a Nate shirt after a hearty session of Cheeto eating.

As ingenious as I thought my assumption was, it still didn't narrow down our victim's identity. Most people liked Cheetos, although not everyone wiped their Cheeto fingers on their shirts. However, the shirt design might help shed some light on the victim's identity—if it had been purchased intentionally and wasn't some hand-me-down. I made a note to let the detectives know and packaged the possible Cheeto dust swab to send to the state lab.

The pants and underwear were a total loss. They were such a mess, I couldn't get a read on them. The only thing I could determine was that there was no semen present anywhere after shining a black light over the two articles. If nothing else, at least we could rule out full sexual assault by a male.

With nothing more to do, I sent a quick email to the team about my meager findings and went home, truly disappointed about my less-than-triumphant return to consulting.

6

I was stuck in the same dour mood the next morning as I went through the motions of teaching my first two classes. My spirits did finally lift a little when my closest friend, Dr. Samantha Jordan, burst into my office and dragged me to lunch so she could tell me all about the anthropological research trip to Belize she'd just scheduled for the coming summer. Even taking in her infectious excitement, I still wasn't myself, and she noticed.

"Okay, what's up? Has living like a nun the past couple of months finally driven you insane?" She wrinkled her nose as she glanced at my plate of chicken Caesar salad, with the croutons carefully removed and tossed aside. "Or maybe it's going sober, Keto, and celibate all at once. You've got to have at least one vice. Maybe you should take up smoking."

I laughed. "That's not the problem. I saw Baxter yesterday."

Her eyes widened. "Why did you let me go on for fifteen whole minutes about myself when you were sitting on that kind of information? Did he grab you and kiss you until you saw stars?"

"Sadly, no."

Besides Vic, Sam was the only person who knew all the details of what had gone on between Baxter and me. I relayed my brief conversations with him to Sam, as well as his side of the infamous phone call, hoping she might glean a tidbit of anything that would give me a clue as to why he was being so distant. Aside from the "her" from his phone call, of course, but I was trying not to dwell on that. I didn't want that to be the reason, but it made more sense than anything else.

When I was finished, she shook her head. "That sucks, especially the part where it's entirely possible he might have moved on." She added gently, "Do you think maybe he misinterpreted your two months' worth of radio silence as *you* moving on?"

I slumped in my chair and said softly, "Oh. I never thought of it that way. I mean, we decided we couldn't be anything more than work colleagues. But at the same time, I needed a break from crime scenes for a while. Those two things were totally unrelated..."

"But maybe they seemed related to him."

Putting my head in my hands, I moaned, "How stupid am I?"

"Well...this is the second time you've kicked the poor man to the curb."

"There was no kicking."

"Maybe not, but there were plenty of poor choices on your part. You truly have a talent for that where men are concerned."

I frowned. She wasn't completely wrong. "I chose Manetti. He wasn't a bad choice."

She scoffed. "And how's that working out for you?"

"Damn. What's with the salt, Sam? I thought you liked Manetti."

"I do, and I would totally go after him if there wasn't all that ongoing weirdness between you two."

"There's no weirdness. You're free to date him whenever you want." I speared a large bite of my salad and shoved it in my mouth.

She stared at me. "You're seriously going to sit there and tell me that you've been playing nursemaid for that hunky alpha male for nearly two months and haven't had even the least bit of an urge to Florence Nightingale his gorgeous ass?"

There might have been one evening when I was feeling soul-crushingly lonely that I had the slightest twinge of nostalgia for Vic, but I didn't act on it. Not worth bringing up. "I haven't." I took another big bite, hoping she wouldn't push me to elaborate.

"And he's made no move on you, either?"

I shook my head. He'd been nothing but a gentleman.

Sam gave me a knowing glance. "Besides always being available literally any time you call or text and going on that gross meat diet with you and taking you to dinner and coffee and out running?"

Why this conversation had turned from Baxter to Vic, I didn't know. "He's bored as hell. He has nothing better to do."

"Mmm hmm," she murmured, taking a bite of the evil-looking blueberry muffin she'd bought.

Over her right shoulder, I saw Ben Seong waving from the register as he was paying for his food. "Oh, there's Ben. And he spotted us." I waved back and added hurriedly, "A quick heads up, he's probably going to ask you out."

Sam's jaw dropped. "Ben the Bug Man wants to date me? I don't know how I feel about that."

I shrugged. "What? He's handsome, he's always cheerful, and he's freaking brilliant. What more do you want?"

"He's a super nerd," she hissed.

Staring pointedly at her, I replied, "Says the anthropology professor who enjoys boiling the skin off random body parts in her spare time. Ben's headed this way."

Grimacing, she demanded, "Did you encourage this?"

"What, him asking you out?"

"Yes."

"I most certainly did."

That morning, Ben had stopped by my classroom under the guise of thanking me yet again for calling him out to help with the scene yesterday. But it was clear that he wanted instead to not-so-slyly ask me if my friend Sam was single. I was more than happy to urge him to go for it with her.

She groaned. "He likes bugs, Ellie. That's just weird."

"Bugs are cooler than boiled feet, nerd. You could do worse. You often do worse. Your last guy was so dumb—" I cut off just as Ben got within earshot. "Hey, Ben. You want to sit with us?"

I bit back a wince as Sam kicked me in the shin under the table.

His face coloring with a blush, Ben replied, "Yeah, I'd love to. Hello, Dr. Jord—uh...Samantha."

"Hi, Ben," she replied, her expression lighting up a little as I noticed her giving him a once-over. His hair was freshly trimmed. His clothes were stylish, for a professor. I knew he'd been working out lately, and it showed. The man looked good; there was no denying that.

I stood suddenly. "Sorry, guys, but I have to run. I just remembered I've got to call the sheriff and give her an update before my next class. Working two jobs is a juggling act sometimes."

Sam threw me a glare while Ben's grin widened. It seemed as though my work was done.

* * *

I finished my classes for the day and had to hurry to arrive in time for the scheduled meeting at the station with the team. I hoped the detectives would have more information than Amanda and I had to share, but that was not the case. Sterling and Baxter had made zero headway, and both seemed angry and frustrated. Ben Seong reported that, by his calculations, the victim had been dead for four days when he was found. But without any suspects to question, the precise date of death wasn't a useful investigative tool.

The autopsy hadn't netted much new information. Dr. Berg had verified that the victim had in fact been asphyxiated. He also found traces of blood matching the victim's blood type under the victim's fingernails. He was sending the blood and skin cells from under the nails to be DNA tested, but he wasn't too convinced there would be any from his attacker. Dr. Berg had also found a thin line of bruising around the victim's neck, which he believed couldn't have been from any kind of ligature. His hyoid bone was unharmed, so he hadn't been manually strangled either. His conclusion was that the victim may have been robbed of air by a plastic bag drawn over his head and held tight around his neck, causing him to claw at his own neck to free himself. Knowing how he died didn't lend any information to who had killed him.

Jayne drew the meeting to a close, thanking everyone for their work on the case and advising us that if no new information came to light within the next day or so, the investigation would be turned over to the cold case division. In other words, our unidentified victim's death would go unsolved.

Everyone slowly gathered their things and began exiting the conference room. Baxter, the first to hit the door, didn't even look my way as he left. After saying goodbye to Jayne, I went to go find Baxter. I needed to make an effort to mend our relationship, whether he wanted to or not. I found him in his cubicle, his attention on his phone. When he heard my heels stop behind his chair, he hid his phone and turned to face me, his expression as blank and passive as it had been yesterday.

"Hey," I ventured, my resolve weakening under his gaze. "I, um...hope you don't think my turning down a few of the investigations lately had anything to do with...um...us. I've been in a weird place, and I really needed a break from all the—"

He cut me off and said flatly, "I didn't think it was strange that you took a break from investigating. I think it's right to put some space between us. Besides, you don't need this job."

That was an odd thing for him to say. He'd always encouraged me to continue to consult for the department. In fact, my consulting gig had been his idea in the first place.

I continued, "Sure, but...I want to make it clear to you that—"

He stood and pasted on a smile—the only time I'd ever seen the man with a fake smile on his face. "Don't worry. We're good." Scooting around me, he strode down the hall and disappeared into the men's room.

I stared after him, heartbroken all over again. We were anything but "good."

* * *

The next day, Vic and I took my nephew, Nate, to Forest Park in Noblesville. Nate had taken a liking to Vic, mostly because he'd been missing one of his few male role models, Baxter. Ever since my half-sister Rachel's kidnapping, Baxter had been a rock for her, walking her through her fears and emotional issues when she could barely leave the house. His younger brother had gone through a similar experience in his childhood, so aside from her therapist, Baxter was the perfect person to listen when she needed a sympathetic ear. However, in the interest of making sure he wasn't seen coming and going from my home, Baxter had been meeting Rachel in coffee shops and restaurants, which weren't the best places to bring a rambunctious nearly-four-year-old boy. Nate had inadvertently gotten left out.

"Agent Vic! Agent Vic! Watch me parkour!" Nate chirped as he ran at the swing set pole, put one foot on it, and vaulted himself off. He pumped both of his tiny fists in the air. "Parkour!"

Vic grinned at him. "Where in the world did you learn parkour, kiddo?"

Already on his way to the next piece of playground equipment, Nate didn't answer.

I explained, "Rachel just discovered *The Office*, so it's on a lot at our house. I think he saw the one with the parkour a few days ago."

Vic stared off in the distance, not a hundred percent his usual self today. He had mostly good days, and I'd learned not to push his buttons on the not-so-good days. He still had a little leftover pain from his injuries, and he was trying to use over-the-counter medication rather than run the risk of becoming dependent on prescription medication. Add that to dealing with everything else he'd gone through, and anyone would be broody and cranky at times.

He finally said, "Hey, I wanted to tell you something..."

He paused for so long, I finally prodded gently, "What?"

My phone rang, and he shook his head. "Nothing. It can wait."

I said, "My phone can wait."

He shook his head again. "You're on an active homicide investigation. Answer it."

I looked at my phone. Oddly enough, the Caller ID showed "Jason Sterling." Surprised, I said to Vic, "You're right, I should probably take this. It's Sterling. Do you mind keeping an eye on Nate for a minute?"

"Sure."

I walked far enough away from the playground to get some quiet and answered the call. "I didn't think you had my number."

Ignoring my greeting, Sterling said, "We turned our homicide over to cold case."

I still didn't understand why I was hearing from him. "Okay...I feel like this call could have been an email."

He hesitated. "Uh...did Amanda say anything to you about me?"

I broke into laughter. *That* was why he called. "What are you, thirteen?"

"You don't have to be such a bitch about it."

Still amused, I replied, "Neither do you."

He went silent until I thought he might have hung up on me, but then I heard Baxter's voice in the background and Sterling mutter, "Gimme a minute."

I took pity on him. "Look, I don't want to get in the middle of this, and she didn't really go into specifics when she told me you guys split up. But I do know that whatever you said to her really hurt her. Some friendly advice? Some women don't appreciate your asshole routine as much as I do."

"So what the hell do I do now?"

I nearly fell over. Jason Sterling was asking me for relationship advice. I let out a snort.

His voice was tight. "Matthews, you know it's a damn catastrophe if I'm asking you this question."

"I'm well aware. I guess my advice would be...basically do and say the opposite of what you'd normally do and say."

"That's not helpful," he barked.

"See, this is what I mean. If she says something that rubs you the wrong way, don't call her out. She's pissed at you right now, and even if you suddenly start being super sweet—which we all know is not going to happen—she's going to say some salty things until you can manage to charm her into forgiving you. If you absolutely can't come up with a non-confrontational reply, then just smile and nod."

"Smile and nod? That's stupid."

I stifled a laugh. "You're seriously proving my point over and over again. The correct response would have been something like, 'okay, I'll try that' or 'I appreciate the tip.' Try one out on me."

His reply was a low growl.

"I'll help you get started. 'Matthews, I appreciate...'"

"Matthews...I...appreciate...the help."

"There. Did that kill you?"

"Damn near," he griped.

"Well, since you managed to say it to your worst enemy and live to tell about it, then you can surely say it to the woman you're crazy about."

"Fine. And...thanks."

While my conversation with Sterling had given me a dose of comic relief, as I headed back to the playground, I couldn't help but slip into a bit of a funk. Despite everyone's best efforts, the case had been a bust. I'd worked on cases that had gone nowhere before, or worse, had gone well on the investigative side and been lost in court. This time felt different.

I threw myself down next to Vic on the park bench. Nate had made friends with a girl about his age, and they were pretending to be frogs, as far as I could gather. I blew out a sigh. "Guess what? My homicide got shoved off to cold case. No ID on the victim, no suspects, nothing to pursue."

Vic frowned. "I'm sorry. I know that's frustrating."

"It feels like I put myself through a lot of bullshit for nothing."

He gave me a pat on the back. "I know it wasn't easy for you to set foot back inside Carnival Cove, but I think you should be proud of yourself for getting back out in the field."

"I was actually talking about my interactions with Baxter." I'd told Vic a little about what went on. Now that our friendship had solidified, I felt like I could talk to him about my relationship with Baxter.

"Ah."

I looked over at him. "I know what you're going to say—there's nothing that can be changed about our situation, so there's no reason to dwell on it."

He smiled. "Do I say stuff like that?"

I went on, "I mean, I know we can't hang out or anything, but he didn't have to ignore me and cut me off every time I tried to have a conversation with him and just..." I shrugged.

"Hurt your feelings?" So maybe Vic was still harboring some ill will toward Baxter.

"Yeah," I said quietly.

He put an arm around me. "Look, I hate to be that guy, but I don't think you two should work closely together like you used to. It's a conflict of interest for him that he can't afford to lean into. And we all know if anyone gives you an inch, you take a mile."

I shrugged away from him. "So you're saying I had this cold shoulder bullshit coming?"

"Maybe, if he thought it was the only way to keep you at arm's length."

"So now you're defending him? Pick a side, Manetti."

He put his arm around me again. "I'm always on your side. I don't want to see you get hurt, and I think if you keep trying to force something that can't happen, all you're going to get is hurt."

"So what do I do? Just pretend he doesn't exist until after the trial is over?"

"I know that's not how you're wired, but you have to find a way to put him out of your mind. You'll drive yourself crazy otherwise."

As much as I hated the idea of it, and no matter how painful it would be for me, the only way to have a chance for a future with Baxter was to give him up.

* * *

Vic and I took Nate with us to do Vic's grocery shopping and give Rachel a little more uninterrupted study time, and then we dropped him at home with her. We went on to Vic's house, where he insisted on making me dinner.

While he was seasoning the steaks he was planning to grill, he said, "I had a breakthrough in therapy today."

There it was. I'd thought all afternoon he'd been gearing up to say something. "That's great. Good for you." I knew from dealing with my sister not to ask about specifics from therapy sessions. You supported the person and congratulated them on their progress and left it at that. If they wanted to tell you more, they would. If not, you didn't press.

Vic opted to tell me more. He faced me. "Turns out, I owe you a big apology."

I gave him a strange look. "I can't imagine what for."

"For using you to try to make Shawna jealous."

Vic had dated Shawna Meehan, another running buddy of his, for a while the previous year, but she'd broken things off. Unfortunately, she'd been one of the victims in the last murder case we'd worked.

I raised an eyebrow at him. "Seriously? You used an out of shape drunk to try to make Workout Barbie jealous. I fail to see your logic."

He frowned at me. "I used a beautiful, brilliant professor who stopped a serial killer and solved a thirteen-year-old murder in under a week while under extreme duress. Do you know how many of my fellow agents begged me to introduce them to you?"

My jaw dropped. "So I could have had my pick of G-men if you hadn't kept me all for yourself? Thanks a lot, Manetti."

"I'm being serious."

"And I'm not because I'm not upset in the least. I used you; you used me. We're even."

"Yeah, but I made such a deal out of the fact that you used me so you wouldn't go running to Detective Baxter. I had no room to talk."

"I've only told you a little of my past history with romantic relationships. This is not the worst thing someone's done to me. Not by a long shot. I'm trying to tell you your apology is not needed." As I studied his pained face, I saw there was something more going on than guilt over treating me badly. My heart sank. "Oh, no...Vic..." I let out a heavy sigh. "You were still in love with Shawna when she died."

He nodded. "And I realized today that I'm still not over her."

I enveloped him in a hug. "Now I'm the one who needs to apologize. How many times did I bust your balls over how you handled yourself during her murder investigation? I wish I'd known how you really felt about her."

"You and me, both. I knew I was jealous over her going back to her old boyfriend, but I chalked it up to a bruised ego. I had no clue my feelings ran so deep."

I let him go and looked him in the eye. "I can't imagine going through what you did, even if you didn't realize exactly what you were feeling. No wonder you couldn't hold your temper and kept cowboying the investigation. If it had been me, I'd have burned the station to the ground trying to get the answers I needed."

"I did manage to get us both fired."

I shrugged. "Eh, we had it coming."

Vic managed a feeble smile.

Knowing the answer, but asking anyway, I said, "So what can I do for you? I can't change the bandage on this wound or be your drinking buddy. And no matter how far or fast we run, we can't get away from this one."

"What you're doing right now is what I need."

I nodded, my heart breaking for him. "Okay." I went back to chopping vegetables, feeling the weight of his loss heavy in the air. I didn't know how long it would take him to work through his feelings, but I was going to be there for him the entire way.

7

One week later

After wrapping up a lecture on collecting shoeprints for my first class of the day, I asked, "Any questions? Finals are fast approaching, and this topic will definitely be on the exam."

A young man with a douchey haircut raised his hand. He didn't wait for me to call on him before blurting out, "I heard the last murder you worked on got sent to cold case."

I had to suppress a growl. Some of these little buggers worked my last nerve. Especially this kid—a local trust fund baby whose mommy was a state senator. He seemed to have no boundaries in any situation. His goal was to become an FBI agent, and he rarely passed up an opportunity to mention it.

"That's not a question," I replied. "And even if it were, it doesn't pertain to class material." I addressed the rest of the class. "Any other questions?" Half the students raised their hands. I frowned. "Any _class-related_ questions?" All the hands went down.

I stewed for a few seconds and then said, "Okay, fine. Yes, the last case I worked went cold. It happens, and it's very frustrating. We had no ID on the victim. His prints weren't in AFIS, so it's not likely his DNA is in CODIS. We can still hold out hope for a match, but it'll take a month to get results back. If we don't know who the victim is, we can't even fathom who might want to kill him, so there's no one to interview or investigate. The sheriff's department has been fortunate lately in closing several complex cases. We did just as thorough a job on the latest homicide, but there simply wasn't any evidence to find."

Trust Fund Baby smirked. "The FBI wasn't involved in this one. Maybe they should have been called in."

I wanted to throat-punch this kid, but instead I tried to think about how much of a kick Vic was going to get out of hearing about this comment later. "The FBI only gets involved when the scope of an investigation warrants a law enforcement presence with resources and jurisdiction beyond that of the county. All the federal reach, better tech, and profiling in the world isn't going to help when there's zero evidence."

My door opened, and my favorite deputy, Carlos Martinez, stepped into my classroom. I tried not to show any emotion as I said, "That's it for today," and began heading Martinez's way.

His interruption had saved me from any more uncomfortable discussion with the asshat FBI wannabe, which I appreciated. However, an in-person visit from Martinez usually meant one thing—he was here to escort me to a crime scene, whether I wanted to go or not.

My stomach plummeted as I reached him and saw none of the usual sparkle in his eyes. "What's wrong, Martinez?"

He lowered his voice. "Sorry to be the bearer of bad news, Matthews, but the sheriff says you have to come with me. Two high profile DBs. This whole thing is gonna suck." He shook his head. "Scratch that. It already sucks."

Apprehension slid up my spine. "What's going on?"

"Check the local news. But do it on the way to my shop."

"Do I have time to change clothes?"

"Make it snappy."

I hurried ahead of him to my office, where I shuttered all the blinds and quickly changed into layered athletic wear. After I'd nearly frozen to death at multiple crime scenes this winter, I kept a selection of warm clothing at the ready both at home and in my office. Plus, I was wearing a new skirt, sweater, and shoes, and they weren't going anywhere near a crime scene, coveralls or not. I slicked my hair into a ponytail and put on a hat as well, also remembering to grab a few snacks and drinks. It was going to be a long day.

I glanced at my phone as we left the science building and headed toward Martinez's waiting cruiser. I didn't have to bother checking the local news, because one text from Vic said it all. *Heads up, the news just reported a double homicide in Carmel at the home of Aurora Bennett. I assume there's no way you're getting out of this one. Good luck.*

I grunted as I sank into Martinez's passenger seat, typing a quick reply, *On my way there now*, followed by the angry cursing emoji.

"Crazy, right? Indy's sweetheart and her hubby dead in their home." Martinez pulled out of the parking lot and turned on his siren, accelerating through the parting traffic.

"He's one of my fellow Ashmore professors."

"Ouch. Sorry."

"I didn't know him that well, but the students really seemed to like him. A lot of them will be crushed."

He nodded absently, but I didn't know if it was because he was concentrating on the road or trying to come up with a reply. After a moment, he blurted out, "Sterling says it's a bloodbath."

I put my head in my hands. I wasn't mentally ready for a bloodbath.

* * *

As we pulled into an expensive neighborhood only minutes from Ashmore, I shook my head. "Damn. One street over, and this would not have been our problem."

Martinez laughed. "I know, right? Could this place be any closer to the county line?"

Ninety-Sixth Street served as the Hamilton-Marion County line. It also served as the southern border of the subdivision where our victims lived. The street was jam-packed with law enforcement, emergency, and media vehicles.

I whistled. "Bet the neighbors are pissed."

"Yeah, you'd think shelling out the big bucks to live in this subdivision would protect you from all this."

I shivered. He was talking about the indignity of your neighborhood being turned into a media circus and the sheer embarrassment of it being the scene of a major violent crime. I was more thinking about the fact that these people, at least before today, had always felt safe in their homes because they lived in a well-to-do neighborhood. I'd grown up bouncing from one bad neighborhood to another with my mother, never sleeping soundly until my stepdad came into the picture and settled us into a decent home. Regardless of the property value here, no one in this area was going to sleep soundly for a good while.

Martinez dropped me off near the criminalists' van, where I could see Amanda unloading our gear. "You have fun in there."

I cocked my head to the side. "Are you not helping us with this shitshow?"

"Nope. Didn't you hear? I'm doing a stint as a TO."

"I hadn't heard, but I can't think of a better person to teach rookies the ropes than you." Martinez had seen everything and still somehow had patience and good humor in spades. I didn't know why they hadn't offered him the job long ago. "Thanks for the ride."

"No problem."

As he rolled away, I approached Amanda. "Hey, long time no see."

She smiled. "Too soon, right?" Lowering her voice, she added, "Can you believe this? I watch Aurora on the news every night. This just feels..." She held up her hands in a helpless gesture.

As I stepped into a clean jumpsuit, I supplied, "Surreal? Like we know her—even though we've never met her."

"That's exactly it. And she's *so* pretty."

Aurora Bennett was gorgeous. She was thin but curvy, her blond mane of hair was always shiny and perfectly curled, and she had the flawless skin and features of a model. But above all that, she was smart, well-spoken, and surprisingly kind and empathetic for a reporter. When she first came on the local news scene when I was in high school, every young girl in the viewing area wanted to be her, including me.

Amanda and I picked up our gear and headed toward the throng of people blocking the sidewalk in front of the largest house on the street. One of the deputies started yelling at people to "make a path" and shouldered his way through to escort us up the driveway.

Another deputy stationed at the front door had us sign the scene entry log. "Take the stairs up, turn left, then the bedroom's on the right."

We took a moment to put on our masks, gloves, and booties, and then did as he instructed, marveling at the breathtaking home as we ascended the stairs. It was decorated lavishly, in dark navy, pastel pink, and metallic gold. The walls of the two-story entryway were covered in enormous flowers, the wallpaper meant to look like a giant mural. We heard familiar voices coming from the open door at the end of the upstairs hallway. My stomach knotted as I heard Baxter's voice, and I reminded myself I was going to be detached this time for both of our sakes. We set our gear down in the hallway.

Amanda and I approached the doorway, clogged by Sterling, Baxter, Jayne, and Chief Esparza, who stood surveying the room. They halted their conversation and turned toward us. Jayne and the chief quietly greeted us. Baxter said nothing.

Sterling piped up, "Watch your step. It's a bloodbath."

"So I've heard." I had a feeling he was going to work my last nerve with that word.

The four of them moved aside so we could enter the room. Unfortunately, the term 'bloodbath' was accurate. Aurora Bennett, award-winning investigative reporter for WIND-TV Channel 7 News, lay still on a lush bed of pale gray silk, dressed in an equally expensive pink satin and lace nightgown, quite literally looking like she'd bathed in a bucket of blood. Her chest and torso were a mess of slashed flesh and ripped fabric, her blond hair crusty and stained dark. I glanced at the tufted white headboard behind her, noting a telltale pattern of several reddish-brown trails made from blood that had sprayed with each swing of the murder weapon.

Aurora's husband, Professor Lance Wakefield, lay face-down on the floor beside the bed next to a bloody chef's knife and a pile of vomit, his hands, clothing, and face smeared with blood. Ooh. That wasn't a good look, especially considering he was an ethics professor. I didn't know him well enough to know if he was capable of something like this. As I stepped farther into the room, my eyes were drawn to the wall to my right. The word "WHORE" was written haltingly on the stark white wall in all caps, in blood, no less. The sinister message took up a good third of the wall. Rivulets of now-dried blood dripped down from the letters, making the writing look like the creepy font used in horror movie trailers.

Amanda was the first to speak. "Wow."

Jayne blew out a breath. "Clearly this is going to be a difficult and delicate situation. It goes without saying, but considering the identities of the victims, we need to lock down all case-related discussions with non-essential staff and especially with civilians. I know you all know how to deal with it, but we will be hounded by the media twenty-four-seven during this case. They'll come at you at home, even, so be mindful."

Sterling waved a hand. "We got this, sheriff. It's not our first murder-suicide—"

"Double homicide," Jayne corrected him, and then she addressed the rest of us. "No one even *think* the words 'murder-suicide' outside this room. If the press get even an inkling that the husband could be a suspect, they'll crucify him, and that's not fair to his family."

"It'll be fair when we prove he did it," Sterling pointed out.

"But first we're going to investigate this scene with no preconceived opinions," she shot back. "The coroner is finishing an autopsy, so he'll be here shortly. You can go ahead and get to work on the room. I'll have some deputies take a look at the rest of the house, but I'll want you all to give it a once-over as well."

Jayne and the chief exited the room, leaving the other four of us alone. The vibe instantly got uncomfortable. This was why I'd always tried to shy away from dating coworkers.

Unable to stand the silence, I blurted out, "I certainly didn't get up this morning thinking I was going to end up in Aurora Bennett's bedroom."

Sterling snorted, thankfully helping me out. "Yeah, my dreams suddenly turned into one big nightmare."

"So what do we know?" I asked. "Who found them?"

Without looking my way, Baxter said, "The sheriff told us to investigate without preconceived opinions. We should follow her instructions."

Sterling rolled his eyes behind Baxter's back, which strangely made me feel less chided by Baxter's refusal to share case information with me. "Aurora's assistant got worried when she didn't show up at work this morning and then wouldn't answer her phone. She drove over here and let herself in and found them. At some point, she fell and broke her wrist, and the EMTs had to chase her down and sedate her to get her into an ambulance."

Baxter shot Sterling a dirty look but said nothing.

Even after receiving a warning from Martinez about the scene and dealing with death on a regular basis, I had to admit that this room was enough to drive a person to hysterics. The sheer volume of blood was horrifying. The state of Aurora's body told of undeniable malice toward her, as did the wall message. Her poor assistant, even expecting the worst, could never have imagined it would be this bad.

Amanda murmured, "I don't blame her. I guess we'd better get to it."

She and I left the room to get our gear from the hallway.

As we gathered the camera, evidence markers, and sketching tools, Amanda made a gagging noise. "It tastes like I swallowed a penny."

"Same," I replied, tucking my voice recorder into my coveralls. The overwhelming smell of blood had lodged a coppery tang in the back of my throat, even through my thick respirator mask. And then there was the aroma of vomit and bodily excrement on top of that. We'd get used to it eventually, but it would take some time.

We returned to the bedroom. This time, Amanda measured the room and started the rough sketch while I took photos. Unlike our last scene, there was no shortage of evidence here. I started with wide-angle shots of the whole room, followed by mid-range shots of both victims, the bloody knife (presumably the murder weapon), the headboard, the wall, and the dotted trails of blood leading from the bed to the wall made by several trips back and forth to collect the "paint" with which to write the crass message. I walked around the otherwise squeaky-clean, well-kept room, looking for things that seemed out of place, keeping up a quiet running commentary for my voice recorder as I went.

Of course it was obvious how Aurora had met her unfortunate end, but upon further inspection, it was pretty easy to figure it out for Lance as well.

I found an open bottle of prescription Xanax on the floor not too far from his body. That definitely deserved a series of shots, as did the crystal decanter of brown liquor on the nightstand with the matching half-full rocks glass next to it. And inches away, the real kicker—a plastic bag of white pills with "7.5 325" imprinted on them, which was pharma code for Percocet. Three types of downers taken together was a recipe for disaster. I glanced over at the vomit next to Lance's head. Yep, I could spot a number of little white pills (Xanax) and slightly bigger white pills (Percocet) amid the chunks in the brown, soupy mixture. He wasn't playing around.

Moving on, I noted the door to the master bathroom was open, and hanging on its handle was a garment bag with a clear front panel containing a man's suit. I noticed blood on the hanger, so I took some photos. There was one perfect droplet on the floor under the bag, so I picked up the bag and turned it around to look for more blood. I shivered and nearly dropped the bag. In those creepy blood letters again, "FUNERAL SUIT" was written on the white fabric backing of the bag. I took several shots of the back of the bag, and then set the bag back on the door handle and unzipped it to get some better shots of the suit, a navy-blue jacket and pants paired with a white shirt and red tie.

I made a thorough sweep of the bathroom, which was nothing short of spectacular with its pristine all-white tile, locker room sized shower, deep soaking tub, and shiny chrome fixtures. No visible blood in here, save the one droplet under the garment bag. I snapped a few photos.

Next to the bathroom was a set of French doors, which I assumed led to a closet. As I was reaching for one of the handles, I noticed some blood smeared on the right one and stopped to take photos. Using one finger to push down on the clean handle, I opened the door. The lights came on automatically to illuminate every woman's dream closet: row upon row of neatly paired heels, sandals, boots, and athletic shoes, all categorized by color and type. Clothing from activewear to formalwear, business suits to jeans, and everything in between hung neatly, also sorted by color and type. And then there was Lance's side, equally well-organized, but with half the number of items. There wasn't a single thing out of place in here, and I saw no blood. I took a few photos.

Sterling was talking through what he thought might have happened.

"He kills her, writes 'WHORE' on the wall in her blood, and then swallows a handful of pills and dies. Seems pretty simple."

"What about the suit?" I asked.

Shrugging he replied, "What about it? Lots of people pick out what they want to wear for eternity before checking out. They think they're doing their family a favor or some shit."

Baxter nodded absently. "Yeah, that sounds about right."

His fast-concurring response troubled me even more than Sterling's dismissive attitude. Those two always argued details of crime scenes. Hell, they often argued key fundamentals like prime suspects. Surely Baxter had some insight beyond agreeing with Sterling's overly obvious assessment.

"Hello again, everyone," Dr. Berg's voice called from the doorway.

We all greeted the coroner as he joined us in the room.

Dr. Berg went on, "The sheriff would like you all to meet with her downstairs for a moment while I perform my initial assessment."

The four of us trooped downstairs, saying hello to Kenny as he and a deputy folded up two gurneys to stuff into the small elevator to transport upstairs. This place was over the top with amenities. In the home's cavernous two-story great room, Jayne stood next to a tall man in a tailored suit who I would recognize anywhere.

"Shane!" I exclaimed as I approached him, removing my mask so he could see my face.

Shane Carlisle, an old buddy of mine from college who was now a detective with the Indianapolis Metropolitan Police Department, broke into a smile. "Ellie. It's been forever. I hear you keep pretty busy catching psychos."

I laughed. "You could say that. How's Kaitlyn?"

"She's great." He smiled proudly. "On an extended maternity leave right now with our six-month-old baby girl."

My jaw dropped. Shane was a dad?

Before I could ask him more about his family or what in the hell he was doing there, Jayne said, "This is Detective Shane Carlisle of the IMPD. He's going to be joining our team for this case." Her tone sounded tight.

Baxter's face went stony. Well, stonier. He was still in that weird, quiet mood.

Sterling was a little more vocal. "What? Why?" He turned to Shane. "No offense, man."

Jayne said evenly, "Since the crime scene is so near the county line and the victim is such an icon of the city, we're getting...encouragement...from multiple sources to bring in an investigator from the IMPD." By encouragement, she meant political pressure. "Detective Carlisle's involvement will give us access to IMPD resources, equipment, and also their dedicated lab. And of course his expertise is top notch." That much was true—Shane had been in homicide for most of his career and had closed a record number of cases for the IMPD.

Sterling shook his head. "We've had enough hot shot investigators brought in to 'help' us over the past few months. We can handle this one on our own." To Shane he added, "Again, no offense, man. I've just had to deal with too many asshole FBI agents lately."

Shane smiled easily. "I get it. I wouldn't want me here, either. The word came down from way above my pay grade. I promise not to get in your way. You all take the lead, and I'll be here to help in any way you need me. And I can assure you, I'm nothing like Vic Manetti."

I didn't disagree with his assessment—if we were talking about the old Vic. However, I still found myself shooting Shane a frown, which dissolved into a rueful smile when I noticed the smirk on his face. I recognized that look—Shane obviously knew about my connection to Vic and was needling me for it.

Sterling must have appreciated what Shane had said, because he nodded. "Okay, if you play nice, I will."

Amanda muttered under her breath, "I'll believe *that* when I see it."

Sterling's eyes darted toward Amanda, his face falling. Damn. The guy had it bad. I almost felt sorry for him.

Jayne said, "Okay, you all, get to work. I'll try to get the media to disperse, but it'll probably be a waste of my breath."

Having successfully covered his disappointment, Sterling jeered, "Hey, Carlisle, hope you're prepared for a bloodbath."

8

As we put our protective gear back on to re-enter the room, I said quietly to Shane, "Sorry about the not-so-warm welcome. *I'm* happy to have you here."

"Not as happy as I am to be in the presence of law enforcement royalty," he replied, doing a little bow.

I rolled my eyes. "Says the hot shot investigator brought in because some highfalutin official thought we couldn't handle it."

"Well, you *are* missing Manetti this time," he joked.

Baxter, who I didn't realize was listening to our conversation, snapped, "We're not missing him," before storming into the bedroom.

Shane's eyes got big as he tried and failed to suppress a grin. "Damn. I guess I'll need to watch my step around here."

I shook my head. "They're just being idiots. You'll be fine."

When Shane and I walked into the room, he stopped in his tracks and whistled. "Yep, this is what you'd call a bloodbath, all right."

Dr. Berg cleared his throat. I winced. I'd forgotten the coroner was in here and had failed to warn Shane of his insistence on decorum.

I got on tiptoe and whispered in Shane's ear, "No gallows humor in front of the coroner."

He hissed back, "You couldn't have mentioned that literally two seconds ago?"

Dr. Berg cleared his throat again. "The cause of death for our female victim is exsanguination, as is evident by the state in which she was left. It's difficult to discern, but there are some minor defensive wounds on her forearms." He took hold of one of Aurora's arms and pointed out a couple of small dark slashes on the underside of her arm, between her elbow and wrist, where she'd tried to fend off her attacker. "Based on the lack of signs of struggle in the room and any other defensive wounding, my assumption is that she was attacked in her sleep."

I suppressed a shudder. I couldn't imagine being roused from sleep by a knife plunging into my chest and having to fight in vain for my life.

He laid her arm back gently onto the bed and went on. "My preliminary determination of the cause of death for our male victim is asphyxia as a result of emesis. Judging by the noticeable amount of partially dissolved medication in the vomit, I believe he was likely in a state of respiratory depression and possibly even coma that prevented him from being conscious enough to properly expel the contents of his stomach. I put both of their times of death between ten PM and midnight. I'll have further information for you after I perform the autopsies, but at first glance, this all seems fairly straightforward. Are there any questions for me at this time?"

I knew Jayne had said to go over this scene without any preconceived opinions, but the evidence was glaring. Who else besides a husband would care if his wife was a whore? I supposed if she had a lover, he would care, but her husband theoretically should care more. Probably. Anyway, if Baxter treated me like a pariah again and wouldn't let me help investigate after the evidence was processed, it wouldn't matter what my opinion was. I hoped I'd be included, especially because this case seemed easily solvable and a good win after the last one being such a letdown.

When none of us replied, Dr. Berg said, "Very well. I'll be back in a bit."

I let Amanda take over with the camera, and I began the task of placing yellow evidence markers next to all the items I'd found as well as affixing a few to the walls near the blood swipes, cast-off, and of course the glaring message. As I placed them, I murmured into my voice recorder, dreading the hours it would take to listen to my ramblings and transcribe them into coherent notes. I still believed my system was preferable to Amanda's frantic on-scene handwritten notetaking. My handwriting was so bad, it would take me forever to decipher it later.

Dr. Berg had turned Lance onto his back so we could study the front of him. The man was a mess. The front of his white button-down shirt was absolutely soaked with blood—his wife's, I assumed, which we would verify in the lab later by a blood typing test—as were his hands, neck, and the lower third of his face.

Sterling came up next to me and stared down at Lance. "You know this guy?"

"Enough to say hello when I pass him on campus," I replied.

"Hmm." He continued to stare at our victim/suspect. "Choking on your own puke. What a way to go."

I glanced from Lance to Aurora and then to Sterling, wrinkling my brow. "Are you trying to say he had the harder death, here? No way."

He nodded. "Absolutely I am. Have you never choked on something? It's terrifying."

My jaw dropped. "More terrifying than waking up to a big knife in your chest?"

"Her death was quick."

"It takes a while to bleed out, Sterling."

He gestured toward Aurora. "Not with that many holes in you." He looked back down at Lance. "Now this guy had several excruciating minutes of trying to suck in air, and all he was getting was puke. Have you ever sucked puke up your nose? It's the worst."

"Well, if that's the worse of these two ways to die, then I'd say he had it coming, considering what he did to his poor wife."

"Damn, Matthews, I'm not defending the guy. I'm only comparing pain of death."

I shook my head. "Do you seriously not know how bad it hurts to be cut by someone with the intent to cause you harm?"

Shane, who'd been listening and was evidently amused by our argument, butted in to ask me, "Do you?"

I pulled back my sleeve to reveal the scar to prove it. "Yep. Serial killer." Out of the corner of my eye, I saw Baxter wince. I was sure he had mental scars from having to clean and bandage said wound.

Shane held up both hands. "You win."

"Logic wins," I said, as much to Sterling as Shane.

Shane asked, "Do you two always fight like this?"

From opposite sides of the room, Baxter and Amanda answered together a weary, "Yes."

Shane grinned. "Then I'm in for an interesting week, I guess."

* * *

After all the evidence markers had been set and a plethora of photos had been taken from every angle imaginable, with and without a scale, Amanda and I decided it was time for a short break. We needed to make a little room while Dr. Berg and Kenny removed the bodies from the scene, so we hung out at the opposite end of the hallway, drinking Gatorade and eating the snacks I'd brought along.

Once they were headed downstairs with the bodies, we resumed our task. We took on processing the headboard and wall behind the bed while the three detectives conferred about going to the pre-autopsy meeting later while they gave the bathroom and closet a once-over. Amanda got out some swabs and collected a few samples of the blood while I measured the droplets and the overall length of the swings.

"The droplets are all two or three millimeters in diameter," I said. "Textbook medium velocity cast-off spatter, exactly what you'd expect from multiple swings of a knife. I'm counting eight or ten swings—there's so much blood it's hard to differentiate some of the patterns, so...that's nine to eleven stabs."

She shook her head. "Damn. That's hardcore. But after seeing how mangled her chest was, I'm not at all surprised it was that many. Definitely not a one and done."

"You want to determine the swing pattern?" I asked. I didn't know if she'd ever processed a scene with a cast-off pattern before. This was our first one since working together.

She stared at the headboard for a bit, then made a slashing motion. "It's fairly straight up and down, but there's a noticeable enough slant from upper right to lower left. And that means...our boy is a righty."

"That is correct."

She continued to study the pattern. "If you take into consideration the placement of the cast-off and the sheer volume of blood on the husband's shirt...I think he was directly above her when he killed her, facing the headboard...straddling her body?" She shivered. "I feel so awful for her."

I nodded. I was thinking the same thing.

The detectives began filing out of the bathroom as Amanda turned her attention to the other wall. She let out an angry grunt. "They shared a home and a marriage. He was the person who should have made her feel safe to be around and let her guard down. I don't care what she did to him, whether she cheated or not. For him to sneak up on her and kill her in her sleep was cowardly and deplorable. Stupid fragile male ego."

Sterling had that defeated look in his eyes again as he listened to her tirade.

Shane said, "Did I hear you say you thought the guy was straddling her as he stabbed her?"

Amanda stiffened and turned around. "Um...yes. I think so. The bulk of the blood on him was concentrated on his front side—which meant he was up close and personal while all the blood was flying."

Shane nodded, his brow furrowed. "Yeah, there was definitely a lot on him." Breaking the tension with a subject change, he said, "Anyone want lunch? I took the liberty of having some delivered for us. A peace offering from the new guy."

Amanda smiled. "Keep bringing us lunch, and we'll never let you go back."

I had to cover a laugh as Sterling looked like he was ready to explode. I started for the door. "I'm more than ready to get out of this room."

Baxter's cell phone chirped as I was speaking. He ripped off his gloves and grabbed the phone out of his pocket, only to stride out of the room, nearly bowling me over as he went. What was with him and all the calls and texts during investigations? He didn't normally use his phone that much...but then again, maybe there was a new girlfriend out there demanding his attention. I put it out of my head. I was giving him up. It was the only way to save my sanity, especially since this case was going to take a lot out of me. I had it together now, but the emotional toll of a scene as graphic as this one was going to eventually hit. The only question was when.

* * *

Sterling hung back at the bottom of the stairs, I assumed to find a place to pout. As Shane, Amanda, and I exited the house, we were ill-prepared for the circus that surrounded us outside. News vans lined the streets as far as the eye could see. Coiffed TV reporters, sound and camera operators, unkempt print journalist-types, and photographers swarmed the neighborhood, and the sidewalks were packed fifty yards in each direction. An army of deputies stood guard to keep the press at bay. We'd be lucky to keep video of our investigation off the air. I'd thought the shades were all drawn when we were in the bedroom, but I wanted to double check there were no gaps a high-res camera with a telephoto lens could see into.

My gut clenched as memories came flooding back of all the media hounding Rachel and I had endured after her kidnapping. Reporters camped out in front of our house for weeks. As we neared the sidewalk to head toward Shane's car, two deputies left their posts and came to escort us through the wall of press. It was truly claustrophobic, like nothing I'd experienced before. I clamped a hand down on Shane's arm to make sure I didn't get lost in the shuffle, keeping my eyes straight ahead and my gaze down. I lost count of the number of reporters trying tactic after tactic to waylay us as we passed them. They all knew our names and called them out incessantly in an attempt to get us to turn and make eye contact with them. Someone asked me how my sister was doing. Someone else asked me about how Vic was doing. They moved with us down the street.

When we reached Shane's car, he turned around with a dazzling smile and addressed the gaggle of reporters. "Guys, come on. This is ridiculous. You know me. If I had something I could share with you, I would. None of us wants incorrect information reported to the public, and you putting pressure on us to let something slip before it's fully investigated is only going to get us all in hot water. We need our full attention on the case, not on worrying about being hounded for a soundbite and chased down the street by a mob. I know you all need a story, but please remember we're human beings."

The 'mob' seemed stunned. Evidently taking his words to heart, they all backed away and shuffled off down the street toward the house again.

Amanda said appreciatively, "Now *that* was a good speech."

Shane grinned as he unlocked the doors to his car and ushered us inside. "I've got that one practically memorized. I'm usually my precinct's mouthpiece."

As he plucked a paper sack off his hood and slid into the driver's seat, I explained, "Shane was a theater major for a hot minute."

She smiled. "Ah."

Opening the bag and passing out burgers, Shane said, "What do you mean 'ah'?"

"It explains the fact that you don't have a panic attack like most of us do when someone shoves a camera in your face."

Shane flicked a concerned glance my way and steered the conversation back to our carefree college days. "What can I say? I've always been a ham. Did Ellie tell you we were friends in college?"

Amanda's mouth hung open. "No, she did not."

He nodded. "It could get pretty wild in the forensics and criminal justice department student lounge."

I laughed, remembering all those late nights doing more hanging out and carousing than studying. "We learned all about laws during the day and then turned around and broke them at night."

He smiled wistfully. "Yeah, we did."

Amanda got a mischievous look in her eye, and I knew what she was going to say next. "Did you two ever date?"

"No," we both replied at the same time.

In college, Shane Carlisle was everything I could have wanted—handsome, brilliant, funny—and there was no denying the way we gravitated toward each other. But he was the first true friend I'd ever had. I never wanted to mess that up, so I made sure we stayed firmly in the friend zone. He'd ended up marrying another friend of ours, and I was truly happy for them. Once they'd started dating our senior year, Shane and I started to drift apart a bit, but that was to be expected. We'd eventually lost touch, but it was pretty clear he'd continued to follow my career, as I had with his.

Amanda frowned. "Oh, well that's no fun."

* * *

As we finished our lunch, my phone rang. It was Vic. Since the street around us was empty, I figured I was safe enough to take the call outside alone.

I said to Shane and Amanda, who were discussing the Pacers' win over the Knicks last night, "I'll be back." I answered the call and said, "Hey, Vic."

He sounded worried. "Hey. Are you okay? I saw you on the news just now, and you looked upset."

I sighed. "Was it when I was getting chased down the street by a few dozen reporters?"

"Yeah, that was it."

"Well, you can imagine how that went for me."

His tone softened. "Is there anything I can do for you?"

I smiled. Even though he was working hard at dealing with his leftover feelings for Shawna, he never passed up an opportunity to support me. "Not really. I need to be a big girl and deal with it."

"Do you get a dinner break?"

"At some point."

"Then call me. I'll come get you and take you out for one of those horrible fast-food fiascos you insist on eating while you're working a case."

I laughed. "Wait. Did I hear that right? Vic Manetti, Mr. You Should Eat a Salad, is condoning garbage food?"

He chuckled, too. "If it helps you get in the right headspace, then yes, I condone it. I'll even stoop to eating some garbage food with you for moral support."

I was truly touched. It would have been a cold day in hell before the old Vic would have approved of this, much less have been the one to suggest it. "That is an offer I can't resist."

"Good. Now just so you know, Aurora Bennett's channel has been live streaming in front of the house for the entire day. Since Sheriff Walsh gave her statement earlier, they've been dissecting every word she said and musing about all aspects of the case. I heard someone even jumped over the back fence and got tackled by one of your deputies. I'm assuming they're going to resort to putting out false information next. I want you to be prepared that it's probably going to get worse as the day goes on."

"Lovely. Just what I need after being trapped all day in that hellscape."

To his credit, he hadn't asked about the scene or any details. "A double is a tough scene to stomach on a good day."

I lowered my voice. "Vic, there's so much blood. It's bad."

He hesitated. "Again, I'm sorry you've got to deal with that all day. Just stay detached. You're welcome to take all your feelings out on me later."

I snorted. "All my feelings? You don't want that."

"Just stay safe, okay?"

"I will."

9

—————

After Vic's pep talk, lunch, and being largely left alone by the media during our return to the house, I was feeling better. Now was the time for the real work.

Amanda and I blocked out four imaginary sections inside the bedroom. We each went over our two sections with a sharp eye, UV lights, flashlights, and magnifiers to search for additional evidence. I found an array of errant blood droplets and a couple of toenail clippings embedded in the carpet, but otherwise didn't gain any new evidence. I gathered, bagged, tagged, and sealed the spilled Xanax tablets and their bottle, this time noting a smudge of blood on the plastic cap. I used a swab to gather a sample of the blood, knowing there was little chance it belonged to anyone except Aurora. However, it did support the idea that Lance likely ingested the Xanax, or at least some of it, after Aurora's death. I went through the same collection process with the chef's knife, using a sturdy cardboard box for safety instead of a paper bag or manila envelope. While I didn't see any patent fingerprints in blood on the handle, I knew there was a good chance the metal surface held onto some latent prints my fingerprint powder and bench magnifier could find at the lab.

As we worked, the detectives droned on, distracting me as I tried to concentrate. I hadn't worked an indoor scene for a while and had forgotten how being cooped up with too many people—on top of the sight and smell of a scene—tended to get under my skin. I got unwittingly sucked into one particular discussion point.

Shane mused, "Does a person go from zero to a handful of pills?"

Sterling replied, "If he wants to die, yeah."

"Anyone heard if he's a known addict?" No one replied to Shane's question, so he went on. "Let's say he's not and the suicide was a spur-of-the-moment decision. He kills his wife—premeditated or not—and then is overcome with remorse and wants to punish himself."

The only one in the room able to speak from an addict's point of view, I piped up, "Or dull the pain or forget what happened."

Shane nodded. "Sure. If we assume all those things to be true, where does the bag of ill-gotten Percocet fit in?"

Sterling rolled his eyes. I could tell he thought this case was a slam dunk and was itching to close it. He didn't enjoy entertaining multiple theories or what-if scenarios, especially when his mind was made up.

Baxter, however, was listening with interest and finally joined the discussion after having been silent for most of the day. "It doesn't. The only time you have street drugs at the ready is when you have a drug problem."

His voice laced with frustration, Sterling said, "Why are we wasting time debating this? Him having a drug problem doesn't prove or disprove anything regarding this case."

Shane replied, "It proves he's been on a slippery slope, and it also proves he knows at least one dangerous person—his dealer."

"So?"

"So, let's say he got that bag of Percocet on credit and his dealer is ready to collect. Maybe the dealer kills his wife to send him a message."

Sterling looked at him like he'd sprouted a second head. "A few dozen Percocet is not murder worthy. I'm thinking a couple of broken fingers at most. Dude, you're wearing me out."

Shane gave him an apologetic smile. "Hey, I'm just spitballing here."

"Spitball this: a know-it-all college professor who's probably nailing his students like most of them do—"

"Hey!" I cried indignantly.

He held his hands out and offered a, "No offense, Matthews," before continuing. "He figures that if he's cheating, his whore wife is probably cheating, too. He has a drink, pops a few pills, works himself up into a righteous rage, and goes a little overboard."

I gestured back and forth between the blood-soaked bed and the wall. "*This* is not 'a little overboard.'"

Ignoring me, he went on, "He's not man enough to take responsibility for his actions, so he shoves some blame her way and chooses death over prison. Case closed, people."

Amanda stood and faced him. "You haven't deviated at all from your original opinion since the moment you walked in here. Why don't you go out and do some actual investigating before you close the case? Ellie and I could do with a little peace and quiet while we work."

I could see Sterling start to go dark, so I slid over to catch his eye. I shook my head slightly. Behind Amanda's back, I pulled my mask down and mouthed, "Be nice."

He blew out a barely controlled breath. "That's a...that's a..."

I nodded encouragement and gestured for him to keep going.

He choked out, "Good idea, Amanda. I, uh...think it's time we...go do that."

I gave him a thumbs-up. Shane and Baxter watched the exchange between us in bewilderment.

Her attention on Sterling, Amanda said warily, "Oh...okay, Jason. Thank you for listening."

I held out both my palms toward her as if I'd done a magic trick and shot a triumphant glance at Sterling. Clearly happy with the outcome of their exchange, he tried hard to hide a smile, but I saw the corner of his mouth pull up.

The three detectives filed out of the room without another word.

Amanda breathed a sigh of relief. "Finally. Now we can get some work done."

Since I was already distracted, I decided this was a good stopping point. I headed out of the room and toward the opposite end of the hall to a clean area where we'd stashed our drinks and snacks. As I neared the end of the hallway, I heard a quiet voice on the other side of a closed door. Baxter.

"I'm coming down tonight." A pause. "It doesn't matter. I want to be there for you." Another pause. "Hey...I love you."

His voice was so tender, so sweet...and at the same time like a knife to my heart. It was true: he'd moved on. Fast. I didn't understand how he'd done it, but it was done. We were done.

I felt like I couldn't breathe. Bolting for the stairs, I flew down them, intending to head outside for some fresh air. Out the window, I noticed the press hadn't dispersed even a little bit. Shit. Going outside would do me no good. Hearing footsteps overhead I assumed were Baxter's, I hurried through the nearest door, which was to a home office. I tried to stay silent. The last thing I needed was someone, especially Baxter, finding me lurking in there. My gaze landed on another crystal decanter similar to the one we'd found upstairs. This one held a clear liquid, prettily displayed on a mirrored tray with three rocks glasses matching the one we'd found upstairs. I assumed this was where the other decanter and glass had come from, since they had seemed a little out of place with the rest of the bedroom décor.

In the throes of my heartbreak, I felt the urge to take a drink for the first time in a long while. An experience I'd had a couple of months ago had suppressed any desire I had to consume alcohol of any kind. The mere thought of drinking had repulsed me and made me sick to my stomach. However, in the meantime I'd yet to experience a big emotional breakdown like the one I seemed to be careening toward at the moment. I fixated on the decanter, my mind playing a scenario in which I poured a double and let it slide down my throat, burning away my heartache as it went. I imagined the welcome haze that would come next, the one that dulled the pain and allowed my brain to relax. I longed for that feeling of release, when all the bad things in my life suddenly became less important and less hurtful. I wanted more than anything to get to that beautiful point where I didn't care anymore.

Tears welled in my eyes as I fought my desire, clinging to the fact that I'd done so well at staying sober for so long. I thought of all the chips I'd earned. I thought of the congratulations I'd received. I thought about how much more present I'd been around Rachel and Nate. I thought about all the hard-lost weight I'd inevitably gain back if I started drinking again. I thought about how shitty I felt all the time while I was drinking.

I thought about how Baxter had been there for me at my rock bottom, giving me the tough love I needed to save me from myself.

I stifled a sob and called my sponsor.

* * *

I felt better after talking it out with my sponsor, Scott, a cop who understood the pressure and craziness I dealt with while working cases. He agreed with Sam—I needed sex or cigarettes or carbs or *something*. Sex was permanently on hold for reasons beyond my control and also because I had decided I was getting too old to hook up with random guys like I had in my twenties. Under peer pressure from my so-called friends in high school, I'd tried my best to become a smoker, but could never get past the way cigarettes made me smell just like my mother. Scott gave me the only advice I could work with. His tongue-in-cheek (but actually serious) recommendation was to grab a box of donuts and eat all of them on the way to a meeting. As soon as I was done with this scene, that was exactly what I planned to do.

My emotions nearly back in check, I returned to the bedroom and began the task of going through all the drawers. There wouldn't be an inch of this room that didn't get fully inspected today. The only thing of note I found was in the bedside table that seemed to be Aurora's—a digital thermometer and a little pink journal that said, "FERTILITY PLANNER."

I held them up. "Guess who was trying to get pregnant?"

Amanda whirled around, jaw hanging open. "Seriously? Who kills the woman they're trying to have a baby with?"

I shrugged, opening the journal to find that she'd made her latest temperature notation the previous day and had made an X in the sex column for sixteen days out of the past thirty, including the previous day. Either these two had an extremely healthy sex life for a married couple, or she was throwing over-the-top effort toward getting pregnant.

Amanda gasped and offered an answer to her own question. "Maybe someone who found out she was trying to get pregnant but hadn't bothered to let him in on her plan."

"Maybe," I replied, moving on to the column where Aurora tracked her cycle. According to her calculations, she was due to start her period two days ago and hadn't yet. It would have been time to take a pregnancy test. My heart hurt even more for her.

Amanda's eyes widened. "Or maybe he found out she was trying to get pregnant by someone else, and that's why he called her a whore."

I couldn't imagine that a couple making such an organized and concerted effort to make a baby together could end up in this situation. It made much better sense that she was more on board with the baby idea than he was, if he was even aware of her plans at all. Something didn't add up.

I nodded. "That's as good a reason as any."

I bagged, tagged, and sealed up the thermometer and the planner, as well as the cellphone in the pretty pink case—now splattered with blood—sitting on the wireless charger on the nightstand. Amanda had already collected the funeral suit, the crystal decanter and rocks glass, and the bag of pills.

"What's left to collect in this room?" I asked.

She replied, "I'm going to swab the sheets, the closet handle, and the wall for blood typing—although I think it's no secret where it all came from. Aside from that, this room's done."

"Sweet."

I moved on to the bathroom and checked through all the drawers, the linen closet, the trash, and the hampers. Nothing out of the ordinary in there—including no used pregnancy tests in the trash—and no blood residue on any of the hanging white towels or in the trash. It seemed as though the crime had been confined to the bedroom. I came out of the bathroom and found Amanda packing up our evidence in tubs for transport.

"Ready to take a look at the rest of the house?" she asked.

"Let's do it."

We divvied up the rooms equally and went in search of any indicators that anything sinister had gone on anywhere besides the bedroom. From what I could tell, nothing had. The house looked as though it was professionally cleaned on a regular basis. Everything gleamed, unlike my house, where everything within a three-year-old's reach was marginally sticky as well as perpetually covered in Golden Retriever hair.

I had kitchen duty, so I went straight for the knife block. It was full of every type of blade a person might need, all the same brand as the murder weapon. There was a conspicuous empty space that would fit the wide blade of chef's knife. After snapping a few photos, I put the whole knife block in a box and sealed it up. Not an earthshattering piece of evidence by any means, but it did prove the murder weapon came from inside the home.

After I'd finished the kitchen, I went to the foyer to drop off the heavy knife block and found Amanda brushing black fingerprint powder over a keypad next to the front door.

I said uneasily, "I suppose even the best security system in the world is useless if your attacker lives in the house."

She shrugged. "Sad, right? I thought it would be best to process the keypads and all the exterior doors, just in case."

While she continued fingerprinting, I asked a couple of the deputies to transport the evidence to our van. The less chance I had of being waylaid by the press, the better. I then roamed around the house, making sure we hadn't left any packaged evidence or tools behind. Being in the master bedroom alone was decidedly unsettling, even though I'd spent the bulk of my day there. I again was left imagining the last moments of Aurora's life—the surprise, the fear, the panic, the pain, the slipping away. All the awful things I'd watched Vic go through.

I shook my head to clear it. I couldn't afford to let my brain spiral down another rabbit hole today. He was fine. He was healing. And I would be fine, too, but only if I kept my head on straight. I left the room without another glance.

10

With the help of two no-nonsense deputies, Amanda and I navigated the media, packed up the van, and headed to the station. At my request, she stopped for donuts on the way. She also needed to decompress after the crime scene, so we got a dozen donuts and gorged on them together during the twenty-minute drive to Noblesville, diets and better judgment be damned.

Once we had transported the evidence inside the station and checked it in with the evidence clerk, I walked a couple of blocks in the warm afternoon sun to an AA meeting at a nearby church. It wasn't my favorite location or clientele. I preferred the meetings geared toward law enforcement officials held in downtown Indianapolis. However, this location was closest to the station and to my house, which meant I ended up there often. I had to refrain from sharing too much about my life and work there, considering the audience. But getting even a little of my woes off my chest helped, and I felt refreshed as I strolled back to the station.

My improved mood didn't last long. I returned to find Sterling and Shane in a near-shouting match in the parking lot.

"I don't have to answer to you. You don't even work here," Sterling barked.

Shane, his voice raised but even, replied, "I do at the moment, and I'm not going to stand back and watch you blow up this case because you can't control your temper."

"I'm direct. It's how I get results."

"Was the result you were going for that two of the victim's coworkers got so pissed over how you treated them that they clammed up and demanded lawyers? We'd agreed to give them a soundbite in exchange for answering a few simple questions, mainly about the victim, and you unnecessarily bad copped them so hard they mistook it as an attack on their character. Next time, I'm talking to the press, and you're going to stand there and look pretty."

"The hell I am. And since it seems like you missed it the first time, I'm going to say it again: *You don't even work here.*"

I rolled my eyes. I'd seen Shane on the news before. He was stellar at dealing with the press. Hell, he'd had them eating out of his hand at lunchtime. He always looked great on camera, he was truthful, and he treated the media with respect even when they were being intrusive as shit and didn't deserve it.

Walking between them to try to defuse the situation, I said to Shane, "I see you're getting the full Sterling experience. That didn't take long."

"Stay out of this, Matthews," Sterling growled.

I turned to him. "You know you suck at talking to the press. You don't even like talking to the press. Shane is good at it. Use him."

Sterling glared at me, but surprisingly did not tell me to go to hell.

I smiled. "This would be a good time to practice using your nice words."

I could tell he was too pissed at me to say anything, but he surprised me by pasting on a super fake smile and nodding. But then in typical Sterling fashion, his face fell back into a full-on scowl as he brushed past me and stalked to his vehicle.

I chuckled and explained to Shane, "You'll either get used to him or want to kill him. Or both. We've all been there."

He gave me a friendly pat on the arm. "Thanks for stepping in. That guy's a piece of work."

Baxter strode out of the building and came our way, frowning and putting a damper on the near-normal mood I'd been able to achieve through refined sugar and emotional catharsis. He seemed a little angry, even. It stood to reason that a person in a new relationship should seem happier, but what did I know?

As he passed us, he muttered, "It's time for the meeting with the coroner."

He did not offer us a ride, not that I was expecting one at this point. I watched him walk quickly toward Sterling's vehicle and get inside.

Shane must have been expecting the offer, because he said, "I guess we have to get there on our own, then?"

I smiled. "It's for the best. It's no fun riding with Sterling."

* * *

Sterling must have driven twice the speed limit to get to the morgue, because he and Baxter were mostly suited up in their protective gear by the time Shane and I got there. I handed Shane a set of gear, and we wordlessly put ours on as Sterling and Baxter finished and left the room.

A couple of minutes later as Shane was about to open the door to follow them, I said, "Hey, if you thought Dr. Berg expected over-the-top reverence at the crime scene, it's nothing compared to how he expects us to behave in his inner sanctum."

Shane's face got a devilish grin about it. "Did you mean for that to sound dirty?"

I laughed. "Has your sense of humor grown up even a little since college?"

"No, and that's why I'm worried about going in there."

"Just speak quietly and keep your mouth shut unless you have a necessary question. I fully expect the DA to bust our balls, but that's what he does. You stand there and take it."

"The people in your county are...unusual."

"You're not wrong," I replied as I pushed past him and through the door.

Speaking of unusual, I was shocked to overhear a very chill DA Wade McAlister calmly discussing the lovely spring foliage with Dr. Berg. I wondered if he was on some sort of medication.

When Dr. Berg saw that Shane and I had entered the room, he cut short their discussion and said, "Let's begin. The autopsies for Aurora Bennett and Lance Wakefield will be at eight and ten AM tomorrow morning, respectively. Which of you detectives will be in attendance?"

Sterling had attended the last one, which meant it was Baxter's turn. Sterling eyed Baxter, waiting for him to volunteer, but Baxter shook his head. "Not me. I have a thing—I mean...an appointment." His cheeks turned pink above his beard. Something squirrely was going on with him.

Quick on his feet, Sterling slid Shane an evil grin and said to Dr. Berg. "I've heard that Detective Carlisle is kind of a nerd for autopsies. He's your man, Doc."

Shane didn't miss a beat, which took a little wind out of Sterling's sails. "I'd be happy to attend."

Dr. Berg's eyebrows furrowed at the undercurrent of nonsense, but he said, "Very well." Folding the sheet down to Aurora's waist, he went on, "Our female victim endured eleven instances of sharp force trauma to the torso and two lacerations to each forearm. The preliminary cause of death is exsanguination, as I mentioned earlier, but I also believe I'll find evidence of traumatic pneumothorax."

I wouldn't be surprised at the presence of punctured lung, given the number and placement of the stab wounds. I actually hoped it was the case, to have allowed her to pass faster than blood loss would.

Dr. Berg went on. "I will have a toxicology screen done for her and will collect vaginal, oral, and anal samples for a sexual assault kit."

I said quietly, "You might also run a pregnancy test."

All three detectives' heads snapped in my direction.

Sterling said, "A what, now?"

I explained, "I found a fertility planner in her nightstand. According to it, she was a couple of days late."

"When were you going to clue us in on that?" Baxter demanded.

Sterling shrugged. "It's not earthshattering news. For my money, her being pregnant is just another nail in his coffin. Good find, Matthews."

It was like the two of them had switched personalities. I didn't like it.

Dr. Berg cleared his throat. "Moving on to our male deceased, I will have a toxicology screen done to determine if he ingested a fatal amount of medication, although based on the amount found in the vomit, there was enough to cause a life-ending event. I'm reporting the preliminary cause of death as asphyxiation brought on by a combination of emesis and coma. Are there any questions?"

None of us had questions, including the DA, who'd been oddly silent and actually rather bored looking the whole time.

Dr. Berg said, "Very well. Ms. Matthews, I have clothing belonging to both of our deceased that I'll send with you."

"Thanks, Doc," I said.

"Thank you all," he said solemnly. Everyone else left the room, and Dr. Berg handed two big paper bags to me. "I hope this investigation goes easily for you, Ellie. I know you must have been disappointed over our last one."

I smiled. "I was. In fact, I shouldn't have complained about the lack of evidence, because this case has a huge amount to process. It'll keep me busy for sure."

"Happy to have you back again, dear."

"Thank you."

By the time I reached the changing room, most of my colleagues were nearly finished removing their protective gear, except DA McAlister, who was taking his time rather than ripping everything to get free like he usually did.

He said, "I don't hate this case. Looks pretty simple, and it sounds like you've collected a substantial amount of evidence against that sick bastard on the slab in there. No trial, either, since there's no one to try."

The DA was uncharacteristically jovial. Then again, he was set up to get off the hook for prosecuting yet another murder case, not to mention missing the complete three-ring media circus surrounding this one. I imagined he was even a little jealous of our mountain of evidence this time. DA McAlister loved his evidence; to him the items we collected were pieces of flair for him to parade around during the trial to wow the jury. Jurors these days expected enough material and scientific proof to link a suspect to a crime without question, like in the crime dramas they watched on TV. That rarely happened, which forced them to make hard decisions. It sucked, and I would much rather take a beating from a defense lawyer on the stand than to have to serve on a jury and decide someone's fate.

Everyone filed out as I was finishing removing my gear, or so I'd thought.

Baxter said, "What's up with you and Sterling?"

I jumped, startled by the ambush and even more so by the fact that he was initiating an interaction with me. Although I had no allegiance to Sterling, I knew he'd hate it if I blabbed to Baxter about our personal conversation. Plus, since Baxter had dropped me like a hot potato, I owed him even less.

Turning to face him, I replied, "Nothing."

"You're less at each other's throats."

"And that's a bad thing?"

"I saw the little exchange you two had behind Amanda's back. Are you of all people helping him try to get her back? I think it would serve you better not to get involved in any personal relationship stuff at work."

As much as I'd been dying for him to deign to speak to me, I didn't want this. I felt my temper slipping, but instead of snapping at him, I decided to take my own advice. I smiled and nodded. "I appreciate the tip." And then dishing him back some of his own medicine, I walked out the door to end the conversation. If he didn't like it, he could go cry to his new girlfriend.

Everything felt chaotic and wrong. Sterling was being nice to me. The DA was chipper. Baxter was a giant ass. Amanda was cynical. Shane was the same, but the bond I'd always felt between us was missing. Vic, even in the midst of working through his own troubles, was a ball of sunshine. Worse than all of those combined, I felt like a struggling alcoholic again, and that was unacceptable.

I met Shane at his car and collapsed into the passenger seat. "I can't remember the last time I had a positive experience in there."

Shane pulled out of the parking lot. "Well, the morgue isn't the most comforting of places."

"It's not the dead people. It's the live ones."

"Ah. Could you consider the fact that you were able to walk out of there a positive? Not everyone can say that."

I chuckled. "I guess I can't argue with that one."

We were quiet on the short drive to the station. I was trying to get my Zen back so I could concentrate on my work. Shane seemed to be deep in thought. We went our separate ways once we got inside. I headed straight to check the victims' clothing in with the evidence clerk and then went on to the lab. After putting on a clean lab coat, gloves, and mask, I sliced open the red evidence tape on one of the bags and removed Aurora's tattered, bloody negligee, placing it on a clean workspace under a lighted bench magnifier. I didn't know what I'd find other than the obvious, but it was a good place to start.

Amanda had texted me to let me know she was on break, so I nearly jumped out of my skin when a voice behind me asked, "Did you take a good look at the blood on Wakefield's face at the scene?"

I whirled around to find Shane standing in the doorway, the same thoughtful expression on his face he'd had earlier. "Didn't anyone ever tell you not to sneak up on someone when they're looking at murdery stuff?"

Shane grinned. "Murdery stuff? Is that a technical term?"

"It is."

He came toward me to see what I was doing. "Oh, man. That's bad. I can understand why you're a little on edge."

I removed my mask, turning around so we didn't have to have our conversation over the massacred clothing. "What were you saying when you barged in here and scared the shit out of me?"

"I wanted to know if you got a good look at the blood on Wakefield's face at the scene."

I wrinkled my nose. "I did. It was super gross and also mixed with puke."

"I mean the pattern of it."

"You mean the giant smear pattern that made it look like he'd been... kissing her or something? Our last case had a victim who'd been kissed or licked or something. I hope that's not the case again."

He made a face. "Gross, and yes, that's what I mean. Instead of one giant smear across his chin, he should have a whole *Dexter* thing going on."

"A Dexter thing?"

"The TV show. You know, like in the Season Two teaser that shows Dexter looking like he's posing for a yearbook photo, but when you get closer you find his face has blood spatter all over it?"

I had no idea. I didn't watch a ton of TV outside of kids' shows and whatever Rachel was bingeing, which since her kidnapping was never anything darker than a sitcom. "Sorry, I don't follow shows about violent crime in my spare time."

He quickly Googled it on his phone and showed me a photo. Sure enough, the actor was cheesing for the camera with carefully crafted back spatter all over his face. "I think Wakefield should look more like this after what he allegedly did."

I stared at him. "Wait. Allegedly?"

"Can I see the photos you took of his body?"

I shrugged. "Sure." I beckoned Shane into the office with me and sat down at the desk, pulling up the photos Amanda had uploaded from the camera to the department's server.

Shane went on, "With pints of blood flying around, there's no way he didn't get some sprayed in his face. There had to have been at the very least one incidence of back spatter, and she would have likely expirated some blood, too. That's not even counting an arterial spray—and after making that many stab wounds there's no way he missed one of the arteries leading to her heart. His whole face should look like he lost badly at paintball." He pointed to one of the closeup photos of Lance's face, gesturing to his clean forehead, nose, and cheekbones. "He should be a mess up here."

"What are you saying?"

"I'm saying, I think if we don't open up to the possibility that this guy didn't kill his wife, we're going to miss something."

11

My jaw dropped. "You don't think he did it."

"I had a feeling in my gut at the scene, and I didn't put it all together until now. I know everything seems to point to him, but there's some evidence that doesn't." Shane pointed to the screen. "And it's right there."

I studied the screen for a moment, thinking back to the scene. Aurora was dead, maliciously so. Lance was there next to her, blitzed out of his mind with booze and drugs, her blood all over him. The murder weapon was next to him, looking as if it could have slipped out of his hand as he fell to the floor. The single word "WHORE" painted a loud and clear message that the killer was upset that Aurora was sleeping around—and who else would even care besides her husband?

But then there was the suit. It had raised a red flag with me initially, but I'd put it out of my mind after collecting so much evidence all seeming to point to Lance. Now with the question of the spatter pattern, I was starting to think maybe there was more to this case. Spilled blood follows certain rules of physics, so we should be able to figure this out.

I nodded. "Okay, let's try to explain the void. What are some ways he could have killed her and walked away without getting it in the face?"

Shane said, "He could have worn a mask."

I may not have been a TV junkie now, but I'd watched a lot of movies in my youth, mostly horror. "Jason Voorhees style?"

He chuckled. "Something like that."

"Interesting. Why would he do that? He wouldn't have had to cover his face in order to sneak into his own house. And if he was planning to kill her, she'd be too dead to ID him, so why bother hiding his identity from her?"

"To elicit fear. To feel a little more detached from the situation. It happens."

"I could buy into that. So where did the mask end up, then? We didn't find one."

Shane shrugged. "In the garbage. In the washing machine. Thrown over the fence and into the neighbor's yard. In his safe. Tucked in a box of old keepsakes in the basement."

"Ooh. Okay. It would be a lot of work, but we could go back out and check those places."

"But why hide the mask and nothing else, including the murder weapon?"

"Fair point. The mask thing doesn't make a lot of sense. Next scenario."

He said, "He could have washed off the blood spatter."

"Then wouldn't his hands have been clean, too?

"Not if he wrote 'WHORE' afterward and did whatever else he did to get her blood all over the bottom half of his face."

I nodded slowly. "True, but regardless, he'd need water and a towel to scrub the bloodstains off, especially the spatter, which would have dried quickly. If he'd done that, there would have been evidence in the bathroom of him cleaning up. The floor, sinks, shower, and tub were spotless, and there were no towels hanging or in the laundry basket that looked like they'd come into any contact with blood. I mean, we didn't break out the Luminol or anything, but there didn't seem to be a reason to. Sorry to shoot down your scenarios."

Shane grinned. "You're not shooting down my scenarios. You're proving my point."

"Oh...well, we can't have that. I'll have Beck go to the scene and look specifically for a mask. I'll also have him check the laundry room for bloody towels and spray down the master bathroom with Luminol." I began typing a friendly email I knew would provoke a scathing reply from Beck. When I got brought in on a case, not only did Beck get shoved out of the way, but he also got demoted from head criminalist *and* had to report to me. He hated every minute I was there. Turning back to Shane, I continued, "Oh, I've got one— what if he'd stood next to her while he stabbed her, rather than over her?"

"Didn't Amanda say the cast-off pattern indicated the killer was strad-dling her? Given the fact that she had some defensive wounding, he prob-ably had to sit on her to hold her down while he went at her."

I frowned. "Putting him in the perfect location for a face full of back spatter."

"Exactly."

"Well, Detective, are you going to share your theory with the team at the meeting?" Sterling was not going to be pleased.

"*Our* theory," he corrected me.

I shook my head. "Noooo. You're on your own with this one, pal." This new wrinkle threw a definite kink into the investigation, but I wasn't sure if I was ready to jump with both feet onto Shane's random killer theory train.

"Actually, I wanted to talk to you about that. It's painfully obvious that you and neither of the other detectives are buddies."

I had to fight a wince. It was painful, all right.

He went on, "And I can say with some certainty that neither one of them is particularly interested in spending any time with me."

"That all seems accurate."

"What do you say to the two of us partnering up? As an outsider, I could really use your local connections, especially for interviewing some of your fellow Ashmore College professors."

"Ooh. Tempting. But you know what? I've got enough evidence to process to keep me busy for a very long time."

"There are other criminalists on staff who can do the monkey work in the lab."

"Lab work is not monkey work."

He wrinkled his nose. "Eh, the second pass kind of is."

I crossed my arms and huffed. "Well, now you've offended me, so I don't want to work with you at all."

He laughed. "Come on, Ellie. Don't tell me you're content to sit here in your Fortress of Solitude and examine the shit in someone else's underwear."

"My job entails so much more than shitty underwear examination."

"I'm sure it does, but the lab has to be the most boring part. Wouldn't you rather be out chasing down leads and interviewing crackpots?"

I did miss that during the last case, but I wasn't sure if I'd missed the investigative side or if what I'd missed was Baxter's companionship and one-on-one attention. "I mean, I like the lab work but...yeah... I guess maybe I'd—"

"Then it's settled. Besides, I need someone in my corner who'll think outside the box with me. I know you'll do that."

But what if Baxter suddenly came to his senses and asked me to investigate with him? I was upset with him, but at the same time didn't want to be the one who broke up our partnership and ran to someone else. "Shane—"

He held up his hands. "Seriously, it's already settled. It was the sheriff's idea. I'm just the mouthpiece."

I stared at him. "Already settled? And she didn't tell me herself because...?"

A smile played at his lips. "She said you'd take it better from me and that if I didn't want my head bitten off, I should ask you rather than tell you."

Stunned, I said nothing.

Undeterred by my lack of excitement, he said as he left the office, "Okay, partner. See you at the meeting."

* * *

I went to the breakroom to get coffee, on the way trying to talk myself down from giving in and grabbing a candy bar to top off all the donuts I'd eaten earlier. If I were being honest, I felt like hell. It was about time for the inevitable blood sugar crash from my donuts. Even worse, my fall off the Keto wagon had made my tastebuds crave even more sweets. That was exactly why I couldn't drink a drop of alcohol ever again. Addictive behavior of any kind was a slippery slope, and my mind and body seemed to love to betray me.

I was almost to the breakroom when I passed Jayne's office. Her door was open, but I kept walking, still stewing over her essentially cockblocking my partner situation. Not that it wouldn't be fun to partner with Shane. It just wouldn't be the same.

"Ellie," she called.

Shit. I stopped and backtracked to her door.

"Come on in. Sit."

I did as I was told, reining in my feelings to appear neutral.

Jayne smiled at me. "Are you doing okay with this case? I know the scene was tough. There's no way we could have handled it without you."

I tried to smile back, but I knew I didn't manage more than a grimace. "I'm okay."

"Good. I want you to take a break, okay? Get away from here before our meeting. Go have dinner with Vic and decompress."

I'd never thought she was a huge fan of Vic's. But then again, they had gotten strangely chummy lately. "Um...okay." I'd tried to put the whole partner thing out of my head, but she was acting weird and I couldn't hold my tongue. "So...Shane. As my partner. Not Baxter."

"Detective Baxter has a partner."

"Who never works with him when we work as a task force and bring in extra investigators."

She stared at me, saying nothing. I could tell she wasn't going to budge on this.

I went on anyway. "I don't get why we'd want to deviate from what always works. Agent Griffin called us the Dream Team, remember?"

Setting her coffee cup down, she gave me a knowing look. "Ellie, do you think I'm blind?"

Damn it. "No." I'd been hoping she was, since we'd yet to have this conversation.

She lowered her voice. "I know you're head over heels for him. And I can see that the feeling is mutual."

My heart gave a hopeful leap. "Still or...before?"

She shook her head, probably realizing she'd said too much. "Look, you two won't be working together anymore. *At least* until the trial's over, maybe longer. You get too close during cases. And while that makes you an amazing team, it's a liability otherwise. We need to put some space between the two of you."

That sounded suspiciously like something Baxter had said to me. My body went cold all over. "Wait...was this his idea? Did he tell you he didn't want to work with me?"

"It's not up for debate—"

"I'm not debating anything. I'm asking you what he said."

"And I'm not getting in the middle of this, except to say, *stay away from him*. You know what can happen to a case you're working when you let your personal life get out of hand. It affects us all, Ellie."

I lowered my eyes. I'd made a mess of things more than once. I couldn't do it again. This time there was too much to lose. And Baxter had made it more than clear he wanted nothing to do with me in any capacity, so there was no use fighting it anymore. "Okay. I'll stay away."

12

———

I smiled across the table at Vic. "I needed this. Thanks."

Grinning, he spread out his hands, palms up. "I'm here to please."

I'd called him after talking with Jayne, and he'd picked me up and whisked me away to a hole-in-the-wall pizza place for dinner. He made a concerted effort to keep our conversation light, except for frankly answering my probing questions about his physical and mental health now that for the foreseeable future I'd have to choose work over hanging out with him in my spare time. After that, he managed to keep the conversation flowing, in no way referencing the case. I wondered if he'd come up with bullet points ahead of time, because there was never a lull.

"I like the new you."

"Well, that's good. I'm painfully aware of the fact that you weren't enamored with the old me," he said dryly.

I leaned across the table to cuff him on the arm. "Oh, get over yourself. I meant that you're more laid back and open to new and different ideas after I nearly let you bleed out."

He frowned at me. "What did I say about you launching into another self-flagellating monologue?"

"Knowing the new you, probably something snowflaky."

"Damn, woman. What's got you so salty tonight?"

I stared at him. "Uh, a double homicide, maybe?"

He eyed me. "I don't think that's all of it. Did you get your feelings hurt again?"

"Maybe."

Letting out an overexaggerated sigh, he asked, "What did he do this time?"

"Where to begin?" As hurtful as his phone call had been to overhear, it actually wasn't what caused me the most grief today. "Ah, I know. The icing on the cake was that he went to Jayne and said he didn't want to be my partner anymore."

"That's the first good thing he's done for you."

I shot him a glare. "You mean other than saving your sorry ass?"

"Oh yeah, I suppose he did do that. I guess he's not all bad." He laughed at my still-sour expression and changed the subject. "But hey, at least there's not too much pressure on the department to solve this case. The news has already done that for you. From their coverage, it sounds like your dead suspect played judge, jury, and executioner on himself and left you some pretty damning evidence. I mean, it sounds like he basically did your job for you." He grinned, clearly enjoying needling me.

I managed to smile back. "Something like that. But my new partner Shane wants us to think outside the box. There's just this wealth of evidence that makes it seem like it's probably okay to think *inside* the box."

"But..."

I let out a breath. "But it's too easy. There are a couple of little sticking points."

He grinned at me. "There it is."

"I feel like Bax—I mean, our team—"

"You mean the Dream Team. You and Detective Baxter."

"*Former* Dream Team."

"Stay on track."

"Fine. I feel like he and I always have had a habit of reading stuff into the homicides we investigate. Like, the most likely suspect is never the one we choose to pursue."

He nodded. "Which is annoying as hell to the rest of your team, not to mention a statistical improbability. But you guys have had some weird ass cases where statistics, not to mention logic, are out the window."

"Don't I know it."

"Okay, so tell me what's weird about this one. What are your sticking points?"

I studied him across the table. His eyes were sparkling, and his posture had perked up. He was excited about talking shop. He'd been off work so long he'd sorely been missing the thrill of an investigation. Sort of cute, in an overachieving kind of way. However, our breakup was largely based on me being angry with him trying to worm case information out of me and the department. Me telling Vic classified information felt a little hypocritical, although I couldn't disregard the fact that his insight would be invaluable.

He interrupted my silent struggling. "I know what you're thinking. But this time, I've got no dog in this fight. There's nothing wrong with you consulting an outside law enforcement official for help."

He was right, and he had, in fact, read my mind. Plus, after all we'd been through, I now trusted him fully. Vic was different after his near-death experience. It had brought out every one of the good things I'd ever noticed in him all at the same time.

"Okay."

He brightened even more. "Really?"

"I agree that this situation is completely different. I'll allow it."

He smiled. "Then tell me everything."

I sent a quick text to Amanda to ask her to send me a few of the pertinent photos and then began regurgitating everything I knew. I ended with touching on Shane's issue with the blood spatter pattern and the nagging questions in the back of my mind about the intent behind Lance's effort to set out his funeral suit. I watched as Vic flipped through the photos she'd emailed and mulled everything over with his FBI profiler brain.

He finally said, "I agree with you it's strange that someone who'd commit such a brutal crime of passion against his wife, premeditated or not, would have the clarity to stop and set out a suit stating it should be his funeral attire moments before swallowing a handful of pills to end himself. I'm not seeing the shift from crazy to lucid and back to crazy so fast. I feel like he couldn't have managed even a moment of that level of organization and clear thought while his wife lay there dying by his hand."

Vic had great insight, but I wasn't backing Shane's theory until I'd gone full devil's advocate on it. "But say he hated his wife and wanted away from her. He kills her, then he feels free. He's calm."

He shook his head. "If he only wanted free of her, he would have killed her and not himself or himself but not her. To commit suicide after murdering someone points to shame and remorse."

"Or simply mental illness."

"True, but if you're so far into your psychotic break that you go through with brutally killing your wife, do you really snap out of it for a good few minutes to go sift through your closet to pick out your funeral wear before offing yourself?"

Shrugging, I conceded, "No, probably not. But I suppose he could have done it after eating the handful of pills. He'd have a little time on his hands before they kicked in. Maybe he was bored and had nothing better to do than sift through his closet."

Vic smiled. "Okay, I'll give you the fact that he had maybe fifteen to thirty minutes before the pills started working their magic. But by that argument, maybe he took the pills first, got a little loopy, and *then* killed his wife."

"You're making this more, not less, confusing. Let's circle back around to the suit."

"Maybe he set it out first, before he killed her and even before the pills. He could have written the message on the bag later as an afterthought."

I considered that for a moment, then flipped to a photo on my phone. Zooming in near the top of the hanger, I said, "Maybe, but after would be much more likely. I found a smear of blood on the closet door handle and another one on the hanger. If he'd gotten the suit out ahead of time, there would have been no blood yet."

Nodding appreciatively, he said, "I'd say that's good reasoning." He looked at the photo and squinted. "Your guy wears a size nineteen dress shirt? He must have gained a ton of weight since the stock photo they used of him on the news."

I took another look at the photo, this time concentrating on the shirt's tag. "Is a nineteen big?"

"It's like the equivalent of a three XL in a T-shirt."

Confused, I said, "That's weird. This must be an old shirt. A three XL would have fit him a few years ago. He's actually lost a ton of weight. I think he had a health issue or something and decided to make some changes." This little development made no sense. I needed more info, so I called Amanda. While it rang, I said to Vic, "Why go to all the trouble of setting out clothes for your funeral, only to— Hi, Amanda. Are you in the lab?"

She sighed. "Aren't I always?"

I chuckled. "Did you process that suit yet?"

"Nope. It's next on my list."

"Can you take a look at the sizes of all the pieces for me, like now?"

"Yes, ma'am." I heard some shuffling and the pull of a zipper, then she said, "Looks like we've got a navy jacket size forty-eight...a pair of navy slacks size forty-six...a white button-down shirt size nineteen neck with a thirty-four/thirty-five sleeve...and a blood-red tie, making one killer funeral suit."

I winced at her words. Thinking outside the box might be a hard sell to the rest of the team. "Thanks a lot. I appreciate it."

"I thought you were supposed to be decompressing, not working."

"I never do what I'm told, do I?"

She laughed. "Not that I've seen. Later."

I ended the call and said to Vic, "Forty-eight jacket, forty-six pants."

He shook his head. "That suit would fit Santa. Your guy would drown in it."

"Ooh. This is getting even weirder. He goes to the trouble of setting out a suit for his funeral, only to grab the wrong one?"

"Nothing about the suit tracks for me. If it had been a straight up suicide with no one else involved, absolutely. People do it a lot, actually— they get their affairs in order in an attempt to make their death easier on their family. Let me think about the suit thing some more, and let's jump to the void on your suspect's face where back spatter should have been. He could have cleaned it off."

"We thought of that." I checked my email. Beck had already replied that the 'wild goose chase' I'd sent him on had wasted his time. He'd barely had enough time to drive over and do a quick and probably not so thorough search, but with Beck, that was as good as we were going to get. "We sent Beck back out to the house. He found no trace of blood in the bathroom and no bloody towels anywhere."

Vic nodded. "Okay. Then maybe Wakefield could have worn some kind of face covering or protection."

"We found nothing fitting that description in our initial search, and we had Beck go over the whole place looking only for that specific type of item. No luck."

"I don't like the void. There's always a reason for a void, and a lot of times it's a squirrely one."

I winced. "Like that someone else may have killed her?"

Vic blew out a breath. "When things don't add up, there's a reason for it. With your guy being a political activist, odds are good he had some enemies out there. Let's say someone else killed her and he walks in and finds her. The first thing he's going to do is check to see if she's still alive or even try to administer first aid, which would explain her blood getting all over him. He realizes she's dead, freaks, and kills himself. He could be completely innocent, yet the circumstantial evidence points straight at him."

"If he didn't do it, then who would write 'WHORE' on the wall?"

He thought for a moment. "She could have had a boyfriend. He could have had a girlfriend. And back to the enemy angle, maybe the killer wanted to cause some catastrophic damage. No matter the circumstances of Aurora Bennett's death, Wakefield's going to get investigated because he's the spouse. He's not even cold yet, and the press has already convicted him in the court of public opinion. Can you imagine what life would be like for him right now if he were still alive? For guys like Wakefield, a ruined reputation is a fate worse than death. Regardless of whether or not they get exonerated later, the damage is already done. And rather than being a commentary on her moral character, your bloody wall message could very well be a brilliant but simple way to ensure the blame is placed squarely on him. Who's going to think twice about a pathetic cuckold killing his whore wife? It's the oldest motive in the book."

"Oh, wow. You're good," I murmured.

Leaning back in his chair and lacing his fingers behind his head, he grinned. "I know." As I rolled my eyes, he added, "I feel like you should be aware of this by now."

13

Vic dropped me back at the station in time for the team meeting. Hoping to get a less uncomfortable seat this time, I charged straight for the conference room, managing to snag a place between Amanda and Shane.

I leaned over to Shane and said quietly, "I've got another possible point for your argument. It's at least a conundrum."

His eyebrows shot up. "A conundrum? Sounds interesting. Lay it on me."

"He grabbed the wrong suit."

"What do you mean?"

"The funeral suit. It's like a three XL. Lance used to be a big guy, so I'm assuming it's one of his old suits and he grabbed it by mistake."

Shane nodded thoughtfully. "Mistake, huh? Yeah, I see it. An innocent husband who just stumbled onto his dead wife is going to be more out of it than a guilty husband who just murdered his whore wife in cold blood, right?"

I shrugged. "Probably?"

"I mean, it doesn't prove guilt or not, but it proves he wasn't thinking straight. What I want to know is, why does he still even have that suit? He didn't lose all the weight overnight. Did he not clear out his closet once he started having to buy new clothes?"

"He's been thin for a few years. I have no clue why he'd keep it so long."

Everyone had taken their seats by now. Jayne said, "It's been a long day. Let's get this finished and then get a good night's rest. Tomorrow won't be any better. Detectives?"

Baxter said, "We started with a timeline of both of the deceased's movements yesterday. Aurora Bennett went to work at her regular time, seven AM. According to her assistant and co-workers, she ate lunch at her desk, went to work out from two to three, and worked late, until around seven PM. She went out three times that day in the news van to do on-site segment recordings. No one we spoke to thought there was anything out of the ordinary going on with her. According to her phone, the only text messages she sent were to her assistant regarding work and a 'K' response to her husband's text that said, 'I'm working late tonight again.' She didn't have contact with any other family or friends. She made a few posts on her public Instagram page, general lifestyle things that may have been pre-scheduled. Her followers' comments were positive—no threats or trolling."

Sterling said, "As for Wakefield, his day started with teaching three classes in the morning. He went running with his normal running partner, another Ashmore professor, Suresh Mahar. Mahar said Wakefield spent the rest of his lunch hour in his office with the door closed. Wakefield taught one more class and left around three. After that, he went to the Wakefield Foundation office, as he does most afternoons, where he's the founder and CEO. He stayed until around seven, and then he and the chief legal counsel, Barry Jeffords, and the COO, Bradley Kerrigan, went to Prime 47 for dinner."

Chief Esparza chimed in, "Dinner at Prime 47? Damn. Wonder if they charged it to their not-for-profit's company card."

Sterling replied, "I asked, but no one would give me a straight answer."

"So, yes."

"Right. And they didn't hold back on buying drinks, because Wakefield got so hammered he couldn't even drive himself home. He caught an Uber and left his car in the Clay Terrace parking lot. According to the home security app on Wakefield's phone, he disabled the alarm system at 9:49 PM. Doorbell cam footage shows him stumbling through the front door a minute later."

Shane frowned. "And the alarm system never got reset, right?"

"Right."

Before Sterling could continue with his report, Shane added, "So anyone could have come and gone from the home after 9:49 PM without tripping the alarm."

I noticed a frown crease Baxter's face. There was no way he believed this case was as cut and dried as Sterling wanted it to be.

"Theoretically, yes." Sterling went on before Shane could cut in again. "Look, it's no secret I've thought from the beginning that Lance Wakefield killed his wife, and after running down some of the people closest to them, I haven't changed my mind. Aurora's assistant said Aurora thought Wakefield was cheating on her, which I called this morning. For a story and for her own personal benefit, she'd been researching some kind of wild parties she worried he was going to. She had no proof, so she hadn't confronted him yet. When asked, the assistant also said Aurora wasn't cheating on him. In fact, she'd been begging him for a baby. He'd been reluctant to agree, which was why she thought he was cheating in the first place, along with him working late and being distracted a lot lately."

Amanda and I shared a glance. Aurora had done a lot more than beg him for a baby.

Jayne rubbed her forehead. "Did anyone corroborate that?"

Baxter said, "Aurora's mother and sister. We interviewed them over the phone. They didn't point the finger at Wakefield, and they didn't seem to know about any cheating on either side. However, they did mention Aurora was unhappy with him dragging his feet in agreeing to start a family. Actually, Wakefield's sister corroborated it as well. She said he didn't want to have a kid because he didn't think Aurora would be willing to let her career take a backseat to a pregnancy or the needs of a new baby. When I asked if she knew about any cheating on either side, she said no, but she did throw in her two cents that if one of them was cheating, it would have been Aurora."

Jayne frowned. "They seemed to be having marital problems, and that's enough motive for murder. I just wish it was a little neater. If he's the one cheating, why is he writing 'WHORE' on the wall? Surely not as an affront to himself."

Shane said, "Um...before we get too far with this, I've got an issue that needs some discussion. Can we pull up a closeup from the scene of Lance Wakefield's face?"

Chief Esparza clicked a few times on the track pad of his laptop, and a giant photo of Lance's face popped up on the white board at the head of the conference room.

Shane stood and walked over so he could point at the photo. "I'm concerned with the void on most of Wakefield's face. I believe if he killed her in the way the other blood patterns suggest, he'd have a significant amount of back spatter covering his face. There's none."

Sterling said, "Big freaking deal. Maybe he was wearing a ski mask."

I'd gone over the "why is there no back spatter" scenarios *ad nauseum* during the past few hours. I wanted nothing more than to go home. I said, "We ran through every possibility for why his face doesn't look like a Jackson Pollock painting and came up with no good reasons." Except for the reason we were about to lay on everyone. "I even sent Beck out specifically to check for that type of evidence."

"That was your first mistake," Sterling jeered.

I went on, "I think it also warrants our attention that the funeral suit Lance set out for himself was several sizes too big for him. It doesn't technically prove anything other than the fact that he wasn't in his right mind, but it could help back up our new theory. And then, considering the fact that their alarm system was disabled from 9:49 on and anyone could have entered the house after that time..."

Jayne looked from Shane to me. "What are you two getting at?"

Shane shrugged. "Lance Wakefield may not be our killer."

As the room erupted into one big argument, including Sterling's gem, "That's the dumbest thing I've ever heard," Shane shuffled back to sit next to me.

He murmured, "*Our* new theory? I thought you said I was on my own with this one."

I chuckled. "Eh, what are partners for?"

Finally Jayne got hold of the meeting again. "This is certainly an interesting twist, and given the circumstances, one that is not outside the realm of possibility. Since the two of you have already taken the time to research some aspects of your theory, I think you should run with it and try to find us some other persons of interest. With the media scrutinizing everything we do, we can't afford to be wrong on this one." She turned to Amanda and me. "Crime scene report?"

Amanda took the lead and rattled off all the things we'd found at the scene. She also reported some conclusions she'd drawn from the analysis she'd done so far in the lab, which included verifying that the blood on the walls and sheets as well as on Lance's clothing and skin matched Aurora's blood type. She'd also determined only Lance's and Aurora's fingerprints to be on the security system keypads, but she hadn't yet processed the prints she'd found on the exterior doors.

Jayne ended the meeting, and even though it would have been perfectly acceptable for me to pack it up and go home, I wanted to have a look at a key piece of evidence before I left, so I returned to the lab by way of the evidence room and checked out the box containing the chef's knife.

Amanda was in the lab cleaning up when I walked through the door. She hadn't said anything to me during the meeting after Shane's and my startling revelation, but now she had plenty to say.

"How did I miss that about the blood spatter?" she demanded. "You and I had a whole discussion about where Wakefield was positioned while he was killing her. Or...while he *wasn't* killing her? This case just got way crazier."

As I put on clean gear and set the knife on a clean workspace, I replied, "That was all Shane. I missed it, too. I think the rest of the blood all over Lance threw me off."

"And the suit? I *processed* the suit, and it didn't dawn on me how enormous it was," she wailed.

"You can thank Vic for that one. I picked his FBI profiler brain over dinner."

"Oh, okay. That doesn't make me feel quite as bad. He's been in law enforcement twice as long as we have."

I laughed. Vic was only forty, but he had ten years on a lot of us around here, which of course made him the butt of plenty of old man jokes, especially when we'd been dating.

She watched as I zeroed in on the knife's handle in search of finger-prints. "I figured you'd be ready to get out of here."

"Well, if our crazy theory has any merit, this knife can't have Lance's prints on it, right?"

"That's right. We can argue spatter pattern all day, but you can't argue with prints on the murder weapon. That would get someone convicted in court. And since I'm going to do the second pass, I'm going to get out of here and not watch you do the first one so my perspective will be fresh."

"See you tomorrow," I said.

Now that I was alone, I turned my full attention to the knife lying in front of me, its sharp point to my right. Along the side of the thick silver handle, I saw two long swipes of blood, but no patent prints. I thought about how the knife would have been positioned in the killer's hand, the opposite way you'd hold it to slice through food. A right-handed person's fingertips would have rested on the opposite side of the handle. I turned the knife over and looked closely for anything resembling a fingerprint. There were no marks other than a thin swipe.

I took a step back from the magnifier and blew out a breath. This knife had been wiped off.

I called Shane. When he picked up, I said, "You need to come to the lab."

By the time I got my phone put away and slipped on a fresh pair of gloves, Shane burst through the door. "Tell me you found something earth-shattering," he said, coming to stand next to me at the table.

"Not exactly, but I did find another instance of lack of evidence. It looks like the handle of the murder weapon has been wiped off. See those faint swipe marks?"

"Wiped off? Why? It would make no sense to wipe your bloody finger-prints off the murder weapon and then turn around and spell out your motive in the same blood on the wall."

"You're right—it doesn't make sense. Just like the void on Lance's face and the giant suit don't make sense."

He frowned. "Damn. No one's going to like it that our latest evidence against Wakefield being the killer is another void."

"Well, I haven't dusted it for latent prints yet, so we might catch a break." Under the bench magnifier, latent prints would be semi-visible, especially on shiny metal. But I hadn't noticed any yet during my examination, so I wasn't holding my breath. "I still say the lack of patent prints is important. If Lance was our killer, there should be at the very least some partials and smudges, considering his hands were bare."

"Unless his bloody gloves are hiding somewhere with his bloody mask," Shane griped.

I gave him a punch on the arm. "Oh, lighten up, partner. We'll find our smoking gun."

He left, and I continued my analysis of the knife. Try as I might, I couldn't see any signs of where to dust for latent prints. So, I dusted the entire handle with black fingerprint powder and studied it again. There were no prints. Nothing about this added up.

* * *

On my way out, I passed Baxter's desk, which was conspicuously empty. Sterling's cubicle was next, and Sterling was there still working, not that I was surprised. He ate, slept, and breathed his big cases. He was a good investigator, holding the best case closure rate in the county for years, but his stubborn streak held him back sometimes. I wasn't going to bother saying goodnight—we weren't on that good of terms yet—but he heard my footfalls and turned around.

"Are you seriously going 'one-armed man' on this case?" he demanded. "The killer used a weapon from inside the home. If it wasn't Wakefield, why didn't the killer bring his own knife or gun or whatever? Who goes to murder someone without the tools to get the job done?"

I sighed. "You just don't like the idea because it came from the new guy."

"I don't like it because it's too far-fetched."

"I could say the same about some of the hunches we followed for that case back in February."

"Maybe it's your influence. You always make Baxter chase all kinds of crazy shit." Before I could defend myself, he added, "Speaking of him, he flew out of here like a bat out of hell as soon as the meeting was over. Where does he have to get to? He's got no life."

I knew what he had to get to, and it rhymed with 'new girlfriend.' I didn't have the energy to be upset about it. After all, what was one more reminder today of the fact that *I* was the one who had no life?

14

"Auntie Ellie, did Mommy tell you Caden is getting a new puppy today?" my nephew Nate asked through a mouthful of blueberry muffin.

I smiled at him and threw my half-sister Rachel a wink across the breakfast table. "She sure did. I bet he's so excited." She hadn't. First rule of little kids—keep everything a yes answer unless it's a hard no. Him finding out Rachel hadn't made it a point to tell me about some random kid's new puppy would have been a personal affront not only to Nate, but also to Caden, his new puppy, and the importance of daycare gossip in general.

"It's a pit mix. A boy. They're getting him from the animal shelter," Nate explained. In the next breath, he asked, "What's a pit mix?"

"It means the pup is a mix of a couple of different breeds but probably looks most like a pit bull." I Googled "pit mix puppy" and showed him a few photos. "It could look like any one of these."

"Aww! They're soooo cute." His eyes widened and ping-ponged between Rachel and me. "Can we get one, too? A boy pit mix puppy? Can we? Can we?"

His enthusiasm always brought a smile to my face. "You already have a puppy, sir." I reached out and patted our giant Golden Retriever, Trixie, who was sitting obediently on the floor between my chair and Nate's.

"Trixie needs a little brother!" he exclaimed.

"You're Trixie's little brother."

Rachel got up and ruffled his hair on her way to put her dishes in the sink. "And besides, Auntie Ellie and I have enough to do around here taking care of you and Trixie. We don't need another animal running around. Speaking of which, let's go get the blueberry smears off your face and hands before you go to daycare. To the bathroom with you!"

I smiled to myself as I cleaned up my dishes and Nate's crumbly muffin mess. Rachel was doing so much better these days. She still had her down days and her frustrated days and her angry days, but all in all she was slowly working through her issues and getting back to life as she knew it. Like the rest of the Ashmore students, she was stressed about her upcoming finals, but her priorities were in check—her mental health always came first, and the rest would all work out.

Rachel poked her head back into the kitchen. "Hey, I saw some of the news coverage on Professor Wakefield's case. Some of the stuff they're saying is really terrible."

We hadn't gotten a chance to talk yesterday, besides me letting her know I'd be out late working on the case. I nodded. "Yeah. Don't believe everything you hear. The media coverage of this case is taking on a life of its own. We haven't told them a lot, and I think they're so hellbent on filling broadcast time that they've started making stuff up. I get it that the area is devastated by Aurora Bennett's death, but they're making it worse by trying to force their content."

Her eyes looked haunted. "Is it really a murder-suicide?"

My heart sank. Once the detectives started interviewing people in earnest, it was only a matter of time before the press would seek those people out and try to get them to dish about their questioning. In this case, the person with the most knowledge of what went on was a news station employee. Based on the fact that WIND-TV 7 had information we hadn't released about the scene, Aurora's assistant had undoubtedly been eager to please her bosses by spilling her guts so her station had the scoop.

I wasn't supposed to discuss specifics of the case with people outside the department, but I did want to clear one thing up. "It's a double homicide. There has been no determination of guilt, and we don't have an official suspect. We have a lot to investigate before making that kind of judgment."

"So Professor Wakefield *didn't* kill his wife?"

I gave her a contrite smile. "Sorry, Rach. I can't say more."

She nodded. "I understand. It's just that...I had him as a professor last year and thought he was a good guy. I hate that they're attacking his character. It's so sad that no one seems to care that he died, too."

"The right people care, I promise. You know we'll do our best."

She frowned. "How's that going to work if you and Nick can't even talk to each other?"

She knew about my involvement in the last case and knew Baxter and I could no longer have personal contact. What she didn't know was how close we'd gotten and how much the whole thing weighed on me. There were a lot of reasons why she didn't need to know.

I shrugged. "Jayne split us up. We can't be partners for a while."

She smiled apologetically. "That sucks. You two nerds make a crazy smart team."

* * *

After I finished teaching my morning classes, I was dragging a little. I'd had trouble falling asleep and had ended up getting out of bed to type out my notes from my voice recorder. I didn't have any epiphanies about the case, but reliving my processing of the scene often put my mind at ease that I hadn't forgotten anything. It had also allowed me to sleep soundly the rest of the night—at least what had been left of it.

I grabbed some coffee from the professors' lounge and went to my office to find Vic waiting by my door. He'd texted me late last night to ask if there was anything he could do for me to make my life easier, and I took him up on it. I imagined he'd intended for his offer to involve walking my dog or taking my vehicle for an oil change or picking up groceries, but I had a task much more in keeping with his skill set. Mostly. In a few short minutes, I was willing to bet he would fully regret his kind gesture.

I said in a mock serious tone, "Hello, Special Agent Manetti. Your mission, should you choose to accept it, will probably make you want to strangle a teenager or two. Are you sure you have what it takes to oversee a lab exercise on fingerprint collection for a bunch of freshmen?"

Vic nodded solemnly. "I think I can handle a room full of intelligent collegians performing a scientific experiment, yes."

He was wearing one of his sharp FBI suits, looking more GQ than G-Man. I said, "Yeah, unless most of them are too busy swooning over you. You could have tried to look a little ugly."

"Next time," he replied, chuckling as he followed me into my office.

I handed him a bag of supplies. "Each student gets three tape lifts. Each table gets one brush and one container of fingerprint dust to share. I've written out the instructions for you to read to the class, and my TA is on standby if you get overwhelmed."

He rolled his eyes. "You know I hunt down career criminals for a living, right? I got this."

"Oh, I should probably warn you that one of the students is a superfan of yours."

"Really? Who?"

Trust Fund Baby was going to pee his pants when he walked in and saw Vic. "You'll figure it out."

There was a knock at my open door. Shane stuck his head in and asked, "You ready?" He noticed Vic and stepped inside to shake his hand. "Hey, Manetti. Good to see you on your feet. When you getting back out there?"

Vic replied, "Not soon enough. I'm stuck at home a few more weeks, and then I'll be a desk jockey for a while."

Shane chuckled. "A lot of my coworkers are missing your visits." In an aside to me, he explained, "You should see how many people in my department drool when this guy walks in. They call him Agent McDreamy."

A grin spread wide across my face as Vic suddenly looked incredibly uncomfortable. "Agent *McDreamy*?"

Vic glared at me. "If you start calling me that—"

"Oh, please. I've called you so many worse things than Agent McDreamy." He was still pouting, so I added, "You can use that angst to keep my rowdy teenagers in line. Let's go."

I led the way down the hall, dropping Vic off at the lab and continuing

outside with Shane. "Who's on your list, the whole philosophy department?" I asked.

Shane consulted the notes on his phone. "Yep. Dr. Suresh Mahar, Dr.
Lamorne Howard, and Professor Leonard Shelton. And Wakefield's TA,
Annaleigh Walters. The other detectives ran down Mahar and Howard
yesterday at their homes, but they mainly talked logistics. I want to do a
deep dive."

I nodded. "Okay. We should find the professors in Bayard Hall. I heard
they suspended classes yesterday after the news about Lance came out, but
they're back at it today."

Bayard Hall, home to the classrooms and offices of the humanities
department, was only a short walk across Ashmore's well-manicured front
lawn from the science building. The towering oak trees weren't yet at their
fullest, but they provided enough shade to shield my eyes from the bright
spring sun. Bayard Hall was the second oldest building on campus,
constructed around the turn of the century from Indiana limestone in
Ashmore's signature Collegiate Gothic style. I felt a pang of déjà vu. Earlier
this school year, I'd crossed the lawn with Baxter on the way to conduct
interviews during the first case we worked together.

Pushing that thought from my mind, I added, "Philosophy guys can be
hard to get a straight answer out of. Oh, and full disclosure, I dated
Lamorne for a hot minute."

Shane grinned. "Did you, now? Are you still on speaking terms?"

"Well enough. He thinks I'm dumb, though."

"Why in the world would he think that?'

I shrugged. "He wanted to philosophize and debate about literally
everything, and I wanted him to shut the hell up. I purposely offered stupid
arguments and backed them up with blatantly made-up facts. He ended up
breaking things off."

"If you couldn't stand talking to him, why didn't *you* break things off?"

"Because his company was very pleasurable when he wasn't talking."

"Ah." He nodded, then said suddenly, "Oh, speaking of that, I have some
fun autopsy news: Aurora Bennett was pregnant. You called it."

My jaw dropped. "No freaking way. And with a baby her husband didn't
want."

"Yeah. Our job just got exponentially harder."

When we got to the second floor of Bayard Hall, I heard Lamorne's smooth, mesmerizing voice drifting from one of the classrooms. When we reached the open doorway, we found Lamorne holding court, garnering the rapt attention of several students who'd dawdled after class. He had quite the flair for idealistic, overly analytical rhetoric, if you liked that kind of thing. He also had a flair for style, especially for a professor. He always looked like he'd stepped out of the pages of a fashion magazine.

Shane and I waited until the one-man show was over and the students had vacated the classroom. "Hey, Lamorne," I called, giving him a tentative wave.

"Ellie, please come in," he said graciously, beckoning us into his classroom. "Lovely to see you."

"You, too. I'm sorry for the loss of Lance. I'm sure everyone in the department is devastated."

Lamorne hung his head. "We certainly are, and for a variety of reasons—"

Before he could launch into a dissertation on those reasons, I gestured to Shane. "About that, we know you spoke with Detectives Sterling and Baxter yesterday, but we have a few different questions for you. This is Detective Shane Carlisle."

Shane nodded. "Good afternoon, Dr. Howard. We're sorry to bother you at work so soon after losing a colleague. Do you have a few minutes?"

Lamorne sat on the edge of his desk. "Sure. Anything to help get justice for Lance and Aurora."

Shane consulted his notes quickly, then put his phone away and concentrated his full attention on Lamorne. "Would you normally interact with Professor Wakefield on a daily basis?"

Lamorne replied, "Monday through Friday, yes. Our offices are next door to each other, and as a department, we all go to lunch together on Fridays."

"Did you notice anything strange in his behavior in the past week? Or maybe couple of weeks?"

Stroking his chin thoughtfully, Lamorne said, "No, nothing specific. But it was kind of like his whole vibe had been off lately. He seemed preoccupied and always in a hurry. He'd normally be one to talk your leg off, but he'd gotten kind of...almost antisocial. It felt like he avoided contact with me, and I saw him do the same with students."

Remembering that Aurora had allegedly thought he'd been cheating on her, I asked, "You mentioned him being in a hurry. Did he seem to be in a hurry to get somewhere else, like he had somewhere to be or someone to meet? Or was he more in a hurry to get away from potential interactions?"

"A little of both, I suppose. I did notice him cutting his office hours short over the past few weeks. He's technically supposed to be available until five on Tuesdays and Thursdays, but he keeps leaving around three. It's not a hard-and-fast rule, but as a department, we pride ourselves on being available for our students outside of class."

Shane said, "Speaking of student interaction outside of class, how did Wakefield handle that? He was a handsome guy. Probably caught the eye of the occasional student. Have you ever known him to become too close with anyone?"

"Is that a question or an attack on Lance's character, Detective?"

I said, "We can't afford to assume anything—good or bad—in a situation like this. And we're not saying Lance was in the wrong. Our students are of the age where their adult hormones can drive them to make childlike choices. Lance could have been in a one-sided relationship and had no idea. Student-teacher crushes rarely end well."

Lamorne relaxed and put on a thoughtful expression. "A student... hmm..." He shook his head. "No. No one comes to mind."

Shane pressed, "Any other ladies on his radar besides his wife?"

"We normally keep our conversations focused on academic pursuits rather than personal ones."

"Do you know about any people who might have been angry with him or wanted to hurt him or his wife? Have you heard about or witnessed him having an argument with anyone?"

Spreading his hands, Lamorne smiled. "We're philosophers. We live to argue and debate."

Another thing that irked me about Lamorne was his tendency to give non-answers to simple yes/no questions. The way I'd found to snap him out of it was to insult him. "He means arguments about real things that matter, not waxing poetic about academic ideals."

He gave me a piteous smile. "Oh, Ellie, 'there is no greater evil one can suffer than to hate reasonable discourse.'"

I snorted. "False. Getting murdered is way worse. We need actual information, Lamorne. Clock's ticking."

Frowning, he said, "Fine. I haven't witnessed Lance being in an argument about anything other than academic ideals. But I've only seen him in action here. I imagine he's made plenty of enemies through his foundation and his outspokenness against unethical corporate practices. Honestly, I wouldn't know where to start with that list of people. But for someone to kill two people over calling out a proven wrong?"

Shane said, "People have been killed over far less. It's standard procedure that I ask this: where were you Tuesday night between ten and midnight?"

Lamorne replied, "I was at home, asleep."

"Alone?"

"Yes."

Shane nodded and handed him a business card. "If you happen to think of anything else to shed some light on what happened, please give me a call anytime."

He turned and headed out of the room, but as I tried to follow, Lamorne stopped me. "Isn't it funny how you think you know a person and what they stand for, but when you hear something incongruent to your image of them, doubt still manages to wiggle its way in and work to reframe your thoughts? I find it fascinating that so many people who knew Lance can all have such differing opinions about his character after watching a little bit of news coverage."

He was clearly working himself up into one of his boring dissertations, and I didn't have the time for it. I shrugged and began walking backward toward the door. "Well, that's the media for you. They've done their job if they've swayed your opinion."

"What about your opinion, Ellie? Which camp are you in?"

"I can't talk about that since I'm working the case."

Evidently my argument to end this discussion wasn't strong enough.

"It's quite a conundrum how as a student—and teacher—of ethics, that Lance's conscious mind could allow him to commit such an act against his wife. But if you look at the incident instead from a psychological perspective, it could be reasoned that he simply had an episode in which part of his mind was able to detach itself from his core beliefs and—"

I interrupted him. "Seriously, Lamorne, I can't talk about this. Like *at all*. Not even in a philosophical kind of way."

"You...oh. I suppose that would be an ethical dilemma for you, wouldn't it? I should have realized that. I apologize."

"It's okay. Thanks for your help. It was good to see you again."

He regarded me thoughtfully. "It was good to see you, too. You know, I'd like to see you again sometime, if you're free."

No way. Being alone was better than listening to him ramble. "I appreciate the offer, but...I'm seeing someone."

"Can't blame a man for trying," he said smoothly.

"Thanks again, Lamorne." I left as quickly as I could without seeming like I was running away.

Shane was waiting for me outside, or more accurately, eavesdropping. He fell into step with me and said, "So who is it that you're seeing? Word was that you and Manetti were an item before his whole blowup with the department, but—"

My jaw dropped. "Wait. You heard about that?"

"You know cops are worse gossips than a bunch of old ladies at a hair salon."

"I do know that, but we're not even in the same city."

"Oh, come on. Hamilton County is just a suburb of Indy. Stop trying to be special. So who are you seeing?"

"No one. I lied to him."

He couldn't contain his smile. "That wasn't very ethical of you."

"Smart ass."

Our chat with the department chair, Professor Leonard Shelton, went about as poorly as a non-suspect interview could go. He was crochety as hell and purposely unhelpful, I assumed due to his belief—that he was more than happy to old-mansplain to us—that society should follow its own moral code with no threat of government intervention. It was clear that he had no use for Lance, his political activism, or any government employee, including Shane and myself. The only actual information he was able to communicate was corroborating Lamorne's statement about Lance cutting back on his office hours and providing his own alibi, a competitive game of chess with his neighbor that had lasted well past midnight.

"He's a delight," I said, shaking my head as we exited Professor Shelton's office.

Shane snorted. "Gotta love a guy with his head shoved all the way up his ass. Now what we need to find out is what Wakefield was doing with those extra four hours per week."

He stopped outside Dr. Mahar's office and knocked on the door. No answer. The other classrooms in this hallway were either empty or the professors in them were not Dr. Mahar.

"He should be here now, according to this." I tapped a sheet of paper taped to the door listing Dr. Mahar's office hours and his cell number. He was a brave man leaving his cell number for the world to see. The only student I trusted with mine was my TA.

Shane took out his phone and called the number. "Dr. Mahar, this is Detective Shane Carlisle of the IMPD. I'd like to speak with you about Lance Wakefield. Can we meet this afternoon?" Shane was silent for a moment, and then said more gently, "I'm sorry for your loss. I didn't realize the two of you were so close. Is it possible for my partner and me to come to your house?" After another pause, he said, "Okay, thanks. See you soon." He ended the call and said to me, "Mahar took the day off to mourn the loss of his BFF."

15

Shane drove us to a modest Carmel subdivision where Suresh Mahar lived. Dr. Mahar welcomed us inside with a wary smile, showing us to a cozy living room crammed with books and décor from around the world. Shane and I took the leather sofa, and Dr. Mahar sank into the overstuffed chair across from us.

He eyed me. "Professor Matthews, are you...here as an Ashmore representative or...?"

"I'm consulting for the sheriff's office," I replied.

"Ah," he said, trying to smile, but failing.

I didn't know Dr. Mahar very well—only to say hello around campus, but he had always struck me as a nervous individual. Today he was more sad and shellshocked than anything, but there was still an underlying level of unease about him.

Shane said, "We appreciate you meeting with us, Dr. Mahar, after already speaking with the detectives yesterday. I understand that you're going through some grief over the loss of a colleague—"

Dr. Mahar corrected him. "A *friend*."

"Sorry, right. A friend. We'll try to get through this as quickly as possible. How long have you known Lance Wakefield?"

"About five years. We met when I moved here to take the job at Ashmore."

"Were you instant friends?"

"Not exactly, but once he mentioned to me about his weight loss surgery...we bonded." Dr. Mahar spread his hands. "The rest is history."

"Can you elaborate?"

"Oh, sure. I had weight loss surgery as well, several years before his. I'd had success and was able to help him through it. We became workout buddies. And then best friends." His voice broke on that last word.

I shot a glance at Shane. This guy was all over the place—happy, then ready to burst into tears. I supposed his reaction could be genuine. If he was a generally happy guy, maybe the grief came in quick waves that kept sucker punching him over and over again.

I changed the direction of the questioning. "How well did you know Aurora?"

He shrugged. "I didn't see her much. At the occasional party they would throw at their home was about it."

"Do you know if they were happy?"

His face grew dark. "If you're taking the media's side, then—"

Holding up a hand, Shane sprang to my defense. "Dr. Mahar, let me clue you in on a little secret—law enforcement and the media are rarely on the same side. Most days, the press only serve to make our job harder, and they're making this investigation exponentially more difficult. We're only interested in the truth—and that means we have to ask some hard questions and look at the case from every angle. I'll warn you that the questions will only get harder from here, but if you really care about Lance and getting justice for his and his wife's deaths, you'll answer them."

Dr. Mahar nodded sadly. "Okay. I...I think they were happy. I know Lance loved her...but I know they'd been arguing lately about..."

"A baby?" I supplied.

He nodded again. "Lance didn't think he was ready to be a father. He didn't know if he had what it took. He definitely knew he didn't have the time—or probably more accurately, he knew he'd have to give up parts of his life to make it work. His foundation work takes up a lot of hours, as does staying in shape, and he does all that on top of a full class load."

I understood. I had the same issue when I was called to work a case. My family time and exercise time always took the first hit.

I asked, "Was that all they'd argued about?"

"I think so."

Shane asked, "Was he seeing anyone else?"

Dr. Mahar shook his head. "Absolutely not."

"You sure?"

"He wasn't a cheater."

"Aurora seemed to think he was cheating."

Dr. Mahar nearly came out of his chair but must have thought better of it and sank back down. "Says who?"

Eyeing him, Shane replied, "I can't disclose that, but the source was likely close enough to Aurora to know her feelings about it. Aurora was actually researching some sort of wild parties she worried he was going to. Do you know anything about that?"

He shook his head again, this time more vehemently. "No. I don't believe any of it. Not out of him."

"Okay, then let's explore the flip side. Did he think Aurora might have been seeing someone else?"

"He never mentioned anything like that to me."

Shane said, "Okay, for argument's sake, let's say that love and relationships had nothing to do with these deaths. Lance didn't kill Aurora, and neither of them had a jealous lover that would have wanted to kill either of them. Who out there had another reason to want to hurt them?"

Dr. Mahar shrugged helplessly. "I don't know. I mean, anyone who knew either of them personally wouldn't have hated them. They were good people. Now, professionally...they maybe didn't come off so well. She made people angry all the time with her news pieces. His foundation's sole purpose is to call out corporations over unethical practices. They've put a lot of businesses out of business and a lot of people out of jobs. I can't imagine the number of enemies they've made over the years."

Lamorne had mentioned this earlier about Lance, but I hadn't given too much thought to the trail of victims left by Aurora's hard-hitting news stories. This was a power couple who'd stepped on a lot of toes and had probably ruined lives. I felt like our suspect pool just exploded with possibilities.

I pushed that aside to focus on the here and now. Lance's workout buddy was our best chance to grill someone about the oversized suit. "Back to Lance's weight loss...he clearly worked hard to lose and keep off the weight. Do you know of a reason he'd keep one of his old suits from before? Did he not purge his wardrobe of his larger clothes when he got new ones?"

Dr. Mahar blew his nose. "He only kept one thing—his lucky suit. He proposed to Aurora in it."

Shane and I shared a glance. I pressed, "So this suit holds a special significance to him."

"Yes, but that's not the real reason he kept it. It's a reminder to never allow himself to get unhealthy again. He put it in the very front of his closet so he'd see it every day."

I thought for a moment. "So, would he ever consider wearing it or putting it on?"

Dr. Mahar made a face. "Oh, no. He would never."

"Might he want to be buried in it since it was special?"

"That's a very odd question regarding your investigation."

I thought fast. "I know. I...heard that the family was grappling with the choice for the funeral and...wondered if that one would be a good choice."

"No, he'd be swimming in it. He'd look ridiculous. He'd hate that."

"I'm sure the undertaker could work some magic with pinning it or something, if you think that's what Lance would have wanted."

He shook his head. "No. Definitely not. He'd worked too hard at getting fit. Putting that suit back on, even in death, would crush his soul. It was no longer a piece of clothing to him—it was an object lesson. If the family needs advice on picking out a suit for him to be buried in, my vote would be the dark gray pinstripe Armani. It was his favorite. He always wore it when he had a big speech to make. He said it gave him confidence."

Again, no smoking gun, but Dr. Mahar's assessment of the suit choice drove home the fact that Lance had been totally out of his mind upon choosing it.

I nodded. "We'll pass that along. Do you and Lance ever work out with a group or attend classes or go to trainers or anything? Or is it always the two of you?"

He smiled. "It's usually the two of us. We either run outside or work out in the campus gym." His smile faded as he added, "Although he does belong to CTC. He plays pickleball there a couple of times a week. I don't play. It doesn't interest me."

Translation: he was terrible at pickleball, and Lance didn't want to play with him. Carmel Tennis Center was the place to go if you were serious about your racquet sports. They were pretty elite. Maybe Dr. Mahar wasn't even good enough for them to let him in the door.

Shane asked, "Did he have other friends besides you?"

"Not best friends." What was with this guy and his need for a best friend?

"Sure. How about regular friends?"

"I think he was friends first with some of the people he now plays pickleball with."

Shane stared at him for a moment. "What about you, Dr. Mahar? Did you have any reason to want to hurt Aurora or Lance?"

"What?" he cried, tears springing to his eyes.

Shane shrugged. "I told you the questions would get harder as we went along. You seem to have had a close relationship with one of our victims. You've got some strong opinions about his character, about his wife's character, and about the validity of your relationship with him. You've got him pretty high on a pedestal in my estimation. It's been my experience that when that sort of thing happens, a fall from grace can make the worshipper really upset."

"I don't *worship* him."

I wasn't too sure about that. Shane said nothing, he just stared at Dr. Mahar and let him make the next move.

Breathing heavily, Dr. Mahar sputtered, "Are you...are you trying to say I killed them?"

"No, I'm just asking if you had a reason to."

"I'm done talking to you without my lawyer."

"Not quite. Where were you Tuesday night between ten and midnight?"

"I don't have to tell you that."

Shane replied calmly, "You do if you don't want to give us a reason to put you on our list of persons of interest."

Dr. Mahar looked like he didn't know if he wanted to explode or burst into tears. "I was here."

"By yourself?"

"Yes. That's not a crime."

Shane smiled. "No one said it was." He stood and started walking straight for the door.

I hurried out behind him, throwing a, "Bye, Dr. Mahar," over my shoulder.

As we got in Shane's car, I said, "Okay, so do we chase the pickleball angle, run down Lance's TA, go interview the people at the foundation, or try to figure out how many hundreds or thousands of people our two vics managed to piss off in the greater Indianapolis area? Oh, or maybe go back and search Mahar's house for the shrine to Lance we both know is somewhere in there? At first I thought he was going to be a big help, but then he started getting creepy."

Shane laughed. "I think Mahar's harmless. I punched so many of his buttons the poor guy didn't know if he was coming or going."

"You certainly did, and you played good and bad cop all by yourself."

"It's a gift." He pulled up Google Maps on his phone. "CTC is a mile from here. I say we at least find out who's in Wakefield's inner pickleball circle. Then we can decide who to bother first."

16

Carmel Tennis Center was a glorified pole barn in a business park north of town. But the modern industrial interior, fully stocked pro shop, and brightly painted courts more than made up for its outward appearance.

A perky blonde whose nametag read "Kayla" smiled from behind the front desk. "Welcome to Carmel Tennis Center." She eyed us—Shane in a suit and tie and me in a silky button down, pencil skirt, and heels—and added, "I hope you two brought a change of clothes, or at least some comfy shoes if you want to do anything more than watch."

Shane flashed his badge. "We came here for information."

She shrank back. "Oh. What kind of...information? From me?"

I smiled, hoping to put her at ease. Not everyone liked talking to cops. "I'm Ellie Matthews with the Hamilton County Sheriff's Office, and this is Detective Shane Carlisle. We were hoping you could tell us who Lance Wakefield normally plays pickleball with."

Kayla's face fell. "Oh...he...he died, didn't he?"

"Yes. We're trying to find some of his friends and acquaintances, and we heard he had a group he regularly met here for pickleball."

She nodded. "He did. Let me check." She tapped on a computer keyboard for a few seconds. "Bradley Kerrigan, Steve Nunley, Jessica

Nunley, and Owen Reeves are who he usually plays with on Wednesday and Saturday mornings."

Shane nodded, entering those names into his phone. "Any of them here now by chance?"

She consulted her computer screen. "No, sorry. Um...anything else I can help you with?"

He replied, "Anything strange stand out to you about Wakefield in the last couple of weeks?"

Kayla frowned for a moment. "Not really. I mean, I don't really interact that much with the customers aside from checking them in and asking them if they'd like a bottle of water."

"Has he missed any of his regularly scheduled games lately?"

She looked at the screen. "Oh, actually, yes. He was a no-show two Saturdays ago and also last Wednesday, and...of course...yesterday." She added quietly, "I suppose I should cancel his membership..."

I smiled. "Thanks for your time, Kayla."

She nodded. We left her staring sadly at her computer.

Shane said, "I'm thinking we track these guys down before opening Pandora's box of people our power couple has pissed off."

I smiled to myself as I thought of what Baxter might have said in this situation—I figured he would have gone with some sort of punny wordplay about Aurora's box and turned it into a bad joke. Shane was a great partner, and I enjoyed being with him, but he just wasn't Baxter. No one was.

* * *

All we had for Annaleigh Walters was her cell number, because Ashmore Residence Life wouldn't give us her campus address without a warrant. Shane was perturbed, but I appreciated the college's insistence on the students' security even though it caused us a bit more work. They'd beefed up security since two girls, including Rachel, had been abducted back in December on or near campus grounds. While we waited for a deputy to get us contact info for the members of Lance's pickleball group, we called Annaleigh. We got her voicemail, and Shane left a message that we wanted to meet her to talk.

I said with a smile, "You might text her too, old man. Young people generally don't use the actual phone function of their phones."

"Oh, right. I can't believe how much things have changed since we were in college."

By the time he'd sent the text, he received the information on the four pickleball players. Owen Reeves was retired and lived not far from Ashmore. The Nunleys lived across the border in Marion County, and both worked in downtown Indy, so we'd wait until evening to track them down. Bradley Kerrigan, luckily enough, was the COO of Wakefield Foundation, where we'd planned to head next. We swung past Owen Reeves's home on the way.

Owen Reeves lived in a mansion on a large plot of land just north of the college. A woman about sixty answered the door and nearly fainted when we told her who we were and that we needed to speak to her husband. Her voice cracked as she ran back into the home and called for him.

A tall, fit older man came to the door with a wary look on his face.

Shane introduced us and asked, "Mr. Reeves, is it okay if we come in and speak to you about Lance Wakefield?"

Owen Reeves seemed to deflate before our eyes. "Yes, come on in."

Once we were settled in a two-story living room with a fantastic view of the home's pool, manicured backyard, and pond, Shane said, "You played pickleball regularly with Lance Wakefield, correct?"

"Twice a week, unless my knees are acting up," Mr. Reeves replied.

"Did you know each other from before, or did you meet at CTC?"

"I've known Lance since he was a boy. His father and I used to work together."

Shane shot me a glance. "Oh, so you've watched him grow up, then."

"I have. And I'm gutted over what the news is doing to that poor boy's memory." His voice broke.

I said, "We are, too, Mr. Reeves. We want to keep an open mind in this investigation so we don't miss something, and the media is not helping. Since you were so close with his father, did Lance ever come to you with any of his problems?"

"On occasion. I can tell you that Aurora's insistence on having a child was weighing on him lately. He didn't think either one of them was ready for parenthood or at a point in their careers where they could take on that kind of extra responsibility. I told him that no one is ever really ready to be a parent and that he better not wait too long or he'll be so old he won't have the energy to chase a child around."

I nodded. "That's good advice. Did he ever come to you about anything else regarding Aurora? Maybe an issue over fidelity?"

He shook his head. "Not lately."

"Define lately."

"Lance used to be a big guy. Heavy. Not long after they got engaged, Aurora cheated on him with her ex-boyfriend. She assured him it was one drunken mistake and that it meant nothing. Lance worried that her eye wandered back to the former football player because of his physique, so he immediately started the process for weight-loss surgery."

Interesting. The story around campus was that health concerns had prompted the surgery, not vanity. "Did she ever cheat again?"

"Not that he knew of. They worked through it, and I think their marriage was pretty solid. They always seemed happy when I saw them together."

Shane grinned conspiratorially. "Every married couple fights about something. There had to have been something to argue about between the cheating all those years ago and the baby in the past few months."

"Well, I suppose he has shared with me about them having the occasional squabble over her trying to wheedle information out of him about the foundation's latest target so she could scoop the rest of the news stations."

Wakefield Foundation took on corporations all around the Midwest for myriad reasons—from unfair hiring practices and racism/harassment/gender inequality in the workplace to unethical business practices of all kinds. They were known for going unflinchingly head-to-head against multi-million-dollar corporations, standing their ground and insisting on change. Sometimes that landed them in court, but they had their own team of lawyers who could hold their own against expensive corporate counsel. No corporation wanted to find itself in Wakefield Foundation's crosshairs.

I frowned. "Him telling her about his foundation's investigations before the information is officially released seems..."

"Unethical?" he supplied, his eyebrows raised.

"Yes."

"That's why they argued about it." He held out his hands. "Don't get me wrong—I loved Aurora like a daughter, but it's too bad Lance couldn't share that part of his life with her for fear of sensitive information getting out. Had his wife been in another profession, he could have spoken in generalities, like he had with me, and been able to talk through the difficult things he was dealing with. Aurora was smart as a whip, so she would have figured out anything he told her, even without naming names or specifics." Frowning for a moment, he added, "She was so rabid to get her stories. He caught her once going through his files in his home office, so he quit bringing foundation work home. You have to be able to trust your spouse."

"Were there any other aspects of their marriage where Lance felt as though Aurora was untrustworthy? Finances? Anything else?"

He thought for a moment. "I don't think so."

Shane cut in. "I need to ask you a couple of tough questions about Lance, only so we can get the whole story."

Mr. Reeves nodded.

"Did he ever tell you that he had a sexual relationship outside his marriage?"

"No."

"Did he ever turn to someone else for comfort, especially since he couldn't speak openly to Aurora about everything?"

He hesitated. "I don't think so. If he did, he didn't tell me."

Shane pressed, "What about his enemies? Did he ever confide in you about being afraid of retaliation over his foundation work?"

"Yes, there were a few times over the years that he'd received threats."

"Did he share any details with you?"

"Again, he didn't name names. He was adamant about keeping all foundation business confidential. I told him he shouldn't keep it quiet from the authorities if he was being threatened, but I don't think he ever made a formal complaint. He seemed resigned to the fact that he'd be a target, and I don't think he took any of the threats too seriously, aside from installing a security system in their home."

"When was the last time he spoke to you about a threat?"

Mr. Reeves thought for a moment. "Oh, it had to be over a year ago. I don't know if there simply hadn't been any threats for a while or if he quit telling me about them so I didn't get upset."

Nodding, Shane asked, "Do you know why he would have been cutting his office hours short at the college on Tuesdays and Thursdays over the past few weeks?"

"I don't know about that, but I can say that he's been missing pickleball lately to put in extra hours at the foundation. He had a very large corporation under the microscope, and he was upset about the initial findings."

"One more thing—and it's procedure only—where were you Tuesday night between ten and midnight?"

He smiled sadly. "Here, icing my knee and trying to sleep after a tough game of pickleball that afternoon."

Shane stood. "Thank you for your time, Mr. Reeves."

"Thank you," I echoed, the grief in his eyes tugging at my heart. I hated family interviews. It felt so disrespectful to make someone dissect a deceased loved one's life so soon after losing them.

As we walked toward Shane's vehicle, he said, "It stands to reason Mr. Reeves would be on Wakefield's side of any argument, but I don't get the feeling he loved Aurora like a daughter."

"Yeah, I got that, too. So we have her family saying he sucked, and his family saying she sucked. Who's going to give us a straight answer?"

"I don't know what you're used to, but no one has ever given me a straight answer in any investigation I've ever investigated for as long as I've been an investigator," Shane said.

I smiled. "Okay, fine. Of course everyone is going to color their version of the facts with their experience and their opinion. Which is why I prefer processing evidence. The shit in someone else's underwear isn't going to give me its opinion. It's only going to offer information."

He laughed. "You mean like the murder weapon offered you information?"

"It told me someone wiped the prints off it. That's good information, and may I remind you, it's information in favor of your argument."

"Point noted."

17

We had to fight past a throng of press on the sidewalk to get to the business complex in Carmel where Wakefield Foundation was housed. The walls of their third-floor office were floor-to-ceiling glass, giving the place a bright and shiny feeling in direct contrast to the vibe that hit me in the gut the moment the elevator doors opened. The whole place felt off. It felt like sadness and despair and anxiety all rolled together. No one would look me in the eye. People flitted around, but with their heads down, staring at the floor. Everything felt chaotic, like everyone had a ton of work to do but no idea where to start. I wondered if they'd had to go into damage control mode after the media's growing war on Lance Wakefield. I'd overheard some of my students talking that morning about an emergency board meeting being called to replace Lance as CEO and rename the foundation. Vic was right—it would have been soul-crushing for Lance to have to live through this.

We managed to get the receptionist to point us in the direction of Bradley Kerrigan's office. We knocked on his closed door, but only waited a moment before a deep voice called, "Come in," from inside.

Badge at the ready, Shane opened the door and introduced us, spouting the standard apology for a second police visit.

Bradley Kerrigan, a big, strapping man, probably mid to late thirties, stood from behind his desk and came our way, hand extended. "Not a problem. Bradley Kerrigan. You can call me Brad." He smiled and gave a firm handshake, but he, too, had that air of anxious sadness about him. I didn't imagine he could escape it, being stuck in this office with the press circling like sharks outside.

I said, "I'm sorry for the loss of your colleague."

"Thank you. Lance was more than a colleague. Our friendship goes all the way back to college."

Shane and I shared a sad smile.

"Please, sit." Brad ushered us to two leather chairs facing his massive desk.

"Thanks," Shane replied. "Mr. Kerrigan—"

"Call me Brad."

"Brad, I wanted to first let you know that we appreciate your cooperation in letting us run your phone and vehicle GPS information and access your home security system log this morning to verify your alibi. It all checks out."

"I'd do anything for Lance." He looked down. "I hate to see what the press is doing to his good name as well as the foundation's. I imagine you noticed we're in a bit of a crisis around here. The grief is bad enough, but we're having to scramble to answer to the press and to the public and to our board of directors."

I said, "We agree that the press is out of line. However, we do need to ask you some tough questions to get to the truth. You were one of the last people to see Lance alive. What was his demeanor like Tuesday evening?"

Brad frowned. "He'd been drinking...heavily. At the end of the evening, I'd...kind of had it with him and said as much." He sighed and wiped a hand down his face. "I wish I could take it back. I just saw him starting to spiral...like my dad...and I got pissed. I shouldn't have left. I should have taken him home and talked it out with him. Maybe then none of this would have happened."

My jaw dropped. "Wait. *You* think he killed Aurora?"

Rubbing his forehead, he said, "I don't want to think it. But so many of the pieces fit."

Shane said, "Let's back up. Why were you, Wakefield, and Barry Jeffords working late Tuesday night, and then why did you decide to cap off the night with a fancy steak dinner?"

"We've got a huge corporate investigation we're working on. We got tired of being cooped up here and needed a change of scenery. There were a lot of difficult issues to discuss, so we figured we'd treat ourselves to a nice dinner at Prime 47." He smiled and said in an aside to me, "I think they call it 'self-care.'"

I laughed at his dumb joke, hoping to establish a rapport with him. "Prime 47 is my kind of self-care."

Shane pressed him, "We heard your latest mark had some issues that were of concern to Lance. Can you tell us about that?"

"No, sorry. I can't disclose foundation business to anyone. It's our policy. Once it gets out that we're investigating a company, we can count on all of our sources clamming up and our leads drying up. We've been burned a couple of times, and it sucks. I'm sure you run into the same problem all the time."

Shane shrugged. "We do, but we can always get a warrant to get our information."

Brad shook his head. "Yeah, maybe not this time. I'm not trying to be a dick here, but we've won that war before."

I said, "Come on, Brad. You won't share information that might help in a homicide investigation regarding your founder, not to mention your friend?"

"It's not my rule. It's Lance's. If it were up to me, I'd help you out."

We were getting nowhere with him, and Shane was right—we could always get a warrant. I decided to skirt around the specifics. "Fair enough. So, these issues got so tough to talk about that he had to self-medicate?"

"Yes. I mean, we all had a few drinks, but...I was pretty sure Lance had started drinking earlier in the day. He was agitated all evening."

"Agitated over foundation business? Or was there more going on?"

"I don't know if he had anything else on his plate. We only talked about foundation stuff that night. He was plenty pissed at Barry and me for disagreeing with him. He finally got belligerent, and that was when I bailed." He rubbed his eyes.

I could sympathize with him. He wasn't the first person to have turned his back on someone, only to have them turn up dead before the issue could be resolved. I softened my tone and said, "Okay, this is tough. Let's switch gears."

He shot me a relieved smile and nodded.

I continued, "As you said, Lance was really big into confidentiality...how did that work with him being married to a nosy investigative reporter? I bet she tried to pump him for information all the time."

"She did, and it often ended in a fight. He had to quit taking work home with him because he caught her going through his files. That meant he had to spend more time here, away from her, which she didn't like either, but that was the only solution."

"Did that end her trying to pry into foundation business?"

"Nope. She came up with more creative ways to stick her nose in it. She'd call and pretend to be someone else to siphon information out of new, unsuspecting assistants and interns. She'd show up in the evening with takeout to supposedly surprise Lance with dinner, but what she was really doing was trying to get a moment alone at his desk. She once spilled a whole container of spaghetti on his lap, and when he left his office to go clean up, I caught her sitting at his desk, reading his emails. They had the fight to end all fights that night."

"How long ago was that?"

"A few weeks ago."

I wondered if that was a ploy Aurora had cooked up to find out if he was cheating on her rather than a ploy to steal a headline. I pressed, "Did he have trust issues with her other than about her being in his business?"

Brad's perma-smile turned into a disgusted smirk. "You mean did he think she was cheating on him? Oh, yeah."

Shane sat up straighter. "Did he know who with?"

"Not that he ever said to me." He sighed. "You have to know, Lance was a very private guy. He compartmentalized every part of his life. I don't know of anyone who knew everything about him. He didn't talk about work with his wife, and he didn't talk about his wife at work. I only knew because he was in here one night drunk off his ass and happened to overshare. We never spoke about it again."

"When was that?"

"Maybe two months ago. It's been a while."

"If he thought she was cheating, do you think he would have decided to cheat, too? Either in retaliation or because of feeling lonely and abandoned?"

"No matter what she did to him, I don't think he'd cheat on her. He really loved her. Plus he's an ethics man, after all."

Shane gave him a confused look. "So you're saying he would never cheat on her, but you think he had it in him to kill her?"

Brad put his head in his hands. "You guys, I don't know what to think. Lance was acting so unlike himself that night. He was just...off."

"Like...he was on drugs?" I asked.

"Sort of, I guess. But...the Lance I know would never take drugs."

"You said he drank too much sometimes. It's a slippery slope."

"Yeah, but drinking's legal, and Lance is a Boy Scout. When the rest of us were partying it up in college, he was the one preaching that 'smoking weed keeps drug dealers in business, which contributes to violence' and all kinds of other ethically bad shit."

I said, "Speaking of partying, did Lance ever talk to you about any wild parties he'd been to lately?"

Brad raised one eyebrow. "What kind of wild are we talking about?"

"The kind of wild that would make you want to cheat on your spouse."

"You mean like a swinger party?"

I hadn't really given it a lot of thought. Any wild party could and usually did end up with someone having sex, but at a swinger party, everyone was pretty well guaranteed to have sex. "Yeah," I replied with more confidence than I felt.

Brad nodded. "Come to think of it, he did ask me one day what I knew about local swinger parties. He asked if I'd ever been to one."

"Have you?"

He scoffed. "I don't need to go to one of those parties to get laid."

Shane's grumble under his breath told me he'd had about enough of Brad's big ego. "Good for you, man."

I shifted in my seat so I could kick him in the ankle while keeping my attention on Brad. Brad was full of himself, but I'd dealt with enough douchebags in my lifetime to know how to use that to my advantage.

I smiled. "I'm sure you don't. But it sounds like Lance might have, especially if he and Aurora were fighting. Was he thinking about the two of them trying out a swinger party, maybe to give their marriage a kick in the pants?"

"Maybe. He wanted to know if I knew how to get into one. Evidently there's a bunch of rich assholes who get together once a week to nail each other's wives, I assume because their own wives aren't giving it to them anymore." He chuckled. "I've heard you have to submit your stock portfolio before they let you in. I'm not sure if that part's true. Sounds like an urban legend to me. That's all I could tell him."

"Did he think Aurora would have been into that, especially since he thought she was already sleeping around?"

"If the guys she could choose from were rich enough, I imagine she'd have no problem with it."

"Did swinger parties ever come up in conversation between you and Aurora?"

"Hell, no. She barely deigned to speak to me."

I mused, "Sounds like you weren't her biggest fan."

"Aurora had no shortage of fans. My only beef with her was that she could have treated Lance better. She knew I felt that way, so she never had much use for me."

"How was she when they first got together? From what I've heard about her, she seemed to be preoccupied with status and looking good. When they met, Lance would have been..."

"A fatty? Oh yeah. He was always fun, though, which I think was what drew her to him initially. Well, that and his inheritance money."

"Ah." I had an idea and stood and walked over toward a credenza anchoring the wall opposite the floor-to-ceiling windows. I picked up an old, framed photo of Lance and Brad. They looked college aged. "What about in college or his early twenties? Any major relationships before Aurora came along?"

As I'd hoped, Brad got up and wandered over to stand next to me. "Nothing too serious."

"You were close all through college?"

"Since day one."

I set the frame down and gestured at Shane. "Same for the two of us. It's funny how much mayhem we caused and still got degrees having to do with criminal justice." I turned to Shane. "You remember the stunt we pulled in Professor James's office?" I slid my eyes meaningfully toward the stack of file folders on Brad's desk I'd noticed the moment we sat down.

Shane gave me a nearly imperceptible head shake and forced out a laugh. "Yeah, that was a stupid one. We were some crazy kids, but now we're law enforcement officials—"

Hoping he'd change his mind and go through with his role in my plan, I cut him off and turned my back on him, picking up another framed photo. "Hey, I know this guy." I lied, pointing to one of about a dozen frat boys in the photo, holding it out for Brad to see in such a way that he'd have to turn his back on Shane also. Leaning toward Brad, I murmured, "I hooked up with him once in a bar bathroom."

Brad's eyebrows shot up. "I didn't take you for a wild one."

"You have no idea." I heard a chair creak behind us, so I kept Brad's attention by pointing to young Brad in the photo. "Aww, look at you. You haven't changed a bit since college." I looked up at him through my lashes. "Mmm. Except...are you taller? And of course you've been working out."

Brad puffed out his chest. "I have." Then he suddenly sobered. "Ellie... you're really nice for a cop."

"That's because I'm not a cop. I'm a criminalist."

He stared at me in awe. "Like on *CSI*?"

I hated that question, but I managed to answer politely, "Yes."

"I like talking to you. Do you think you and I could go—"

Shane hopped up and elbowed me aside, sticking his hand out to Brad. "I think we've covered everything, Brad. Thanks for making time for us."

Brad nodded, peering around Shane to maintain eye contact with me. "It was my pleasure."

Shane backed up into me, effectively pushing me toward the door. "Have a good afternoon."

As Shane ushered me out of the office, I said, "Bye, Brad. Nice to meet you."

Brad called after us, "You have my number, right?"

Shane replied, "Got it."

When we rounded the nearest corner and were out of earshot, Shane griped at me, "What the hell, Ellie? Not cool."

I scoffed. "Hey, I made sure we got the information we needed, didn't I?"

Lowering his voice, he replied, "I didn't like the way you did it, or that I had to be a party to it."

"Oh, come on. Those files were in plain sight. No harm, no foul."

"It wasn't completely above board for me to take a photo of them, though."

"Neither was Brad asking me out during a police interview," I argued.

"That's on you. You were totally chatting him up."

Shrugging, I said, "Yeah, my unfortunate superpower is being able to get losers to open up to me. I'm not proud of it, but it's come in handy during my last couple of cases."

"We can't submit the photo as evidence."

"We could, but it would likely get thrown out. But who cares? The information on it is fair game, and that's all we need. Knowing what corporations these guys were investigating could point us to tons of people who might have wanted to get back at Lance."

He frowned. "It could. But it's just as likely those files aren't the new cases they're working on."

"Now I feel like you're being a party pooper on purpose."

"Fine. Let's talk to the other last person to see Wakefield alive. Try not to flirt with this one, okay?"

18

Wakefield Foundation's chief legal counsel, Barry Jeffords, would have been nearly impossible to seduce. He looked like Santa, and he was every bit as kind and jolly. I didn't know how he went up against sleazy, corporate lawyers and won.

The first five minutes of our conversation with him were practically a verbatim reenactment of the conversation we'd had with Brad Kerrigan.

When we got to the part about Lance's drinking getting out of hand and Brad getting mad and leaving, Barry shook his head sadly. "Brad's father died recently. He'd been a lifelong alcoholic, and Brad resented him for it. As he had with Lance, he'd told his father how fed up he was with his drinking the last time he saw him. I fear this has brought it all back up for him again. He's put on a happy face here at work to get through the day, but I'm worried at some point he's going to crash and start feeling it all."

I knew exactly what he was going through. I'd done the same thing to my mother, and I'd never stopped blaming myself for the things I'd said to her, even though they were true.

Shane nodded. "It's understandable for him to be upset by Mr. Wakefield's drinking. What did you make of it?"

Barry's face fell. "Well, I knew he'd been hitting the alcohol a little harder than usual lately. And...um..." He cleared his throat. "I saw...a bag of pills on his desk earlier this week. They, um…caught my attention because they weren't in a prescription bottle."

A chill ripped through me. "Can you describe the bag of pills in more detail?"

"It was a Ziploc sandwich-sized bag. The pills were small and round. Chalky. They looked like old-school Tylenol, but I don't think that's what they were." He sighed. "I should have said something. But at the end of the day, Lance is my boss…was…my boss. Brad could call him out for something like that, but I didn't feel like I could. I should have gone to Brad. Mixing drugs with alcohol never ends well. I suppose this situation is no different."

Shane said kindly, "Hindsight is twenty-twenty, Mr. Jeffords. Please don't blame yourself for something that was out of your control. Let's talk more about Tuesday evening. Mr. Kerrigan said the three of you had to have a difficult discussion over a corporation you were investigating? Can you elaborate?"

"Somewhat. I'm sure Brad filled you in on our company-wide stance on confidentiality. I can tell you it was a doozy of a discussion. Lance was hopped up about some information he'd learned, and Brad and I were trying to make sense of it. That's how we work. Lance is the conspiracy theorist, Brad wants to give everyone the benefit of the doubt, and I can see both sides, so that makes me the referee a lot."

I said, "So Brad and Lance were fighting a lot Tuesday night, and not just about alcohol?"

Barry winced. "It was more like two against one on this particular investigation. Brad and I didn't see where Lance had a leg to stand on with his accusations. He had some damning things to say, and he wanted to make a move pretty quickly to expose the corporation in question. We needed a lot more clarification, and we told him we weren't budging until we got it. He also refused to tell us where he'd gotten his information, which is not how we operate. We have to be able to back everything up with an overabundance of evidence, or we'll get crucified. Corporations fight dirty when they have something to hide, so our work and our evidence has to be above reproach."

Shane said, "It's going to be hard to stay above reproach with the media sullying the Wakefield name, isn't it?"

Barry sighed. "It's already a nightmare. Our board moved earlier today to replace Lance as CEO in the interim with the board chairman. They also voted to change the name to Hamilton Foundation. Hopefully that will be enough to keep us from being dragged through the mud with poor Lance, but I'm not holding my breath. If our donors and benefactors give up on us, we're through. I may be contemplating early retirement this time next month."

I frowned. "Are there any employees, board members, or donors who might benefit from Lance being out of the picture?"

"I can't imagine so. I suppose you could say the board chair got a paying job out of this, but I wouldn't want it for all the money in the world. I think he accepted the job only because no one else would touch it. He has to sink with the ship either way, so he might as well go down swinging."

Shane asked, "Have there been other instances when corporations have tried to go to the press and slander the foundation, or maybe even threaten it privately or its employees personally?"

Barry nodded. "The foundation does get the occasional threat of bad press. We've also had instances of myself and Lance receiving personal warnings after particularly spectacular findings are released. They all turned out to be empty threats."

"Did you report them to the police?"

He hesitated. "No, we extend our confidentiality policy even when people behave badly. Reporting threats to the police would only serve to over-sensationalize our mission, which is simply to keep corporations honest and fair." More quietly, he added, "You and I both know restraining orders aren't worth the paper they're written on."

He wasn't completely wrong. If someone wants to hurt another person, a piece of paper isn't going to stop them. But I still believed in doing everything in your power to prevent yourself from being hurt, and I thought Barry and Lance were placing too much risk on themselves—not to mention their families—by ignoring threats of bodily harm.

I asked, "Have there been any threats made lately to the foundation or to Lance, specifically?"

Barry replied, "Not to my knowledge."

I pivoted the conversation. "How well do you know Aurora?"

"Only from making small talk at a handful of foundation events over the years."

"And I don't suppose you and Lance were close enough that he spoke to you about their relationship."

"No."

Shane said, "Is there anything else you thought seemed strange lately in regard to Mr. Wakefield or his behavior?"

Barry thought for a moment. "No, aside from what I've already told you, the only thing I noticed was him being here in the office more. But we've had a bigger caseload lately with this last investigation, so that's not a surprise."

Shane gave him his card. "If you think of anything else, please call me."

"Will do."

Shane again had to part the gaggle of press hanging out in front of the Wakefield Foundation office building. "No comment" was not what they wanted to hear from him, so they dogged us all the way to his vehicle.

Once we were safely out of the parking lot, he said, "I've been kicking around this idea…"

I leaned my head back against the seat. "If it's going to give us more potential suspects than we already have, I don't want to hear it."

Shane grinned. "It's going to do the opposite. I promise."

"Then I'm all ears."

"Okay. If Aurora Bennett is the sneaky go-getter Reeves and Kerrigan both say she is, having no qualms about going through her husband's work files and emails—"

I interjected, "And no qualms about getting pregnant when her husband didn't want a baby."

"And that…do you think she quit poking around in the foundation's business after their nasty fight over the email? She had to have known he was in the middle of a big investigation with him spending so much time at the foundation office and acting differently lately. I know she chalked it up to him cheating, but surely she'd also have wondered if he had a new company to go after."

"Ooh, good point. Him thwarting all of her attempts would only make her work harder to find another angle."

"Exactly."

I wrinkled my nose. "Do we have to try to figure that out, too?"

"I think I have. We know she somehow found out about the swinger parties—evidently not from Brad, but maybe through reading her husband's emails. Doesn't matter how, but what was the first thing she did afterward?"

I was getting tired and hungry and didn't feel like playing a guessing game. "I don't know. Cry to her assistant?"

He shook his head. "She researched it like it was her next headline news story. If she even had an inkling of who the foundation was going after next, she'd go after them, too. I say we match up the names on the files from Kerrigan's desk with the latest story leads she was working on."

I smiled. "Aww, look who decided to come around and use the bootleg photo he took."

"Don't get used to it. And no more delinquent behavior out of you."

19

We grabbed some fast food on the way to the WIND-TV Channel 7 studios downtown. It took a while in rush hour traffic to get there, but it also gave us enough time to obtain warrants to recover Aurora's story notes and scour her office for anything else that might help us figure out who'd want to kill her. We passed the drive time talking about Shane and Kaitlyn's first six months as new parents.

When we arrived at the studio and produced our warrants, the head of security escorted us through a big bullpen full of cubicles, its perimeter lined with offices sporting nameplates of the higher-ups. I didn't know what "normal" was at a TV news studio, but the vibe in here seemed fine. Maybe they were close enough to showbiz that they subscribed to the old "the show must go on" adage, even with losing a major player. They definitely weren't exuding soul-crushing sadness like at Wakefield Foundation. While our double homicide was set to wreck everything the foundation stood for, it was ratings gold for the studio, thrusting them into the limelight and allowing them to play gatekeeper for one of the biggest news stories of the year.

Aurora had been a big enough deal to snag one of the offices. The security guard left Shane and me alone in her office and said he'd find Aurora's assistant so we could speak to her. We both put on a pair of gloves and began going through Aurora's files and drawers.

After pawing through notebook after notebook in one filing cabinet, I griped, "For a woman in her mid-thirties, she was surprisingly all about paper."

Shane said, "You know how it is—people don't mind if you take hand-written notes while you're interviewing them. But stick a voice recorder in their face or get out a laptop and start typing their every word, and they'll clam up."

"I suppose."

There was a quiet knock at the door. "Come in," Shane called.

A young woman with a short Afro opened the door and stuck her head inside. "I'm Iris Gerard, Aurora's assistant. Jeremy said you wanted to see me."

Shane smiled. "Yes, please come in and have a seat, Ms. Gerard. I'm Detective Shane Carlisle and this is my partner, Ellie Matthews. I'm sure you've been interviewed more than you'd like, but we have a few more questions for you."

Iris Gerard couldn't have been more than twenty-five. She was fresh-faced, or at least she would have been if she didn't look like she was in pain. Between her broken wrist leaving her left arm in a sling and the misery apparent in her eyes, she seemed fragile. It made perfect sense after seeing what she'd seen yesterday, only to have dragged herself to work today.

He continued, "I'm very sorry for the loss of Ms. Bennett. Were you two close?"

She cleared her throat. "Yes, well, sort of...Aurora and I spent a lot of time together, and I feel sometimes like I knew her better than she knew herself. But we weren't, like, *friends*. She was my boss. We didn't see each other outside of work."

"You had a key to her home."

"Because I often went by and dropped stuff off for her."

"Did you know her husband?"

"A little. I've talked to him at a few parties and at their home."

"What did you think of him?"

She looked away. "I...didn't like him."

I thought back to Sterling's report about what he'd gathered from speaking to her and asked, "Is that the opinion you formed from personal interaction with him, or is your view of him largely based on what Aurora told you about him?"

She frowned. "Both, I suppose."

"Did the scene inside their bedroom have any bearing on how you feel about him?"

"How could it not?"

I didn't blame her. We'd all jumped to the same conclusion at first glance.

Shane said, "Let's put all that aside for a moment. Tell us more about what Aurora would share with you on the daily about her life. You told our colleagues that she worried her husband was cheating on her. Was that something she talked about a lot, and were you the only person in the office she shared it with?"

Iris's brow furrowed. "She was pretty preoccupied with it in the last month or so. It bothered her to think that he was having sex with someone else when she always made it a point to make herself available to him."

I added, "Because she wanted a baby."

"Exactly. She didn't want him wasting his energy—or his sperm—on some rando."

I was a bit taken aback by her bluntness, but a witness who wouldn't hold back was a total jackpot. I went for it. "Fair point. Did he keep turning her down or something? Were they having sex at all in the past month?"

"I mean, it's not like she regularly blabbed to me about her sex life, but she did complain that it had been a few weeks since they'd done the deed, and that wasn't normal for them." That statistic didn't match with all the X marks in the sex column of Aurora's fertility calendar.

Shane, who'd been clearly uncomfortable with my line of questioning, changed the subject, sort of. "You also spoke about some wild parties Aurora thought her husband was attending. Did she ever find out if he actually went to one?"

"No. And not for lack of trying."

I asked, "Were they swinger parties?"

"Yes, and that's what I thought was kind of weird about him hiding it from her. Aren't you supposed to go to one of those as a couple? Otherwise there's an odd number of people..." She scrunched up her face in thought for a moment. "But I guess then the extra person could be part of a threesome."

Shane got our questioning back on track. "Those kinds of parties aren't illegal if everyone is a consenting adult. Why would Aurora research them as a potential news story? Or was that just her cover for doing personal research on the job?"

She frowned. "At first it was personal, but once she dug a little bit, she found out there were people attending who would be ruined if the public found out their dirty little secret."

I said, "What keeps the other people at the party from outing them? Do they have to sign NDAs at the door?"

"No, they keep their identities secret with masks."

Ooh, creepy. "Then how did Aurora know some of the attendees would be ruined if they got outed? She'd have to know their names to know that."

She shook her head. "I don't know how she finds out some of this stuff. She just does."

"Can you gather all of her notes for us for the stories she was working on?"

"No problem. I'll warn you it's going to be a hodge-podge of hand-written notes, emails, video and audio recordings, photos, and maybe even a cocktail napkin or two. I try to keep her information organized, but sometimes I can't keep up."

I smiled, dreading sifting through all that, and lied, "Not a problem."

Iris left, and we went back to work going through Aurora's belongings. Her desk drawers didn't hold a lot of interesting things—mainly meal replacement bars, office supplies, and makeup. But the locked bottom door, which I'd found the keys to in the main drawer, was another story.

"Hey, she's keeping an old iPhone locked up in a drawer. It's so ancient it's got a home button. Check it out." When I wiggled it at Shane, the screen came to life. I wrinkled my nose. "Wait, she's using this?" My jaw dropped. "Oh, I get it. Sneaky."

Shane nodded. "Yep. Old phones make great burners if all you're using them for is cheating."

I studied the phone for a moment. "I suppose we could give her the benefit of the doubt and assume she could have used this to contact shady sources she wouldn't want having her real number."

"Maybe she used it for both."

"Well, it'll be easy to find out. I'll make a 3D print of her fingerprint and put it on the button to unlock it. It works. I've done it before."

"Sweet."

"I want to see your warrant, Detective Carlisle," an icy voice snapped from the doorway. A middle-aged woman in a red power suit and matching heels stalked over to us and read over the warrants Shane produced. "Fine. But if you learn anything from any of Aurora's research, I'd better not hear about it on another channel's broadcast. I know how you people operate."

Shane gave her an easy smile. "Beth, you know exactly how I operate, so you should know I would never do that."

Beth leveled a glare at me. "I don't know her."

He said, "I do, and I can assure you she treats all evidence with confidentiality."

She gave me another second's worth of side-eye before turning to Shane with a pout. "It's...been a tough couple of days."

I interjected, "Not for your ratings, though, right?" and immediately regretted it. Damn, I could usually hold my tongue a little better than that. This case had me off-balance.

Beth squared her shoulders at me. "Who are you, anyway?"

Shane said quickly, "Ellie Matthews. She's the lead criminalist on this case."

I assumed she was the head of the station because she didn't hesitate to assert her authority. "Oh, then maybe you should collect evidence and leave the talking to the real investigators."

She wasn't wrong, but she didn't have to be such a bitch about it.

"Easy, Beth," Shane said. "We're all on the same team...but she does bring up a good point."

Beth turned her wrath to him. "If you're getting at something, say it, Detective."

"Okay. Does anyone here have a reason to want Aurora out of the way?

Who benefits from her death...or from being the station with the inside track on the most explosive story in years?"

Her face turning the same shade as her suit, she exploded, "Are you crazy? Aurora was my star reporter, with three years left on her contract. You think I'd trade her bright future for a few days' worth of coverage for her death? That's asinine."

"I didn't say you, specifically. I'm asking a question that needs to be asked. And you have no room to talk. You guys are crucifying Wakefield over this with no proof. If you don't tone it down, you could easily get slapped with obstruction."

"Freedom of the press still exists."

Shrugging, he pointed out calmly, "So does ethical journalism, but not so much around here this week."

I wanted to give Shane a high-five for that one, but I didn't feel it was the appropriate time.

"Get what you need and get the hell out of my studio," she bellowed, turning on a pointy red heel and stalking out of the room.

I said, "I think you made her mad."

Shane's eyes bulged out. "Me? You started something I had to finish."

That was nothing new between the two of us. In college I was always causing trouble, usually with my smartass mouth, that he would step in to defuse. "Sorry. You know I can be a hot mess sometimes."

"I thought maybe you'd grown out of it."

"Not so much."

We continued through the room but didn't find any more items to take into evidence.

Iris returned with a box full of notebooks and papers, which she handed to Shane. She dropped a flash drive in my hand. "This is everything she was working on, I think. If I find anything else, I'll let you know."

"Thanks," I replied. "Do you know if one of these stories was so big someone would kill to keep a lid on it? Had she run into any opposition with her digging?"

She shrugged. "Just the usual. She got nasty calls and emails all the time telling her to back off. It comes with the job."

Shane handed her his card. "Can you find out all you can about the ones she got in the past couple of weeks and make a list for us?"

"Actually, I'm already working on it for Detective Baxter."

That was interesting. I'd thought Baxter was on Sterling's side, which would've meant he wouldn't waste time looking into who other than Lance had a reason to kill Aurora. Maybe the old Baxter was in there somewhere.

She went on, "It's taking me a while to wade through Aurora's old voicemails to find the threatening ones, and that's if she didn't delete them, which she probably did. She always laughed off stuff like that. She thought it was funny when she pissed people off. It was also how she knew she was getting somewhere."

We thanked Iris and left the building. On the drive back to the station, I started digging through the box she'd given us.

I hadn't gotten very far when Shane suddenly blurted out, "You've worked closely with Detective Baxter. What's his deal?"

Hoping to stop a blush from coloring my cheeks at the mention of his name, I looked out the window and replied, "What do you mean?"

"I thought he was supposed to be so level-headed and brilliant, but I don't get that vibe from him. Basically all he's done is agree with Detective Sterling and brood a lot. I can't imagine you enjoying that, unless that's why you guys aren't partners anymore."

"Uh...he's usually not like this. Must be something personal going on."

"Well, he shouldn't bring it to work."

In Baxter's defense, at least part of his personal problem—me—was already at work, and he could do nothing about it. But I knew what he had going on wasn't all about me, and Shane confirmed it.

He continued, "And he especially shouldn't come in late, wearing the same clothes and looking like he didn't sleep. We need to be sharp."

I held in a grimace. Shane didn't need to know my feelings about the issue, but I couldn't help uttering a catty retort. "Are you implying he did the walk of shame this morning?"

Letting out a snort of laughter, he said, "Not unless his girlfriend is a dominatrix or something. He looked rough. Definitely no post-coital glow."

I'd forgotten how much of a gossipmonger Shane was. In college, he always knew everyone's relationship status, down to the minute, and what everyone was saying behind everyone else's back. He was great at getting people to tell him things. While that was an invaluable skill for a detective, he'd clearly yet to master the art of keeping what he'd learned to himself.

"He's nothing if not level-headed. I mean, he's thinking outside the box at least a little if he's planning to investigate the threats Aurora received. If he's got something going on, he'll figure it out. I'm sure he won't let anything affect his work."

That was a lie. Whatever was going on had already affected his work. I just wanted to shut this conversation down before I said more than I should. I was thankful for the reminder to not let Shane in on anything I didn't want to be public knowledge. One slip about my former relationship with Baxter, and everything could crumble around me. I trusted Shane with my life, but not with my secrets.

Worse, now I had moved past being hurt by the thought of Baxter staying up all night with his girlfriend and had begun, instead, to worry about him. What Shane had said about the way he showed up at work that morning was so unlike him. Even when we'd had cases where we were literally under the gun, Baxter was the one who insisted we get at least a little sleep and a shower and change of clothes to feel refreshed.

I reminded myself that worrying about whether or not Baxter was letting his personal life affect our case was also affecting our case. I pushed him out of my mind and went back to looking through Aurora's story notebooks. After flipping through several, I found what seemed to be the newest one.

I said, "She was looking into at-risk teens being lured into gang activity. That could be a dangerous angle if she played hardball with the wrong person."

Shane thought about it for a moment. "If this were gang retaliation, it would be clear who did it so no one else would want to pick up the story and run with it. Plus, they would have gone with intimidation first. And not in the form of a strongly worded email or voicemail. It would have been old school and in person. She wouldn't have laughed it off."

"True." I kept flipping through notebooks and came to a note on TC Pittman Enterprises. I pulled up the photo Shane had taken in Brad's office. No matches there. I grunted to myself and kept flipping.

"What?" he asked.

"Oh, nothing. Just bummed I didn't find any matches yet to the files from my hard-won photo."

"Wouldn't it be funny if that photo was of zero use to us?"

"Yeah, hilarious."

20

Back at the station, I went to the lab to make a 3D model of Aurora's fingerprint to unlock her second phone. Shane went to find a computer to look through the flash drive Iris had given us.

I pulled up an image of Aurora's right index finger that Dr. Berg had collected during the autopsy and sent it to our 3D printer. While I waited for the printer to fashion my fingerprint, I texted Vic.

I hope my students didn't eat you alive.

His reply came almost instantly. *More like they were eating out of my hands.*

So next time I need a substitute teacher, I should ask you?

There was a hesitation this time before his response. *I think I'll stick with my day job.* After a moment, he sent another message. *One kid—IDK his name, the one with the stupid haircut—asked me out for coffee so he could learn 'literally everything there is to know about the FBI.'*

I'd called that one. *I can't think of anything worse than alone time with that fool. I hope you said no.*

I did, but I let him down easy.

Good. Gotta go. Talk soon.

I removed the 3D image of the fingerprint from the printer and placed it against the button on Aurora's cheater phone. Nothing happened. I repositioned it and only had to wait a moment before the phone came to life. I went straight for the text app.

There were three numbers she texted with fairly often. Her last text, from the day before she died, was her reply, *Can't wait.* I clicked on that thread and found that she was responding to the message, *See you at 2 today?*

As I started scrolling back through the conversation, I noticed the bulk of their exchanges over the past week were similar, like Aurora and whoever had the phone number ending in 2583 must have had standing meetups (or hookups) that they checked to make sure were still on. Mostly it was 2583 doing the checking and Aurora confirming. The texts from 2583 kind of reminded me of the reminders I got from my hair stylist on appointment days. But then I read a text that definitely did not remind me of the ones I got from my hair stylist. I texted Shane and insisted he come to the lab to read these with me. The one I saw from last week had me shivering. *I can't wait to see you. Are you sure you'll be home alone tonight?* Knowing where and how she died, that one chilled me to the core.

"What's up?" Shane asked, taking a seat next to me in the lab office.

I handed him the phone. "I've got a bad feeling about whoever's on the other end of this conversation."

Shane read aloud, "*I can't wait to see you. Are you sure you'll be home alone tonight?* Her response was, *Don't worry. You'll have me all to yourself. Lance is working late again.* Oh, shit. That sounds murdery."

"That's what I thought. Any idea what she was doing at two PM the day she died?"

He thought for a moment. "A workout, I believe. Detective Baxter put together a timeline for her day, and I think that sounds right."

"So this 2583 number belongs to her workout buddy?"

"Or another kind of buddy. Maybe 'workout' is code for 'sex.'"

"Ooh, that's definitely possible. Keep reading." He took a breath to read aloud, but I stopped him. "Read to yourself and give me the highlights. This conversation is giving me a creepy vibe."

"So you summoned me in here to screen these texts for you."

"Basically."

He smiled and shook his head, turning his attention back to the phone. After a moment, he said, "You know, it's a lot of the same—afternoon meetups around two PM, but not necessarily every day. A couple of times they schedule to go out for coffee. And then there are a decent amount of evening meetups, all at her house, and most of them reference Lance being away."

"So this is definitely her cheating burner."

"I'd say so."

I thought for a moment. "I guess we could find out for sure. Let's cross reference her fertility calendar with these dates."

* * *

While I retrieved Aurora's fertility calendar from the evidence room, Shane went to get us some coffee. We met in the conference room, where we kept all the communal files on the case.

When I entered the room, Shane turned his laptop screen my way and said, "Hey, check this out—looks like Aurora did find out something pretty huge from reading Wakefield's email." The photo was of a computer screen with an email to Lance from a man named David Jarvis. Shane read, "'I would be pleased as punch to welcome you and your beautiful wife as my guests at the recoupling parties I enjoy with my intimate acquaintances. I can assure you the guest list is top-notch, and anonymity is king. Attire is masked, black tie.' Evidently all Wakefield had to do was send an email to recoupling317@gmail.com saying David Jarvis would vouch for them, and they were in."

I made a face. "Recoupling? Is that rich people speak for swinging?"

"I guess."

I flopped down in a chair next to Shane and sighed. "Add David Jarvis to our never-ending list. Let's tackle this calendar."

Shane went old school and drew out a calendar of the past month on a sheet of paper. I read off all the X marks for sex from the fertility calendar for him to write down. So I wouldn't have to look through all the icky texts, he slid the makeshift calendar and pen to me while he read off the dates and times for the meetups. Thank goodness for text timestamps. One of the simplest bits of technology, timestamps were invaluable during some investigations.

He put the phone down. "Well, what have we got?"

I studied the calendar we'd put together. "Aurora and 2583 had a lot of sex...but to their credit, they didn't hook up every time they spent time together. Looks like we've accounted for every X on her fertility calendar with one of their meetings. I'd say 2583 is her baby daddy, not Lance."

Shane shrugged. "Unless she doubled down with Lance on days she'd already been with 2583."

"Eww."

"Standard cheater MO. Women will make sure to have sex with their husbands at least once a month so if there's a surprise pregnancy, they can account for it."

"That's awful."

"Cheating is awful, but a lot of people are really good at it."

I frowned. "So is 2583 our prime suspect now?"

Shane already had his laptop out looking up the phone number. "He's a better suspect than anyone at this point." His eyebrows shot up. "Nice. Evidently this guy didn't need to use a burner. The phone is registered to Max Stevenson." He pulled up Facebook and typed in the name. "Bingo. He's a personal trainer at a small boutique fitness center in Carmel."

My face fell. "Tell me it's not called GLSTN." I pronounced it "Glisten."

"It's G-L-S-T-N...oh, wait. That's how the cool kids would spell 'Glisten.'"

My lips curled in a sneer. "Yeah."

"What's wrong with it, other than the stupid name?"

"We had to interview someone there during our last case." I added under my breath, "Dumb bitch."

He chuckled. "What, did she steal your boyfriend?"

"Not for lack of trying. And she called me fat."

"Oh, a serious bitch, then. We still have to go there and try to track down this trainer. You know, you probably won't even see her."

I wrinkled my nose. "I think she's there all the time. She lives and breathes fitness."

"Well, if it's any consolation, you're not fat and you have no boyfriend to steal, so what could she possibly say or do to you this time?"

"Oh, she'll find something."

* * *

I drove us to GLSTN so Shane could ride shotgun and work. He began the process of running a background check on Max Stevenson, meanwhile weeding through the other texts on Aurora's phone.

Shane said, "I think these other two numbers she'd been texting belong to her confidential sources for her stories. They never speak in specifics, although one of them will sometimes gloat about a 'hot new tip' for her. The bulk of the texts are simply meeting or drop off locations and times, and a few are demands for cash."

"Demands for cash are kind of a red flag, right?"

"I think in this context it's money owed for services and information. From what I can glean, Aurora seemed kind of tight and often late with her payments and neither of these people appreciated it."

My eyebrows shot up. "Worth killing her over?"

"Nah, we're talking like twenty to a hundred bucks. Chump change."

"Can you get names for these two?"

"Working on it right now..." he murmured as he typed on his laptop. "First one is a burner." He began typing again. "And...damn. The other one is, too. These informants aren't screwing around."

"I imagine they're lowlifes, right? She's looking for dirt on dirty deals and gang activity and corruption. She won't get that kind of information from soccer moms."

"I suppose not." He clicked a couple of times on the trackpad. "Here's background on Max Stevenson..." After staring at his screen for a few minutes, he griped, "The man doesn't have so much as a parking ticket. Totally normal financials." He picked up Aurora's phone again.

"Maybe he's good at being slippery. He was boning Lance's wife, at least sometimes in Lance's house, and we don't think Lance knew it."

"And that's why I'm worried. He could be dangerous." He stared at the phone for a moment. "Oh, wait. This isn't good. There's a Facetime call to his number at nine PM the night of the murders. I don't know that it's a good idea for you to come along when I speak to him."

I frowned and jerked my chin at Max Stevenson's driver's license photo on the laptop screen. "I've interviewed much scarier people than that human Ken doll."

"I feel like the sheriff wouldn't appreciate it if I delivered her favorite employee to a murderer."

"Look, he's not going to murder me in the middle of GLSTN. Too many Witness Barbies. And besides, I have you, and you have a gun."

"What's with the Barbie and Ken fixation?"

"You'll see."

* * *

When we walked inside GLSTN, Shane took one look around and said, "Oh, I get it. Everyone in here really is a Ken or a Barbie. Nothing on them is real: hair color, skin color, body parts, eyelashes, fingernails."

I nodded. "Welcome to hell."

Shane walked up to the reception counter and asked the young doe-eyed girl sitting there if we could speak to Max Stevenson.

The girl's eyes grew even wider. "Oh...Max had a...a death in the family. He's off work for a while to grieve."

"We actually need to speak to him about that. Can you give us his home address?"

Speaking of hell, I heard a voice squeal from a few feet away, "OMG, Elaine?"

I turned to find Eve Shelton walking toward me, GLSTN-ing in a hot pink sports bra and matching spandex leggings that looked like they'd been painted on. I cringed inwardly and corrected her. "Ellie."

She wrinkled her pert nose. "Ellie? Oh." She thought for a moment and added, "Really?"

I nodded. "I'm pretty sure."

Shane coughed to cover a snicker.

Without missing a beat, Eve went on, "How've you been? It's been *forever*."

I smiled. "And somehow not long enough."

Her brow wrinkled for a moment, but then she slipped her fake smile back on. "How's Vic? I haven't had a chance to catch up with him since..." Her smile finally faltered and disappeared.

"He's okay. He should be back to work soon."

"Can he, like, work out at all? Is he..." She leaned in with a look that fell somewhere between concern and disdain and asked quietly, "Is he out of shape?"

Shane had to fight a grin from forming on his face.

I said, "We're running together."

Her expression turned full-on worried. "Oh, no. He's not in good shape at all, then."

Shane had to walk away for a moment after hearing that comment.

I turned to the receptionist. "Can you hurry up with that information, please?"

Shrinking at my snappy tone, she placed a Post-it on the counter. "Here —here you go."

Shane finally got himself under control and returned to the counter. He said to the girl, "We're also going to need to speak with some of his closest co-workers, starting with your manager. Can you round up some people for me?"

The receptionist jumped up from her seat and hurried down a nearby hallway.

To my dismay, Eve had yet to buzz the hell off. She pressed, "Are you working another murder case? And did you bring that cute detective from before? Wait. Are you working...Aurora's case?"

Ignoring her questions, I said, "How well do you know Max?"

"Oh, he and I go way back."

I nodded, unsurprised. "I see. Eve, have you met Shane?"

As I walked away, she was already batting her eyes at my married partner and cooing, "I haven't had the pleasure."

I decided to wander down the hallway and peek into the classrooms. People were doing different group exercises in each one—some were cycling, some were treadmilling, some were working out with weights and bands and other contraptions. They were all definitely GLSTN-ing.

The last room was evidently their breakroom. The receptionist was in there talking to a man and two women, one of whom I recalled interviewing last time I was here. I hoped this was her attempt at rounding up people for Shane and me to speak to, and since I didn't want to be in here for a moment longer than I had to, I burst in and got the ball rolling.

"Hi, everyone, I'm Ellie Matthews with the county sheriff's office. My partner and I are here to get some information from you about a case we're working on."

The nervous receptionist slunk out of the room, but I wasn't letting anyone else leave. I got out my phone. "Can I get your names, please?"

One of the women frowned. "What's this about?"

"An active homicide investigation. I'm sure you all wouldn't want to stand in the way of that. Now, names?"

They each gave me their names, and only the frowny woman seemed to do it grudgingly.

I went on, "So Max Stevenson...he's a trainer here?"

The non-frowny woman I recognized from last time, Britney, said, "Oh, yeah. He's the best. Totally sweet."

The man, Malcolm, said, "But he's a hard-ass when it comes to his boot camp sessions. In a good way."

I asked, "When you say 'sessions,' do you mean group classes or one-on-one?"

The frowny woman, Celine, said, "You get whatever you'll pay for. His one-on-one time is expensive, but it's worth it."

Evidently Aurora thought so.

I said, "So he's not here this week."

Malcolm nodded. "Yeah. A death in his family. He's pretty torn up."

"Right. Let's go back to before the death in his family happened. Did you notice him acting strangely at all or not like himself? Stressed? Upset?"

Britney shook her head. "No, Max is one of those guys who's pumped to be alive. He's a very positive person. I don't know that I've ever seen him stressed or upset." She nodded sagely. "Must be all the endorphins. As a group, most of us GLSTN-ers are pretty happy folks!"

I was willing to bet Britney and Eve were besties.

I pressed, "If he wasn't acting strangely, then was he deviating from his normal schedule at all? Like missing work or leaving early or anything like that?"

Celine said, "Not that I noticed. He's here a lot, and I don't think last week was any different. Why do you ask?"

Had these three really not put two and two together and figured out the 'death in Max's family' and my homicide investigation had something in common? Especially with Aurora having been a member here and the coverage of her murder everywhere you looked?

I finally said, "You guys do know that by 'death in the family,' Max means his pregnant lover, right?"

Malcolm's eyebrows shot up. "Max got Aurora pregnant? No freaking way. Oh, that's so sad, though."

Britney gasped. "We didn't know about the baby. She wasn't showing, like, at all."

Well, so much for Max covering up his affair. Maybe he only cared that Aurora's husband didn't know about it.

"One more thing. Was Max here on Tuesday night, and if so, what time?"

Malcolm said, "I talked to him around seven. I think he was still here teaching a class when I left at nine."

Celine said, "Same. Only I left at around nine-thirty."

Britney shook her head. "Sorry, I wasn't here that night."

They gave Max an alibi up until nine-thirty, but that didn't help him.

I smiled. "Thank you for your time. If we have more questions, we'll be in touch."

I exited the room to go find Shane and get the hell out of there. Eve still had him cornered in the reception area, but he was also speaking to the owner, who I recognized from before. I figured he could take it from there, so I hurried past them and out the front door while Eve was busy looking the other way. I didn't know why that woman made me feel like I was a teenage outcast with no self-esteem again, but she did. I got a sudden flicker of the urge to blot out my feelings with a drink, but I paced the parking lot until it subsided.

Shane found me in my car, doomscrolling the Instagram hashtag, #whomurderedAurora. According to most of the posts and a disturbing number of memes people had taken the time to create, the consensus was that it was Lance. No surprise there.

"Hey, why'd you run off?" Shane asked as he got in the passenger side.

"Because I wanted to throat-punch Bitch Barbie real bad, only I don't have time to get arrested today."

He laughed. "After what she said to you, a throat-punch would have been considered self-defense. Come on, let's grab a decent coffee and decompress. I'm going to have some deputies bring Max Stevenson to the station for formal questioning."

21

Once I'd been placated with good coffee and a couple of Shane's new-dad fiasco stories, I was able to return to the station feeling refreshed, or at least as refreshed as a person working two jobs, one of them a double homicide, could get.

Max Stevenson was already in the interrogation room when we got back to the station. Shane and I let him stew for a while and watched him from the room next door.

I said, "It didn't really strike me from his photos, but in person, this guy reminds me a lot of Lance Wakefield. I wonder if that's why Aurora picked him for an affair when she was trying to get pregnant."

Shane studied our suspect through the two-way mirror. "You're right, they do look kind of alike. The baby would look pretty much the same with either dad. She could pass the kid off as Wakefield's, and no one would be the wiser. Maybe she planned to use this guy to get pregnant and then toss him aside, like that old song by Heart."

I huffed out a laugh. "Yeah, I guess." I sobered. "Seriously, though, that particular type of con could cause a man to go off the deep end and want to hurt or even kill the woman. It would at least warrant him calling her a whore. It fits."

"It all fits...but look at the guy. Tell me what you see."

I took a hard look at Max Stevenson. He was tall and handsome and of course amazingly muscular. Thirty-ish, dark hair, brown eyes...brown eyes full of pain. He looked like he hadn't slept in a while. His skin was sallow and blotchy like he'd been crying. His hair, which had been perfectly styled in the photos I'd seen of him, was a total mess and was even greasy, like he hadn't showered. He evidently hadn't shaved, either, and had a couple of days' worth of dark stubble across his jaw. His clothes were rumpled and stained.

"I see what you mean. He's grieving."

Shane made a move toward the door. "And we're going to make it worse."

We went to the next room and took a seat across from Max Stevenson. He barely registered our presence and only seemed to be half-listening when Shane introduced us and began explaining why we'd had him brought into the station. He only seemed to snap out of it when Shane said Aurora's name.

Max's eyes flicked up and fixed on Shane. "You brought me here because you think I killed Aurora? I...I loved her. I didn't kill—" He couldn't even finish his sentence for trying to choke down a sob.

Shane replied, "Then make this easy and give us a solid alibi for Tuesday night between ten and midnight."

He wiped a hand down his haggard face. "I left GLSTN at nine forty-five and went straight home. I live alone, but...isn't there some way you can GPS track my phone or something?"

Shane nodded. "There is, and we'll certainly do that. What did you and Aurora Bennett talk about during your Facetime call on Tuesday night at nine PM?"

Max's eyes filled with tears. "That was the last time I heard her voice."

"And what did you talk about?" Shane prompted.

"She said she had some big news to tell me. We made plans to meet for coffee the next day, but..." He shook his head sadly.

My stomach lurched. There was a good chance he didn't know about the baby yet. We were going to need to tell him, because I'd played our hand at GLSTN to his co-workers to get them to talk. In retrospect, that was a poor idea, although the news would come out once the case went to trial. That was, if we could find someone to try.

I said, "You obviously knew Aurora better than most people. Who might have wanted to hurt her?"

He sighed. "Given my relationship with her, I'm sure you'd expect me to say her husband. But he was a decent guy. He wasn't horrible to her. They just were no longer on the same page. She wasn't in love with him anymore. She was going to ask for a divorce, but she couldn't get him to give her enough of his time to have a tough conversation like that."

Shane said, "From what we've heard, she'd been asking him for a baby."

"She did. He said no. That was a sticking point for her. Part of her decision."

"Did she then ask you for a baby?"

"Sure, we'd talked about it. We didn't feel it appropriate to act on it until she left him."

Aurora evidently didn't have enough patience for that. And women like her weren't the type to leave rich, high-powered, successful men like Lance Wakefield for middle class guys with no connections like Max Stevenson.

I asked, "What would have happened if she ended up deciding not to leave him?"

He shrugged. "That wouldn't have been ideal, but I suppose we would have continued to see each other."

"I mean if they'd reconciled and decided to stay together. How would you have reacted?"

"Not well...what are you getting at?"

Shane said, "I believe she's asking if it would have thrown you into a murderous rage."

Max answered matter-of-factly, "No, I don't rage easily, and I wouldn't have killed the love of my life because she decided to go back to her husband. If I had to let her go to make her happy...well, that's how much I love her." He blew out a hard breath. "Loved her."

If Max Stevenson wasn't giving an Oscar-worthy performance disguising his psychopathy and was truly speaking from his heart, that was the most beautiful thing I'd ever heard.

I said quietly, "I'm sure she would have chosen you."

A ghost of a smile crossed his face.

Shane said, "Okay, let's say you didn't kill her and her husband didn't kill her. Someone did. Did she confide in you that she'd been threatened lately or maybe had felt like she'd been followed or watched?"

"She did say she'd gotten some scary phone calls at work in the past few weeks. Someone using a voice changer had said she needed to watch her back and stay out of their business. The only problem was, they didn't identify themselves, so she didn't know which story to back off."

Shane flicked a glance my way. "So she went full speed ahead on everything."

"That's Aurora." He frowned. "Anything for the story."

"Did she happen to tell you what she was working on?"

He shook his head and smiled sadly. "She always said I can't keep a secret to save my life. It's true. I gab all day with my clients, especially when we're resting between sets during one-on-one sessions. I get to learn about what she's been working on along with the rest of her fans." His face fell. The poor guy was devastated.

I couldn't handle him finding out about the baby from an unsympathetic person. As much as I didn't want to deliver the news, I felt like I was the best person for the job. "Max, you said Aurora had some news for you... and I think we know what it was. It's going to be difficult for you to process, but I don't want you getting blindsided with it out in public. Um...she was pregnant. She probably found out Tuesday."

Max stared at me, the color draining from his face. "She was..."

I nodded. "I'm so sorry you had to find out this way. And I'm especially sorry for your loss."

Tears filled his eyes. "She was already..."

I nodded. "We found a fertility calendar beside her bed. She very much wanted to have a baby."

"Is it...mine? I guess...there's really no way to ever know..." His shoulders slumped even more.

"Um...we did the math. We cross-referenced her fertility calendar with the texts between the two of you scheduling meetups. If it were me, I'd be confident you're the father."

He started to smile, but then he suddenly burst into tears.

Shane and I shared a glance. Shane whispered in my ear, "What do we do now?"

"Wait it out?" I whispered back.

We sat there while Max sobbed. Several minutes passed. He finally went still, slumped over the table with his head buried in his arms.

I ventured, "Max, is there someone we can call to pick you up?"

Shane shot me a frown. "We still need to verify his vehicle and phone GPS before we do that."

Max raised his head a couple of inches. "Whatever. It doesn't even matter now."

"What do you mean?" asked Shane.

Max wiped his face with the hem of his shirt. "There's no Aurora. No baby. She was everything to me. And a baby with her? That's more than I could have ever hoped for. Certainly more than I deserve. I have nothing. I don't care anymore. You can lock me up for this. Or not. I'll be in hell wherever I am." He put his head back down on the table.

I didn't think it was possible, but my heart broke even more for him.

Shane said, "Give us a minute. I'll grab your phone and start the process. Shouldn't take too long." He stood and snagged me by the arm, ushering me out into the hallway. Once the door closed, he said, "Uh, we can't let him go."

"Why? He obviously didn't do it."

"I agree. I'm saying his ass needs to be on psych watch."

"Oh, right. Fun. And I caused it." I put my head in my hands.

Shane shook his head. "The situation caused it. They'll give him some good drugs and a warm bed at the hospital. Trust me, he'll thank us for it."

"I seriously doubt he's going to be thanking us for anything anytime soon."

22

Shane got assistance for Max in motion while I gave in and ate three stale donuts in the breakroom. They didn't even taste good—I just couldn't stop. After that, I headed for the conference room to start digging through Aurora's notes before our upcoming meeting.

Shane came into the room and took a seat next to me. "Stevenson is being taken to the nearest hospital. Poor guy didn't even put up a fight."

I sighed. "I feel so bad for him. I hope he can find a way to make peace with everything."

"Well, let's do our part and nail to the wall the son of a bitch who killed his girlfriend and his baby."

We pored over her story notes, stopping when we thought we had something to add to the bullet points on the whiteboard. We came up with the gang recruitment, the swinger parties, and three businesses: TC Pittman Enterprises, Axion Pharmaceuticals, and Adler-Jamison Engineering.

Vic called, and I took an opportunity to take a break. "Hey," I said wearily, wandering out in the hallway so I wouldn't bother Shane.

"You still at it?"

I yawned. "It's only eight."

"Dangerously close to my bedtime. I called because I've got some thoughts to share about your case, if you want them."

"Are you kidding? I'd love it if someone could make sense of this thing for me. We've got so damn many possibilities for reasons people would want to kill these two. Our investigation is a hot mess." I walked back into the conference room. "Let me put you on speaker and you can share your thoughts with Shane, too." I put my phone on the table and said to Shane, "Vic."

Shane said, "Hey, Manetti."

Vic replied, "Hey, hope you don't mind me butting in."

He laughed. "Not in the slightest. Tell me you've cracked our case."

Manetti said, "I wish. First, the suit. I'm sure you think I'm weirdly fixated on it, but...what if it's the wrong suit because Lance Wakefield wasn't the one who picked it out? What if..." He hesitated. "This seems a little out there because of the way he died, but it could make some sense. It's possible that the killer killed both of them."

Shane and I shared a glance. I'd never thought along those lines.

Shane said, "According to one of Wakefield's friends, he'd kept that suit as an object lesson to not get fat again. He had it as the first one in the closet, right inside the door, where he'd see it every day. For someone who didn't know what it stood for, it would have simply been the easiest suit to grab. I can see it."

I said, "True, but then his cause of death makes no sense. Can you force-feed someone a handful of pills?"

Shane said, "As drunk as Wakefield supposedly was, he would have been easy to handle physically, and probably easy to talk into something crazy. For example, the killer could have held his wife at knifepoint and forced him to take the pills or else."

I didn't like that angle. "At the risk of sounding like Sterling...if the killer wanted both of them dead and went to their house to do it, why didn't he bring a weapon with him? I could see being able to sneak up on one person, alone, and be able to kill them either without a weapon or with whatever you found when you got there. But the second person...you'd need to pop them fast with a gun or something, because once they heard the ruckus from the first murder, they'd be on high alert and on the offensive."

Vic said, "About that, I think that could all have been by design. If the killer wanted to make people think Wakefield did it, he—or she—couldn't stab Wakefield, too. He had to die by his own hand, or at least look like he did."

I asked, "Why do people need to think Lance Wakefield did it?"

Vic replied, "To end Wakefield Foundation. To make it go away."

"Then just kill him. Aurora doesn't even factor in."

"That's not good enough. Think about it—if you want to obliterate Wakefield Foundation, you don't murder Lance Wakefield. It would turn him into a martyr and fire up his supporters. Plus, there are plenty of other people at the foundation to carry on his work. However, if you kill his wife and make it look like he did it, you turn him into a monster. He's ruined, and everything he ever touched is ruined."

Shane nodded. "He's right. If the foundation's damage control fails, it's only a matter of time before the place is toast."

I said, "Which is what all those businesses they ruined over the years have been wishing for."

Vic said, "Exactly. So did that help you figure some things out, or did I throw a wrench into your whole line of thinking?"

I chuckled. "A little of both. We still appreciate you, though."

Shane said, "Yeah, thanks, man."

Vic replied, "You're welcome. Good luck."

I ended the call and sighed. "I lied to him. That was a wrench I didn't want."

Shane mused, "Well, if he's right, and this was about ruining Wakefield Foundation, it would shrink our possible suspect pool considerably to only have to worry about his enemies."

"Except she was the one getting threats."

"True. I guess we can't rule out her haters yet. You know, he may have been getting threats as well and keeping them to himself."

"Then we need to get access to his email accounts, phone records, and the foundation's list of targets."

Nodding, Shane said, "We should have his phone in evidence, right? I think the other detectives went through it, though, and didn't find anything of note."

"If they were looking through it to find evidence against him, they may have missed something."

"That's fair. I'll go get it and spin through it. I'll put in a warrant for the foundation's confidential information, too. We might get lucky and not get blocked like Brad promised."

He left the room, and I continued to paw through Aurora's notes.

Minutes later, Shane returned with a cellphone in hand and asked, "What's the date on the email from David Jarvis? I'm not seeing it, and I've gone two months back, inbox and trash, in three different email accounts— one for Ashmore, one for the foundation, and a personal one. It's nowhere."

I pulled the photo up on the laptop. "March twenty-fourth."

He studied the phone for a moment. "Nope. Nothing."

"Wait." I looked at the photo more carefully. "This email was sent to 1234.john.smith.9876@gmail.com. Surely that's not what Lance named his personal email account."

"No, his personal account shows his real name. We need to get into that John Smith account. It sounds like a burner email." Shane sighed. "I guess I'll go write up yet another warrant."

"You have fun with that."

I was getting a headache from trying to decipher Aurora's messy penmanship, so I wandered to the lab to see what all had been processed. I found Amanda hard at work, examining a pair of men's slacks under the bench magnifier. It didn't smell very fresh in there.

"Lance's poopy pants?" I asked.

"Yep. He shit himself good." She beckoned me to follow her to the office. Once we were in there with the door closed, she removed her mask and took a deep breath of much fresher smelling air. "Whew. I'll admit I put those off. I was hoping maybe you'd come back and do the second pass so I wouldn't have to. I roped Beck into doing the first."

I smiled. "With the way this case is going, I think I'd prefer the poopy pants."

"That bad, huh?"

"I'm sure you'll hear all about it at the meeting in a few minutes, but there are just so many people out there with a reason to want to see one or both of our victims dead. If it weren't so depressing, it would be impressive how many people they've managed to drive insane between the two of them."

"I wish I could tell you more about the killer," Amanda said. "But all I can tell you is that they were good at not leaving anything incriminating behind. I've got no prints in the house other than Aurora's and Lance's, and as you saw, there were no prints at all on the murder weapon. I think whoever did this had some experience."

I stared at her. "Like a contract killer?"

She shrugged helplessly. "Maybe. Whoever it was, they were meticulous. They had to have worn gloves, and they probably changed them at some point. Maybe changed clothes, too. After being at the center of all that carnage and writing all over the wall in blood, an amateur couldn't have slipped out of the house without leaving so much as a smudge."

"You're right. The rest of the house was pristine. You should voice your theory at the meeting."

"It's only a working theory, and I've told you. Isn't that good enough?"

"You sound like Shane. He was nervous to bring up his 'Lance didn't do it' theory."

She pointed out, "Well, it wasn't initially well received."

"He knew Sterling wouldn't be receptive." Ooh. That was a knee-jerk response, and I wished I hadn't said it to Amanda of all people. Not that it was an incorrect statement, but I'd decided to try not to talk shit about Sterling to her since he was trying to win her back.

"True, but overall...have you noticed the positive change in Jason's behavior?"

"I have. He seems to be making a real effort to improve his people skills."

"Right. Especially with you. Did you guys bury the hatchet?"

I didn't want to tell her what he and I had discussed, because I wasn't sure she'd appreciate me essentially meddling in her love life. Then again, me helping Sterling try to be a nicer version of himself wasn't a bad thing.

"Kind of, I guess." I ventured, "Are you thinking about giving him another chance, considering?"

She frowned. "He'll have to do a lot better. And for longer. I'm hoping this change in attitude isn't all about him trying to win me back."

Uh oh. I knew he was hoping for a quick fix, but Amanda wasn't the type of person to fall for anything short of true sincerity. Seemed like she'd seen right through him. He was going to have to up his game and commit to it for the long haul. If he really cared as much as he said he did, then I believed he'd do it. He was nothing if not thorough once he made his mind up about something.

I let out a nervous laugh. "He'd be stupid not to try, right? And he's not stupid."

She tried to fight a smile but couldn't. "Not completely."

* * *

I figured I'd better give Sterling a heads-up, lest he fall into his regular habit of becoming grumpier and meaner as a case dragged on. I found him in the breakroom.

"Hey, I'm not trying to be a gossip, but...well, I guess I am. You didn't hear this from me, but Amanda has noticed the effort you're making."

He grinned. "It's about damn time."

I laughed. "Slow your roll, Romeo. She also said she worries it's a play to get her back and your good behavior won't last."

He scoffed. "No one can be nice forever."

"You're going to have to be if you want a chance with her."

Frowning, he said, "You know me. Nice isn't who I am."

"It's probably more about respect. She knows the real you, and she knows you call things how you see them. I don't think she wants you to be something you're not. She just wants you to not be such an asshole when it's not necessary."

He nodded slowly. "That makes sense, I guess."

"Do you like her enough to soften your edges a little?"

"I'm crazy about—"

Baxter opened the door and eyed us suspiciously. "What are you guys talking about?"

"Your mom," Sterling jeered.

I gave Sterling a pointed look.

Realization dawned in his eyes. "Oh, this is...I get it. My bad."

I nodded in reply.

Baxter glanced from one of us to the other. "What is up with you two? Are you...?" He trailed off, glaring at us.

How dare he insinuate I would even consider Sterling as a rebound? I had yet to figure out the right comeback when Sterling came to my rescue.

"Hooking up again? Absolutely." Sterling rolled his eyes. "Come on, dude. You know us both better than that. Take your bad mood somewhere else."

Baxter left the room without another word.

Sterling said to me, "Hey, thanks for the tip."

"No problem."

Who could have guessed that being at odds with Baxter would create a weird bond between Sterling and me?

23

When I got back to the conference room, Shane was cleaning up our stuff so the others would have room at the table for our meeting. "I ended up calling the Nunleys since we got busy tonight and didn't have time to drop by to see them. Dead end there. They were brought into the pickleball group by Owen Reeves and only knew Wakefield through small talk at their weekly games and what they've heard about him from Reeves."

"At least we didn't have to drive all the way to their house to find out nothing."

"Not my favorite way to conduct an interview, but I had a feeling they weren't in his inner circle. What have you been up to?"

I chuckled. "Having a couple of really weird conversations. Oh, and Amanda says she has been finding a noticeable lack of any kind of transfer evidence from the killer. She's wondering if it might be the work of a professional."

Nodding, he said, "That's not a bad idea. But here's one: I think we need to get ourselves into one of those swinger parties."

I made a face. "That's not a bad idea. That's a terrible idea."

"Come on, hear me out. I've done a little digging, mostly in Aurora's notes, but a little on my own. These parties are every Friday night, and they're held at a big lake house in Geist."

"Yeah, I thought it was odd when that email said they were weekly parties. At once a week, don't they pretty quickly run through everyone on the guest list and have to re-recouple?"

He shrugged. "Maybe. I mean, if you think about it, how is it different from going to the same bar every Friday night to find a hook-up? In theory, it's safer, because you have to know someone to get in."

I wasn't convinced. "It's a much weirder dynamic and not at all organic."

"Sure, but where else are the elite going to find suitable partners to bang?"

Staring at him, I said, "Um...at home."

"Do you not understand swing culture?"

"I do, but I don't get the draw."

He squinted at me. "I feel like you were edgier than this in college. Is being a stuffy professor spilling over into your sex life?"

What sex life? "Shut up, Shane."

He laughed, then sobered. "I only want to know if you're up for the challenge of going to one undercover, should the need arise."

"No, no, no. No more undercover for me." I shivered at the thought of my last undercover mission.

"Multiple people have told me you're pretty amazing at it, and I was front and center for your stellar performance with Brad."

"Yes, I speak fluent loser. I can get idiots to open up and talk. Rich, successful people? I'm not so sure."

"People are all the same. All anyone wants is someone who'll listen to them."

"I don't think conversation is the reason people go to these parties."

"I suppose it can be, especially if they're presented with a sympathetic ear. After all, lots of times men pay hookers simply to talk to them."

My jaw dropped. "Did you just compare me to a hooker?"

"No, I'm comparing the situation."

"Then it seems like a situation I don't want to be a part of."

Our conversation ended when Baxter and Chief Esparza came into the room. The chief and I exchanged hellos, but Baxter didn't look up from his phone or acknowledge my presence in any way as he found a chair and sat down. No real surprise there, considering our weird interaction several minutes ago.

Shane said, "Oh hey, Detective Baxter—before I forget, Eve Shelton said to say hello."

I balled my fists to rein in a bubble of rage, but relaxed when Baxter made a face and said, "Who?"

Shane replied, "Eve Shelton. Pretty blonde trainer at GLSTN."

"I'm supposed to know her?" Baxter said, his attention still on his phone.

"She seemed to think so."

Baxter just shrugged and didn't look up, totally unimpressed.

I, on the other hand, had to clench my jaw extra hard to keep my expression neutral. The poor teenage outcast who'd gotten her feelings hurt by the pretty popular girl was doing a little happy dance inside me. Eve didn't make enough of an impression on Baxter for him to have remembered her. He might have been studiously ignoring me, but at least he hadn't forgotten I existed.

Everyone else filed in quickly, and Jayne seated herself at the head of the table. "I know you've all been working tirelessly today. I hope we can bring some information together and get a break in the case. First, Detective Carlisle, your report on the autopsies?"

Shane said, "Lance Wakefield did in fact die from asphyxia as a result of choking on his own vomit. His blood alcohol level was high—point two-one, but it was likely higher before his death. What was left in his stomach and esophagus consisted of whiskey, Xanax and Percocet at various stages of digestion, steak, and salad. Further tox screen pending. No wounding on the body. Aurora Bennett died of exsanguination. No surprise there. She was also pregnant."

The chief frowned. "How pregnant?"

I said, "According to her fertility calculator, barely. She was two days late. We don't know for sure if she'd taken a test yet, but she'd told her boyfriend she had big news to tell him. Then again, news is her life, so—"

Jayne cut in, "Boyfriend? Have we talked to him?"

Shane replied, "Yes. We've got a lot to unpack from today."

"Let's not get ahead of ourselves, then. Continue with the autopsy report."

Shane went on, "Aurora Bennett's blood alcohol level was minimal. There'll be a tox screen done, but Dr. Berg found no drug residue in her stomach. Only popcorn, chocolate, and red wine."

Sterling barked out a laugh. "The lonely, pathetic woman diet."

I said, "In our defense, that's the lonely, pathetic women's standard 'I'm too tired to fix myself dinner' dinner. Aside from the inevitable heartburn, it's strangely satisfying."

I thought I saw a flicker of something pass over Baxter's face and wondered if he was taken aback by the fact that I called myself lonely and pathetic or over worry that I might have been drinking again. Or maybe I was reading way too much into his general frowny disposition.

Jayne said, "Ms. Carmack, Ms. Matthews, your report?"

Amanda said, "All of the evidence we collected at the crime scene has gone through at least the first examination. I'm sorry I don't have more to report, but there really isn't a lot we've learned from processing the evidence. The murder weapon had been wiped clean of fingerprints, and all fingerprints we collected at the scene were from the home's occupants. For making such a messy scene, the killer didn't leave much behind."

I could tell Sterling was itching to voice his opinion about the killer being Lance, which would have also explained why there was no extraneous evidence from an outside person. But to his merit, he let her speak and didn't argue.

"Thank you, Ms. Carmack." Jayne asked, "Detectives Sterling and Baxter, your report?"

Sterling said, "I went through Lance Wakefield's and Aurora Bennett's financials, which are, interestingly, completely separate from each other. No joint accounts. Hers look pretty clean aside from an obscene amount spent on personal care and one instance a few weeks ago of taking out three thousand in cash. His are a little suspect—he's been making monthly withdrawals of between five and eight thousand in cash for the past year. Not enough to put up a red flag with his bank, but more than he should need for walking around money. Even if he's got a major drug habit, it's way too much. And speaking of drugs, I'm working with vice to try to run down who might have sold him the big bag of Percocet. Nothing yet. I've spoken to his bosses at the college, who haven't been particularly impressed with his work ethic or his attitude lately, but at the same time couldn't provide any insight into why he killed his wife. I read through all of his Wakefield Foundation emails and picked out staff members he'd berated and argued with over the last couple of months. I interviewed all of them, and none would say a word against him. They weren't singing his praises, either. Everyone I asked if they thought he could be a killer could see it going either way."

Sterling was surely frustrated. He'd run people down all day and had nothing to show for it. However, to his credit, he was less outwardly angry than I'd expected. I guessed he was trying to rein it in, at least in Amanda's presence.

I was right. After clearing his throat, he continued in an oddly tentative tone, "I've had impound grab his vehicle. Um...Amanda, would you mind taking charge of processing it for us?"

She gave him a strange look. "Sure. It's my job."

He beamed at her. "Thank you." I hid a smile. He'd definitely taken my suggestions to heart.

Baxter, who seemed marginally annoyed by their exchange, began his report. "Now that we know a little more, I returned to the scene and took a look around. I didn't find anything new, but since there are still reporters camped on the sidewalk and a steady stream of gawkers rolling by, I recommend we keep some deputies there to deter anyone from trying to break in."

Jayne nodded. "Will do."

Since Baxter was speaking, I was able to take a good, long look at him without anyone thinking I was staring. Shane's assessment was right, and I was disturbed by what I saw. Baxter looked nearly as haggard as Max Stevenson. His cheeks were sunken, like he'd suddenly lost weight. His normally meticulously trimmed beard was uneven and overgrown. His hair was a mess, like he'd pulled it in all different directions. But what I couldn't get past was the haunted look in his eyes. I knew what he looked like when he was scared, hurt, and angry, but this was none of these. It was something deeper. Something had rocked Nick Baxter to his core.

He went on, "I had Aurora's assistant gather all the threats she'd received in the past few weeks. I'm in the process of vetting them for intent versus empty scare tactics."

Jayne asked, "Where are we with beneficiaries on their life insurance plans?"

Baxter consulted his notes. "Neither of them listed each other as beneficiaries. Aurora Bennett's beneficiaries are Avery Bennett-Alonzo and Austin Bennett, her sister and brother. We reinterviewed them today. Both have solid alibis for that night. Lance Wakefield's beneficiary is Annaleigh Walters—"

Shane's eyebrows shot up. "His TA?"

"His niece. We haven't talked to her yet. She's not answering her phone, and we're waiting on a warrant to get her address. Ashmore won't cough it up."

Shane said, "We left her a couple of messages to get in touch with us, but haven't heard back, either."

Jayne looked concerned. I couldn't blame her—last time an Ashmore student wasn't answering her phone when the cops called, it was her own niece, and it didn't end well. "I don't like the fact that she's not responding."

The chief stood and headed toward the door. "I'll go run a location on her phone and send out a deputy to track her down. Be right back."

Visibly relieved, Jayne went on, "Detective Carlisle and Ms. Matthews, how is your investigation going into possible other suspects?"

Shane turned to me and grinned. "Where to begin, right?"

As I smiled back at Shane, I noticed Baxter's perma-frown deepen, which kind of irked me. He was the one who refused to partner with me, so he should have no opinion about me sharing an inside joke with my new partner.

Shane said, "We found a burner phone in Aurora Bennett's desk at work. From that, we managed to track down her trainer, Max Stevenson, who she was in an extra-marital relationship with. He's also most likely the father of her baby."

"And where is he now? Do we have him in holding? Have you officially interrogated him?" Sterling demanded.

I said, "Why do you care? I thought you were convinced the husband killed her."

"Well, on the off chance it's not him, I want a backup plan."

Shane said, "To answer your questions, Max Stevenson is on his way to a psych hold, and yes, we've spoken to him."

Sterling snapped, "And?"

"And he didn't do it," I said.

"Matthews, let the adults talk."

I shot him a disappointed look, and he held up his hands. "Sorry. Old habits."

Shane stared Sterling down. "She's right. I don't believe he did it, either."

Sterling wasn't giving up, but he said in a calmer tone, "I want a crack at—"

Baxter cut him off. "I listened in from next door. They're right. He's not the guy."

I hadn't known that Baxter was in the next room when we were speaking to Max. I didn't have time to wonder why as Shane continued his report.

"But he did give us a solid lead. He confirmed what Aurora's assistant had told us about Aurora getting threats to back off a story she was working on. If we can figure out which one, we can concentrate on that and maybe even tie it to one of Wakefield Foundation's investigations. We have all of her notes and a couple of contact numbers for her confidential sources."

Jayne asked, "Have you found anything in her notes yet that we might start working on tonight?"

I said, "We didn't get too far into them because we kind of went off on a tangent when we found out about Max Stevenson." I gestured to the list Shane and I had made on the white board behind me. "But we do know she'd been investigating gang recruitment, TC Pittman Enterprises, Axion Pharmaceuticals, and Adler-Jamison Engineering, and then of course we already knew about the swinger parties she thought her husband was going to. Or maybe did actually go to?" I looked at Shane. "I guess we don't know if he ever attended one."

"Swinger parties?" Chief Esparza said as he reentered the room. "What the hell? I was only gone for two minutes."

I explained, "Those wild parties Aurora thought Lance was going to behind her back are, in fact, swinger parties."

"You're sure about that?"

I nodded. "Aurora had a photo she'd taken of an email from..." I tried to make my tired brain recall the name, which I hadn't bothered to write in my notes. "Oh, yeah—David Jarvis. He invited Lance and Aurora to one of their weekly 'recoupling' parties. Lance evidently didn't pass along to her that she was welcome there as well."

Jayne raised an eyebrow. "Recoupling?"

"Their term for swinging, evidently."

Shane said, "According to her assistant, Aurora was rabid over finding out everything she could on these parties. And even though the attendees are promised anonymity—the attire is masked, black tie—she'd somehow managed to uncover some of their identities and knew if their names got out they'd be ruined. To me, that's a lot of motive to kill someone with the ability to reach millions of people."

The chief frowned. "That is a lot of motive. Maybe we need to get into one of those parties."

I said, "According to Brad Kerrigan, we'd need an invitation, not to mention a killer stock portfolio, and no one's going to invite a cop to one of these."

Sterling shook his head. "The parties aren't illegal, they're just weird."

Shane said, "I'm sure there's a fair amount of nose candy that gets passed around there. Probably the occasional roofie as well, especially if some of the women get cold feet. It won't be easy for us to get in, but I agree that we should give it a shot."

Baxter asked, "Why don't we just interview these people the old-fashioned way?"

Sterling shrugged. "People will admit all kinds of stuff during pillow talk they'd never breathe a word of during an interrogation."

Shane added, "Plus, we only know the names of a few of the regulars from Aurora's notes. We could find a lot more possible suspects by being able to ID them in person."

Baxter frowned. "Which may or may not work, considering everyone will be wearing masks."

I said, "And who exactly is going to volunteer to go to the party and get to the point of pillow talk with these people?"

Sterling wiggled his eyebrows at me. "You are."

I snorted. "Like hell."

"As much as it pains me to say it, Matthews, you're the only woman on the team who's had undercover experience and is young enough to fit the bill. No offense, Sheriff."

Jayne frowned at Sterling. "I suppose you're not wrong."

I stared at Jayne, shocked she didn't put a stop to me going undercover again. Maybe she didn't think this would be a dangerous situation.

Sterling nodded. "Then it's a go."

Shane said, "Ellie needs a husband. You volunteering?"

I cut in, "First of all, no one is going to believe that pairing for a minute, and second of all, I never agreed to this."

Ignoring me, Sterling shook his head. "I'm out. What you see with me is what you get. I'm man enough to admit I'm shit undercover. Why don't you do it?"

Shane chuckled. "You don't want me. This particular situation will have my middle-school sense of humor in overdrive. I won't be able to keep a straight face."

Sterling said, "Well, Baxter has no game with women, so where does that leave us?"

Baxter scowled at Sterling, although he didn't say a word in his own defense. I had to clamp my jaw shut so I wouldn't react.

Shane turned to me. "How about Manetti? You guys are believable as a couple."

"He's still on medical leave."

"This isn't going to be a physically grueling op."

I made a face. "It is if he's going to have to bang some rando to get to the pillow talk stage."

Grinning, Shane said, "You sound like that could make you jealous."

"I sound like someone who doesn't want to go to a sex party."

Sterling held up his hand. "All in favor of Matthews and Manetti running point on this op?"

They all held up their hands. Even Baxter and Jayne. Traitors.

* * *

Everyone filed out of the conference room, leaving Shane and me alone. I paced the room as I tried to wrap my head around what I'd somehow managed to get myself roped into. "A masked black-tie swinger party. So, like, are we talking a full *Eyes Wide Shut* scenario, here?"

Shrugging, Shane replied, "Yeah, I guess."

"That was an orgy, though, wasn't it?"

"Well, I imagine it could turn into one given the right circumstances."

My stomach lurched. Flinging my hands in the air, I announced, "I'm out." I turned on my heel and started to storm out of the room.

Shane grabbed my arm before I could get away. "I'm kidding. I promise it won't be as bad as you're imagining. We'll get there reasonably early, during the mingling, drinking, and flirting stage—before people start pairing off. And then we'll extract you before you have to put out. You should only be in there an hour, tops. We'll listen in on everything, and all you'll have to do is say the word if you get in over your head."

If I had to be in a place I felt uncomfortable, which I knew would be the case, there were no other people I'd rather have watching out for me than Vic, Shane, Baxter, and even Sterling.

Once Shane left the conference room, I stewed for a while about what I would say to Vic. I hated I had to ask him to do this undercover thing with me. I knew he'd agree simply because I was the one asking. If it became dangerous and he happened to get hurt, his recovery would be set back, which I didn't know if he could mentally handle again. And I didn't know if I could mentally handle being the cause of it.

I finally worked up the courage and dialed Vic's number.

"Hello?" his voice, although groggy with sleep, had a worried edge to it.

"Oh, damn it. I'm sorry, Vic. I forgot you'd already be asleep."

He grunted. "It's fine. What's up?"

I didn't know how to begin. "Um...I was just in a meeting that went really poorly."

"You didn't get fired again, did you?" From the concern in his voice, I could tell he was only half-joking.

"Worse. I got voluntold to run point on another undercover job."

"Ah. Not what you wanted to hear."

"It gets worse from there. They tasked me with talking you into doing it with me." I added hastily, "But you can say no."

"Me? Really?"

I figured he wouldn't be upset by the news, but it was still presumptuous of them to assume he'd drop everything to help. Not that he had anything more pressing to do, but for me it was the danger factor.

I said, "Yeah. We have to pose as a married couple."

"I'm sure we could pull that off easily enough."

"At a swinger party with the area's rich elite."

Manetti laughed. "Oh, shit."

"Yeah. It probably won't be super dangerous, but if you don't think you're physically up for it—"

"I'm up for it," he said, a slightly defensive tone creeping into his voice.

"Okay, just think about it and make sure."

"I'm sure."

"Okay."

He laughed again. "You're gonna hate this."

"I already do."

24

As Shane and I were about to call it a night, Sterling burst through the door of the conference room. "I just got the weirdest phone call."

I piped up, "Aren't you used to that? I mean, isn't 'for a good time, call Jason Sterling' written in every bar bathroom stall in town?"

Shane burst out laughing.

Sterling nodded, appreciation apparent in his expression. "Ooh, Matthews with the quick comeback. I might take offense if my news wasn't way more embarrassing for you."

"What?" I asked warily.

"Brad Kerrigan just called me to give you a message to call him. He said he wants to 'hook up with you' sometime soon."

"Eww. Pass." I shuddered. "And yes, you win for the most embarrassing statement uttered in the last two minutes."

Shane rolled his eyes. "You were kind of putting it out there earlier."

I cuffed him on the arm. "I was doing my job."

Sterling said, "And you're going to continue doing your job by agreeing to go have coffee with that assclown."

"What? No."

Shane frowned. "I know I was the one who jerked you out of his office as he was trying to ask you out, but it's actually not a terrible idea. He was opening up to you earlier, and if he's asking to see you again, maybe it's for the purpose of talking about the case."

My eyebrows shot up. "Are you unaware of what the phrase 'hook up with you' means?"

"It can mean 'meet you' instead of 'sex you.' It won't hurt anything to call him back and find out his intention. If it's just coffee or a meal, I say go for it. See what else you can find out from him."

Sterling added, "And if he actually wants to sex you, are you really in a position to turn down a proposition, Matthews? I'm sure you don't get those too often."

Glaring from one man to the other, I griped, "I hate both of you."

* * *

It turned out that Brad simply wanted to go for coffee and talk further about the case. I agreed to meet him the next morning at a coffeehouse in Carmel during a break between my first two classes. I had a feeling something odd was up, though, like Brad knew something big he'd yet to share. So, I bet Shane and Sterling twenty dollars I'd come back with an earth-shattering piece of information.

I wasn't stupid, though—I insisted on meeting Brad at the coffeehouse rather than allowing him to pick me up at Ashmore, which he offered to do. No way was I getting in a car again with a person of interest in a murder. I'd learned my lesson. I'd also told Shane and Sterling exactly where I was going and when, in case anything went sideways. And I'd brought along the voice recorder I used while processing scenes. I made sure it was on and recording, then slipped it in my pocket as I entered the bustling coffeehouse.

"Oh, hey, Ellie. Good timing," Brad said, smiling at me from the register. "What can I get you?"

I joined him at the counter. "A plain latte with coconut milk. Hot, please. Thanks."

He turned to the barista. "You heard the lady."

He paid for our drinks, making a show out of stuffing a five in the tip jar, and then we found a table and sat down.

I smiled at him. "How are you doing?"

He sighed. "Hanging in there. Thanks for meeting me."

"No problem."

Out of the corner of my eye, I noticed someone sit down at a table across the room from us and had to work to hold in my reaction. What the hell was Baxter doing showing up here literally seconds after me and plopping himself down in my line of vision? And he was making no effort to hide the fact that he was watching us.

Brad traced a couple of lines in the woodgrain of the tabletop, oblivious to pretty much everything else. He couldn't see Baxter from his vantage point, and I needed to keep it that way. I didn't want to spook him into clamming up. I had a bet to win, after all.

I said, "So what did you want to talk about? Did you remember something else we didn't get to discuss earlier?"

"Not exactly..." He looked at me earnestly. "If I tell you something...can you use it against someone?"

Oh, he knew something. I was so winning this bet. "What do you mean?"

"Order for Brad," a barista called from the counter.

Brad began to push his chair back, but I hopped up and beat him to it. "I'll go. You relax. You seem stressed."

I passed Baxter's table on the way and stopped in front of him. "Are we in a staring contest I didn't know about? Because you're definitely winning." When he only scowled at me in reply, I added, "More importantly, what the hell are you doing all the way out here?"

"Your partner's job, because he's not getting it done," he griped.

"Oh, you mean the partner I'm with because you want nothing to do with me?"

Ignoring my jab, he said, "He's not watching out for you."

I frowned. "That's not his job. I'm a grown-ass woman."

He clenched his jaw and ground out, "Who's out on a date with a person of interest in a double homicide."

"I feel like you'd know I have better taste than that. This guy knows something but hasn't given it up yet. He wants to talk to me because I'm not a cop. On that note, can you get the hell out of here? You're exuding bacon. I don't want him to think we're together."

"You're the one who came over to my table."

I rolled my eyes. "To tell you to quit being so weird."

He shrugged. "Well, I'm not leaving."

"Whatever. Just don't butt in."

As miffed as I was by the possibility of Baxter's presence spooking Brad, I couldn't help but feel absolute joy over the fact that Baxter did still care about me. Or at least he cared about my safety. I'd take what I could get.

I picked up the drinks and returned to the table with Brad. "Sorry about that. Where were we?"

He shook his head and sipped his coffee. "Ah, I was just talking out my ass. I guess more than anything, I need to talk to someone who understands my situation."

I placed my hand on his arm, knowing Baxter was watching and hoping he didn't like what he saw. "I'm all ears, Brad."

"I guess I...I don't know. I'm really worried about what's going to happen to Wakefield Foundation—er, I mean Hamilton Foundation. Damn. That's going to take some getting used to."

"Right. Barry Jeffords said the board was scrambling to do some damage control, starting with a regime change and a name change. Do you think the board president will be easy to work for?"

"Should be. We kind of have to answer to him anyway, so it won't be too much different. But I will say that he usually just agrees to whatever Lance says. He's never put pressure on us to work his own agenda."

"That's good, I guess...if he's strong enough to be an effective leader, especially with the place in such turmoil. Have you had a bunch of corporations start coming after you, trying to strongarm you into going back on your assessment of them?"

"We've had a couple of people call to gloat over the irony of our founder committing one of the most unethical acts ever, but there have been no suits levied against us." He sighed. "Yet. What's going to hurt most is if our investors lose faith in the foundation. A whole foundation shouldn't be ruined by the actions of one person..." He drifted off, his brow furrowed.

"Well, when his name's on the door, it's kind of different. If one of the rest of you did something bad, it probably wouldn't be such an issue."

He looked me in the eye. He really wanted to say something, but he couldn't seem to get it to come out.

I said, "Earlier you said to me, 'if I tell you something...can you use it against someone?' What did you mean by that? Do you know of someone who did something bad?"

He started breathing heavily. "I...no. I didn't mean it."

"I think you did."

Shaking his head, he asserted, "No. I say a lot of dumb stuff."

"Do you do a lot of dumb stuff?"

"Sometimes," he muttered.

"Do you think asking me out for coffee to talk was dumb?"

"Very possibly."

I grabbed both of Brad's hands across the table. As I did this, I noticed Baxter sit up straighter and frown more, but I kept my attention on Brad. "Look. It's painfully obvious you know something. If you tell me, I can't promise it won't be used against whoever you're talking about, but I can promise I'll protect you from whoever you're scared of."

He gripped my hands. "It's big."

"Then get it off your conscience. It's going to eat you alive otherwise."

"You promise not to tell anyone?"

"No, I promise to keep you safe. There's a difference. However, I do promise not to tell anyone who's not on my task force team."

He let out a long breath and released my hands. "Okay. Um...so...you know Barry? He, um...he kind of...made friends with a few of the big corporations we've investigated over the past year or so. And um...they were paying him to...sweep some stuff under the rug. I'm pretty sure Lance found out about it, because the dynamic between the two of them at dinner the other night was off-the-charts uncomfortable. I, uh...didn't say anything earlier because..." He hitched out a sigh. "I didn't want you going in and using what I'd said to question Barry. He's a smart guy. He'd know I was the one who narced on him."

I hardly knew where to begin. I lowered my voice. "Are you saying Barry might have had something to do with Aurora's death?"

"I hope not. I hope it was totally unrelated and just bad timing. But if you'd been at that table with those two like I was..." He shook his head.

"So you feel like you might need protection from Barry?" I asked.

"It's possible. I don't know how much he knows about what I know."

"And how exactly did you find out about his connections to these corporations?"

"I'm the COO. I'm at the center of these investigations. If there's information that's in our system one day and gone the next, I notice."

"So you've noticed information disappearing for a while now?"

"Yeah. I finally traced it to him."

I nodded slowly. "Okay, let's do this: give us twenty-four hours to do some digging on Barry." When he opened his mouth to interject, I held up a hand and assured him, "He won't know it. We won't question him or anyone close to him. Once we're ready to move in on him, we'll put a deputy with you for your safety. Does that sound good?"

He sat back in his chair, his face showing relief. "Yes. That's great."

"I just need one thing from you."

"What's that?"

"The names of the companies Barry was 'friends' with. If we're going to nail him, we have to know."

"Uh...I can't really—"

"Don't bullshit me, Brad. I know you guys are all about the confidentiality, but if you don't give me a starting point, our only option is to go straight to Barry, and I know you don't want that."

He blew out a breath. "No, I don't. Okay..." He leaned in and lowered his voice. "TC Pittman Enterprises and Greenstar Plastics."

Bingo. TC Pittman was one Aurora was looking into as well.

I smiled. "Thank you."

He smiled back. "I should be thanking you." He suddenly stood. "Whew, that's a weight lifted. I gotta bounce, but maybe I can see you again, soon?"

"You can count on it." I got my phone out and began composing a text to Baxter.

Brad squeezed my shoulder as he left the table and walked out the nearby side door of the coffeehouse. Baxter was frowning at me with pretty much everything he had, but once he read the text I sent him, his expression morphed into shock. He bolted up from his table and hurried my way, dragging me out the door with him.

25

Once we were in his SUV and following two car lengths behind Brad's Tesla, Baxter snapped, "I told you this guy was dangerous, and I was right."

I chuckled, finishing up a text to Shane about taking a hard look into TC Pittman Enterprises and checking for any mention of Greenstar Plastics in Aurora's notes. "To be fair, he's more stupid than dangerous."

"Sometimes that's worse. Bring me up to speed on what you learned on your date."

"Well, for starters, I learned my buddy Brad is a damn fine actor. But he's just dumb enough to say a little too much, which is what tipped me off. He threw Barry Jeffords under the bus with both hands."

"For what?"

"For doing favors for certain companies Wakefield Foundation is investigating. I assume these companies offer bribes in exchange for making unflattering information disappear. For my money, it's actually Brad who's doing this, and he's trying to throw us off long enough to get his house in order. That's why I wanted to be sure someone was on him immediately. And I was right about that, considering we're going in the opposite direction of his office." Wakefield Foundation was south of there, and we were headed north.

"Do you think he also killed our two victims?"

"Wait—*two* vics? Hang on. First, you're one hundred percent in Shane's and my camp about Lance being innocent? I hoped you were leaning that way since you were tracking down people who'd threatened Aurora at work."

"Of course. The evidence clearly points to Wakefield not having killed his wife. Don't tell him I told you this, but even Sterling is starting to come around."

That was interesting. In not having spoken to Baxter about the case, I hadn't known his thoughts about it, aside from what I'd been able to glean during team meetings. But now that I thought about it, he hadn't really voiced an opinion of his own—only having offered a one-time, distracted, rather disinterested agreement with Sterling at the scene when we all thought it looked like Lance had killed Aurora.

"And you're saying you think Lance was also a murder victim? His death wasn't a suicide?" I couldn't imagine he'd been talking to Vic, or even to Shane, to have heard about Vic's theory. But Baxter was plenty brilliant enough to come up with it on his own—I just hadn't thought he was putting in the effort to be brilliant this time.

"I'm thinking more like an assisted suicide. Who better to talk you into ending it all with a handful of drugs than one of your best buddies?"

My jaw dropped. "No." I thought for a moment about Brad being that kind of bad guy. "I'll agree that Brad is one slippery son of a bitch, and I guess I could imagine him peer pressuring someone into taking pills. But Aurora's murder? I'm not seeing it. He doesn't have that...serial killer-y thing about him."

"Because he's not a serial killer."

"I mean that violent, unhinged vibe they have. You know what I'm talking about."

"I do, and I also know many sociopaths are great at hiding it."

"Again, I don't know that he's bright enough to hide something that monumental. Aurora's murder was so...straight out of a slasher film. I feel like the killer needed to have some kind of pent-up rage going on to do that much damage to another human being."

He shrugged. "Maybe, maybe not. If she fought him—which her wounds indicate she did at least a little bit—he'd have no choice but to keep stabbing until he got the job done. The gruesomeness you assume came from rage could have come from sheer panic and self-preservation."

Wow. There was the Baxter I knew. I had to admit I got a little turned on.

He went on, "If Kerrigan is taking bribes from corporations both vics are investigating and one or both of them knows it, he's got to take them out. He kills them, he kills their investigations. Then he works from the inside to clean up any loose ends."

"He did admit to me that as the COO, he's in the middle of every one of the foundation's cases." I thought for a moment about the conversation Shane and I had with Vic last night. "But as the COO, he shouldn't want to make it look like Lance killed Aurora. If Lance's reputation gets ruined, the company goes down with him and Brad's job and his cash cow disappears. You make Lance a victim, and the company takes no hit."

"True, but we don't know what Kerrigan's endgame is or how deep he's in with these corporations. Maybe there's a reason someone wants the foundation to fold or at least be shaken up. Maybe the master plan got messed up somewhere along the way and Kerrigan figures he's got an equal shot at either winning it all or going to jail. At this point, his best bet is to make sure Wakefield is ruined and damage control the hell out of the situation to keep the foundation running. The board made some swift moves yesterday to do that. Kerrigan may have feigned ignorance, but you can't tell me the COO isn't heavily involved in steering the foundation back on track after a disaster like this."

I'd never thought of it that way. "Ooh, you're right." We stopped at a stoplight, still a couple of cars back from Brad's Tesla. I turned to Baxter. "Where have you been?"

He flicked an uncomfortable glance at me. "What do you mean?"

"The old Nick Baxter. I thought he was gone for good."

His face became stony. "If you're thinking this little joyride is going to change anything about us working together, don't. It's purely necessity."

Necessity, my ass. I'd driven myself to the coffeehouse, so it wasn't like him leaving to follow Brad would abandon me or even risk my safety, because it was Brad he'd been protecting me from. And he totally could have tailed Brad by himself—he certainly didn't need me. We also could have had this discussion over email, text, phone, or Facetime. I didn't believe for a second he didn't want me here, just like old times.

He added, "And speaking of necessity, maybe we shouldn't talk about anything that's not case-related."

"Whatever you say."

It got uncomfortably quiet, the minutes ticking away as we followed Brad toward Westfield, a smaller town just north of Carmel.

I finally said, "I can't ride around all day. I have a class in thirty minutes."

His grip on the steering wheel tightened. "We're in the middle of an active double homicide investigation. Cut class like you normally do."

"I can't. It's too close to finals."

"You can, and that's what your TA is for. You just for some reason don't want to."

"Do you think you're in a position to throw shade at how much effort someone else is putting into this case?"

He shifted in his seat. "I'm putting in plenty of effort."

"You mean when you're not on your phone. You're like a teenage girl with that thing."

Between gritted teeth, he said, "I'm keeping in contact with the dozens of people I've interviewed."

"Is one of those your new girlfriend?" I muttered under my breath.

"Excuse me?"

"Nothing. You were right about not talking."

Finally, after what seemed like hours—it was four minutes, tops—Brad pulled into the parking lot of a strip mall in Westfield. We pulled slowly into the lot, waiting to see where he parked. He got out of his car and approached a dark SUV. Baxter parked at the opposite end of the lot, but with a vantage point where we could see Brad and the SUV. Brad knocked on the driver's window, and the window rolled down. The man inside was hard to see. All I could make out was a bald head and sunglasses. Not helpful.

"Who's that guy?" I asked.

"How should I know?" Baxter snapped, taking photos of them with his phone. He then buried his attention on his phone again, as per usual.

I'd had it with him. "Seriously, Baxter, have you been taking asshole classes from Sterling?"

"Ellie..." He huffed out a breath, pausing what he was doing to rub his eyes.

Even though his tone was sharp, I loved hearing him say my name. It had been so long since I'd heard it.

He went on, "Look, I'm under a lot of stress right now. I apologize for being short, but you're not exactly making it easy."

I wasn't. I knew that. I replied quietly, "I'm sorry, too. I'll ease up."

Brad and the bald guy were still talking, although it looked more like an argument than a friendly conversation.

Baxter said, "I had Sterling run the guy's plates. The vehicle is registered to a local security firm called Dynasty Elite Security."

"Security...hmm. Is Brad so important he needs a bodyguard?"

"I don't feel like a bodyguard would speak to his client like that."

That was probably true. Brad and Baldy's discussion-turned-argument had degraded into what looked like a full ass-chewing, based on the contrite and kind of scared look on Brad's face.

I said, "Brad definitely did something stupid. It's a question of what."

"Talking to you was pretty stupid if you're right about him taking bribes and screwing the foundation. It would stand to reason that he'd want to give his partners in crime a heads-up. Maybe this guy works for one of them. I'm having Sterling dig for it as we speak."

"I could see Brad going rogue and not mentioning to his cronies until after the fact that he was going to out them to the cops to save his own ass."

"He could be banking on the fact that we won't care about anything that doesn't have to do with our case."

"Except it could have everything to do with our case, seeing as how the foundation and Aurora were both investigating TC Pittman."

"We're close. We'll figure it out."

We waited until Brad and Baldy's conversation was over, which left Brad slinking back to his car and Baldy taking out his phone and making a call.

I said, "You want to switch gears and follow Brad's buddy?"

"Yes, but alone."

I sighed. "I thought we weren't going to do this again."

There was a hint of a smile on his face, or at least no frown, as he said, "Didn't you say you have a class to teach?"

"Oh, yeah."

He pointed to the strip mall in front of us. "Go sit in the coffeeshop there. A deputy will be here in a few minutes to pick you up and drive you back to Ashmore."

The fact that he'd made plans for me to get back to work, per my wishes, wasn't lost on me. "Thank you, Nick."

26

Teaching the same lesson on toolmark collection for a second time that morning turned out to be way less exciting than tailing Brad with Baxter. I wished I hadn't made such a deal about getting back to campus. If I'd kept my mouth shut, he might have let me continue to ride around with him. Even though we'd exchanged a few barbs, we'd managed to talk out some interesting theories I wanted to follow up on that afternoon. It was the most he and I had spoken in two months, and I'd finally begun to see glimpses of the old Baxter. It was nice to know he was still in there, but he was far from cured of whatever was bothering him.

In my time between class periods, I dropped by my friend Sam's office.

"Hey," I said, letting myself in and plopping down in the chair facing her desk.

"Ooh, it's Ellie Matthews, from the TV," she cooed, fanning her face.

I groaned. "Was I on the news again?"

"Yeah, they had reel of you and some hot guy in a suit leaving the Wakefield Foundation office, and they had you two walking into that swanky gym...what's it called, Shimmer?"

"GLSTN," I replied, shaking my head. "They were in our faces at the foundation office, but I had no clue we were being filmed at GLSTN. Did I at least look okay?" My head was not in this game. I was destined to make a big mistake.

"Beautiful, as always. Who's the hottie?"

"My old buddy Shane from college. They sent reinforcements from the IMPD to join our team."

She snickered. I'd told her how much law enforcement agencies loved other law enforcement agencies invading their turf. "Is he single?"

"Nope. New dad."

"Too bad, and eww."

"Why 'eww'?"

She shrugged. "I'm not into dads. Hey, so it's true that Lance didn't kill his wife?"

"What?" We'd never made a statement either way.

"It's all over the news. You took Aurora's lover into custody last night, right?"

"*What*?"

Sam eyed me. "Are you not hearing me, or are you not comprehending the words that are coming out of my mouth?"

"I'm freaking out, that's what. We didn't—" I stopped myself before I inadvertently gave anything away about the case. "I have to make a call."

I'd worked late last night, and I'd overslept and had to rush to campus that morning. I didn't have time to pay attention to the news, but evidently they'd been working overtime to suddenly change their narrative on our case.

I locked myself in my office and called Shane. Before he had time to get out a, "hey," I cried, "What's going on with the media? One of my friends said they're broadcasting that we have Aurora's lover in custody."

He grunted. "I just saw that." Sighing, he explained, "I think they've been following us without our knowledge. They've got soundbites from Owen Reeves and several Wakefield Foundation employees singing Wakefield's praises. And then they've got all the GLSTN trainers—including your nemesis Eve—protesting too much about Max Stevenson's great personality and also outing their affair...and the baby. Oh, and don't forget the tearful sit-down on the morning show with Suresh Mahar bemoaning the senseless death of his poor BFF Lance Wakefield."

I hadn't given much thought to the fact that we'd largely been left alone by the press after that first day at the crime scene. They'd traded hounding us in favor of sneaking along behind us and reinterviewing everyone we spoke to, figuring civilians would give them a lot more information than we would, which clearly they did. It was infuriating.

"So what now?" I asked.

"We go on with our investigation. It doesn't matter what the world thinks."

I shivered. "It's going to matter to poor Max Stevenson when he gets out of psych hold and finds out he's Public Enemy Number One."

"Now don't you think he'll be thanking us for that psych hold? Maybe by the time he's out, either the media will have moved on to their next victim or we'll have the real killer in custody."

"I hope so, if only for his sanity."

Shane softened his tone. "Look, we got this. It changed nothing about our investigation when the media was witch-hunting Wakefield. The fact that they have a new witch will keep them busy for a while and hopefully out of our hair. That said, we've got a lot of new information to wade through, so get here as fast as you can."

I sighed. "Will do."

A few minutes later, as I was gathering my stuff to leave, Sam knocked on my door. "Lunch later?"

I made a face. "Sorry, freaking case. I'm going to have to turn over the rest of today's classes to my TA and head to the station right now. Maybe tomorrow?"

She looked away. "I've got lunch plans tomorrow."

Sam was an oversharer. "Lunch plans" sounded to me like a date she didn't want to tell me about. "Why you being so cryptic?"

"I'm not being cryptic."

I eyed her. "False."

She huffed. "Fine. I'm seeing a man for lunch."

"What man?"

Blushing, she blurted out, "Ben, okay? I'm having lunch with Ben the Bug Man. Happy now?"

I smiled. "Thrilled, but you don't seem to be."

She looked up and down the hallway to make sure no one was listening. "He's so nerdy. He's *so* into bugs."

I rolled my eyes. "I'm not having this conversation again with you. If you don't like him, then don't go out with him."

Her face fell. "But what if I do like him?"

"Then get the hell over the fact that you think you're too cool for him. Which I'm sorry to tell you, you're not."

Her jaw dropped. "Hey!"

"How many body parts have you boiled the skin and other jiggly parts off this month?"

She hesitated before answering, "Two."

"That's two too many, and that makes you a nerd."

"It's my job."

"And bugs are Ben's job. We can't all have glamorous jobs like me, where I get to study dead people's shit-stained underwear."

"I feel like this conversation has taken a turn."

I shrugged. "This is the most normal conversation I've had all week."

"You need to get a life. Speaking of which, did you ever get laid or at least eat a carb?"

"I ate some carbs."

She made a sympathetic face. "I feel so sad for you."

"Me, too."

* * *

Talking to Sam about Ben Seong jogged my memory about our recent John Doe case, which I ended up thinking about all the way to the station. I was still troubled by the fact that we weren't able to even identify our victim. The events surrounding that case and the current case couldn't have been more different. Although I hated the constant media scrutiny and meddling, at least it meant that people were interested in justice for the victims. No one had given two shits about our poor John Doe, but he was every bit as dead as Aurora and Lance.

At the station, I found Shane slumped over his laptop in the conference room, papers scattered all around the table. "This must be where the party is."

He looked up, bleary-eyed. "Oh good, you're here. Now both of us can be bored as shit and totally confused by legalese."

I took the chair next to him. "That does not sound like a party."

"Trust me, it's not, but there's good news. Turns out Kerrigan was blowing smoke up our asses about the warrant blocking. I got the foundation's full files on TC Pittman Enterprises, Greenstar Plastics, Axion Pharmaceuticals, and Adler-Jamison Engineering. And we got Wakefield's laptop."

My eyebrows shot up. "Whoa."

"It's a brick at the moment, but cyber is working on getting around the password."

"Any of those four businesses have dirty little secrets they're willing to kill to keep?"

"Yes and no. TC Pittman went belly-up last week, but from the looks of it, they were heading that way long before Wakefield got involved. It wasn't a huge company, and the owner was skimming. The foundation called out the fact that several male employees repeatedly sexually harassed the one woman who worked there."

"So you're saying they had it coming and had no one to blame but themselves."

He nodded. "Basically."

"Where are Aurora's notes? I seem to recall something about sexual harassment in there."

"In the box there." He pointed to the other end of the table.

I went over and pulled her latest notebook out of the box and flipped to the information I'd found about TC Pittman. "She referenced the sexual harassment, but not the skimming." I looked up. "Wait. If TC Pittman paid Brad to sweep the bad stuff under the rug, why is it still there in the information the foundation gave you? He told me he figured out 'Barry' was doing the whole bribe thing because information was in their system one day and gone the next."

Shane frowned. "Maybe this stuff wasn't the worst of what they did."

"Maybe Brad took their money and screwed them over. They'd have no recourse."

He shrugged. "They could have killed him or kneecapped him."

"Brad screwing them over would be a much worse offense than Aurora or Lance doing their jobs. Wouldn't that make the TC Pittman guys less likely to want to kill Aurora and Lance?"

"Aurora *and* Lance? Are you all in now about Manetti's idea of the double murder?"

"Baxter came to that conclusion as well, so I'm thinking both of them can't be wrong. Anyway, let's keep going. I'm not convinced TC Pittman has much of a motive."

"Then you're going to like Greenstar Plastics even less. Wakefield Foundation found that they had some safety non-compliance in their plant. The powers-that-be at Greenstar fixed every one of the issues and then some. There's a news article chronicling their plant renovation with a photo of Wakefield, Kerrigan, and the CEO of Greenstar shaking hands and smiling. I guess I wasn't under the impression that there were instances in which the companies being investigated were cooperative about it. But most importantly, this is old news. It was last year."

"I don't remember seeing the name Greenstar in Aurora's notes. Did you have time to look through them that far back?"

"I wasn't super thorough, but yes. I didn't find a mention of Greenstar, either."

I frowned. "I think Brad punked us."

Shane let out a groan and ran a hand through his hair. "Damn it. He did, didn't he? Sorry I didn't figure that out sooner. I wasn't keeping track of which companies Kerrigan gave up versus the ones Aurora was investigating. The other two look squeaky clean, which was a red flag to me that they weren't, so I thought I was onto something overall."

"Sounds like you are onto something. Tell me."

"Well, it's kind of like the void on Wakefield's face and the murder weapon with no prints. Axion Pharmaceuticals was being investigated for drug testing on the homeless—which they make no bones about doing, and it isn't illegal. The foundation was concerned Axion wasn't getting legal consent for testing, considering a decent amount of homeless people are mentally ill. But according to everything I've read so far, Axion provided all the necessary forms and even did some acuity testing to prove competency. The foundation has yet to officially clear them, though. I don't know if that's because information went missing or because they're not done looking into them or because they're in crisis mode this week."

"Hmm." I flipped farther through the notebook until I got to Aurora's notes on Axion. "According to this…she was looking into the consent issue as well. Wait. There's something here I couldn't make out before—her handwriting is a nightmare. This…" I held the notebook out for Shane and pointed to one word. "Does this look like 'Annaleigh' to you?"

He squinted at the chicken scratches. "I think so?"

"Did anyone ever find her?"

"Yeah. A deputy tracked her down last night at a Starbucks. She said she was on her way home from work and hadn't got around to answering her messages for the day."

My eyebrows shot up. "Work? She's already a TA and a grad student at Ashmore. She's got another job on top of that? She's a busy young woman."

Shrugging, he said, "That's what she told him. She's not allowed to use her phone during work, so she doesn't always get back to people quickly. She texted me an apology last night and said she could meet with us tonight at nine, after she gets off work."

"Don't we—I—have a sex party to go to tonight?"

"I think we'll be in and out plenty before nine."

"That's what she said."

He grinned. "There you go. You're already in the spirit of the party. And speaking of which, as luck would have it, a VP from one of our other companies, Adler-Jamison Engineering, should be there."

Staring at him, I said, "Hold on. How do you know that? I thought the guest list was a secret."

"I found a spreadsheet of a guest list from two weeks ago in Aurora's flash drive files." He opened up an Excel file and turned his laptop so I could see it. I didn't recognize any of the names, but then again, I didn't run in that kind of circle.

I did a slow head shake, stunned. "How on earth did she get her hands on that?"

"Ah, that's where it gets even more interesting. I looked through the email on her burner phone—just like her husband, she had a secret burner email account as well—and found where she'd emailed someone about obtaining a guest list for her. The email account is RexXanthe69@gmail.com. I haven't been able to find any Rex Xanthes in the area."

"Probably because it's a fake name made up by a teenage boy."

"I put the cyber team on tracking down the person behind the name. Whoever it is, they were very cryptic in every email, insisting to meet in person to get the details and a fifty percent down payment for services. Want to guess how much?"

This was becoming a lot to process. "No."

He chuckled. "Fifteen hundred bucks, which is fifty percent of three thousand, which is the amount of cash she took out of her account three weeks ago."

"Oh. That's an expensive list." I thought for a moment. "But maybe not if you wanted to know if your husband was cheating on you. What's your marriage worth?"

His eyes widened. "Uhh...I feel like this is a trick question."

I waved a hand. "It was rhetorical."

"Good. After Googling a few of these names, I can understand why someone might want to silence her to keep this list from getting out. There are CEOs, big local philanthropists, and even a megachurch pastor named here."

Rolling my eyes, I griped, "If you don't want to be outed for rocking out with your cock out, do it the old-fashioned way—screw somebody else's wife in private."

"I still don't think you understand swing culture—it's more exciting than a boring old affair."

"Can we stick with talking about the case?"

"Technically, we are, but fine." He looked at his notes. "The investigation into Adler-Jamison Engineering has to do with discriminatory hiring practices. Easy to point fingers, tough to prove blame. The investigation is still open, but the foundation doesn't seem to have any actual proof of anything."

I felt a little ill as I read Aurora's notes. "Aurora wrote down 'racist assholes' and 'misogynist bastards.' Also, 'I need a shower after being here.' She made a note that there's only one woman working there who isn't a secretary, and no people of color. Oh, and someone named Stephanie Adler is by Aurora's account a fat bitch and a dirty whore. Her notes on this place are considerably less professional than any of her others. Her visit there must have been pretty nasty."

"Nasty enough to make someone want to murder her?" Shane asked.

"Maybe, especially if they're worried her negative opinion of them could spill over into a defamatory news story and sway public opinion against them."

"But how bad would that hurt them, really?" Shane asked. "Say they're branded as racists. Sure they're going to lose a few customers, but keep in mind we live in Indiana. There's no shortage of racists here. Their customer base shouldn't take that much of a hit. And once the next big news story drops, people will forget this one. If the company had done something illegal and had to pay damages and fines on top of losing customers, that's a different story. As bad as it sounds, this would be easy enough to bounce back from."

"Sad, but true," I said.

"Adler-Jamison shouldn't be the only business represented tonight that's been bitch-slapped by Wakefield and consequently had their names dragged through the mud by the media. We've also got the possibility of running into the owner of Elliston Luxury Watercraft, the COO of Pink Armadillo Cosmetics, and the CFO of Britton-Hawley Group. Oh, and there's even a Wakefield Foundation board member on the list."

"Interesting. There's got to be someone Lance was going after if he was angling for an invite to one of these parties—especially to go without his wife. Isn't that a party foul in the swinger scene?"

"Like Iris said, as a single he could have got in on some threesome action."

"Have I mentioned how much I don't want to go to this thing?"

27

Shane got a text from cyber and went to go confer with them while I continued to slog through Aurora's notes and computer files. I was hitting dead end after dead end, so I decided to take a break and track down Baxter. I wanted to ask if he'd managed to speak to Brad's friend Baldy from Dynasty Elite Security.

I found Baxter in the breakroom, sitting by himself and nursing a cup of coffee, staring at a spot on the table. He flicked his eyes at me when I walked in but said nothing. Everything suddenly flew out of my head, and I panicked. He'd apologized and been kind of sweet by making sure I got back to work earlier, but we'd also exchanged some pretty harsh words. I didn't know what to expect now. Looking for something to busy myself while I got my act together, I went over to the counter and got out a mug for some coffee.

I pulled the pot off the warmer. It had a tablespoon of coffee left in it at best. "There's no coffee?" I grumbled, mostly to myself.

Behind me, Baxter muttered, "I took the last of it, I guess."

That wasn't like him, not that he'd done anything normal in the past week. I threw a look at him over my shoulder. "And you didn't make more?"

He shook his head.

"Thanks," I said, heavy on the sarcasm as I got out the can of off-brand coffee grounds and a new filter. The air was dead and tense between us, so I blurted out what I was thinking. "I wish they'd shell out a couple more bucks for decent coffee around here, as much as we need it to keep up the crazy hours."

He stood and pushed in his chair. "After the undercover thing tonight, you don't have to keep working this case. We've got it from here."

Anger flashed through me. I plunked down the coffee can on the counter and turned to face him. "You know what, Baxter? I'm really trying to not let how you've been treating me get under my skin. You've been dismissive and have pretty much ignored me when you're not berating me for something. I understand that we shouldn't be partners anymore, but you've gone as far as to mess with my job, and there's no reason for it. Are you mad at me about something?"

His expression didn't falter, but his eyes registered something I couldn't put my finger on. "Should I be?"

I stared at him. "No."

"Good." He turned to leave.

"Wait. We need to talk."

"We don't," he insisted, his hand on the doorknob.

"Okay, then *I* need to talk. There's no reason we can't have a simple conversation—"

Wheeling around to face me, he said quietly, "No conversation between the two of us is going to be simple. And there are hundreds of reasons— every case you or I have ever worked on in our careers. If there's a hint of even friendship between the two of us, our last case blows up. Two people dead and Manetti nearly killed, and no one gets punished for it? Unacceptable. Worse, that news gets out, and every slimy lawyer in the state will be filing petitions to overturn every conviction either of us had a hand in."

"That's a little dramatic, don't you think? It's not like we broke any laws or took bribes. You're not going to get branded a dirty cop over a relationship that was over before it started."

"It's too big a risk to take."

"I disagree."

"You might have the luxury to play with fire since you have another job to fall back on. This is my career we're talking about."

He left me alone in the breakroom, angrier than I'd been when we started this conversation. And I hadn't managed to ask him about Baldy. I decided to stay put for a bit and cool down before accosting him again. I finished making the coffee, waited for it to brew, and then poured myself a full cup. After taking a few sips, I was sufficiently calm, so I headed to his cubicle.

And he wasn't there. "Damn it," I griped, looking for him over the rows of cubicles in the room. His jacket was missing from the back of his chair, and his computer screen was in sleep mode. Maybe he'd left the building. I sighed. My eyes fell on his desk, to the file folder of his notes on our case. Our files were all community property, and it wasn't an invasion of privacy for me to borrow his notes without asking. I could see him getting shitty about it with me, though, given his attitude lately, but I didn't let that stop me. I picked it up to search for any notes about his conversation with Baldy.

When I picked up the file, I bumped his mouse, which brought his computer screen to life. I happened to glance at it as I was thumbing through the notes and noticed the article that was pulled up on his internet browser. The headline read, "Local Residents Apprehensive over Upcoming Marie Collins Release." A chill ran up my spine as that name rang a warning bell in my head.

My legs going to jelly, I sank down in Baxter's chair. Marie Collins was the woman who'd kidnapped Baxter's younger brother when he was a kid. She'd been in prison for the last fifteen years paying for that crime. As I read through the article, a hollow feeling grew in my stomach. According to the local newspaper in Baxter's hometown of Boonville, Indiana, Marie Collins was scheduled to be released tomorrow, having served a fifteen-year sentence for kidnapping and confining an 'unnamed four-year-old boy' for seven months. When Rachel had been kidnapped, Baxter told me the story of his brother's kidnapping, but no one else here besides Jayne knew about it. Of course it was common knowledge in his hometown, a good three hours away, but he'd made it a point to keep it quiet around here.

I put my head in my hands, everything sliding sickly into focus. No wonder Baxter was acting so strangely. He'd told me how his family had been tormented by this incident, and I imagined the impending release of the monster who caused it was flooding them with terrible memories. His brother, Shawn, at only nineteen, was ill-equipped to emotionally handle the idea that the woman who'd ripped him from his loving family was going to get to resume her life again. If it were me, I would worry she'd try to retaliate against me and my family or possibly even kidnap another poor, unsuspecting child. I imagined there was no shortage of "what if" scenarios running through poor young Shawn's mind...not to mention the minds of the rest of his family members.

Now the phone calls I'd overheard made sense—Baxter was telling someone he loved her and wanted to see her. Rather than a girlfriend, I realized now he'd been talking to his mother. He'd told me that she'd spent most of the seven months Shawn had been gone in a state of deep depression, unable to get out of bed and do anything. If that feeling came crashing back, she would be in for a hard time.

And coming to work in the previous night's clothes, looking like he hadn't slept? Rather than a walk of shame, Baxter's appearance was the product of a six-hour trip home and back that had him driving most of the night and struggling to stay awake. Poor Baxter. Here he was, juggling working a double homicide and consoling his family from two hundred miles away, and then having to deal with me coming at him over not treating me exactly the way I'd expected.

I had to talk to him and get him to agree to let me help him. He needed someone in his corner, and I wanted to be there for him. I had to figure out a way to get him alone so we could have this conversation, where he couldn't run away from me and we wouldn't be interrupted, or worse, seen or heard. My plan would have to be foolproof.

* * *

I'd just sat down in the conference room to resume my work when Shane burst in, all smiles. "Hey, we got something."

I spun in my chair to face him. "What? Tell me it's enough that we can abandon this ridiculous party tonight."

"Sorry, not enough for that. Cyber got into Wakefield's laptop, which means I got into his super-secret email. Turns out he's been emailing RexXanthe69, too. A *lot*."

Raising an eyebrow, I asked, "A lot, as in they're sexting over email?"

"No, a lot as in RexXanthe69 is doing a *lot* of hacking for Wakefield."

"Ooh. Way more interesting. Hacking who?"

"Pretty much every business Wakefield Foundation has investigated in the last year. Wakefield had the files hidden in a folder called 'Old College Dissertations.'"

My jaw dropped. "No freaking way. That is so—"

"Unethical?" he supplied for me. "Shit yeah, it is."

"Wow. Hacking is a serious breach—one that could dig deep enough to find skeletons no one's ever supposed to know about."

"Exactly. It's one thing for Wakefield Foundation to conduct above-board investigations by way of interviews, requests for information, and even impromptu walk-throughs of operations. But hacking for company secrets to use against them? That's worth killing over."

"Especially since Brad couldn't make those particular secrets disappear, because Lance kept them all on his personal computer."

Shane nodded. "Wakefield was more in control of these investigations than anyone realized. All the cash withdrawals from his personal account coincide with requests for RexXanthe69's services. And their little code was pretty easy to break—they used the company's initials, like 'I'll have AP for you by the end of the week.'"

"Lance used his own money so he could be the keeper of the big secrets. Maybe he was getting kickbacks, too." I frowned. "Does this mean our suspect pool just got bigger, considering he was buying hacked information about more than just the four companies we're already looking into?"

"That is what that means."

I groaned. "I hate this case."

* * *

Shane and I sat in the conference room, working to match up hacked information on seventeen businesses to seventeen emails between Lance and RexXanthe69.

I complained, "I wish they would have spelled out the full names of these businesses and Lance's instructions for what dastardly deeds

RexXanthe69 should look for proof of. It would make for much better evidence in court."

Shane shrugged. "Nothing in a murder investigation can ever be easy. I assume they had a similar arrangement to the one RexXanthe69 had with Aurora—he gets the fifty percent down and the instructions in person. Less of a paper trail that way."

"Which is probably a good thing, since Lance was evidently too dumb or too lazy to not sign out of his super-secret email account."

"In his defense, his computer is password-protected, so there's one layer of security."

"Still." I sighed. "Also, I'm bummed that there's no dirt from the last hack job Lance ordered."

"For Axion Pharmaceuticals?"

"Yeah. That whole deal with testing on the homeless is so icky. I'd love to find some nasty evidence on Axion that could shut that shit down. I was hoping for a happy ending."

Shane blew out a breath. "I'm afraid there's no part of this case that's going to be a happy ending."

"True. And here's another unhappy ending—the last email exchange between the two of them is from three weeks ago, long before Lance died. RexXanthe69 promised to get him the info on 'AP' by the end of the following week, but never made good on it. Lance emailed RexXanthe69 several times after that asking where in the hell his info was, but RexXanthe69 never responded."

"RexXanthe69 took the money and ran?"

"That's dumb, because Wakefield was keeping this hacker flush with cash. Why walk away from that?"

"Maybe RexXanthe69 got caught and is in jail."

I frowned. "I never thought of that. How would we find that out if we don't know RexXanthe69's real name or address?"

Shane replied, "Well, he or she has to live kind of close if they're exchanging cash on a fairly regular basis. We can look at arrests for hacking and cyber-attack in the last three weeks. There can't be that many of them."

* * *

While Shane went to chase that information, I went to the lab to find out if Amanda and Beck had uncovered anything that might help us narrow down the identity of the killer.

I walked in and asked hopefully, "Any smoking guns in here?"

Amanda turned from the bottle of Xanax she was processing and removed her mask. "Unfortunately, no. You find any?"

"We know Aurora and Lance both used the same hacker to obtain information for them. Evidently RexXanthe69 has been a busy little bee, hacking into the private computer systems for all eighteen businesses Wakefield Foundation has investigated over the past year. We wondered how the foundation got enough dirt on so many places to ruin them. Now we know."

"Damn. That's unethical."

"You think?"

Beck, who was across the room repackaging some clothing evidence, interjected, "RexXanthe69? I think I know that guy."

My jaw dropped. "What?"

He mused, "I mean, if that's who I assume it is. But it's got to be him. That's totally his sense of humor."

As I texted, *Come to the lab now*, to Shane, Baxter, and Sterling, I asked Beck, "How exactly do you know this guy?"

"I don't know him, know him. But I've fought alongside him through many bloody battles. We're part of the same guild."

Amanda's face was a mask of utter confusion. "What in the actual hell are you talking about, Beck?"

He rolled his eyes. "*Xanthe's Quest*, only the biggest, most popular MMO at the moment. Duh."

She and I both shrugged and shook our heads.

He heaved out a sigh. "It's the new *World of Warcraft*."

"Oh," I replied, still not completely knowing what in the hell he was getting at.

The three detectives burst through the doors.

Sterling griped at me, "This had better be—" He stopped dead in his tracks when he realized Amanda was in the room. "I mean, what have you got for us to see?"

"It's for you to hear," I replied. "Beck, tell them how you know RexXanthe69."

Clearing his throat, Beck explained, "Well, as I said, I'm a member of his guild in *Xanthe's Quest*. We've never met personally."

"Then you *don't* know him, Becky," Sterling snapped, unable to hold his tongue where Beck was concerned.

Beck grimaced and stood straighter. "I've spoken with him during battles. He once told me I had excellent sword-fighting skills. He's a legend, and also a well-known Twitch streamer, so that's some pretty high praise."

None of the detectives seemed impressed.

Shane said, "So does that mean you can contact him, then? Maybe through the game?"

I said, "If he's a streamer, doesn't he have a pretty big online presence? He'd be easy to track down that way."

Shrugging, Beck replied, "Not exactly. He's an anonymous streamer—he never shows his face during a stream, and no one uses their real names on Twitch. Trying to contact him through the game would probably get us the fastest response, but...he's been offline lately. No game play, no streaming. No one knows if he got mad and quit or went on vacation or what."

Baxter's face became concerned. "How long has it been since he went offline?"

"I don't know. Like, two weeks? Our guild has been lost without him. He's our general. When he comes back, he's not going to be pleased with our progress."

Sterling asked, "Can you get on the game from one of the computers here?"

Beck replied, "Yeah, I do it all the time."

Frowning, Sterling said, "While you're supposed to be working?"

"No, during breaks," Beck said defensively, realizing his mistake.

"I thought you spent your breaks pretending to smoke."

Beck's cheeks colored. "Not always...I—I mean, sometimes I check in on my guild."

Amanda and I shared an amused glance. We hated Beck's all-too-frequent smoke breaks. Everyone knew he only pretended to smoke so he was allowed more breaks than the rest of us.

Shane said, "Send him a message that we need to speak to him ASAP. If he's still showing as offline, start asking your guild people if they know how to contact him in real life. Meanwhile, we'll run down his social accounts."

Baxter had looked like he was deep in thought throughout this entire conversation. He finally said to Beck, "Does the word Westerley mean something to you?"

Beck snickered, as if Baxter's question was totally stupid. "Uh, yeah. It's only the name of the entire realm."

Baxter's eyes widened. "I think I just figured out who our Carnival Cove John Doe was."

28

Everyone started talking at once, and Sterling had to whistle to break up the cacophony.

Baxter turned to me. "You emailed me a photo of the shirt our John Doe was wearing, hoping it could help with determining his identity. I researched it and found that it was a reference to *Xanthe's Quest*. Since it's the most played game out there right now, it wasn't helpful at the time, but now..."

Sterling said to Beck, "How do we find out this nerd's real name?"

Beck shrugged. "If he's been thorough with his anonymity, you won't."

I knew from experience you couldn't say stuff like that to Sterling during a homicide investigation because he'd turn it into a personal crusade.

As if on cue, Sterling promised, "Oh, I'll find him," and stormed out of the lab.

Baxter hurried after him, and Shane and I wandered back to the conference room. I couldn't decide whether I was excited or bummed about Baxter's revelation. We were closer to finding out our John Doe's identity—maybe, if Baxter's hypothesis was correct—and it would be pretty major to be able to tie his death to our current investigation. But that didn't get us any closer to figuring out who killed our now possibly three victims.

As Shane and I sat back down at the conference table, I said, "Well, Sterling will be out on *Sterling's Quest* for a while, and I'm sure he won't come back until he learns RexXanthe69's real name or dies trying. So what rabbit hole do you want to go down now?"

He wrinkled his brow. "Well, since it's highly likely these deaths all have to do with the hacking that was done, I say we research the hell out of these companies and see if something pops."

I nodded and grabbed a laptop. Before I dived in, though, I fired off a text to Baxter. *Did you get any information out of Baldy or Dynasty Elite Security?* I didn't want to have another face-to-face conversation with him until I'd had time to think about exactly what I wanted to express to him.

His response was, *Who's Baldy?*

The bald guy you followed this morning. IDK his name.

IDK either. The Dynasty receptionist couldn't or wouldn't tell me who was driving that vehicle today. Everyone has access to the keys, and they don't have to sign vehicles out. Said she couldn't tell who the guy was by the photo.

I replied, *Sounds like bullshit to me.*

Agreed. They've got something shady going on, like maybe their thug roster is full of ex-cons. I did manage to verify they only provide personal security—no businesses, so no tie there.

Well, that was a dead end, unless we could get Dynasty to cough up their employee list. We could get a warrant, but if they were as shady as Baxter thought and they knew we were looking for Baldy, it was likely they'd protect him.

Shane said, "By the way, there were exactly zero hacking and/or cyberattack arrests in the past three weeks in Marion and the surrounding counties. Evidently it's not a big thing in central Indiana. Since our guy isn't in jail, I'd agree there's a decent chance he's your John Doe."

"Let's hope so."

I took half the businesses in Lance's hack file and Shane took the other half. We both managed to weed out a few, including Greenstar Plastics, but we were still left with E&X Distributors, McIver-Ramirez Financial, DKE Fittings Corp, and Whitacre Honey Farm in addition to the ones we'd already been researching.

I said, "What in the world could a honey farm do that's so dastardly?"

Shane explained, "They repackaged bulk honey from Costco with their own label at triple the price."

"Well, I guess that's one way to make money. Is it really illegal, though?"

"It is when you put 'Local honey, product of Indiana' on the label."

"Eh. Kind of pales in comparison to McIver-Ramirez Financial's Ponzi scheme."

He laughed. "It certainly does. As does DKE Fittings Corp's price gouging after their only competitor went bankrupt and closed up shop. At quadruple the price, the part in question still came in at under fifty dollars."

"Wow. But the clear winner—or should I say loser—is E&X Distributors for overworking their truckers and falsifying their mileage and time on the road. Tired truckers being forced to drive put thousands of people's lives at risk. Both McIver-Ramirez and E&X went under because of Wakefield uncovering their sins. Lots of motive."

"DKE Fittings Corp survived, but they also sent plenty of threatening emails to Wakefield personally, so they're still worth a look. Whitacre Honey Farm is no longer, but they weren't a real farm, anyway. I think the whole operation was one middle-aged woman with a Costco membership, a funnel, and sticky hands."

I laughed. "She could take her brilliant business model and go repackage some other food and sell it. Somehow, I don't see her as a threat."

"You may change your tune once you hear her go full Karen on a voicemail message Wakefield saved." He clicked on a file on Lance's laptop, and an enraged woman's voice filled the room: "*You son of a bitch! My livelihood is gone because of you, Wakefield. You have everything, and yet you felt the need to rip my small business away from me, the only thing that was keeping me going. Now I have nothing, while you sit there in your Armani suit with your bimbo wife and laugh it up. I hope you die and rot in hell! And that news bitch, too!*"

I snickered. "Damn. Karen mad."

"I'd say so."

"But murderously mad?"

"How many cases have you had where people have killed over far less?" he asked.

"Fair point, but she'll have to wait until tomorrow. I'm betting if her failed small business was all she had, she's not invited to the big, fancy sex party."

"You are correct."

I made a face. "Speaking of, I'm going to need to eat before I go, or I won't be very charming. I'll be back."

* * *

I needed to clear my head, so I grabbed some fast food and went home, hoping my family would be there. They were. I got a very warm welcome from a sweet little boy, a sweet big dog, and even my sweet-but-sometimes-salty sister. She'd made so much progress emotionally in the last four months, but still some days were not the best. This was one of the good days, and I was glad I took the time to go home.

"I know I can't ask, but how's the case coming along?" she asked as we sat down around the living room coffee table and had an indoor picnic.

"It's coming along. Vic and I get to go u-n-d-e-r-c-o-v-e-r at a posh party tonight in Geist." Before long, Rachel and I were going to have to come up with a new system of censoring our speech in front of Nate, because he was starting to get the hang of spelling easy words like dog and cat.

"Wow. Can you fool posh people into thinking you're one of them?"

I laughed. We always joked that we were trailer trash from way back, which was a completely accurate assessment. When we were kids, our mom dragged us from one shitty place to the next. More often than not, home was a roach-infested rental trailer, which was a step up from the time we lived with her drug dealer boyfriend in a sketchy downtown Indy neighborhood.

"I'm certainly going to try."

Her expression had become worried. "Will it be...d-a-n-g-e-r-o-u-s?"

"No, it shouldn't." Shouldn't being the operative word. There was no reason to panic her. "Besides, I have Vic there."

"I thought he was still off work."

"He is, but we needed him to play my h-u-s-b-a-n-d, because I don't think anyone else wanted to."

As if on cue, Nate piped up, "I saw Caden's new dog...d-o-g today. I can spell, too."

Rachel and I burst out laughing. Before long, this kid would be outsmarting both of us.

While we finished dinner, Nate told us all about his friend Caden's new puppy, which his mother had brought to preschool for Caden to do show and tell. Getting to pet this puppy only fueled Nate's desire for a new puppy of his own, but Rachel and I stood in a united front.

I showered and fixed my hair and makeup, hoping my look would be in keeping with whatever dress Jayne had found for me. When I left, I gave Rachel and Nate a hug. I noticed that Rachel held on longer than normal. I hated that she worried about me. It was my job to worry about her.

* * *

When I got back to the station, I literally ran into Sterling as he barreled out of the men's room.

"Watch it," he bellowed, not even looking my direction as he gave me a shove out of his way.

"You watch it, you ass." I lowered my voice. "What if I'd been Amanda?"

He stopped and pounded the side of his fist against the wall. "Damn it, I'm sorry. I'm pissed as hell I haven't found this RexXanthe69 punk yet."

I figured as much. "You'll find him. I have no doubt you'll get the job done. You know, you don't have to waste your time tonight going to the party just to listen over the coms. We can give you the highlights later, and I'm sure Baxter will record it."

"Are you kidding? Miss you being all awkward and uncomfortable and trying desperately not to get boned, live? Not on your life."

It had been bad enough during my last undercover mission to have Baxter in my ear while I was trying to pick up a guy, but now I'd have Sterling, too. So much for trying to talk him out of going tonight. If I hadn't been nervous already, now I really was.

I frowned. "Great. Just don't distract me with a bunch of your nonsense."

"I wouldn't dream of it."

Not buying that for a second, I headed past him to Jayne's office to get into my dress for the evening. Vic had arrived just before I did and was putting on the tux the department had rented for him.

I knocked on Jayne's open door. "Reporting for undercover duty," I said, a little nervous hitch in my voice I wasn't expecting.

Jayne stood and came over to put an arm around me. "You'll do just fine. How could you not in that thing?" She gestured across the room at her coat rack to where my borrowed clothing for the evening was hanging.

The dress was stunning. I wasn't convinced I could pull it off. For starters, it was made entirely of gold sequins. No blending into the crowd in this thing. And the neckline was going to put my assets on full display, whether I wanted them there or not. It was also for the most part backless. Thank goodness there was a little drape to the skirt, otherwise there would be literally nowhere to hide my mic pack. In theory, it was the perfect dress for a sex party—unless you weren't there for the intended reason. Oh, and it was worth two thousand dollars, on loan from one of Jayne's friends. If I broke it, I'd have to buy it.

Jayne pulled the blinds in her office and helped me stuff myself into the dress and zip up. I had the slightest amount of wiggle room, even though it was a size smaller than the last new dress I'd bought a couple of months ago, so that was one positive in this shitshow. Regardless, I'd still have a long night of gut clenching and proper posture ahead of me. I used a garter holster to strap the mic pack to the back of my upper thigh, hidden in the space under my left butt cheek.

Jayne stepped back and smiled. "Absolutely beautiful."

"You're sure I'm not overdressed?" I looked down at all the exposed skin I wasn't used to seeing. "Or underdressed?"

"You're perfect. Now get out there and do your job, and don't let one of those skeevy old men try to take advantage of you."

"Anyone lays a hand on me, and Vic will be on them in a heartbeat."

"While I appreciate that, we want to first and foremost keep your cover intact. Just stay at arm's length."

"Oh, trust me, that's the plan."

As I walked toward her door, she said in a tight voice, "Please be safe."

"I will."

I turned down a hallway to find Baxter, Sterling, and Shane coming my way, laden with gear and heading toward the door to the back parking lot.

Sterling's eyebrows shot up. "Damn, Matthews. Not bad." Quite a lavish compliment coming from him.

Shane said, "You clean up nice. I think you'll be believable as a socialite with a side of kink. Have you been practicing your bored rich lady face?"

I mean mugged him. "I have resting bitch face. Does that count?"

"Close enough. Good luck tonight."

Baxter said nothing. He didn't even look my way as he passed me in the hall. The three of them exited the building. Disappointed, but quickly admonishing myself for feeling that way, I turned around to find Vic coming out of the men's room looking like a complete and total movie star in his tuxedo.

I griped, "Oh, this isn't fair at all."

"What?"

"You're covered from neck to toe, in layers, no less. You get to wear pants. You get to have pockets. You can wear normal underwear. You're not in imminent danger of turning an ankle in your shoes." I huffed. "And you're *still* prettier than me."

He leaned his head back and laughed, but he sobered quickly and looked me in the eye. "That's absolutely untrue. You're gorgeous."

"Eh, whatever," I grumbled.

"What, am I not the person you wanted to hear that from tonight?"

I frowned. "I didn't say that."

"You didn't have to." He held out his arm to me. "Come on, wifey. Let's go not get laid at this party."

29

Vic drove the two of us to the party in a rented luxury sports car. Compared to my last undercover mission, where I'd spent a whopping twenty dollars on drinks and got to wear my own clothes, this operation was rather expensive. It put added pressure on me to get the job done, even though my head was less in the game this time than ever before—partly because I'd hatched a fairly stupid plan of my own to try to accomplish this evening. Every time I'd tried to talk to Baxter lately, there had either been other people around or he'd managed to get away from me. I'd thought up a way to get him alone for a few minutes and have no one question it. Now I just had to find the right time to set everything in motion.

Once Vic parked in the cul-de-sac near the home, he and I put on our masks, switched on our coms, and let the detectives know we'd arrived. We'd passed their SUV a couple of houses down, lined up with a dozen much nicer vehicles, inconspicuous enough with its tinted windows.

Shane said, "Ellie and Vic, an FYI, the two of you will be on different channels so your conversations will record separately. It'll also help so you won't be distracted by hearing each other's conversations. If the two of you need to communicate, you'll have to find each other and speak in person. Okay?"

"Okay," I replied, beginning to get a little nervous.

"Got it," Vic said, giving my arm a squeeze. "You ready for this?"

"As ready as I'll ever be," I muttered, opening my door to get out of the car. Between my too-tall heels, the too-close-to-the-ground car, and my nearly-too-tight dress, I needed some help getting out. Noticing my struggle, Vic ran around to my door and took both of my hands, pulling me up and out of the car and not letting go until I was steady on my feet. "See what I mean about my stupid outfit?" I griped.

He chuckled. "What's that old saying? 'Beauty is pain'?"

"This is already my least favorite undercover op, and it hasn't even started yet."

Vic tucked my hand in the crook of his arm and led me toward the door. "I haven't done one in years, so I'm kind of looking forward to it."

I grumbled under my breath and tried to prepare myself for what was on the other side of that door. Vic and I were met by a bouncer outside who checked our (fake) names off his list, then by a butler inside who took my wrap and welcomed us warmly to the soiree. Once Vic and I entered the great room, it was time to part ways. And, of course, the first thing that happened to me was that one of the waitstaff descended on me and tried to shove a champagne flute into my hand. I had to tell her no three times, the last time so firmly she shrank back from me, aghast. Great. My lack of proper upbringing never failed to rear its ugly head when it mattered. I took a deep breath and scanned the room for my first mark. I didn't immediately see him, so I walked slowly around the room, trying to get close enough to eavesdrop on a few conversations but not get sucked in.

A little flustered and a lot sickened by the premise of this party, I was off any game I ever had for picking up random men. Plus, it wasn't exactly easy to accost guys and flirt my heart out when the man I had feelings for was listening to my every word.

"Matthews, quit stalling. Get this show on the road," Sterling barked in my ear. "Manetti's already got two different offers for blow jobs."

I glanced across the room at Vic. Damned if he didn't already have two women hanging on his every word. Not that I was surprised—anytime we were out together, women swooned over him.

"Not helpful. We're here to get information, not hummers," I muttered, getting a snicker from Shane. "Now get out of my head."

I forced myself to calm the hell down, focusing my mindset on the investigation rather than the situation. I stood up straighter and walked purposely toward my first mark, Douglas Busing, age fifty-six, married with three grown children, and VP of Adler-Jamison Engineering. Pushing seven feet tall, he was an easy one to spot. I hoped his personality was more attractive than his photo, or it was going to be a challenge to feign interest in him. As I got closer, I noted that his photo was much more flattering than the real thing. Despite his height, he probably weighed less than I did. His suit was inches too short for his arms and legs, and his mask seemed to be a child-sized version. No way this dead-eyed, slack-jawed weirdo was going to get any action tonight. I'd seen corpses more lifelike than this guy. His skin was even similar to dead people I'd examined—sallow, dry, and practically see-through.

I decided to go with a meet-cute to break the ice. He was standing near the massive fireplace taking up most of one wall of the room, so I weaved around some furniture and positioned myself out of his line of sight. As I neared him, I turned around and bumped into him from behind.

Whirling around, I placed a hand on his arm. It was like grabbing onto a skeleton in a suit. I abruptly released him so I could slide into character. "I'm so sorry." Looking up at him through my lashes, I smiled. "Oh, hello there."

"No need...to apologize."

His voice a gravelly monotone, he spoke so slowly I thought he might have a head injury. But then he lifted the glass he was holding and chugged three fingers of Scotch in two gulps, and I understood why he seemed to be in slow motion. If I had to guess, I'd say he'd also taken a pill or two at some point tonight. He reminded me of Lurch from the old *The Addams Family* reruns I remembered seeing at my grandmother's house when I had to stay with her during my mother's frequent weekend benders.

"My name...is Douglas." He offered his hand.

"Nice to meet you, Douglas. I'm Ellen." I shook his clammy, flaccid hand and forced down a shudder.

"A lovely name...for a lovely woman." If he didn't start talking faster, this interview was going to take all night.

"Um...so what do you do?"

"I prefer to do anal...but I'll consider—"

I held up a hand, willing my dinner to stay put as Sterling choked on a laugh that spiraled into a coughing fit in my ear. "I meant for a living. The night is young. Let's not get ahead of ourselves."

Lurch seemed disappointed, but he answered politely, "I'm a VP...at Adler-Jamison Engineering."

Did he not understand the element of anonymity or the purpose of the masks at this party? Douglas was a common enough name that no one could definitively identify him as being a partygoer, but there was no question about the identity of Douglas, VP at Adler-Jamison Engineering.

I smiled. "How interesting. Isn't your company in hot water over unfair hiring practices?"

His eyebrows rose above his too-small mask. "Uh...no?"

"So you're not under investigation for that by Wakefield Foundation *and* by Aurora Bennett of WIND-TV?"

"Slander...all lies," he slurred.

"I bet you've been pretty angry at Lance Wakefield and Aurora Bennett for a while, am I right?"

"They both...got what was...coming to them." Lurch reached out one of his long, spindly arms in front of me to snag a drink from a passing waiter's tray. In doing so, he brushed the back of his hand across my left breast. I was pretty sure it was on purpose, but I didn't react.

Sterling said, "Stay on that, Matthews. Sounds like he's got an axe to grind."

I said, "Oh, absolutely. It seemed like they were both going after your company with both barrels—did it feel personal to you?"

Lurch nodded. "Lance and our CFO...used to be...an item."

Shane exclaimed, "Jackpot! Keep it up, Ellie."

"Did they have a bad breakup?" I asked.

"Very bad. It was before...my time at...the company."

"How long ago was that?"

"Five years."

Sterling said, "Our dead couple just had their four-year anniversary last month. What do you want to bet Wakefield dumped the CFO for his wife?"

Shane said, "Or that he was cheating on Aurora with the CFO. In her story notes, she called the CFO a fat bitch and a dirty whore. Maybe she knew about it."

I said to Lurch, "That's been a minute, but I'm sure people still talk. What do the other employees say?"

His words were all starting to slur together. "There's talk they had...a nooner...every Friday...on her desk." Leaning down toward me, he added, "There's a desk...in the study...I'd like to bend...you over."

"Ooh, tempting," I choked out. "But back to our conversation. Do you think Lance Wakefield and Aurora Bennett were targeting your company to get back at your CFO?"

"Possibly." He gulped his fresh drink, again in record time.

I needed to work fast—he was well on his way toward blackout drunk territory. If he didn't slow down, he was going to drink himself into missing out on all the action later. Then again, I hardly blamed him for engaging in a little self-medication. The thought of coming to a party with your spouse with the express purpose of cheating on them by the end of the evening had to weigh heavily on some of these people. At least I hoped it did.

"Did they have a long-running feud going on? Would she have retaliated?"

He shrugged. "Possibly."

"'Possibly' doesn't give us shit to go on, Matthews. Do better," Sterling griped.

"Does your CFO attend these parties?" I asked.

Lurch shook his head, his body listing to one side as he did so.

Between Sterling's bossy interjections and the clock ticking on Lurch's impending loss of consciousness, I was losing my focus. "Did she, uh...ever mention being jealous of his wife?"

"I don't recall." His eyelids started looking heavy, like Nate's when he was exhausted and fighting falling asleep.

"Um..." I couldn't think of anything else to ask.

As if reading my mind, Shane said, "Ask if she has a history of being violent or abusive."

I blurted out, "Does she have a history of being violent or abusive?"

Instead of answering, Lurch stumbled toward me, hands out and going for my breasts as his knees buckled. I managed to block his grabby hands in time and shove him in the direction of a nearby couch, where he landed, passed out cold.

"What happened, Matthews? You cut out, and there was a bunch of rustling," Sterling said.

Vic appeared at my side, his expression a mix of worry and surprise as his eyes ping-ponged between Lurch and me. "Are you okay? I saw this guy try to grab you, and by the time I got over here, he's out for the count. Did you clock him?"

Shane's worried voice said, "He tried to grab you?"

I smiled, thankful Vic was here, even though he'd run the risk of blowing his cover to come to my aid. "I'm okay, guys. Our boy had too much to drink and tried to use my breasts as a handle when he started keeling over. I managed not to get myself groped."

Visibly relieved, but pissed, Vic mumbled something about, "If Slenderman here wasn't already unconscious, I'd—"

"Let's get back to work," Baxter said. "Your next marks are Walt Elliston, owner of Elliston Luxury Watercraft and Robert Hawley, CFO of Britton-Hawley Group. And not to be that guy, but I just stalked Stephanie Adler's social media and found out she has the mother of all alibis for Tuesday night. She was in the hospital having a baby. That lead is toast."

"That would account for the 'fat bitch' comment," Sterling said.

I bit back a growl of frustration. All that nonsense with Lurch for nothing.

Vic and I went our separate ways. I milled through the crowd looking for my marks. Walt Elliston was a grandfatherly-looking man whose yacht dealership was investigated by Wakefield Foundation last fall for employing undocumented workers, but it was ultimately deemed above board. No matter the outcome, there could still have been bad blood over the witch hunt Lance put his company through. Robert Hawley was tall, handsome, and built like a linebacker, and thankfully more my age at thirty-nine. Britton-Hawley Group had been investigated a while back over allegations of fraud in a handful of their advertising campaigns. The ad agency stuck to their guns, saying the purpose of advertising is to build up their customers' brands and gloss over any negatives. It was such a gray area, the foundation wasn't able to definitively prove anything. Britton-

Hawley Group only suffered a quick black eye until the media moved on to the next story.

Walt Elliston's captain's hat and mouthful of false teeth were all I needed to pick him out of the crowd. I approached him and said, "I hear you're the man to see about luxury watercraft."

"Yes, darlin', I certainly am," he drawled in a fake Southern accent. According to the background I'd read on him, he was born and raised in the Indianapolis area, and no locals had that kind of exaggerated hick accent. In the southern end of the state on the fringe of the Mason-Dixon line, maybe, but not here. Poser.

He seemed nice enough, though, so I relaxed a bit. I smiled. "I'm sorry to hear about your good name being dragged through the mud by that awful watchdog Lance Wakefield. He tried to do the same thing to my husband's company a while back. What an awful, arrogant man."

Walt waved a hand. "Water under the bridge, ma'am. What do you say the two of us find a quiet place to talk?"

Ooh. Number one rule for women—never go to a less populated area with someone you don't know.

Even Sterling was on my side with this one. "Stranger danger. Find a reason to stay where you are."

I put my hand on his arm. "I know you're itching to get on with the point of this party, but I need to stay and get some food in me to keep my stamina up."

"Oh, there'll be plenty of time for that. Let me have you all to myself for a minute." He took hold of my upper arm.

I'd had enough. "Hands off, old man."

His jaw dropped, and he immediately released his grasp on me. "What? I wasn't trying to do any harm, darlin'. No need to get your panties in a bunch."

Shane asked, "Ellie, you okay? You can abort this one if he's making you feel uncomfortable."

I narrowed my eyes at Walt. "I call the shots. Not you."

The old man gulped. I couldn't tell if he was scared of me, turned on, or a little of both. "Yes, ma'am."

"Now, I want to know what you know about Lance Wakefield and his foundation."

"He's dead."

"I know that. I want some dirt. That foundation needs to be dismantled, and with him gone, it'll be much easier to do."

He guffawed. "Sounds like you've got a mighty big score to settle, I reckon."

"You have no idea."

"Well, I'm sorry to tell you, but I don't know any dirt. When the foundation investigated my business, they were polite and courteous. I didn't feel like it was a witch hunt. I didn't have anything to hide, so I wasn't upset about being scrutinized. I think we need those kinds of organizations to keep us honest."

I stared at him. "So you abuse and objectify women in your spare time, but when it comes to business you're a freaking choir boy?"

"Damn, Matthews, ease up," Sterling warned.

Walt's larger-than-life smile faded. "You, little lady, need to learn yourself some manners. You're not worth the trouble." With that, he turned on his heel and left me alone.

"Great job, Matthews. You drive your first mark to drink himself into a coma and piss off your second."

Shane said, "It's fine, Ellie. You'll get the next one."

I huffed out an exasperated breath. "One more old creepy guy tries to feel me up or kidnap me, and I'm out of here." Waylaying one of the wait staff, I grabbed three mini beef Wellingtons from her tray and began inhaling them. They were heavenly.

Sterling replied, "Suck it up, buttercup. You're not leaving until you find something we can use. And you do realize you're at a *sex* party, not a tea party, right?"

Shane said, "Stay aloof enough that no one touches you. You were too nice to that guy at first, and I'm afraid he saw it as an invitation."

Baxter asked, "Have you found Robert Hawley?"

I swallowed before replying, "Nope. Haven't seen him anywhere." I popped the third Wellington into my mouth.

Baxter said, "Then your next mark needs to be Hal Casper. He's on the board of Wakefield foundation. Thick white mustache, probably about your height, barrel chest. Should be easy to spot."

Around my last mouthful of the most delicious appetizer I'd ever had, I mumbled, "Fan-freaking-tastic. Another old guy. Does he have any interests besides being a rich asshole and making women feel uncomfortable?"

Baxter said, "He's a dog lover. Lead with that."

I decided now was the time to make my move. Pretending not to have heard him, I waited a beat and griped, "So that's a no?"

Sterling piped up, "You deaf, Matthews? Baxter just said he's a dog lover."

I said, "Hello? Anyone there?"

There was a loud tapping sound in my ear as if someone were thumping a microphone. Shane said, "Did you hear any of that, Ell—"

Interrupting, I said, "I guess I'm on my own, then. Thanks a lot, guys."

I heard chatter about how my com must have been malfunctioning and noticed Vic coming my way. I had to hide my glee when I heard Sterling snap at Baxter (the unofficial tech guy) to go find me and fix it. There was a muffled conversation in the background about how Baxter would gain access to the house.

Vic came close to me and murmured in my ear, "Is your earpiece dead? The team can hear you, but they said you don't seem to be hearing them."

I replied quietly, "That would explain the sudden radio silence."

"Detective Baxter is on his way to fix it. Go down the hallway to the right and find the study. It'll be the last door on the left. It's got an exterior door. He'll be waiting there for you to let him in."

"Roger that."

30

I had to seriously control myself in order to stroll rather than skip down the hallway, thrilled my dastardly plan had actually worked. I knew it was beyond unprofessional to halt an undercover op for a personal matter, but Baxter had given me no choice. Making sure no one saw me disappear into the study, I locked the door behind me. First things first, I removed my mask and slipped a hand up my dress to switch off my mic pack. Seeing a shadow outside the French doors, I hurried over and unlocked them to let Baxter inside.

He looked everywhere but at me, refusing to make eye contact. Holding out his hand, he grumbled, "Give me your earpiece."

"Nick, look at me."

His head snapped up, eyes flashing. He mouthed, "Is your mic on?"

"No."

His expression grew dark. "Is your earpiece even broken, or is this a total waste of my time?"

"Look, I'm sorry for ambushing you, but—"

Cutting me off, he barked, "We're in the middle of an undercover op. Bringing me in here was reckless, and you should know better. What the hell do you want?"

He wasn't wrong. I didn't have time to dance around what I needed to say. I blew out a breath. "I know what's going on with your family right now."

"What?" he breathed, going pale.

"I know that Marie Collins is getting out of prison tomorrow. I assume your family is understandably upset by that." I took a step closer to him and softened my tone. "And I know you're upset."

He had to struggle to hold his stern expression. "You shouldn't have done this. I'm getting out of here before this whole thing blows up in our faces."

I caught his arm. "Not until you talk to me. Please let me help. I can tell you're about to fall apart."

He pulled away from my grasp, his expression going flat. "We never had the time to really get to know each other. You don't know me as well as you think."

"You're joking, right? We've been to hell and back together. We know each other."

"We've worked closely, what, about six weeks out of the past six months? Don't forget the rest of the time we weren't even on speaking terms."

I knew he'd do everything in his power to fight me on this, but I'd promised myself I wouldn't give in and snap back. This was too important. I smiled. "Even so, you've always been there for me when I needed you. Let me do that for you this time. I want to help you get through this."

The brave face he'd been wearing since the last case fell away. He looked like a sad little boy. "I can't let you."

I took another step toward him and put my hands on his arms. He didn't flinch away this time. "Everything and everyone else can go to hell. I only care about you. I won't stand by and let you go through this alone because of some stupid rule."

Eyes glistening, he said, "This is my problem, and I don't want to drag you into it."

"I want to be in it. I want to be with you. We're a team. No wonder we haven't solved this damn case yet. We're with the wrong partners."

He hung his head. "I know. And I'm sorry I keep pushing you away, Ellie. I'm sorry for the way I've been treating you. It's killing me, and I feel like I'm doing everything wrong. But...I don't know what else to do. I just...I can't deal with being around you and trying to pretend you mean nothing to me on top of dealing with my family issues. I'm too spent."

"I know you are." I reached up and cradled his cheek with my hand. "Lean on me for once. We'll figure the rest out later."

"What's going down with my family...it's bad. There are things you don't know."

"Then tell me. You know I'm the last person who has room to judge on family drama."

He sighed and placed his forehead against mine. "Not here. We'll talk soon." He smiled slightly, for what felt like the first time in forever. "Thanks for ambushing me."

"Anytime."

His blue eyes bored into mine, and he came closer so he could brush my lips with his. That was all the invitation I needed. I pressed my lips back against his. He wrapped his arms around me, his hands warm on my bare back, and deepened our kiss, hot and lusty. Backing me up against the wall, he leaned into me, his body tight against mine. I let out a little moan, fully lost in the long-awaited, absolute bliss of being near him again. It was intoxicating.

He was different. Our kiss was fiery and urgent, unlike any we'd shared before. I supposed he must have noticed a difference in me as well, my pent-up sexual frustration spilling out into our kiss. Much too soon, he released his hold and backed away from me. We stared at each other for a moment, both of us breathless.

He gave me a genuine smile and turned and exited through the French doors.

I was so relieved, not to mention euphorically happy, I nearly burst into tears of joy. But I hadn't brought any makeup with me, so if I cried, I'd be a raccoon, which would be noticeable even with my stupid mask. Baxter had kissed all the lipstick off my lips, not that I minded in the slightest. I took several deep breaths to calm myself, put my mask back on, and bit my lips, hoping to coax some natural color into them.

I turned my mic pack back on and said, "Com check, boys."

Shane said, "Can you hear us now?"

"Loud and clear. Heading back out into the fray."

Head held high, I felt like I could take on the world. I slipped out of the study and rejoined the party, zeroing in on my mark. Gross. This guy was round and bald and a total alcoholic, evidenced by the tip of his knobby red nose peeking out from beneath his mask and the stench of gin rolling off him as I got close. Thankfully, in situations like this, the alcoholic in me was repulsed by the thought of ingesting alcohol, lest I turn back into one of these losers. A high horse to be on, I knew, but cautionary tales solidified my commitment to sobriety way more than AA meetings ever did.

Eye to eye with Hal Casper, I smiled. "Hey, there. I'm Ellen."

Hal leered at me, looking me up and down. Creep. But I supposed, to be fair, this was literally a meat market, and I was offering myself willingly, at least as far as he knew.

"Hel-*lo*. I'm Hal. Wanna party?"

Sterling jeered, "That was fast. But I guess pickings are probably getting slim if he's settling for you, Matthews."

Ignoring Sterling, I smiled at my mark. "Maybe. Tell me about yourself, Hal."

"I'm rich and I'm hung, and that's all you need to concern yourself with, sweetheart."

Sterling lost it, dissolving into belly laughs. Shane told him to shut up.

I said, "Mmm, and humble." I scanned the room and spotted Vic. I pointed to him and said to Hal, "Make your case for why I should choose you over him tonight."

Hal blanched for a moment, then straightened up to his full height, a whole half-inch taller than me now. "I've got more clout in this town than that pissant could ever hope to have."

I leaned closer. "I'm listening."

"I'm the CEO of a multi-million-dollar company I built from the ground up."

"So are half the men here, *sweetheart*. I need more."

A vein popping out in his forehead, he sputtered, "I'm a known philanthropist. I'm on the board of several non-profits."

I smiled. "Now we're talking. A man with a conscience is a real turn-on. Tell me, how are you changing the world?"

"I give a shit ton of money to cancer research."

I let my smile fall away. "So does everyone. Boring."

"I...I'm...on the board that's been working tirelessly to map out, pave, and maintain all the new exercise trails popping up all over the county."

"So even more douchey runners and bikers will want to move here. Great."

Sterling interjected, "I'm telling Manetti you said that."

Hal blustered, "Now, now...I'm not finished. I'm on the executive board of an organization that calls out corporations over bad business practices."

"Oh," I cooed, cringing inwardly as I ran one finger along the plunging neckline of my gown. My not-so-subtle trick worked. Dude's eyes were locked on my cleavage. "Tell me more. Have you dismantled any evil corporations lately?"

"We're working on several...although we're kind of at a standstill...with the, uh..." He trailed off, evidently mesmerized by my rack. My trick had worked a little too well.

I put my finger under his chin and raised his face to meet mine. "You're at a standstill? With your connections, surely nothing gets in your way."

He frowned. "Nothing can compete with our CEO being at the epicenter of a murder-suicide."

"Oh, you're part of *that* organization." I leaned closer. "So how well do you know that Wakefield guy? What do you think made him snap?"

"I'm not sure about that, but I can tell you he was getting too big for his britches."

I didn't feel like that would make a person snap, but it could make someone else want to kill him. "How so?"

"Taking on a holier-than-thou attitude with the board and his staff."

My jaw dropped. "Why did he think he was above the rest of you? I mean, didn't he come to these parties, too? You two had a not-so-holy vice in common."

He shook his head. "He was invited but never showed up. I would have liked to get my hands on that hot little piece of ass wife of his. He probably thought she was too good to let anyone else have her. Controlling bastard." His gaze returned to a spot much farther south than my eyes. "Let's talk about you for a while. Is this your first time swinging? Have I got myself a virgin? Haven't had one of those in a long time."

Eww, but if that was what turned him on, I had to lean into it. I had an idea. "It's my first time swinging, but I'm no stranger to fooling around behind my husband's back. In fact, you know my go-to guy who's always up for anything."

"Who's that?"

"Brad Kerrigan."

He snapped his eyes up to meet mine, clearly unimpressed. "He's a jackass."

"Oh, I'm well aware. There's exactly one reason I'm screwing him, and it isn't his personality. In fact, I sometimes resort to gagging him because he talks too damn much. Usually business, and it's super boring."

Hal's mustache twitched. "He talks business in the bedroom? What has he told you?"

"Not that I ever really listen too much, but he bitches a lot about how Wakefield goes on these psychotic witch hunts that make the foundation look like it's run by zealots. Oh, and that the board has their collective noses so far up Wakefield's ass they can't see that he's making them look like chumps."

"Brad said that?"

"Yeah, and he said that when he takes over, things are going to change. That he supposedly knows something that can get the whole board tossed out so he can replace them with level-headed people without an agenda who'll make the foundation reputable again. I guess it's kind of sweet that he thinks he can make some real change in—"

"He's a damn dirty liar!" Hal roared.

Several people turned their heads toward us, including Vic, who was all the way across the room. He gave me a worried look.

I focused my attention on Hal, dragging him over to the nearest chair and settling him into it. Against my better judgment, I sat on his lap. I could feel how close I was getting to him opening up, and I couldn't risk losing him. I needed to hit him with some hard questions, and fast. The hour Shane had promised was up, and people were pairing up and getting handsy. This was my last chance.

Running one finger down Hal's sweaty jowl and trying not to gag, I cooed, "Look who's getting all hot and bothered. Save that for later, big boy."

He let out a breath and placed a hand on my knee, visibly relaxing. "It boils my blood to hear something like that out of someone we've had to bail out of trouble more than once."

"Ooh, my Braddie is a baddie? He just got way more interesting."

"He's not bad—he's stupid. He doesn't want 'level-headed people without an agenda' on the board. He wants lenient people who'll cover for his buddies and bury the truth. We finally had to call for his resignation after it came to light that he'd taken a bribe to destroy some of the foundation's evidence."

Shane demanded, "They all know about the bribes?"

I asked Hal, "So why does he still work there?"

"Wakefield made him return the money and swore to us he'd keep the fool in line. They were friends."

Shane said, "More likely, he wanted to keep an eye on him. Keep this guy talking."

I said, "Wow. That's risky. What's going to happen to Brad now that Wakefield's gone?"

Hal frowned. "I don't know if I want to tell you that, considering you're sleeping with him."

"Not anymore, now that I know he's a bitch boy who takes bribes and lets his buddy get him off the hook. I hope you're going to fire his ass and turn him in to the cops."

His hand on my knee started inching up my thigh. "I thought we were going to talk about you for a while."

"We did. I told you I cheat on my husband with Brad. That's pretty personal, don't you think?"

"I'd like to get a lot more personal than that."

Out of the corner of my eye, I saw Vic heading my way, muttering in the direction of where his com mic was hidden. He had three beautiful women hot on his heels. I hoped he wouldn't get all protective and ruin the last remaining minutes I had before I'd be forced to extricate myself from Hal's clutches.

Sterling piped up, "Manetti says you're about to get groped and wants to bail. I don't think you can squeeze much more out of this turd, anyway, and all Manetti's doing at this point is fending off horny housewives. Wind down your conversation and ditch this bozo, and then we can all get the hell out of here."

I swung for the fences. "Okay, let's get really personal. Do you think the whole Brad situation pissed someone off and made them want to kill Wakefield's wife to get back at him?"

Hal squinted at me and wagged a fat finger in my face. At least he'd had to take his hand off my knee to do it. "I didn't mean that kind of personal. I don't want to hear another word about anything except how you plan to pleasure me later."

Baxter said, "It's time to abort. Get out of there, both of you." Since I'd learned he still cared about me, I hadn't had the time to think about how my current situation would affect him. Based on the tightness of his tone, not well.

Sterling snorted. "Wait, give her one more minute. Let's hear it, Matthews."

I wrinkled my nose and stood. "Hard pass. Good luck finding anyone with enough self-loathing to polish your knob, Hal."

"Bitch," he spat as I walked away.

I sidled up next to Vic, who'd positioned himself about ten feet away from where I'd been sitting with Hal. Vic looked like *he* was the one who needed saving from being groped. I said to his entourage, "Scat, girls. He's mine."

The three women also made it clear that I was a raging bitch, which made for a lot more cackling in my ear.

I said to Vic, "Did you happen to spot Robert Hawley? I haven't seen him anywhere."

"No, I only saw your other three marks, the ones you already talked to."

I nodded. "Three out of four ain't bad. Ready to call it a night, Casanova? I realize your dance card's probably full for the evening, but you're my ride."

Vic laughed and chin-nodded across the room. "Yeah, I'm out—some lady just took the party to the next level."

I followed his gaze to a woman who'd undone the ribbon at the neck of her halter dress. She stood among a group of fully clothed people, naked from the waist up. Except for the ridiculous peacock-themed mask covering her face, of course.

I griped, "Mask on, tits out. Again, I have to ask—what is wrong with these people?"

Sterling said, "And *again*, you shouldn't have to be reminded that you're at a *sex party*, Matthews. They're not going to break out Pictionary as the entertainment."

I ignored him, unable to rip my gaze from the woman's breasts. "Those are fake as hell, but damn, they're perky." Glancing around the room at all the ladies there, most of them nipped and tucked and not a wrinkle anywhere, I said, "Any takers on a bet that I'm the only woman here with her original equipment?"

Vic said, "Guys, don't take it. It's a sucker bet. It's plastic surgery central in here."

Baxter griped, "I'm only going to say it one more time. Get. Out."

31

Vic seemed deep in thought as he drove me back to the station. Or maybe he was tired. It was past his bedtime, and even though he hadn't complained once, I knew tonight had been stressful for him. I could tell he'd been on high alert, keeping an eye on me to make sure I was safe the whole time.

He finally looked over at me and said, "Your earpiece wasn't really broken."

I let out a soft laugh. "Nothing gets past you, does it?"

He smiled. "I might have fallen for it if you hadn't come out of the study with a noticeable absence of lipstick. You know you're playing with fire having secret trysts, right? And I thought your boy wasn't even giving you the time of day lately."

I shrugged. "I know. But I had to find out where his head was."

"And did you find out?"

"Yep. Sure did." I couldn't wipe the smile off my face.

"While you were off canoodling, I spoke to several ladies who had a lot to say. I learned that Walt Elliston's wife's hobbies include alcoholism, drunk driving their yacht around Geist Reservoir, spray tanning, and sleeping with her pool boy."

"Oh, nice work, Columbo."

"Wait, I'm not finished. I also found out that Douglas Busing's wife enjoys abusing Prozac and her monthly attempts to slit her wrists."

I gasped. "That's terrible, but...it tracks." I couldn't imagine what their home life was like.

"All either of them wanted was someone who'd pay attention to them. I gave Mrs. Busing the number of my therapist and texted a buddy of mine at the Indiana DNR to have his conservation officers watch out for Mrs. Elliston's yacht. Both of those ladies could use a dose of tough love." Vic was such a good guy. While on a mission to try to charm secret information out of sad, rich ladies, he'd made it a point to help them at the same time.

Shaking my head, I said, "All they're getting tonight is the wrong kind of love."

He gave me a pointed look. "You just about got some, too. What were you thinking giving that asshat a lap dance?"

I scoffed. "First, there was no dancing. I was sitting as still as I possibly could so he didn't get too much of the wrong idea. Besides, I had it handled."

"You nearly *got* handled."

"Yeah, and if I hadn't done what I did, I would have had jack shit to show for my evening." I waved a hand. "Moving on."

"Agree to disagree. Hal Casper's wife knows nothing of what he does all day, nor does she care. All she wanted to talk about was how much I was worth. Since when is four million in net worth laughable?"

"Since the rest of them could add a zero to that."

"Oh. So much for trying to keep my backstory believable." He shook his head. "Lastly, I learned from Lana Higgins, COO of Pink Armadillo Cosmetics, that her company threatened a lawsuit against Wakefield Foundation a few months ago. One of their employees propositioned her for sex in return for him making sure Pink Armadillo passed their investigation with flying colors."

"Oh, let me guess—his name rhymes with Brad Kerrigan?"

"Sure does. The foundation paid her off to keep a lid on it."

"Of course they did. And way to bury the lead, Manetti. Nice job getting your marks to open up to you without having to resort to a lap dance."

* * *

The first thing I did when I got back to the station was hightail it to Jayne's office to get out of that dress. It did its job, but I was beyond done with it.

"So, how did it go?" Jayne asked warily as she helped me out of the dress.

"Good. Vic and I both got some serious dirt on Brad Kerrigan. I don't think he's the killer, but he's mixed up in this somehow. If we keep leaning on him, I think everything will eventually come together."

"And you got away unscathed?" she asked. I assumed she'd already been briefed by the detectives about the party.

"Yes, but not for lack of trying by a few dirty old men."

"Mmm."

I was never so happy to have my old clothes back on. And I was starving. Those three appetizers I managed to snag were long gone, as was my dinner. "Trust me, I'm fine. We knew it was going to be a shitshow, and it didn't disappoint."

She said, apologetically, "If it hadn't been important, I never would have—"

I held up a hand. "Would you have thought twice about sending someone who's not me?"

"No."

"There you go. I'm tougher than I look." I smiled. "Probably thanks to you. Throwing teenage me in a cell with a couple of crack whores in full jones mode was definitely character-building." I'd met Jayne when she caught me shoplifting and decided I needed to be scared straight. It worked, and I owed her everything for her tough love.

She gave me a wry smile. "Get back to work, smartass."

* * *

I found Shane in the conference room. "You're taking me out for food. Lots of it."

He snickered. "What's the matter? Rough night?"

"Something like that."

He grabbed his keys and phone and followed me out the door and down the hall. "After your new boyfriend Hal said Wakefield had promised to keep an eye on Kerrigan, I figured there was a good chance it meant he'd had him hacked. It didn't take me long to find everything I needed in a file he'd named 'Wildcats,' which is the mascot from his and Brad's alma mater, Northwestern."

"Nice of him to make it so easy for us to find."

He shrugged. "Maybe by design. There were only certain people he needed to hide this information from, and if things went badly for him, he'd probably want investigators to have no trouble finding it."

"That's morbid."

"So's keeping your friends close and your frenemies closer."

"No wonder Lance was such a secretive guy. There weren't a lot of people in his life who gave him a reason to be trusting. But enough about that—what did you find?"

Shane grinned as he held the door open for me and we stepped out into the crisp night air. "It turns out Kerrigan is the proud owner of a shell corporation called Big B Ballerz that's funded by an international bank account in Dubai."

"That sounds shady as hell."

"It is. And when we track down the owner of another account—also out of Dubai—that dropped a million dollars into Kerrigan's Big B Ballerz account last week, I'm thinking we'll find someone with a lot to lose."

I gaped at him. "Someone was willing to give that douche a million dollars to make some information disappear? This is huge."

"Which is why you should go out with Kerrigan again and try to get him to turn on them."

I stopped with my hand on the door handle of Shane's sedan and stared at him over the roof. "Are you nuts? He's not going to choose me over a million dollars. No one would choose me over a million dollars."

He gave me a patronizing smile. "Aww, I would."

"Seriously, though. What incentive does he have?"

"Well, it's only a matter of time before we can prove all this and put him in prison. His incentive will be to not get put in a pound-me-in-the-ass prison."

"Oh, right. I suppose we have him there."

"Perfect. First you call Douchey McGee and get a date with him tonight. Then I'll buy you a fourth meal."

I glared at him. "You dick. I've already earned the fourth meal. And besides, it's late."

"It's barely nine on a Friday."

"I'm too tired to be charming."

Shane shrugged. "Sorry, but we're kind of under the gun here. Tick tock." He got in his car, and I had no choice but to get in with him.

On the way to meet Annaleigh, I texted Brad and asked him to meet me for coffee later at the same place we'd met that morning, the coffeehouse near Ashmore with late-night hours that catered to college kids. Shane was going to wait outside in his car, just in case things got dicey. Now that I had my "date" lined up, Shane made good on his promise and got me a big but bunless cheeseburger, which I inhaled on the way to meet Annaleigh Walters at her campus apartment.

When we knocked on the door, a slender young woman with large glasses poked her head out and said warily, "Show me your badges." I vaguely recognized her from campus.

Shane showed Annaleigh his badge. "Shane Carlisle, IMPD. I'm the one who texted you."

"Right," she replied, eyeing me. "Oh, I know you."

I smiled. "Ellie Matthews. I'm a criminalistics professor at Ashmore, and I'm consulting on the case."

She nodded and let us into her apartment. It was adorably decorated in the latest Instagram vibe, warm and glowing with funky lamps and fairy lights strung around all the windows. She offered us her tiny couch and perched nervously on a leather pouf ottoman across from us.

Shane said, "First of all, we want to say that we're sorry for the loss of your uncle. I'm sure it's been very difficult on you."

Annaleigh sniffed. "It has."

I ventured, "Especially with finals coming up and you working as a TA and also at another job. Are you finding time for yourself?"

She seemed to brush aside her feelings. "I'll take a break when my work's done."

Shane nodded. "We don't want to cause you any more stress, but we assume you were closer to your uncle than most people. Do you know of anyone who'd want to hurt him or your Aunt Aurora?"

"Plenty of people. He was a crusader for justice. You're going to make enemies doing work like that. She was a social-climbing bitch who pretended to care about issues to get ratings."

"Not a fan of your aunt's work?" Shane asked.

"She's not my aunt. She's just married to my uncle."

Shane frowned. "Where were you Tuesday between ten PM and midnight?"

Snorting, Annaleigh said, "Please. She wasn't worth killing. I was here. My roommate can vouch for me."

"Okay. Had your uncle received any specific threats lately? Or did he express any concern to you for his safety?"

She stiffened. "My uncle was careful."

Shane said, "Not completely, and you didn't answer my question. Aurora's death was very clearly at the hands of someone else. Your uncle's death at first glance appeared to be a suicide. But we're beginning to believe it could have been staged to place the blame on him for killing her, maybe to discredit him and, by extension, his foundation. Because that's exactly what's happening right now."

I didn't know Annaleigh, but I knew how to spot a young woman keeping a secret, and she had one. "Annaleigh, you know something. And unless you had a hand in your uncle's death, why would you not want to help us so we can find whoever did this to him?"

Her expression turned angry. "How could you even say that I might have hurt him?"

I shrugged. "I don't know, maybe because you're his sole beneficiary? That's a lot of motive."

"I don't care about his money. I care about what's right."

"And what's right is getting justice for your uncle. What's more important than that?"

She looked like she was about to cry. "Justice for a lot of people with no voice and no one to care about them."

"Like who?" I asked.

She shook her head.

Shane and I shared a look. This one was going to be a tough nut to crack.

Shane said, "It sounds like you and your uncle were working on something together, and that something may have been what got him killed. Are you not worried the same thing might happen to you?"

A single tear spilled down one of her cheeks.

I said gently, "Annaleigh, we can protect you. It's our job. Please let us do that."

She got up and started pacing the room.

Shane added, "We think there are three deaths tied to whatever's going on. These people aren't fooling around."

Annaleigh stopped pacing to bark out a mirthless laugh. "Oh, there are way more than three deaths."

Shane said, "We're really going to need you to start talking, Annaleigh. You're teetering very close to obstructing justice, and I'm not going to let that happen."

"Are you threatening me?" she snapped.

Shane didn't back down. "It's not a threat. You just said you know about more deaths tied to our case, and if you don't tell us, you are obstructing our investigation. I will not hesitate to arrest you."

Shane's scare tactics were only making Annaleigh dig her heels in. I went at this the way I would have with Rachel. "Look, Annaleigh, it's obvious that you care deeply about this cause you and your uncle were working on. We get that. But it kind of sounds like you're going at it on your own now, and you need an ally. Especially if there's something illegal going on, we can get to the bottom of it a lot faster with the resources we have. Bring us in on what you're doing."

She shook her head. "We've worked too hard on this for you guys to come in guns blazing and blow it all up."

"Is this a Wakefield Foundation thing or something else?"

She didn't reply.

Between the murder and the bribery and the hacking and all the crazy nonsense surrounding Wakefield Foundation, it had to be the common denominator. I thought back to the hundreds of files and notes we'd read through earlier and had an idea. "You said there have been deaths. Is it E&X Distributors? Did they cover up some vehicular accidents?"

She shook her head. "I don't know anything about them."

I had to fight an eyeroll that this interview had degraded into a guessing game. I thought more about her statement about people with no voice and no one to care about them, and what corporation would have a million spare dollars to hand over to Brad Kerrigan. "What about Axion and their drug testing on the homeless?"

She flinched. Bingo.

Shane saw it, too. "Did a drug test go horribly bad, Annaleigh?"

Her bottom lip began quivering. We had her.

I sent a text to Baxter and Sterling to have them start looking into anything they could find on Axion Pharmaceuticals and their drug testing on the homeless, plus any suspicious disappearances of homeless people in the area.

Shane stood. "Well, thanks for your time, Annaleigh. You've given enough away that we at least know where to start looking. If you want to continue to keep your secrets, that's fine, but it'll be on you if we're forced to 'come in guns blazing and blow it all up' because we didn't have the information we needed. Goodnight. I'd consider hiring a personal security guard if I were you."

Annaleigh let out a whimper. "Wait. Wait." She sighed and put her head in her hands.

Shane sat back down on the couch, knowing he'd finally pushed the right button with her, and waited for her to speak.

She raised her head, her eyes brimming with tears. "My uncle got some really damning intel about Axion's drug testing on the homeless...and it went far beyond lack of consent. He'd heard from a source—not a very reputable one—that they'd killed a few people during one round of drug testing and had...disposed of the evidence. He didn't want to believe it, but he made sure to do his due diligence and check it out."

Shane said, "By having his personal hacker breach their computer system."

"Yes, and by getting me a job at Axion."

My eyebrows shot up. "You were feeding him company secrets from the inside?"

"Yes."

Shane gave her a strange look. "Isn't that—"

"Dangerous? Very."

"I was going to say unethical."

Her nostrils flared. Clearly it was a touchy subject with her. "Ah, the age-old debate between morals and ethics. If you could stop the senseless killing of innocent people by simply hacking someone's computer, would you do it?"

Shane said, "Fair point, but both are still felonies. And working as a mole inside a pharmaceutical company could warrant civil charges as well."

She huffed out an angry breath. "Again, what I'm doing pales in comparison to Axion using homeless people as guinea pigs to test dangerous drugs. Axion banks on the fact that if they get sick, no one will care."

I added, "And if they die, no one will miss them."

"That's exactly what Uncle Lance was afraid of." She heaved out a shuddery sigh. "But he never found out for sure. He went to his usual source to do some deep digging, but the guy never came through with the information. He'd never done that before. And when Uncle Lance tried to contact him, the guy ghosted him. We figured Axion found him poking around and paid him more than my uncle to keep his mouth shut."

Shane and I shared a glance.

Shane asked, "Do you know how to contact this guy?"

"No, my uncle did all that. I did the exchanges with him—cash payments, written instructions, flash drives with the information. Uncle Lance didn't want the guy to know his identity." Annaleigh was the only person we'd run across who'd met RexXanthe69 in person.

"Why?"

She smiled nervously. "Well, he's a hacker. He could ruin my uncle, too."

I nodded. "Do you at least know his name?"

Shaking her head, she said, "No. We all remained anonymous for our own protection."

Shane pressed, "But you could identify him if we had a photo, correct?"

"I could."

"Maybe even work with a sketch artist to come up with a composite?"

"I could try."

Shane stood again. "We'll get an appointment for you tomorrow morning with a sketch artist. Meanwhile, don't you think it's time to tender your resignation at Axion?"

Annaleigh looked at him like he was crazy. "No way. I'm seeing through what my uncle started."

"Your uncle is dead because of this."

When the poor girl's chin started quivering again, I jumped in and said, "You've done a great job, Annaleigh. You've risked your life to get to the truth and put a stop to more abuse of the homeless. Let us take it from here. The charges will stick better if it's done legally. Even if you found a literal smoking gun, it would be inadmissible in court because it didn't get collected using the proper channels. Do you understand that *you* could actually be the one to blow up this case at this point?"

She seemed to deflate before our eyes. "I understand."

"And I know it won't be fun, but I think you should be put in protective custody."

Hanging her head, she murmured, "You're probably right."

As Shane stepped away to make the call, I said to Annaleigh, "I want to ask you one more thing. Did your uncle ever mention anything negative about Bradley Kerrigan?

She snorted. "Only that the Bradster was trying to turn a profit by screwing the foundation."

"Did he get into any specifics?"

"He said he protected him from getting fired over it so he could keep tabs on him. He paid attention to what companies Brad was trying to protect, and that's how he knew who to go after the hardest. In a way, it made his job a little easier. But it really hurt Uncle Lance to know his oldest friend had turned on him."

I nodded. "I imagine so."

32

By the time we'd passed Annaleigh into protective custody, it was time for me to meet the Bradster. I was tempted to slug his stupid smug face when I met him at the counter of the coffeeshop. I was way too exhausted to keep my cool for long. I ordered the biggest vanilla latte they made and one of their giant chocolate muffins, carbs be damned.

Of course Brad was a dick about it. "That stuff will go straight to your hips."

So Shane could hear us, I was wearing my com setup, but minus the earpiece, so at least I didn't have to endure any rude backchat in my ear as I had at the party. Thinking about Sterling reminded me that I needed to practice what I preached and play nice, even if it felt like it was going to kill me.

I gave Brad a fake smile. "Thanks for the tip."

As we sat down at a table together, he said, "I was stoked to hear you wanted to see me again so soon. I like it when a lady takes charge."

"Then you're going to love this conversation."

He winked at me. "I'm more looking forward to what might happen after our conversation."

I smiled genuinely. "I can honestly say the same thing." It was time for the gloves to come off. "So, when you told me Barry was taking bribes, you really meant *you* were taking bribes."

His face fell. "Not where I thought this was going."

"Buckle up, buttercup. We need to chat."

"I don't think I want to chat about this."

"Because you have something to hide?"

He spread his hands innocently. "I've got nothing to hide."

"So spill it about the bribes."

"Did you not look into Barry's background?"

"We did. We also looked into yours."

He smiled, but it didn't reach his eyes. "Why mine?"

"Spare me your fake surprise."

His smile turned into a leer. "I don't fake anything."

Shaking my head, I said, "You fake everything, except being a dumbass."

The leer became a frown. "You don't know me."

"I know there's a cool mil stashed away in a Dubai bank tied to a shell corporation called Big B Ballerz that's tied to you. Why did you spell Ballerz with a Z? That's so lame."

Sitting very still, he said, "I've never heard of that company."

"Really?" I asked, my voice dripping with sarcasm. "Okay. Would you like to hear our one-time offer for partial immunity or keep lying and get arrested for two to three murders?"

He thought for a moment, then replied calmly, "You have nothing on me, otherwise I'd be arrested already and not out on a second date in one day with you."

"I have the fact that you gave a law enforcement official false information about TC Pittman and Greenstar." I leaned back and crossed my arms. "Did you think you could snow me because I'm a girl?"

He leaned in and murmured, "Oh, honey. I did snow you because you're a girl. I gave you the exact information I wanted you to have, and I made you think you charmed it out of me. You think I'm some kind of amateur at getting women to think and do what I want?"

I shrugged. "Stupid women, maybe. I had a tail put on you when you left here this morning. It's been there all day, and you've had no clue."

His face fell. "A tail?"

"Yep. We saw your little meeting with your security buddy. We then saw you go home and pack a couple of bags, go to the bank, and buy hair dye at CVS. If that doesn't scream, 'I'm fleeing town,' I don't know what does. You planning to *Gone Girl* yourself, or what?"

He scoffed, but his eyes were strained. "Great work, Scooby-Doo. I would have got away with it, too, if it hadn't been for you meddling kids. Since when are common errands considered criminal behavior?"

I leaned in. "Since we're *this close* to being able to link the money in your Big B Ballerz account to whoever paid you. Once we do that, we take everyone down."

Brad's face went pale, but he somehow managed to keep up the bravado. I had to give him credit—he had brass balls. "That's impossible."

"Clearly, you're scared, because otherwise you wouldn't be skipping town. What I haven't figured out is if you're more afraid of the police or your partners in crime. Because you looked like you were about to pee your panties when your bald buddy was yelling at you this morning."

He clenched his jaw. "Again, it sounds like you have nothing on me."

"You know we can help you not get kneecapped or worse if you'll work with us."

He only stared at me in response.

I sat back in my chair. "You're not going to admit to anything, are you?"

"Nope." He got up and left the table.

I shrugged, calling after him, "It's your funeral."

I waited until I saw Brad pull out of the parking lot before exiting the coffeehouse and throwing myself into Shane's car. "Guess what? He's still being an asshole. But I guess you heard all that."

Shane put his car in gear and careened out of the parking lot, turning on his lights and siren and accelerating at an alarming pace. "Doesn't matter. Sterling figured out the identity of your John Doe. I sent his DMV photo to Annaleigh, and she confirmed his identity as the hacker."

The siren was giving me a headache, and my latte and muffin were starting to bubble in my belly. "That's great. Why are we speeding, and can we stop doing it?"

He turned off the siren and eased off a little on his speed, leaving his lights on to help part the traffic. "We're heading to his place so you can process it."

"Now? But it's late and I'm so exhausted," I whined. "It'll be there tomorrow."

He shot me an amused glance. "You are familiar with how policework works, right?"

"Look, I've had a rough day, bookended by dates with the Bradster. So if I want to bitch and moan for a minute, I'm going to do it."

He grinned. "That's fair. You definitely had the worst day of any of us... probably of all of us put together."

"Thank you. So who is RexXanthe69 IRL? I have to know."

"Elvin Butler, twenty-four. Hacker, hermit, and...haver of no friends."

"Good grief. *Elvin*? Did his parents hate him or something? How many times a day did he get his ass kicked in school?"

"His parents are dead. No other family, no friends. That's why you had no missing person's report to match up with your John Doe. No one missed him."

I sighed. "That's so sad. Poor guy."

"Poor guy? He was a hacker for hire. An agent of chaos."

"Loneliness does weird things to you. He was probably an angry young man who never felt like he was heard."

"He didn't have to turn to a life of crime."

"You have become significantly less empathetic in your old age."

Shane chuckled. "Okay, okay. I'm sorry the dude's dead. But he was asking for it."

"Wow. That was not better."

When Shane and I got to Elvin Butler's dilapidated rent house near the fairgrounds in Indy, Baxter, Sterling, and Amanda were already inside. It wasn't the freshest-smelling home, but at least there were none of the regular murder-type odors. I doubted we were looking at our primary crime scene. However, unless Elvin had made it a habit to trash his home like a drunken rock star in a hotel room, the place had been tossed.

I said to Sterling, "Good job finding our John Doe. That was fast."

I could have sworn I saw him puff his chest out just slightly when Amanda nodded in agreement and murmured, "It was."

Sterling said, "I talked to more nerds today than I ever have in my life. Finally I found one who knew our hacker's real first name. Lucky for us, Elvin's a weird enough name that there are only four of them in the state. Two are senior citizens, and one is five years old. DMV records show our Elvin drives a 2004 Honda Civic hatchback, but it's not here."

Amanda handed me my case. "We've already taken a quick look around, and I took some photos. This isn't the primary. No blood, urine, or anything, so I'm not bothering with a jumpsuit or booties or a mask. And since someone clearly beat us here, I doubt if we find any kind of evidence at all, unless we get some fingerprints."

Sterling added, "Oh, and whoever did it must have had our vic's keys, because there's no sign of forced entry on any door or window, and the place was locked up when we got here. The landlord had to bring a key over."

I glanced around the room and sighed. "This place is a nightmare. If we all pitch in, it'll go a lot faster. Glove up, boys, and let's get this over with."

Sterling grunted. "I didn't see you doing my job today, Matthews. I'm not doing yours now."

I turned on him. "I didn't see you having to go out for coffee with a moronic douchebag not once, but twice today. I also didn't see you have to pour yourself into a ridiculous dress and walk the line between flirting and getting sexually assaulted by a bunch of disgusting old men." I dropped my case onto the floor. "You want to go? Let's go."

Sterling held out his hands in defense. "Clearly, I misspoke. Where do you want me to start?"

Giving myself a moment to calm down, I took a pair of gloves out of my case and put them on before asking, "What exactly are we looking for?"

Baxter said, "Reasons someone might want Elvin Butler dead."

"So his computer, for starters."

Shane was already crouched next to a large folding table holding Elvin's command center—five monitors and dozens of accessories including keyboards, game controllers, mice, speakers, and webcams. He said, "Looks like he had two PC towers, and they're both missing. Someone ripped them from their cords and wires."

Sterling shoved aside some of the refuse littering the table. "I see a laptop charger, but no laptop. Someone wanted him silenced and his information gone."

I walked over for a closer look and spied an open bag of Cheetos. "Hey, I was right about the Cheeto dust on his shirt." I tapped the bag, and a couple of roaches skittered out. I jumped back with a squeal. When everyone—except Amanda, who knew about my issue with roaches—stared at me, I shivered and added, "I really hate roaches."

"Good to know," Sterling said, smirking. "Well, this might be a bust, but let's get at it. Amanda, would you want to look in the kitchen with me?"

"Sure," she said, following him to the next room.

Shane piped up, "I'll take the bedroom."

That left Baxter and me alone in the living area. He smiled shyly at me.

"Just like old times," I murmured.

"Yeah."

Neither of us could seem to stop grinning at each other, but we couldn't just stand here forever.

I said quietly, "I guess we'd better get to work."

If I'd thought it was hard to concentrate before when I was worrying about why Baxter wasn't paying attention to me, it was ten times harder now that it was clear that all he wanted to do was pay attention to me. Our reconciliation was so new, I hadn't had time to process it. Forcing myself to focus, I took the command center. For the thousands of dollars of electronic equipment here, there was nothing with any kind of memory chip in it. The gaming chair had once been nice enough, but it was food-stained and beat up, like the rest of the place. The only other furniture in the room was a wobbly coffee table, a dingy recliner, and a broken-down couch.

Baxter was pawing through the couch cushions with a look of disgust on his face. Up to his elbow in the corner, he muttered, "I'm taking this one for the team only because I like you."

"Thanks," I replied, trying and failing to keep a dopey grin off my face.

I moved on to the coffee table, which was laden with empty fast-food containers and snack wrappers and not much else. I'd decided this room was a bust when Shane came striding out of the bedroom, on his phone. "I'll be there in ten minutes, honey." He hung up and announced, "My sweet little bundle of joy just puked all over Kaitlyn, our new couch, and a throw rug. I'm going home."

I tried not to laugh. I remembered those days. "Ooh. Even this place is less gross than that. Have fun."

As he headed for the door, he said, "You'll need to do the closet and bathroom. I looked through the dresser and under the mattress and bed. I found nothing but a lot of frightening stains."

"I didn't want to know that. But hey, between that and the mess you have waiting for you at home, you might just beat me at having the worst day."

He nodded tiredly. "I just might."

Once he was out the door, I said to Baxter, "So do we need to flip a coin for closet versus bathroom?"

Baxter looked up from his phone, thinking for a moment. "I honestly can't decide which one would be worse, based on his assessment of the rest of the room."

We headed into the tiny bedroom and looked around. It was as gross as the living room, and since the only flat surface to catch trash was the dresser, a good amount of food wrappers and drink cans were thrown haphazardly on the floor. It didn't look vandalized like the living room, though.

Baxter opened the accordion doors to a fairly empty closet. "Is it too late for me to call closet?"

I laughed. I'd missed this so much. "Absolutely not. Go for it."

While he dug around in the closet, I steeled myself for a nasty bathroom. It didn't disappoint, but there wasn't a lot in there. Elvin didn't strike me as much of a man of hygiene, and, as such, he didn't have a lot of extraneous bathroom products. Razor, deodorant, soap, shampoo, toothpaste, toothbrush, comb. Not a lot going on in there. I peeked in the toilet tank, but he had no secret stash floating inside.

Baxter had pulled a few boxes from the closet and had set them on the bed to go through them. I said, "Let me grab a clean pair of gloves, and I'll help you."

When I entered the living room to retrieve my case, I caught Sterling and Amanda jumping apart. I looked from her blushing face to his smirking one and shrugged. "No judgments." As I picked up my case, I continued, "Anyway, Shane went home, and we're pretty close to finished, except for a few storage boxes and the fingerprinting."

Amanda said, "I took care of fingerprinting the front and back doors already. I got a few usable prints—all loops, so there's a decent chance they belong to our victim."

Sterling said to me, "If all you have is some boxes to go through, you don't need us anymore. We're going to head out."

"Uh…" I croaked, turning to Amanda. "Shane was my ride, so I'd assumed I'd go back with you." Not that I didn't want to be left here with Baxter and get to take another drive with him today, but we still didn't need to be seen together alone, especially him dropping me off at the station late at night to get my car.

She replied, "Nick drove. I'm sure he'd be happy to take you back with him."

Sterling joked, "Well, he may not be happy about it."

I forced out a laugh and played along with our running 'Baxter's in a foul mood' bit. "That's what I'm afraid of."

Sterling said, "Sorry, Matthews, you're going to have to suck it up. We're going out for a drink, and you're not invited."

My eyebrows shot up. "Oh."

Amanda frowned and elbowed him.

I laughed for real this time. "No offense taken. You kids have fun."

33

I joined Baxter back in the bedroom. Setting my case on the floor, I whispered, "Guess who's going out on a date, like right now?"

He glanced up from the boxes he was perusing. "Can it be us?"

Smiling, I said, "I wish." The front door squeaked and then slammed shut. "Sterling finally talked Amanda into going out for a drink with him. I have no other choice but to ride back with you."

"No choice, huh? Does that mean we're alone?"

"It does."

Ripping his gloves off, he took two strides and had me in his arms. He kissed me with the same intensity he had hours earlier, and I got every bit as light-headed again. His hands roamed my body, and I knew exactly where we both wanted this to go.

I pulled back. "Yes, absolutely, to whatever you have in mind, but please not here."

While kissing my neck, he said, "Not here? So I've misread it that it's a fantasy of yours to fool around in a crime scene?"

"Gross. No. Why would you think that?"

He stopped kissing me to look me in the eye. "Ellie, I'm joking."

"Oh. Bad Nick Baxter gallows humor strikes again. You don't know how happy I am to hear it." I took his face in my hands. "I missed it so much. I missed *you* so much."

"I missed you, too."

He leaned down and covered my lips with his, this time sweetly and softly, but it was no less intense. We had to figure out a way to be together. It would crush me to have to give him up again.

When we finally broke apart, he said, "Before you came in and derailed my train of thought, I found something pretty interesting." He took a new pair of gloves out of his pocket and put them on before reaching into one of the boxes and pulling out an ornate wooden box with a large carved dragon perching on the lid, as if ready to strike. The look was completed by red jewels for the dragon's eyes.

I made a face and donned a new pair of gloves. "If by interesting, you mean strange, then I guess this thing is very interesting."

"The interesting part is what's inside." He opened the box and held it out to me. There were several flash drives nestled in the red velvet lining.

"Wonder what a hacker would keep on a bunch of flash drives hidden in a box within another box in his closet?"

Smiling, he closed the box and handed it to me to package as evidence. "You up for pulling an all-nighter with me to find out?"

I frowned as I took out a big grocery bag and put the box inside. "I'd love to, but we both need sleep. You, especially, after driving all night Wednesday."

He eyed me. "Wait, I didn't tell you that yet. I didn't tell anyone that. How in the hell did you know?"

"I'm a really good investigator," I joked, scrawling the pertinent information on an evidence tag to affix to the bag and then sealing the bag shut with tape.

"I know that, but this is different. You had no way of knowing."

"Ah, see, you're not fully aware of how the female mind works sometimes. When you started avoiding me, I couldn't rest until I figured out why. It kind of consumed me for a while."

He shook his head and removed his gloves. "Ellie, I'm so sorry. If it's any consolation, I think it hurt me about as much as it did you."

"I know. I can see it now. As for the trip, Shane said you came to work yesterday morning in the same clothes you'd left in the night before. At first, I thought you'd done a walk of shame from your new girlfriend's house or—"

"Wait. You assumed I'd moved on and found someone else that fast?"

I cleared my throat and removed my gloves. This was going to take a minute to unpack. "Yeah, about that...full disclosure—I did overhear a couple of your private phone conversations." When his face fell, I held out my hands in defense. "Please don't think I was being some psycho ex-girl-friend. I did not intentionally listen in. I just happened upon you having a conversation and...didn't walk away quickly. I realize that was a gross inva-sion of your privacy, and I apologize. You know how I always warn you I make bad choices where men are concerned? This is one of those times."

I hadn't really thought through how I'd go about coming clean to him about my lapses in judgment. Judging by the look on his face, he wasn't impressed with my antics. But at this point our relationship couldn't survive on anything less than the truth. He was worth it to me to have a difficult discussion.

When he spoke, I realized what I'd thought was disappointment was actually hurt. "You thought so little of me that you believed I'd throw away everything we had after a couple of months? Was it because you were thinking of doing the same thing with Manetti...or maybe with your old buddy Carlisle?"

His harsh words cut through me, but I managed to take a moment to try to digest them before snapping at him. This reminded me a lot of our conversation at the party earlier. I could imagine how as he'd had to harden his heart against me, he'd probably dreamed up all kinds of scenarios of me falling back into old habits with Vic. And I'd seen him frowning over plenty of my interactions with Shane this week.

I said, "No, I was not. I didn't want to think you'd do it either, but at the same time I understood why you might have. I ghosted you and the whole department for two months, turning down job after job that would have allowed us to legally see each other. I bet after a while you were good and pissed at me for that."

Seeming a bit taken aback, he frowned. "I was. I knew it was best that we stay apart for long enough to let our feelings cool down. But I would have liked to have had a say in the decision and not just be forced to sit there and wonder if there was another reason you didn't want to be around me."

I sighed. "I'm sorry I made you feel that way. It wasn't intentional. It was me not being able to deal with...everything. I didn't have myself together enough to do my job, pretend you were nothing but a work colleague, and stay sober all at the same time. I couldn't afford to screw any of those things up. Not even a little."

He nodded, seeming to soften at least a little bit. "Oh."

I went on, "And then when I got a less than warm welcome back from you, I kind of panicked. You were different, and literally on your phone the whole damn time, which is so unlike you. I knew something was going on, and that's when I heard you on the phone at our John Doe scene telling someone you wanted to see her. I put all that together and figured you were starting a new relationship. Then at the Bennett-Wakefield scene, I heard you tell someone you wanted to be there for them...and you said, 'I love you.' That solidified my theory." I let out a breath. "And it also broke my heart. It's no excuse for not believing in you, but it's all I have."

He stepped toward me and took my hand. "I can understand how you'd put all that together."

"But can you forgive me for it?"

"If you forgive me for what I said about you and Manetti and Carlisle."

I smiled up at him. "Already done."

"And for not just telling you what was going on with me in the first place. In hindsight, it would have saved us both a lot of grief."

"Where's the fun in that?"

He squeezed my hand. "I still don't understand how you shifted theories from me having a girlfriend to me and my family freaking out over Marie Collins's release."

Shrugging, I said, "That was the easy part. I went to your desk to ask you a question about the case, accidentally bumped your mouse with a file, and saw a news article about her pull up on your computer. It was a total lightbulb moment. Suddenly everything made sense. Especially your shitty attitude."

He huffed out a soft laugh. "I've been under duress."

"I know. So...are we good?"

He smiled and reached out to cradle my face in his hands. "Better than good," he said as he kissed me.

* * *

We packed up our gear and locked up Elvin Butler's home. We didn't talk a lot on the way back to Noblesville, but Baxter never let go of my hand.

As we were approaching the station, I said, "So, how do we play this going forward? I mean, at least you can quit *White Fang*-ing me now."

Baxter chuckled. "I'll be happy to be done with that. I guess I was shit at it, because you never got the hint and left me the hell alone."

"You should have known I'm too stubborn for it to work."

"I should have. I guess I still have to be aloof, though, right?"

"I hate to break it to you, but aloof does not even begin to describe you. You're full on crankypants."

He cringed. "Have I been that bad?"

"There was a point at which I thought you and Sterling switched personalities."

"Oh, right. You asked if I'd been taking asshole lessons from him. That hurt."

I laughed. "Yeah, sorry. I'd had enough of your sass and couldn't hold back any longer."

"You weren't wrong."

"Hey, you're allowed some bad days when you've got stuff going on."

He nodded, a frown marring his handsome face. He'd yet to bring up the specifics of his family's situation, and I hadn't pressed. We'd had our fair share of emotional conversation tonight. He knew he could come to me when he was ready, and I had no doubt he would.

Parking next to my vehicle and turning to face me, he said, "I take it we probably shouldn't finish what we started earlier. At least not until we have more of an idea how this is going to work."

I nodded. "You're probably right."

He smiled at me. "We'll figure it out, I promise."

* * *

I slept like the dead. All the angst of the last couple of weeks had disappeared. Of course, as soon as Baxter shared with me about what was happening with his family, there'd be more angst to replace it. But we were together again, and we could get through anything. I couldn't act too happy at work, because people would know something was up with me. This was my doing, though, so I'd have to sack up and give a non-stop Oscar-worthy performance. It was going to be exhausting.

But not more exhausting than being awakened on a Saturday morning at six to go in early for a meeting because our case absolutely blew up during the meager six hours of sleep I'd managed to get.

34

Special Agent Steve Griffin, the FBI agent who'd taken charge of our last case, stood at the head of the conference table. "Good to be working with all of you again," he said with a smile I would have liked to slap off his face. "I want to commend your team for your hard work and stellar investigation. Axion Pharmaceuticals, one of the largest drug manufacturers in the country, is about to be ripped apart and dismantled thanks to you. Once we were alerted to the possibility of them being involved in foul play by Detective Carlisle, we began reinvestigating a tip we'd received about them from last fall."

I leaned over to Shane, who was sitting next to me, and murmured, "We have you to thank for this?"

Shane shrugged. He hadn't been wrong to loop the FBI in on this matter, but I didn't have to like it.

Griffin slid me some side-eye and continued, "Overnight we found reason to believe Axion Pharmaceuticals altered documentation of the deaths of over a dozen of their test subjects to show that they were released from the program alive and well. Detective Baxter and Ms. Matthews, the flash drives you took into evidence from Elvin Butler's home were invaluable to our investigation. Great find, Dream Team."

I nodded, keeping my eyes on Griffin so as not to make any contact with

Jayne. I couldn't imagine she'd be pleased about the Dream Team getting back together, even unintentionally, when she expressly told me not to.

"The flash drives contain backup copies of every hack job Elvin Butler did for Wakefield Foundation, so in addition to the current case, we'll have numerous instances of corruption to investigate in the coming weeks. I'm certain we'll find even more evidence as our agents continue to dig." Griffin cleared his throat. "To that end, the FBI will be completely taking over the portion of your investigation dealing with Axion, since it's a national company. The homicides, however, we're going to leave to you."

I was shocked to hear this, and judging from the looks on their faces, everyone else on my team was as well. Agent Steve Griffin was a control freak with a tendency to micromanage. Most of us had had some kind of altercation with the guy. He'd fired Vic, forced Jayne to fire me, and if he'd gotten his way, would have had Baxter fired as well. I didn't believe for a second that he'd step aside and let us run our part of the investigation.

Ever the blowhard, Griffin wasn't even close to done talking. "My team did some further digging into the wire transfer of a million dollars to Bradley Kerrigan's international account. It came from an account tied to a shady subsidiary of Axion called Leosedonas Corp, which is headquartered in Dubai. On the same day from the same account, another million-dollar transfer was made to yet another international account belonging to a man named Clive Sanderson, who happens to be employed by Dynasty Elite Security here in Hamilton County. Small world, isn't it?"

My jaw dropped. I turned to Baxter. "Is that Baldy?"

He nodded once, giving away no emotion toward me.

Addressing the room, I said, "Then he's our guy, right?"

Jayne, who'd been moved down a seat from her regular head of the table, suddenly got up and left the room, answering her phone as she went.

Griffin replied, "Oh, yeah, he's your guy. Slight problem—he's in the wind. We had to lean pretty hard on his boss, but he finally came around and decided to be helpful. He said Clive Sanderson didn't show up for a job last night and wouldn't answer calls or texts. He also has one of their vehicles, license plate DNY014." Baxter and I shared a quick glance. That was the plate on the black SUV we saw him driving yesterday. "We pinged his phone, and it's nowhere. House seems empty, vehicle is gone, and the

GPS seems to have been disabled. We think he knew he was in trouble and ran."

Now I understood why the FBI was more than happy to let us handle this part. It was going to take hours upon hours of manpower, and that was if we even found Clive Sanderson at all. With a head start, a killer instinct, and a million dollars, he had the upper hand. This case was never going to get closed.

"The sheriff is having Bradley Kerrigan brought in for formal questioning. We'll hit him with both barrels—for his bribe for covering up Axion's transgressions and for his involvement with Clive Sanderson. From what we know about Kerrigan, we don't believe he's a hardened criminal. He'll cave on something, and I'm betting it'll be rolling on Sanderson to save his own ass. Either charge is enough to hold both of them, and then we'll have time to work on anything they don't readily confess to."

Jayne returned to the room and announced, "I hate to break up this meeting, but we need to move. Bradley Kerrigan is missing and there's blood in his house."

* * *

As Shane sped to Brad's home, he and I had a lengthy conference call with the sheriff and the other detectives so she could bring everyone up to speed. After it was over, Shane griped the rest of the way about the fact that Brad had disappeared right under our department's nose. Baxter had had a deputy track Brad all day yesterday, and Jayne had okayed the continuation of the surveillance until further notice. The deputy on duty had followed Brad home from our coffee date. Since then, he'd been parked in front of Brad's house all night and hadn't seen Brad or anyone else come or go. After being given the order to bring Brad in this morning, he'd knocked on the door and waited for Brad to answer. Nothing happened. He'd peeked in a few windows and noticed blood on the living room carpet, then called for backup. He and another deputy entered the home, found that Brad was gone, and called Jayne.

"This is bullshit," Shane reiterated as we parked in front of Brad's house. "How did your deputy miss a whole grown-ass man disappear?"

Reaching into his jacket pocket, he pulled out a roll of Tums and popped two of them. After chewing them, he washed them down with what was left of the coffee in the cup he'd brought from the station and winced.

Shane was rarely in such a foul mood. In his defense, he looked like he'd been up all night, which was entirely possible, given the fact that he'd had to go home and clean up what sounded like an obscene amount of baby puke.

I said, "Jayne mentioned something about blood drops leading to a back door. Brad could have snuck out the back. You wouldn't be able to see that from here."

As we got out of his vehicle and headed toward the house, Shane said, "Snuck out? I was under the impression he didn't leave of his own accord. There was blood."

I frowned. "I'll reserve my judgment until after I see exactly how much blood. I'd put money on the fact that Brad's going to come up with some dumbass scheme to try to throw us off his trail, like pulling a *Gone Girl* or something. No one with a million dollars in the bank dyes their hair at home unless they're running from something."

Once we got to the front porch, Shane put booties on and went inside while I stepped to the side to gear up. I'd be the one elbow-deep in the blood and whatever other yuck there was to be found inside, so I started getting into my jumpsuit.

Baxter and Sterling came up the sidewalk, both of them stone-faced. Baxter bumped into me as he passed me. I thought it was odd, considering I wasn't blocking the door or anything. I felt his hand on my hip and wondered what in the world he was doing, but then I felt a heaviness in the pocket of my coveralls. He'd put something in there, reverse-pickpocket style. Clearly, he meant it to be unnoticed, so I had to resist the urge to immediately pull out and look at whatever he'd given me. I put on my booties and mask and then crouched down to take a few pairs of gloves out of my case. When I did so, I made sure no one was looking and slipped the item out of my pocket and down into the case to conceal it while I took a good look. It was an old-school flip phone with a charging cable. Interesting. I made sure the volume was off, detached the charging cable, and placed the phone in my pants pocket for safekeeping.

After making sure I had my hat, mask, gloves, and booties in place, I entered the house to find Shane standing in the living room, standing over a decent-sized patch of bloody carpet, berating a contrite-looking young deputy. Baxter and Sterling were standing on the back patio just outside the open sliding glass door.

Shane demanded, "How did this happen? Were you not watching at all?"

The deputy replied, "I can't be in two places at once, and since I was told that Kerrigan was a flight risk with packed luggage in his vehicle, I figured I'd best keep an eye on that vehicle. The only vantage point for that is from the street in front of the home. Yes, that left the back of the home vulnerable, but I made the best decision I could with the intel I had."

In an effort to shift Shane's focus, I asked, "Shane, where do you think Brad may have exited the house?"

He flung a hand toward the sliding glass door. "Are you blind? Can you not see the damn trail of blood droplets leading outside?"

"*Bro*," I said in a warning tone.

He shook his head. "I'm sorry, Ellie." He turned to the deputy. "Sorry, man. I'm off my game today." He wiped a hand down his ashen face. He was sweating like a pig even though it was borderline cold in there.

I eyed him warily. Back in college, when Shane got grumpy, pale, and sweaty, it usually meant one thing. "Let's get you some fresh air."

"I don't need—"

Cutting him off, I said, "Yeah, you do. Go. Step around the blood." I ushered Shane out the back patio past Sterling and Baxter, out into the yard.

Shane said, "I just need a minute to—" He suddenly leaned over and vomited.

I nodded. "Yeah. Thought that was coming."

Sterling snickered and elbowed Baxter. "Hey, Nicky, he's doing your thing."

Baxter grunted in response. He had his phone in hand, frowning at it. I worried it was more bad news of his family issues, especially considering today was Marie Collins's release day, but I couldn't show it. There was nothing I could do for him while we were in the middle of processing a crime scene, so I pushed my feelings aside and concentrated on the situation I could do something about.

I waited until Shane seemed to be finished. "Feeling better after—"

Shane doubled over and retched again.

Wrinkling my nose, I said, "Ooh, guess not."

Sterling was loving every minute of this. "Nope, he's not better yet."

I snuck a glance at Baxter, also worried that him watching someone else vomit would trigger his gag reflex. It didn't seem to. In fact, Baxter had put his phone away and was standing there smirking in Shane's direction, not seeming to feel any empathy for him.

Shane let out another nasty-sounding retch.

"Whoa," Sterling said. "How do you have anything left to puke out, man?"

Shane shook his head, keeping his mouth clamped shut to stave off another wave of nausea.

Something dawned on me. "Wait a minute. Your kid puked everywhere last night, and now you're doing it? I think the Carlisle house has come down with the stomach flu. Go. Home."

Shane croaked, "I can't leave a...new crime scene."

"I don't want what you've got. Get out of here."

Sterling said, "Matthews is right. If you stay and get us all sick, we're screwed."

Shane started to protest, but I stopped him by saying, "Seriously, go. Now."

His shoulders hunched in defeat, or maybe from stomach cramps, Shane shuffled around the side of the house.

"You're welcome," I said to Sterling and Baxter as I breezed back inside. "If it hadn't been for me, that would have happened in the middle of your crime scene, boys."

35

Amanda was suited up and was just taking the camera out of its case when I re-entered the living room.

"What do you think?" I asked her. "Murder, kidnapping, or convoluted escape plan?"

She snickered. "Ooh. So many choices. That's a lot of blood for a convoluted escape plan. It would take real commitment."

I shrugged and kneeled down to get a closer look at the floor. "It's not a life-threatening amount of blood. A nasty flesh wound at best."

"True. Plush carpet like this soaks up blood and makes it seem worse."

Something caught my eye from this angle. There were lines pressed into the carpet, and they looked familiar.

I gasped. "Look." I pointed to the floor in front of me, drawing a line toward the sliding door that coincided with the blood droplets. "You have to be in the right light to see it clearly, but these are caster tracks. Like from a desk chair."

She gasped as well. "Like from our John Doe scene?"

"They look very much the same."

Amanda took several photos, from different angles to catch the sunlight streaming in on the pile of the carpet to best show the tracks. She asked hopefully, "Do you think they continue somewhere outside?"

"Only one way to find out." I grabbed a flashlight and a scale out of my kit.

As we trooped out the door and into the yard, Sterling said warily, "Don't tell me one of you is sick now."

Amanda called over her shoulder as we walked toward the trees that framed the back property line, "No, we're looking for chair tracks."

"What? Again?" He hurried after us.

I hadn't realized a parking lot butted up against Brad's back property line. You couldn't see it through the trees and brush. We walked through the tiny, wooded area and ended up in the church parking lot next door.

"Well, isn't this convenient?" Sterling griped.

Amanda and I searched for chair marks in the patchy grass shaded by the trees. It had rained overnight Thursday, so the ground was perfect for it. I was just beginning to get frustrated that we hadn't found anything when Amanda let out a yelp.

"Here!" She pointed to the ground in front of her. Sterling and I raced over.

I shined the flashlight on a roughly three-foot-by-three-foot patch of weedy dirt. "Looks like similar marks to the John Doe scene to me."

Amanda began excitedly taking photos.

Sterling squatted down for a closer look. "Great find. Again, I'm not sure that this is enough to tie the two murders together in court, but it is in my mind. Whoever killed Elvin Butler kidnapped and/or killed Brad Kerrigan."

I asked, "And do you think that person is Clive Sanderson?"

"I do."

"In that case, we need to alert the state lab to run the tire tread we found at Carnival Cove against the type of vehicle Sanderson took from Dynasty and against any personal vehicles he owns. If we can find the stolen vehicle and check it for signs Elvin Butler was in there, that's an excellent nail in Sanderson's coffin."

We looked for tire marks, but the asphalt was clean enough that there were none to be found. Undaunted, we headed back to Brad's house to start processing the inside. Baxter met us at the door, and we filled him in on our find.

He nodded. "That's good. I'm pretty confident Brad Kerrigan was alive when he left here." Gesturing to the carpet, he said, "I'd say he lost a pint or two of blood. The equivalent of participating in an overly aggressive blood drive. Unless his assailant gave him a cookie and some orange juice after wounding him, he'd have been semi-conscious at worst. Probably fatigued enough to have trouble walking across his backyard but perfect for manhandling into a chair and getting dragged to a second location without a whole lot of fight. Especially since he seemed significantly intimidated by our guy during a simple conversation."

Amanda and I got to work on processing the room while the detectives searched through the rest of the house. Any deputies that had been inside earlier were now stationed outside to corral the growing number of news vans setting up camp on the quiet street.

As she began taking more photos, Amanda said, "Have you been paying attention to what's going on outside?"

"I was literally just worrying about that. How are we going to get out of here without Shane this time?"

She shrugged. "'No comment' is always a good place to start."

"Even that is a bit much for me sometimes."

After a few moments, she said quietly, "I hope you don't think I'm stupid."

Thoroughly confused, I looked up from collecting a sample of the blood from the carpet. "What? I would never think that. What are you talking about?"

"I mean about..." She lowered her voice to a whisper. "About kissing Jason. In a crime scene no less. How unprofessional."

I had zero room to judge. "Well, when you work with the homicide team, you don't have a lot of options for romantic venues." I took the swab of blood and performed a quick typing test, which confirmed it was Brad Kerrigan's blood type, A negative.

She blurted out, "It doesn't mean we're back together. I mean, we did go out for a drink last night. It might seem like we're back together, but we're not."

I stood and smiled. "Don't protest too much, there."

"I'm not. I got swept up. He wanted to go celebrate his win. He said it would mean a lot if he got to celebrate it with me."

"I'm sure it did. He's trying really hard to do better. And not just around you."

She regarded me thoughtfully. "You know, if you of all people are giving him your seal of approval, does that mean I'm being too stubborn?"

"Absolutely not. No one else's opinion matters. Do what feels right for you. If you're still on the fence, make him sweat a little longer. He's a big boy. He can take it."

She seemed to mull that over as we continued our tasks in silence. I collected fingerprints from the sliding door while she measured the living room and began making a rough sketch. Just as I'd bagged and tagged the last of the print cards, Baxter and Sterling rejoined us in the living room.

Sterling said, "The packed bags the deputy noted yesterday are still in the trunk of Kerrigan's vehicle. We also found a used package of hair dye and accessories in the bathroom trash. No signs of struggle anywhere but in this room. You might want to grab photos of the dye and the bags, though."

Amanda said to me, "Do you mind getting the photos so I can finish the sketch?"

I picked up the camera. "No problem."

I went and got a couple of quick shots of the bags in Brad's Tesla, then headed upstairs and found the master bedroom. It was nice enough. Mannishly decorated, but clean and neat. The closet seemed a little empty, with a dozen or so hangers dangling at odd angles, as if clothing had been hastily ripped from them. The bed looked as though it hadn't been slept in. I entered the bathroom and found the trash can Sterling had mentioned with the telltale hair dye.

I was snapping photos when I heard soft footfalls on the carpet behind me. I turned to find Baxter standing in the doorway between the bedroom and the bathroom.

"I assume by now you found my gift."

I set the camera on the sink so I could remove one of my gloves and retrieve the phone from my pocket. Waggling it at him, I pulled my mask down and replied, "I did. I've never had a burner before. So, since there are only maybe two uses for one of these, are you planning to ask me to become drug dealers with you or help you cheat on your wife?"

He laughed and moved so he stood very close to me. "I thought it would be nice to be able to keep in communication with each other and not have any official record of it."

Nodding slowly, I said, "Oh, smart. You know, I've always heard cops make the best criminals."

"Very funny."

"So we're going to talk on the phone like it's 2003?"

"It has texting, too."

I flipped it open and raised an eyebrow. "Eight buttons for twenty-six letters? Pass. Texting 'OK' on this thing will take three minutes."

"Well, if you don't like my gift, I'll just take it back." He reached to grab the phone out of my hand.

Before he could get to it, I clasped it to my chest. "Not so fast. I never said I didn't like it." I smiled up at him. "I think it was a very sweet gesture. I can't wait to talk to you on it like it's 2003. Thank you."

He leaned down and said, "You're welcome," as he nuzzled my ear.

Trying to keep my cool, I asked, "Did anyone see you come up here, Detective?"

"Nope. Sterling and Amanda were too busy flirting." He planted a soft kiss on my neck.

A shiver snaked through me. "Still. We can't..." I lost my train of thought as he trailed his lips down my skin an inch and kissed me again. "Nick..." I breathed. A couple more seconds of this and I wasn't going to be able to think straight.

"Ellie..."

It took amazing willpower on my part to take a step back. I sighed. "I'd hate to see the hell we've gone through trying to stay apart be for nothing because we suddenly started being careless. The last two months nearly drove us both crazy. We get caught, and it's back to that."

He nodded. "You're right." A smile crept onto his face as he backed out of the bathroom. "It's just that you're so sexy in those coveralls."

I laughed. "Oh, now I know you've lost it. I look like a clown in this thing."

Shrugging, he said, "Not when I imagine you're wearing that dress from last night underneath it." He exited the bedroom, and I had to concentrate hard to settle down and focus on collecting the hair dying accessories and the empty box from the trash as evidence.

When I got downstairs, Jayne was speaking to Baxter, Sterling, and Amanda.

I heard her say, "We've got a warrant to search Clive Sanderson's residence. We've got addresses for his mother and girlfriend to interview them. I'd also like us to make a trip out to Carnival Cove and look around."

Sterling asked, "You really think he'd dump a second body there?"

She replied, "It worked for him before. As far as he or the rest of the world knows, we never figured out Elvin Butler is our John Doe. Besides the fact that we're having trouble finding any next of kin to notify, it's in our best interest to keep it quiet while the FBI works on Axion."

Sterling said, "We should split up. Baxter and I will each take a criminalist so if we need a place processed, they can do it quickly. It'll save time and be less driving around since we're down a vehicle with Carlisle gone."

Jayne nodded. "That's not a bad idea."

"I'll take Amanda."

I was just starting to get excited about the prospect of a whole afternoon of investigating with Baxter when Jayne flicked a glance at the two of us. Damn. I knew what she was thinking before she could get the words out. "No, you take Ms. Matthews and visit the girlfriend and Carnival Cove. Detective Baxter, you take Ms. Carmack and go see Sanderson's mother and look through his home."

Baxter nodded.

Sterling fumed. "Sheriff, you know we don't work well together."

Jayne wasn't budging. "You do today. I'll hold an impromptu press conference to keep the media vultures busy while you all sneak away. I don't want anyone following you this afternoon. Go around back." She walked out the front door, leaving the four of us in an uncomfortable silence.

Sterling frowned at me.

"What?" I demanded. "You're glaring at me like this is my fault." Technically, it was, but he didn't know that.

"This afternoon is gonna suck."

"That's one thing we can agree on."

36

Driving down to the east side of Indy to talk to Sanderson's girlfriend was a total waste of our time. She was a hot mess, and everything she said, which wasn't much, felt like a lie. Sterling was so pissed off he could barely see straight, and he nearly bit my head off when I suggested we take a break and get lunch before heading to Carnival Cove. I managed to talk him into getting food, and we sat in his vehicle and ate in a tense silence until Baxter called.

"What?" Sterling barked around a mouthful of his sandwich as he put the call on speaker.

Baxter said, "I thought we should trade information on what we found out so far."

"We found jack shit. The girlfriend was a total bitch. Your turn."

I explained, "She covered for Sanderson and said he was with her during all of the murders. One of them she confirmed before we told her the date."

Baxter replied, "We made some decent headway. His mom said he does side work unrelated to his job at Dynasty. She insinuated that they helped him make the connections to get the side work."

"You mean contract work," Sterling said.

"I do."

"Then say it, man."

After a beat of silence, Baxter continued, "She's also the proud owner of a new-to-her 2004 Honda Civic hatchback."

Although I felt I knew the answer, I asked, "Elvin's?"

Baxter replied, "That's the one."

Amanda chimed in, "Nick had it impounded while the poor woman stood there and cried."

Sterling muttered, "The 'poor woman' shouldn't have raised a killer."

Amanda snickered. "Someone's grumpy."

While Sterling tried not to lose what was left of his cool, I said, "You have no idea."

Baxter got the conversation back on track. "We're headed to Sanderson's house. I'm hoping to find Elvin Butler's laptop there, since the car's not quite enough to get him for murder. If we're really lucky, we'll find something there with Aurora Bennett's blood on it and be able to tie him to her murder, too."

Sterling rolled his eyes at me and huffed. "Good luck with that." He ended the call.

I said dryly, "I take it you were done with our conversation."

He said nothing, diving back into his sandwich with an angry ferocity.

* * *

Vic had texted me while we were eating. He'd heard about the case exploding from a couple of FBI buddies of his. He didn't come right out and say it, but I knew he was wishing he could join in another of our investigations. Especially considering how much help he'd been to us already.

I replied, *Don't tell anyone, because I'll deny it, but I'm glad the FBI took over that part of this case. That's a long-term project I don't want to take on.*

They'll be investigating it long after I'm back, so I may get sucked into it after all.

Called that one. *I get to head back to Carnival Cove this afternoon. Yay.*

You okay with that?

No, but I'll deal with it. We're hoping to find our missing guy there, but I'm kind of hoping to not find him, if you know what I mean.

I do. Call me anytime.

As we got closer to Carnival Cove, I was starting to worry more and more about Brad. With an open wound that probably wasn't being treated, he'd continue to lose blood and start developing an infection. And that was if Clive Sanderson didn't inflict any more pain on him or decide there was no reason to keep him alive. If we didn't find Brad soon, chances were good we'd have a fourth homicide on our hands.

I sighed. "'It's your funeral.' Those were the last words I said to Brad Kerrigan. Why in the hell did I say that to him?"

Sterling shrugged. "Because you say stupid shit sometimes." He must have been at least partially hangry, because his attitude had improved after we ate. It still wasn't what you'd call positive.

I frowned at him. "Not helpful."

He said matter-of-factly, "This isn't your fault. You tried to get him to take our help. He made the choice not to."

"Still, I kind of gave up on him. I could have insisted."

"What, and dragged him kicking and screaming into the station? No way he would have gone for that."

"We should have arrested him."

He shook his head. "It was too soon. We didn't have enough to hold him, which was why you were the one talking to him in the first place. Even if we'd tried to lock him up, his lawyer would have had him out in ten minutes. Same outcome. We would never have been able to keep him overnight."

"I know, but...it still sucks."

"Hey, speaking of things that suck, why in the hell did we get stuck with Carnival Cove?"

I wrinkled my nose. "If I had to guess, it would be because I kind of know my way around. That, or Jayne thinks it's funny to screw with my head."

Glancing over at me, he asked, "What is your problem with that place?"

"I found a dead body there. Surely you remember."

"You see dead bodies all the time. I'm not buying it."

I sighed. "Fine. I have a...clown phobia, okay?"

He hooted out a laugh. "Well, well, well. That's an interesting piece of Ellie Matthews trivia. Tell me another."

"Okay, here's one: I hate being partnered with you."

"Aww, that's hurtful."

"Good."

* * *

Sterling and I walked every part of the Carnival Cove property. My feet were killing me.

He must have been feeling the same way. "I've had my exercise for the week. There are zero bodies out here. Let's go."

As much as I would have liked that, there was a lot of ground we hadn't covered. "We haven't looked in the buildings yet."

"Most of them are locked up tight."

"Yeah, most of them. That means *some* of them are not, and I feel like you know which ones those are, considering you had to search them all two weeks ago. Why are you suddenly so against being thorough?"

"Since..." He huffed out an angry breath.

"Since you didn't get to spend the afternoon with Amanda and you're pouting over it. I get it. I'm not her. But the faster we do our jobs, the faster you can get back to her."

Little did he know, I could one hundred percent empathize. Getting to walk around outside on a nice afternoon all by ourselves would have felt like a date if I'd gotten to do it with Baxter. I wouldn't even have minded the clowns.

We started working our way through the buildings, beginning with the pump rooms for the waterslides, in the area we'd found Elvin Butler. Those buildings had no windows, and the steel doors were locked and didn't seem to have been messed with. We then moved on to Kiddie Land, my least favorite place, to check a couple of snack bars. The back door to the second one we came upon looked like it had been jimmied. Sterling unholstered his gun while I swung the door open for him. We entered a dark storage room.

We made our way through and found another door, this one a bit ajar.

When I pushed that one, a gun appeared in my face before I could get out of the way for Sterling to go through.

"You came to the wrong place," a man said. Clive Sanderson—Baldy—in the flesh. He was unfortunately much, much bigger than he'd looked sitting in his vehicle.

I'd had a gun pointed at me twice before, but I couldn't imagine it was something that would get easier the more times it happened. My breathing started coming fast and hard, and I couldn't do a damn thing to get it under control. It only got worse when Sanderson came closer and pressed the cold muzzle against my temple.

"Give me your gun," he ordered Sterling.

Clenching his jaw so hard it looked like he might chip a tooth, Sterling handed over his service pistol. Once he'd relieved Sterling of his weapon, Sanderson mercifully took a couple of steps back from me and trained the gun on him instead. Not that I wanted the gun pointed at Sterling, but I was overwhelmingly relieved it was no longer pointed my way.

"And your phones," Sanderson added.

I reached into my pocket with shaking hands and handed him my iPhone. While his head was turned grabbing Sterling's phone, I managed to pull my burner out of my other pocket and slip it into the end of my sleeve, figuring his next move would be to pat us down.

It was. Sanderson had us both walk a few steps into the kitchen and place our hands on a nearby counter. He ran his hands all along my sides, pockets, waistband, and legs. He made sure to check very carefully to find if I had a gun strapped to my ass cheeks or in my bra, which pissed me off.

My anger allowed me the clarity to get a grip on myself. I snapped, "Hey, pervert. Hands off."

"Shut up, bitch."

He moved on to Sterling, quickly finding Sterling's ankle holster with a spare gun, his keys, badge, and wallet, so he took all that, too. "Turn around. Get those hands up," he barked.

As we turned to face him and put up our hands, Sterling said, "This is a bad idea, man. People know we're here. If we don't check in soon, they'll come looking for us."

"That's why I'm going to drive your vehicle into the White River with your phones in it. They'll track you and check there instead."

Clive Sanderson didn't seem to be the brightest bulb. Maybe he was the muscle and Brad was actually the mastermind of their little duo. I said, "If *you* drive it into the river, how are you planning to get out? The White River is high right now from all the rain, and the current can be pretty fierce in places. Are you a strong enough swimmer to bet your life on it?"

Wrong thing to say. Before I knew what was happening, Sanderson busted the back of a meaty hand across my left cheek, bringing tears to my eyes. Sterling must have seen an opportunity, because he went for the guy. Sanderson, a much bigger man than Sterling, grabbed Sterling with one hand and clocked him on the head with the butt of his pistol. Sterling dropped like a sack of potatoes.

Oh, shit. I was on my own. Sanderson turned a murderous glare on me.

I held out my hands in front of me. My face stinging and my jaw starting to throb, I choked out, "Let's just take a breath here. You've committed several crimes already, and I don't feel like you should add any more violence, especially against law enforcement. Maybe you should just run."

"And let you live?"

"Yes, absolutely."

"I've got a better idea."

37

"No, no, no, no—" The door of the walk-in freezer where Sanderson had us trapped slammed shut, leaving us in total darkness.

Sterling, who'd just regained consciousness, croaked, "Ow, my head. Where in the hell are we?"

I'd been prepared to be instantly chilled to the bone in here, but the temperature was decent. "The snack bar's walk-in freezer. At least it's not cold."

"That's because there's no power out here, genius," he barked. "And how in the hell did I get tied up?"

I lied, "Sanderson tied us up while you were knocked out."

The truth was that Clive Sanderson had held me at gunpoint and forced *me* to zip tie Sterling's ankles and wrists, then my own ankles. He then bound my wrists and dragged us one by one into a walk-in freezer, where he already had a very unhealthy-looking Brad Kerrigan bound and lying on the floor next to an overturned office chair. At least Amanda and I had been right about how Sanderson transported his victims. I wished there were something I could have done besides let all of that happen, but Sanderson had a gun, a mean slap that had knocked one of my molars loose, and a hundred pounds of muscle on me.

"Brad, are you okay?" I asked. "We were at your house earlier. We know you've lost a fair amount of blood."

"Oh, that. Yeah, I'm good," he said, his last word ending in a groan.

My eyes were fighting to adjust to the pitch black, but I still couldn't see a damn thing. "It's really dark in here."

"No shit, Matthews." Sterling snapped. Sterling with a head injury was going to be insufferable.

Brad said, "You get used to it."

"It smells awful, too," I added.

"That's my bad. I've been here a while."

"Ah." I turned to Sterling, or at least where I assumed Sterling was. "So, I've got a phone in my front pocket, and I can't reach it. That means you're going to have to do it."

Brad said, "Who, me? I'll put my hand in your pocket."

"Not you, *Brad*," Sterling said. "Matthews, how in the hell do you still have a phone?"

"It's an extra," I hedged.

"And why in the hell do you have an extra phone? You banging some married guy now?"

"It's a long story. Just get it. It's in my front left pocket."

"Do you think I can see right and left in here?"

I let out a tired sigh. "You're just going to have to feel around for it."

Brad laughed. "That's what she said."

Sterling and I both barked, "Shut up, Brad."

I scooted toward Sterling and turned until we were essentially spooning, with my left hip in the air, hoping that would be the easiest position for the phone extraction. I felt his fingers brush my stomach. "Lower and to our left."

Brad evidently couldn't help himself. He chortled. "That's what she said."

Sterling barked, "Say it one more time, man, and see what happens. One more."

He felt around again. I felt his fingers nudge the phone.

"That's it. Now push it straight up out of my pocket."

He pushed the phone up, and I felt it pop out of my pocket. He didn't catch it in time, and it clattered onto the floor.

I said, "I'll get it from here." I felt around behind me and grabbed the phone off the floor. But now how to use it? I'd only had a moment to take a look at it, and even though it had few buttons, I had no idea which ones did what. "Shit."

Sterling said, "What?"

"Um, I just got this phone. I don't know how to use it without looking at it."

I imagined Sterling rolling his eyes into the top of his head as he said, "Turn around and I'll be your eyes. I'll tell you what to push."

I didn't want Sterling getting a good look at my phone, lest he see that there was only one phone number programmed into it. "Let's do that the other way around. I'll tell you what to push."

"Whatever. I don't care. Let's get this show on the road."

I wriggled around and placed the phone into Sterling's hands, then I rolled to where I could see the screen. "Okay. I'm pretty sure I have no bars, but it doesn't say 'no service,' so let's try a nine-one-one call. On the part with the keypad, there's a round button at the top."

"Okay." He pressed the button.

"I didn't tell you to press it."

"Damn it, Matthews. You suck at this."

"So do you, you ass. Listen. There's a weird-shaped button to the lower left of that button. Press it."

He pressed the button. "Done."

"That opened up the phone app. Now we need to use the square buttons under the one you just hit. Nine is on the right, third row down."

He pressed the nine.

I continued, "The one is at the top left. Push it twice."

"I know the number for nine-one-one, Matthews."

I let that one slide. "Now hit that same weird-shaped button to the lower left of the round button. It's green, so I think it means 'call.'"

"Tell me again why you don't know how your own phone works?"

"Shut up and hit the button."

He hit the green button, and it showed that the call was being made. Then...nothing. It went back to the home screen.

I sighed. "It dropped the call."

"Let's do it again."

I groaned, then walked him through the process again. And again, the call dropped nearly instantly.

"Damn it," he said. "What about a text?"

I sighed, thinking about how long that was going to take. But then again, what else did we have to do? "Okay, let's do that."

"Text the sheriff."

I hesitated. "I don't have her number on this phone. And I don't know it off the top of my head."

"I thought you guys were tight."

"We are, I just...I've got Baxter's number."

"Close enough."

After making him press several buttons in vain, I finally figured out how to open the texting app. He cussed me with every mistake, which wasn't helping. Finally we got to where we could start the text.

I said, "What do we want to say?"

"We want to say, 'Get your ass over here and rescue us.'"

"That's not specific enough. Let's send a quick one that says, 'Need help at CC.' Then we can let him know what's going on in another text."

"*If* we can get two texts through. Don't forget you've got no bars."

We went through the excruciating process of typing in the letters—with the L and Cs taking three consecutive button taps to come up. I then had him add "kidnapped" at the end, which he griped about. He thought that was too embarrassing, even though that was, in a word, what had happened to us. "Tied up and locked in a freezer against our will" was more typing than I was willing to engage in with Sterling.

He hit the green button to send the text, and we waited. And waited and waited.

I said, "Maybe he's in the middle of something." I assumed he had the ringer off for this phone. He probably wouldn't have been checking it, either, since it would have been hard for me to get away from Sterling long enough to use it without him seeing me.

"Maybe it didn't go through. Does it tell you when it doesn't go through?"

I looked at the screen. "It doesn't say either way."

"Piece of shit. Why do you even have this thing?"

I didn't answer.

It dawned on me that Brad had been quiet for a while. Granted, Sterling and I had both told him to shut up, so if he was actually doing what we asked, he was doing a great job. But the Brad Kerrigan I knew couldn't keep his mouth shut that long.

"Brad?" I said, looking his way but unable to even see the outline of his body.

No response.

"*Brad*," I said louder. "You sleeping or passed out?"

Sterling whistled through his teeth. "Hey, Kerrigan. Wake up!"

Nothing.

Sterling said, "Go over there and see if he's still breathing."

"No way. I can't see a thing, but I can smell that there's piss and shit over there. I'm not rolling anywhere near him. If you need to know how he's doing so badly, go find out for yourself."

"I have a concussion. And you should care more about your boyfriend over there."

"What exactly would we be able to do for him with our hands tied? He was talking just fine a few minutes ago. He probably just passed out."

Sterling growled, then asked, "Did Baxter ever respond?"

I looked at the phone screen. "No."

"We're stuck in an insulated metal box. We're going to have to get out of here to get enough of a signal for that text to go."

He was right. It was stupid to just sit here and do nothing, especially with Brad's condition deteriorating.

I said, "Okay, surely we can figure out how to do that."

"Help me stand up and get to the door."

"You're probably woozy, especially after lying down for so long. I'll go. You help me. Wait, first let's get the phone back in my pocket. If we lose it in the dark, we're screwed."

I got on my knees and scooted toward him. I bumped into him and could tell that he'd managed to get into a sitting position. I wriggled around until my pocket was near his hands. "Okay, I'm here." He easily slid the phone back into my pocket. At least one thing had gone right.

I leaned against him for support and made it to my feet. It was a bitch to hop with my feet bound over toward where I hoped the door was, but I finally made it to a wall. I turned and put my back against it to feel for a handle.

"Aha!" I cried, feeling a knob. "Found it." Something wasn't right with the knob—it was slanted in an extreme downward angle. As I ran my fingers over it, I felt jagged metal, as if it had been damaged.

Sterling said, "Did you find the door handle? Or is it a knob? If it's a knob, you push it. It's a safety feature so assholes like us can't get trapped in places like this."

I tried pushing, pulling and turning the knob. Nothing. "I think Sanderson busted it. It won't budge."

Sterling bellowed out a string of curses.

I said, "Our only other choice is to get him to come to us. Maybe the two of us can bum rush him. You think he'd unlock the door if we told him Brad was dying?"

"I think it's his plan to have Brad die in here, and for us to watch...or listen. Whatever."

"Oh."

"You could offer to exchange sex for our release."

"Are we really to that point yet?"

"I think we're close, Matthews. And I said offer. Maybe it won't need to get to completion."

I grunted. "Gross." I thought for a moment. "What if I ask him if I can use the restroom?"

"That's stupid."

"It always works in movies. All we really need is to get me one step across the threshold. Once the phone is out of this box we're in, the text should send immediately." I started pounding my fists on the door and yelling, "Clive! Clive! Hey!"

I went through four rounds of pounding and calling, punctuated by Sterling grumbling that it wasn't going to work. Finally I heard a metal tapping coming from the outside of the door. In my mind, I imagined Sanderson tapping his gun against the door and shivered. I knew this plan would involve me getting that gun pointed at me again, but I had to push through it if I wanted to get us out of here.

Sanderson's voice from the other side called, "What do you want?"

"I have to go to the bathroom!" I shouted.

There was a beat of silence on the other side. Then he said, "I'm sure there's a bucket in there somewhere."

"I can't see anything!"

"Find a corner. Your buddy did."

I made a face. "I'm a girl! I can't just go in a corner! Come on!"

Sterling muttered, "Offer to show him your tits."

"That is for emergencies only," I whispered.

"And you wouldn't call this an emergency?" he hissed back.

Sanderson said, "Okay, okay. Get away from the door. If you try to rush me, I'll shoot you."

I shot Sterling a triumphant glance, forgetting he couldn't see me. Oh well, we both knew I won that one.

Using the wall for support, I made a couple of hops to the right of the door. "Okay!" I called.

The door swung open. In contrast to the absence of light in the freezer, the late afternoon sunlight streaming in from the windows in the outer room was so bright I could barely see. A hand clamped around my arm and started pulling. I struggled to get my feet under me and began hopping as fast as I could, trying to keep up with Sanderson and keep focused on the important thing—with every hop there was more chance of that text going through. But I had a little more in mind. He'd given me an inch, and I was going to take a mile.

38

I said breathlessly to Sanderson as I hopped along beside him, "Can we do something about these restraints? I'm going to need to get my pants down."

"I'll take care of that for you."

I fought the chill of fear rushing through me. "Mmm, that's not going to work for me. I'm a shy gal. And I'll need the use of at least one of my hands."

He stopped walking suddenly, and I would have toppled over if his hand wasn't as strong as a vise grip on my arm. "You really think I'm dumb enough to do all that?"

Yes. "Do you really think I'm a physical threat to you? You know I'm not a cop, right? I'm a criminalist."

"A what?"

"A CSI, like the TV show. Only I don't even have a gun. I spend most of my time in a lab. The detective only brought me out here because we thought we were going to find Brad dead and I'd have to start processing a scene."

His grip loosened a smidge. "Oh."

I tried to play up that I was merely a fluffy little girl. "And I have zero hand-to-hand combat skills. If I tried to hit you, it would hurt me way worse than you." I trailed my gaze down his veiny, bulging arms. "You look like you've been carved out of stone."

He hesitated, seeming to be mulling it over.

I added some sweetness to my tone, hoping to drive home that there was no way I was any threat to him. "Can you decide faster? I *really* have to pee. I drank a venti iced latte on the way here, and I didn't plan on my afternoon playing out like this."

Grumbling, he used his free hand to remove his gun from the back waistband of his pants. Pointing it at me again, he let go of my arm and reached in his pocket, producing a switchblade knife. I sucked in an involuntary breath as he switched it open, the tip shooting way too near my wrist for my comfort. He sliced open the zip tie, and I felt a wave of relief as blood flowed back into my hands. I guessed my adrenaline had been masking how painful my bondage had become. He then stuck the barrel of the gun into my side as he leaned over and cut the zip tie around my ankles.

Backing away, he gestured to a nearby door with the gun. "There you go."

I opened the door and walked in, only to have him follow me. Damn it. I said, "Now that you very kindly removed my restraints, I can handle everything from here." There was at least a little light coming in from a couple of rows of decorative glass blocks near the ceiling. I gestured around the room. "No windows, only one door. I'm not going anywhere."

Again he appeared to be weighing his options. Gun still trained on the center of my chest, he walked past me and checked the two stalls. After giving me another hard stare, he walked backward out the door.

I heaved a sigh of relief and bolted for the stall by the wall. In case he decided to come in and check my progress or was listening outside, and because I didn't want to have a real bathroom emergency after he tossed me back in the freezer, I did actually use the toilet. I sat and grabbed the phone out of my pocket, holding back happy tears when I saw a return text from Baxter: *On way with backup. Exact location?*

I typed as quickly as I could, which was not very quickly, *Kiddie Land snack bar freezer. No sirens. CS has gun and knife.* I finished my business and washed up, giving the phone one last check for another message. There wasn't one, which was fine, as I hoped Baxter was currently speeding our way and not bothering to take the time to stop and text me back. I replaced the phone in my pocket and pulled my sweater down to cover it.

Going over to the door, I knocked and said, "I'm finished."

The door opened, and Sanderson was there, again with his gun pointed straight at my chest. He zip tied my wrists but thankfully left my legs so I could walk. Again gripping me by the arm, he marched me right back toward the freezer.

Hoping I could derail him for a bit and keep my legs free for as long as possible, I said, "Thanks for being cool about letting me use the restroom. I feel so much better."

He only grunted in reply.

I went for it. "So, I have to ask—you seem like you've got this contract work you do down to a science. Why bring dumb, bumbling Brad Kerrigan into the equation to screw it up? You surely didn't need his help."

"Wasn't my choice," he muttered.

That tracked with the fact that they'd both been paid by Leosedonas Corp to do Axion's dirty work. What I needed to find out was what exactly Brad did to make this guy mad enough to kill him.

"I guess he was the only one who could help with the cover-up end of the job. Makes sense. Too bad he's such an asshat, and because of him, now you're on the run. I hope Axion Pharmaceuticals is going to compensate you for your extra trouble. As far as we could see, Leosedonas Corp paid you and the Bradster the same fee. I feel like you had to do a lot more to earn yours."

He slammed me up against the wall. The back of my already throbbing head bounced against it. "That's enough out of you."

So much for small talk. "Okay," I croaked.

Surely it wouldn't be long before Baxter led the charge to save us. As the thought of him coming to my rescue played in my head, it suddenly dawned on me that was not at all what I wanted. In fact, the last thing I wanted was for Baxter—who'd be in a panic because I was in danger—to lead the charge in here and get hurt by stupid Clive Sanderson. I couldn't allow that to happen. But what could I do? I could only hope he had tons of backup and kept a cool head. I didn't know if he had enough in him to do that at this point.

We were back at the freezer. Sanderson grabbed me and shoved me toward the door. I didn't remind him I still had the use of my feet. Instead, I shuffled obediently to the wall beside the door and waited for him to open it for me, desperately trying to come up with an idea to stop him. I had nothing. Sterling's proposition idea popped into my head. My heart sank as I realized it had finally come to that.

As Sanderson opened the door, I took a deep breath to start to speak. But my words died on my lips as Sterling hurled himself out of the freezer, taking Sanderson down like a linebacker. This time Sanderson was the one whose head took the damage, rocketing backward against the tile floor with a sickening thunk. I snapped into action, running over and kicking Sanderson's gun out of his hand as Sterling started punching him mercilessly and incessantly in the face. I didn't know how Sterling had gotten out of his zip ties, but I was damn happy he had. Sanderson went limp, and I kicked the gun back so Sterling could pick it up.

Sterling hauled himself off of the bloodied and unconscious body of Sanderson, swaying a little as he did so. His hand, drenched in Sanderson's blood, seemed steady enough on the gun he had leveled at Sanderson's chest, just in case he came to.

"You okay?" I asked.

"Yeah," he said, panting. "I saved your ass. You remember that, Matthews."

I smiled. "You did. I've never been so happy to see you in my life."

* * *

After Sterling cut the zip ties off my wrists, I helped him tie up Sanderson. I also gave him a hug, which he protested, but he hugged me back. Sterling stayed inside and kept an eye on Sanderson while I went outside to flag down our rescuers, who'd just started to converge on Kiddie Land. Baxter raced straight toward me, but at the last minute remembered to rein it in and slowed his pace, stopping a few feet from me. I used all the strength I had left to not give into the rush of emotion and jump into his arms. I didn't know what I was more relieved about—that I was no longer in the clutches of a murderer, or that Sterling had managed to gain control of the situation before Baxter found himself in harm's way.

His face a mask of concern, Baxter asked, "Are you hurt?"

My words tumbled out. "I'm fine. Sterling is inside with Sanderson in custody. We're going to need three ambulances. Brad Kerrigan is alive—I think—but not well. Sterling turned Sanderson's face into meat. And I'm sure he won't cop to it, but Sterling most likely has a concussion."

His eyes grew wide. "I'll catch up with you later." He took out his phone and began hurrying toward the snack bar.

I found a nearly intact lounge chair and collapsed into it, stretching out in the afternoon sun and letting the chaos whirl around me as I appreciated my freedom.

* * *

I was in such a lovely meditative state, I didn't even realize I had company until Baxter's voice said, "What happened to your face?" I opened my eyes to see him and Sterling standing over me. Baxter's expression was tense.

Sterling guffawed. "Sanderson bitch-slapped her."

While Baxter clenched his jaw and tried not to react, I said to Sterling, "You've got no room to talk. He pistol-whipped you."

Sterling fired back, "Which was all your fault. You started running your mouth and got slapped for it. I stepped in to defend your honor and got concussed for it."

I shook my head, which was a mistake. Now all of it was throbbing. "I feel like it's more accurate that you saw me getting slapped as an opportunity to step in and try to take Sanderson down. So you're welcome for the distraction, which you did not put to good use."

"Need I remind you I saved your sorry ass?"

"After I tricked a stone-cold killer into letting me out of the freezer so I could call for help."

Jayne came up to us, worried but weary. "Maybe I should have listened and not put the two of you together this afternoon."

Sterling said to her, "We managed. Just promise you'll never do it again."

She smiled. "Done. Detective Sterling, you go get checked out by the EMTs. Ellie, come with me. Agent Griffin wants to speak with you."

The last time I'd had a headache this bad, I'd got stuck being interrogated by Agent Griffin. Not how I'd wanted to spend my afternoon. I got up from the lounge chair, but I must have done it too fast, because my head started spinning. I started leaning, in danger of going down, but Baxter caught me and held me upright.

"Ooh, must be a little dizzy from all the excitement," I said, hoping not to freak anyone out.

Jayne eyed me with a frown. "On second thought, both of you are going straight to get checked out."

Baxter said, "I'll take them over."

Baxter helped me to the nearest ambulance and sat me down on the back of it, mumbling about coming back to check on us later. Sterling plopped down next to me, looking more exhausted by the minute. I imagined all he wanted to do was sleep, but judging from the giant goose egg on his head you could see clearly through his hair, he was in store for a barrage of testing at the hospital. I was hoping to get checked and released by the EMTs and be able to go home.

I said to Sterling, "You never told me how you managed to get free from your zip ties."

He replied, "When you left, I searched the room for something sharp and found a rusty pair of pliers on a shelf only a few feet from me."

"Wow. Talk about luck—"

He cut in, "What the hell's going on with you and Baxter?"

"Nothing," I said, a little too quickly.

Sterling narrowed his eyes at me. "Then why do you have a new burner phone with hardly any numbers in it except his?"

"It's for work," I said.

"Bullshit." He studied me for a moment, and then realization dawned on his face. "You guys are doing it."

I hissed, "Keep it down." Then I added quietly, "To be clear, we're not doing it."

"But you want to," Sterling said, obviously pleased with himself for figuring out our little secret. His face suddenly fell. "Wait—except you can't because of that last case. You're on opposite sides of it, so it would be all kinds of wrong if—"

I cut him off. "Exactly. Which is why you can't tell anyone what you figured out."

He smirked. "Sounds like I have dirt on you and Boy Scout Baxter."

My jaw dropped. "Are we really going to do this after what you and I went through together today? I thought we'd turned a corner in our relationship."

He snickered. "You think I would give up something like this to hold over your head?"

"Maybe, if you took a moment to remember the only reason you're back with Amanda is because of me."

His smile faltered. He still managed to scoff. "Yeah, right. She likes me for me."

I scoffed back at him mockingly. "She didn't like you for you a couple of weeks ago, before you begged me for my help to win her back. What do you think she'd say if she knew you were holding the two of us hostage with your newfound information? You think she'd think that was the right thing to do?"

He glared at me. "Probably not."

"Then do we have an understanding?"

After a moment of hesitation, he said, "I guess."

"And you're not going to bust Baxter's balls over the fact that you know *or* the fact that he's with me."

Sterling snorted. "You mean that he got my sloppy seconds?"

Borrowing a phrase from him, I said, "Say that one more time and see what happens."

Rolling his eyes, he said, "Fine."

I breathed a sigh of relief.

He added, "But if I see even a little PDA between the two of you, the deal's off."

"Fair enough." I stuck out my hand, and we shook on it.

39

Vic's FBI buddies had also made him aware of my incident, because it wasn't long before I saw him striding my way, his face tight with concern. I'd just finished my painful debriefing with Agent Griffin, so the bear hug Vic gave me was much needed.

"You were held in a freezer by a contract killer?" he demanded, his grip on me tightening.

"Yeah…" I replied, not really knowing any way to sugarcoat it.

He let me go and studied my face, zeroing in on the place where Sanderson clocked me. "What's that bruise? And you've got the start of a black eye."

I huffed. "Seriously? A black eye? That asshole." I hated black eyes. The swelling and pressure drove me insane.

Vic was struggling to keep his temper in check. "Sanderson did this to you?"

I nodded. Again, it sounded as bad as it was.

"He's lucky I'm not on this investigation."

I smiled. "Trust me—Jayne is pissed enough for all of us." She hadn't noticed my face at first, with everything going on, and had bought my lame excuse of too much excitement for nearly keeling over. She'd later conferred with the EMTs about their examination of me and lost her shit.

He smiled. "In that case, I wouldn't want to be Sanderson right now."

Vic waited for me while I told the story of the past couple of hours to countless law enforcement officials, including Internal Affairs, who demanded to know every detail about Sterling's one-sided fist fight with Sanderson. Vic didn't seem to mind hanging around, since he essentially got to be a part of the investigation of a crime scene without having to do any actual work. He conferred with all the colleagues he'd been missing over the past couple of months, and he was even able to offer some insight since he'd been helping Shane and me along the way. It made me happy to see him so happy.

In the midst of the madness, I found a moment to call Shane. When he croaked out a sad hello, I said, "Hey there, partner. Feeling any better?"

"I've spent the day with my head in the toilet."

"Ooh. Then your day went a lot like mine."

"Oh, hell. Did I get you sick?"

"No. Jayne partnered me with Sterling."

He let out a painful-sounding laugh. "I bet that made you wish you'd gotten to spend the day with your head in the toilet."

"It did. Especially once we caught up with Sanderson."

"You found him?"

"Eh, more like he found us." I told him the long, sad story.

When I finished, he whistled. "I missed all that?"

"I wouldn't say you missed anything."

I could finally hear a smile in his voice. "I'm just happy you're safe. I hear this bug is only a twenty-four-hour commitment. I'll come in tomorrow and help you with the paperwork."

"Sounds like a party."

* * *

Once I was cleared to leave the scene, Vic took me back to his house, got me some dinner, and generally fretted over me. He paced the floor while I ate and then for a good while after that while I returned several messages to myriad law enforcement officials who had extra questions for me.

"I'm *fine*, Manetti," I finally snapped, when I caught him staring for the thousandth time. "No concussion, no open wounds. My pride's not even hurt, because Sterling and I outsmarted that asshole in the end."

He crossed his arms and frowned at me. "Oh, so I should quit worrying about you like you quit worrying about me the past couple of months after I repeatedly told you I was fine?"

I glanced toward his dining table, where his near-death experience had occurred, and had a minor ugly flashback as I said, "That was different."

"Not to me."

"You didn't stand there and watch you die."

"Neither did you."

"Ah, but I thought I did. It counts."

He sat down beside me and took my hand. "When are you going to forgive yourself?"

"I'd like to say as soon as you're back to a hundred percent, but we both know the real answer is when hell freezes over."

He nodded. "Thought so."

Vic's doorbell rang, and he left me to go get the door. I thought I was hearing things when I heard Baxter's voice. I wasn't. I turned to find him walking into the living room, a sweet smile on his face when he locked eyes with me.

Vic said, "I'm going to give you two some alone time."

I gaped at Vic, who was the last person I'd ever thought would play Cupid between Baxter and me. "Wait, you set this up?"

He shrugged. "When you find the right person, you have to go for it, right? Sometimes you need a little help from your friends to make it happen."

Vic disappeared up the stairs as Baxter came to sit next to me on the couch. We did nothing but hold each other for several minutes.

He finally leaned back so he could look at me. "You okay?"

I smiled. "I am now." My smiled faded. "But we can't keep meeting secretly at Manetti's house, of all places."

"I know. I'm still trying to figure out how this is going to work, but I promise you...it will work."

I leaned my head on his shoulder. "Um...about that. Sterling knows."

He let out a low growl. "Not what I wanted to hear. He's going to drive me nuts lording it over me."

"No, he's not. He's not going to talk about it at all, and he's not going to hold it over either of our heads. I threatened to tell Amanda, and he backed off."

"If that turns out not to be enough, he owes you a serious solid for covering for him to IA."

"I wasn't covering. Sanderson is a freaking giant, and he was packing a gun and a knife. Sterling had one chance to take him down and no weapons. He had no choice but to punch him until he was out for the count. It wasn't excessive force. Speaking of Sterling, has he had his head examined yet?"

"Yes, and they're keeping him overnight for observation. He'll be on leave for a while until that concussion heals."

I joked, "You should see the other guy."

"I did. Your assessment of his face looking like meat was hideously accurate."

"And Brad?"

"He's going to be okay, which is good news for us. He was so thankful you and Sterling saved his life, he sang like a canary. He copped to everything we assumed about him and more. He started off his life of crime by taking bribes to delete and destroy files at the foundation for some of the companies they were investigating. When he realized Wakefield had additional information he was hiding from the rest of the staff, he took a page out of Aurora's book and broke into Wakefield's email, where he found the interactions with RexXanthe69. He then told RexXanthe69 that the email account had been compromised, opened up a new account, and used that to lure him out so Clive Sanderson could kill him and steal whatever sensitive information he'd managed to hack on Axion."

I frowned. "Damn. Brad's smarter than I gave him credit for."

"Not completely. He's the one who broke into Elvin Butler's place and stole his laptop and computers. Amanda found them at Sanderson's house with both Kerrigan's and Sanderson's fingerprints on them, so we have solid evidence to connect them to Butler, rather than just Kerrigan's word."

"Nice."

"Kerrigan bought the bag of Percocet and planted it on Wakefield's desk so Barry Jeffords would walk in and see it, establishing Wakefield's alleged drug problem that Kerrigan hoped would have kept us chasing our tails for a while."

"Again, a fairly well-thought-out plan."

He shrugged. "It was Sanderson's idea. During his interrogation, he said that he didn't trust Kerrigan from the start. He was so afraid Kerrigan would double-cross him that he insisted Kerrigan kill Wakefield so he'd have some leverage against him."

I felt ill. "Wait. Brad killed Lance Wakefield?"

"He did. He admitted to slipping drugs into Wakefield's drinks at dinner, keeping him occupied downstairs while Sanderson murdered Aurora Bennett upstairs, and then bringing him upstairs so he'd find his wife dead. Wakefield lost it, and then his good buddy Kerrigan gave him a handful of pills to 'calm him down,' knowing the combination would kill him."

"You called that yesterday." I shook my head, which ushered a fresh wave of pain through it. "You're good."

Blushing slightly at my compliment, he went on, "Kerrigan said he was the one who set out the funeral suit, grabbing the first one he saw in the closet. He said Sanderson also forced him to write 'WHORE' on the wall, which strangely enough was almost a dealbreaker for him."

"*That* was the worst part of the situation for him?"

"He said it was the act of having to collect and use Aurora's blood that made the whole thing real."

Sighing, I said, "I don't even know what to say about that."

"It's crazy, I know. Anyway, he agreed to testify at the murder trials and at the FBI's Axion trial, plus he agreed to plead guilty to Lance Wakefield's murder. He'll be in WITSEC for a little while, and then he'll be in prison for a long while. He'll be placed in minimum security, which is all he's asking for at this point."

All along, I didn't believe Brad had it in him to truly hurt anyone. Bribery and deceit, yes. Straight-up murder, no. What he did to Lance wasn't violent like what Sanderson did to Aurora—he technically didn't kill him by his own hand, so he could easily get a lesser sentence out of it. But in my mind, what he did was worse.

I huffed out a breath. "He killed his best friend. He shouldn't get to ask for anything."

Baxter nudged me with his shoulder. "Now aren't you glad I crashed your date with him?"

I frowned at him.

"Too soon?"

"A little."

He smiled and stroked the side of my face that wasn't hurt. "I heard Sanderson slammed your head against a wall, too. Why didn't you tell us that earlier?"

"Because I knew you and Jayne would go apeshit on him, which wouldn't do you any favors once his interrogation rolled around."

"Because we care about you."

"I know. But I'm not concussed. It's fine."

"It's not fine." He blew out a breath and turned my wrists over to examine the nasty-looking ligature marks from the zip ties.

I said truthfully, "Those look a lot worse than they feel."

"I should have been there with you."

"I was happy you weren't."

His eyes snapped up to meet mine. "What?"

"Honestly, I think there's some merit to the idea that it wouldn't be in our best interest to be partners again. If we'd been at Carnival Cove together, you would have been worried about me and I would have been worried about you, and we wouldn't have had cool enough heads to get out of there. Hell, I was worried about the fact that you were the one I went to for help and would undoubtedly come in guns blazing to try to rescue me. I didn't want you in Sanderson's line of fire, even if it meant that I still was. Thank goodness Sterling came flying out of that freezer when he did, because I was about to do something really stupid to try to take down Sanderson before you got the chance."

He looked at me like I was crazy. "I'm a trained police officer. Why would you think it was up to you to try to save me?"

I reached up to cradle his cheek in my hand. "Because I know how impossible it is for me to live without you."

"I could say the same about you." He leaned down and gave me a tender kiss. "I should go."

I nodded and ventured, "How's everything going, otherwise?"

Shaking his head, he said, "Getting worse by the second."

"You want to talk about it?"

"I don't want to put anything else on you today."

"I'm not fragile, Nick. You should know that by now."

He sighed. "Marie Collins was released today at noon. Her sister's house, where she plans to live until she gets on her feet, got vandalized pretty bad this morning while the sister was gone picking her up from prison. Shawn left home early this morning and didn't show up for work this afternoon. Now he won't answer his phone. The police are looking for him, but I'd prefer to find him first and talk to him. If he did in fact do it, his best course of action is to turn himself in, but I know he's not in the right headspace to be thinking that clearly right now."

My heart hurt so much for Baxter and for his family. "So let's go find him. Now."

Shaking his head, he replied, "I can't go anywhere. I'm buried in paperwork for this case. So are you."

I shrugged. "It'll be there when we get back."

"If I leave without filing my reports for this case, I won't have a job when I get back."

I smiled. "There are a couple of really cool inventions that make it possible to get work done from anywhere. I don't know if you've heard of them, but they're called laptops and the Internet. I'll drive." I stood, fighting a dizzy spell as I did so.

He stood and steadied me. "I'm not letting you behind the wheel of a vehicle."

"Then you drive and dictate your reports, and I'll type. You're not getting out of this, Baxter."

Frowning, he said, "All that aside, I can't ask you to drop everything and go with me. It's too close to finals—you said so yourself. We could be gone for days."

"You think I could actually concentrate on my job if I stayed? Plus aren't *you* the one who said that's what my TA is for?"

"Ellie."

"Nick."

He grinned at me. "I'm not going to change your mind, am I?"

"I don't even know why you bother to try anymore."

RELATIVE HARM
Book #5 of the Ellie Matthews Novels

When her partner's family is implicated in a brutal murder, expert criminalist Ellie Matthews must race against the clock to find the real killer... and save the people she loves.

Ellie knows she can't live without her partner, Detective Nick Baxter. So when Nick's brother is accused of vandalizing the house of his former kidnapper and goes on the lam, she insists on accompanying Nick home to help with the family crisis.

Marie Collins has just been released from prison after serving her time for kidnapping Shawn Baxter when he was a toddler. Reviled by the whole town, no one is surprised at the defacement of her property, and Ellie and Nick are able to bring Shawn in to face the consequences of his petty crime. Thinking the situation successfully handled and preparing to leave town, Ellie and Nick are blindsided when a dead body is found in a barn. On Baxter property. And the victim is Marie Collins.

Now the entire town thinks they are guilty of murder, and they must dig into Marie Collins' past, unearthing disturbing secrets and a list of potential suspects that keeps getting longer. But they are playing a dangerous game. Because this killer has gone through hell to get their revenge...and they won't let anyone undo their good work.

Get your copy today at
severnriverbooks.com/series/ellie-matthews

ACKNOWLEDGMENTS

Thanks to the Severn River team for making my first novel with them a great experience! Special thanks to Julia Hastings and Amber Hudock for guiding me through the process and Randall Klein for working with me on the story outline. Also a big thank you to my son, William Fardig, for collaborating on character arcs with me!

ABOUT THE AUTHOR

Caroline Fardig is the *USA Today* bestselling author of over a dozen mystery novels. She worked as a schoolteacher, church organist, insurance agent, banking trust specialist, funeral parlor associate, stay-at-home mom, and coffeehouse owner before she realized that she wanted to be a writer when she grew up. When she's not writing, she likes to travel, lift weights, play pickleball, and join in on vocals, piano, or guitar with any band who'll have her. She's also the host of a lively podcast for Gen Xers called *Wrong Side of 40*. Born and raised in a small town in Indiana, Fardig still lives in that same town with an understanding husband, two sweet kids, and three exhaustingly energetic dogs.

Sign up for Caroline Fardig's reader list at
severnriverbooks.com/authors/caroline-fardig

Printed in the United States
by Baker & Taylor Publisher Services